ONE

YEAR

LOVE

Collecting Books 1-4

Devon Hartford

COPYRIGHT NOTICE

Want to get an email when Devon's next book is released?

Sign up here:

http://eepurl.com/B7crf

DEDICATION

To everyone who voted for the Golden Handcuffs T-shirt. You know who you are. You guys liked the image so much, I had to write a book to go along with. :-D

Book 1

Chapter 1

DRAKKEN
When I close my eyes before sleep every night, I hope that I never wake up.
When I open my eyes every morning, I want to die.
Every waking moment of my life is tinged with misery.
Because of what happened in the past.
(...)
To her.
I cannot fix it.
I cannot change it.
I do my best to forget it.
But I always remember it.
Most of all, I remember her.
And it hurts...
Every morning I slide my stone face into place and take another step forward, hoping to put my past one step further behind. Hoping to forget so I can resume living.
But the past hangs on.
I try to outrun it, but no man can run forever. Not even me.
One day, my past is going to catch up with me.
When it does, it will destroy me.
Unless I destroy it first.
I just pray that no one else gets hurt...

Chapter 2

RIVER

When I notice the hot shirtless guy jogging along the wide sidewalk on Santa Monica Boulevard, I nearly poke myself in the eye with my mascara wand.

Startled, I jerk back from my car's rearview mirror and gasp at the sight of Mr. Eye Candy.

In a good way.

Unfortunately, my mascara wand decides now is a good time to jump out of my fingers and dive directly toward my tailored white spa uniform.

"Shizz!" I blurt, frantically grabbing for the disaster-hungry wand. Black spatter on your white uniform is never a good look. "Ack!" I wince as my spazzy hand hits the tip of the wand, causing it to pinwheel in the air.

I'm never going to catch it.

At the last second, the wand hits the edge of the steering wheel and bounces sideways, landing in the passenger footwell.

Phew, that was close. I breathe a sigh of relief.

Who says doing your makeup in your car is a bad idea? I mean, besides everybody?

It's not like my car was moving. I'm stuck in traffic at a red light. Otherwise, I might have lost an eye. I never do my makeup when the car is actually moving for this exact reason. Way too many head-turning hotties in Los Angeles. But none like this guy.

Since I'm still waiting for the light, I focus on ogling Mr. Eye Candy.

As always, he's nearly naked. Today he wears negligible navy blue running shorts and neon blue running shoes. His sweat-slick tan skin caresses his flexing abs as he takes long graceful strides.

He runs with obvious ease, as if running is easier for him than walking is for the rest of us.

My eyes lick the chiseled V arrowing into his low ride shorts. His muscular pecs and arms bounce and clench with every stride. A headband keeps his thick flyaway hair out of his sculpted brow. I can't tell what color his eyes are from this distance, but it really doesn't matter.

He's certifiably hot by anyone's standards.

The first time I saw Hottie-McJogs-A-Lot was two weeks ago when I took the long way to work. That morning, I didn't have time to make myself breakfast, so I was going to stop at Trader Joe's to buy some munchies. When I saw McJogs, I forgot all about food. The only munchies on my mind were the ones in McJogs' running shorts.

Needless to say, I've been taking the long way to work ever since so I can eye-lick McJogs' eye candied self every morning. I never get tired of watching him run in the morning sun.

Naughtiness overtakes me and I imagine his muscular body pounding something other than the pavement.

I squirm in my seat.

I swear, the squirming gets worse every time I see him. Yes, I've been obsessing about him. Luckily, the stoplight is still red so I can continue goggling at McJogs.

My cheeks turn as red as the stoplight.

As he approaches my car, my heart speeds up and my pulse pounds in my throat.

Will he finally notice me this morning?

I've been waiting patiently day after day.

But a girl can only wait so long. Sometimes you have to drop the proverbial handkerchief so the guy will pick it up for you. And by drop, I mean jump out of my ratty Chevy Cavalier and chase after McJogs so I can proposition him for a pounding.

Too bad that's never been my style.

I need to find a parking space quick. Then I can stand idly on the sidewalk and drop my handkerchief. Not that I have one.

A tissue will have to do.

If I could find one in my purse. But I don't have time to look inside that disaster area.

"Crap!" I bark out loud.

Maybe I'll just fall over on the sidewalk and pretend I'm having a heart attack so he'll give me mouth-to-mouth. But all the spaces along Santa Monica are filled with cars and I'm still stuck at the red light.

McJogs is now only two car lengths away from mine.

I openly stare at him.

He's really hot.

If he was less hot, I might be able to tear my eyes away and forget about him. But he isn't. His angelic beauty literally *forces* me to stare.

I chew my lower lip and catch myself moaning out loud, "Mmmm, abs…"

Good thing he can't hear me with my windows rolled up.

I squeeze my knees together, mindful of keeping both hands on the steering wheel. They have a mind of their own today. Who knows what my fingers will do if left to their own devices…

Then my world turns upside down.

McJogs slows and winks at me.

Holy shizz.

He waves a cute salute.

It's the cutest salute ever saluted.

I slap my hand over my eyes.

Our first eye contact ever!

Can you say, finger quotes, Match made in heaven?

I just hope McJogs doesn't realize how long I've been staring. And stalking.

I spread my fingers just enough to see his face. Sunshine literally beams from it.

The Angel Choir sings, "Ahhhhh!" They're in top form today. Which is perfect because McJogs' beauty would make Michelangelo weep with envy. The Sistine Chapel ain't got nothing on McJogs.

I'm about to roll down my window when sudden doubt freezes me in place. Does McJogs' smile say, "What's your name, beautiful?" Or does it say, "Don't you know we're in West Hollywood and I prefer penises, but I'll totally be your gay best friend?"

Only one way to find out.

Indecision freezes me again.

Idon'tknow Idon'tknow Idon'tknow

I'm quickly running out of time...

I sink in my car seat, melting into a puddle of embarrassment and girlish excitement. I totally want to chase him, but at 23, I'm not the desperately giddy teenaged girl I was at 19.

Screw it.

Who says being an adult means being boring? I'm gonna ditch my feminine pride and just run after him. They say morning is the best time to exercise, and I haven't gone to the gym today.

It's now or never.

I reach down to unbuckle my seatbelt, my finger hovering over the red plastic button. Then I remember the tow trucks.

Tow trucks, you ask?

L.A. Tow Trucks are like vultures. They hover around during rush hour, waiting to pounce on people who leave their cars where they shouldn't. Like the middle of Santa Monica Boulevard. During morning rush hour.

Crap.

I can't do it.

I can't run after McJogs and leave my car sitting in the street.

I want to.

But I can't.

I have responsibilities. I have a job I need to keep. Being mature sucks. Being a teenager was much more fun.

When McJogs zips past my car, I sneak peeks at his butt in his short shorts as a consolation prize. And what a prize it is. He has an incredible ass. He's as good going as he is coming.

Coming...

I *used* to know what that was.

I pound my fists against my steering wheel in frustration, mad at myself for not doing something more spontaneous and courageous.

I watch McJogs longingly in my rearview mirror as he pounds, pounds, pounds down the sidewalk. McJogs sure can run fast on those powerful legs of his.

Imagine all the pounding he could do in the bedroom…

I squeeze my knees again and my thighs literally quiver as the smoldering ember between my legs heats up and threatens to combust.

Wow, I seriously need to get laid.

If I want that to happen, I need to do something about it.

Screw it.

I'm going after him.

No time like the present.

I unbuckle my seatbelt, throw open the car door and…

Trip all over my seatbelt, which somehow managed to snake around my ankle.

"Damn it!" I shout as I land on my hands and knees. "Ow!"

Something tells me I'm not supposed to chase after McJogs today.

I'm so frustrated, I can't get my ankle free from the seatbelt no matter how hard I kick my foot. So I twist around until I'm sitting on my ass. I huff and grunt as I wrestle with the seatbelt around my ankle.

"Let go!" I shout.

I finally free my leg and stand up. I dust off my knees, which are now scuffed dirty brown. I twist around and see that the ass of my uniform is scuffed too. Why does anyone ever wear white?

Obviously, I wasn't the one who picked the color for my uniform.

I glance past all the cars waiting behind mine, looking for McJogs. He's long gone.

I drop into my car seat and sigh heavily.

The rusty door hinge squeaks loud enough to wake the dead when I pull it shut.

I should've gone after McJogs the second I saw him. But I waited too long.

Indecision won this battle.

Lately, my indecision has been winning *every* battle. Maybe it's for the best.

I'm not ready to date anybody.

Cage…

Not even a hottie like McJogs.

Cage…

But I *want* to be ready.

Cage…

Everyone tells me to give it time.

Cage…

They say I'm not done grieving.

Cage…

They say I should wait at least six months.

Cage…

Or even a year.

Cage…

Part of me wishes I was over Cage. But I'm not. The sadness I still carry with me every second of the day lives just beneath the surface of my skin. Some days I feel like you could poke me with a pin and the heartache filling every cell in my body would blow me apart like a popped balloon.

I don't want to feel fragile anymore.

I don't want to feel weak.

But I do.

Not even the distraction of gawking at McJogs can push the feelings away for very long.

I sigh again.

I'm so sick of the pain. I want it to be over and done with. I want to live and breathe and smile and laugh and chase hot guys like McJogs. Why can't the dark cloud that storms over my heart and ruins my good mood twenty times a day go away forever?

I want my sunshine back.

Cage…

Stupid storm clouds.

Finally, the stoplight ahead turns green. The cars in front of me accelerate up to speed and I begrudgingly follow.

Sigh.

As always, my transmission slips a bit as my car gets up to speed.

"Hold together, Sheena," I say to my car. I call her Sheena the Chevy. "You can do it, girl!"

Eventually I make it up to 35 mph like everyone else.

I really need to get Sheena fixed, but I never have enough spare cash to cover it.

As I pass IHOP, and Santa Monica Boulevard curves to the left, a huge red bomb explodes in the corner of my vision.

I slam on my breaks and my tires screech. My Chevy swerves toward the sidewalk as I avoid the nut job driving the liquid red Lamborghini who blasted into my lane without warning.

A woman waiting at a bus stop is standing in the street scanning the distance for the next orange Metro bus.

I'm going to hit her.

Why did she have to pick now to look for the bus? I frantically wheel my car to avoid running her over. My elbows flail around the steering wheel like nervous birds. My brakes are locked and my car has no traction. The woman's eyes pop from her face and she stumbles backward onto the sidewalk as my car hurtles toward her.

At the last second, my car regains traction and turns the six inches necessary to avoid murdering her.

My Chevy bounces up the curb and thumps loudly before stopping halfway up the sidewalk.

What was that thump?

Ohmygodohmygodohmygod—

Did I kill someone?

My eyes dart around nervously, checking for dead pedestrians. My heart thunders in my ears at about 1,000 beats a minute.

The racing Lamborghini's engine screams so loudly it drowns out all sounds. Up ahead, it swerves around more cars and blasts through a red light. More tires screech as cross traffic nearly cuts the Lamborghini in half, but the sports car is too quick and it's gone in a flash of red mercury.

One of the cars that almost hit the Lamborghini is a Pink Dot delivery car. It's a blue VW bug with a splatter of pink polka dots, giant plastic eyeballs for headlights, and a giant plastic beanie hat on the roof. Its comical horn blares indignantly at the long gone Lamborghini. The quacking screech of the horn would be hilarious under ordinary circumstances, but there's nothing funny about the disaster nearly caused by the idiot driving the blood red sports car.

The people at the bus stop are all on their feet, tensed and ready to flee to safety. They all gawk at me, jaws hanging slack, staring at my motionless car like it might suddenly vault toward them and mow them down. A random guy helps the woman I almost killed to her feet. Thankfully, she isn't hurt.

I smile at her meekly through my windshield.

She gapes at me in horror.

Maybe next time she won't stand in the middle of the street. More importantly, none of this was my fault.

Who the hell was driving that red Lamborghini?

What rich shithead thinks he's king of the road?

And why did I bother to get out of bed this morning?

Chapter 3

RIVER

Twenty minutes later, I pull into the parking lot of the luxurious and exclusive Beverly Hills Resort where I work as a massage therapist.

My heart has calmed to a mere 500 beats per minute.

It's going to be a long day.

Sitting proudly in the roundabout that circles below the elaborate overhang fronting the main entrance to the hotel is a red Lamborghini.

My stomach clenches and my hands start to shake with rage.

Is it the same car?

If it is, I need to key it or slash some tires. Sadly, I already know the owner values his paint job more than human life and would sue me into bankruptcy if I did. Not that I have any money to begin with. Either way, whoever the asshole is who drives it, I pray he dies a slow death as soon as possible.

I hope I never meet him.

If I do, I will politely kill him.

I shake my head, trying to ease the anger so I can focus on my day. I can't bring my bad mood with me to work. Nobody likes an angry massage therapist. There's a reason people don't call us massage therapisseds.

The gate to the underground parking garage opens and my Chevy descends into the shadows beneath the hotel where the rest of the staff and the non-asshole guests park.

I try my best to dust the scuffs off my knees and ass, but no luck. I hope nobody notices. I take the elevator up to the main lobby and walk across it.

"What happened to your ass?"

I spoke to soon.

The ass noticer is my work besty Finch Barksdale. Finch is a bellhop at the Beverly Hills Resort. Right now, she stands behind the concierge desk in the main lobby wearing a burgundy blazer, gray slacks, and her blonde hair in a tight chignon.

I flash her a glare as I stride past, "Don't ask."

Finch falls into stride beside me and mutters, "Did some hot guy pin you up against a dirty brick wall and do dirty things to you?" Finch hasn't had sex in forever.

I roll my eyes. I'm really not in the mood to make jokes after my run in with the Lamborghini. I continue walking.

Finch says, "I notice your knees are dirty too. Did the guy make you get down on your knees and suck his woolly mammoth?" She lifts one arm in front of her and curls it like a pretend elephant trunk. She then makes her best impersonation of a screeching elephant honk, "Wer-GEEK!"

I frown. "A, Ew! And B, have you ever even seen a penis?!"

"Not that I can recall," she winks.

I shake my head and try not to grin as I walk down the hallway that leads to the spa.

Finch hollers at my back in a low voice, "You can tell me all about it later! Wer-GEEK!"

I blurt out a laugh and keep walking.

Chapter 4

RIVER

Ten minutes later, I'm in the massage room working on Mrs. Mueller. I've successfully wrestled my anger under control, and I'm totally focused on the task at hand.

"Oh!" Mrs. Mueller winces on the massage table.

I ease up slightly as I press down with my forearm and glide it along the muscles of her lower back.

"Careful, River. I'm not as sturdy as I once was." She laughs merrily. Mrs. Mueller is in her seventies and in great shape for her age. "I think I threw my back out on the court today with one too many backhands."

"Maybe you should cut back on the tennis from five days a week to three," I smile as I continue to stretch out the knots along her spine.

"Why would I do that when I have you taking such good care of me?"

I grin, "Aw, thank you, Mrs. Mueller." A half hour later, I finish her massage. "All done," I beam. "How do you feel?"

She sits up and wraps the towel around her back demurely. "Like a young woman of forty." She sighs contently and arches her back while leaning from side to side. Her face lights with excitement. "My kink is completely gone! Tell me your secret, River!" She says it like I know the winning lottery numbers or I'm about to tell her the secrets of the universe.

I smile, "It's all in the fingers." I wiggle all ten.

"You truly have magic hands, my dear." She walks behind the Japanese shoji screen in the corner to dress.

Making people's pain go away is the coolest job ever. I only wish all my clients were as nice as Mrs. Mueller.

She emerges from behind the screen in fresh tennis clothes.

I blurt, "You're not going back to the court for another game, are you?"

She smiles, "No. But this outfit makes me look sporty, and I have a lunch date."

"Oooh" I coo, "did you meet someone?"

She grins, "I did indeed." Mrs. Mueller's husband died five years ago, and she's been dating a lot lately.

"Is he handsome?"

"For sixty-five, he is absolutely dashing."

"Sixty-five!" I chide. "Mrs. Mueller, you're such a cougar!"

She chuckles, "I don't think you can call me a cougar when my younger man is old enough for a senior discount. And how about you, young lady?" She arches her eyebrow, "Are you chasing any younger men around town?"

"Younger? I'm only twenty three!" I laugh. "They don't get much younger than me."

She waves her hand, "Oh, piffle. I'm sure you could find an innocent eighteen or nineteen year old in need of corrupting," she winks.

"Mrs. Mueller!" I chide, giggling.

"If that's too young for you, send them my way," she chuckles dismissively.

Mrs. Mueller asks me about my dating life all the time. She knows I'm single, but she doesn't know anything about Cage. My clients don't need to know about my dreary personal life. Heck, I wish I didn't know anything about it either.

"Well then," Mrs. Mueller prompts, "have you been chasing any men of a more appropriate age?"

Cage...

I jut my bottom lip and puff a stray lock of hair out of my eyes, pushing thoughts of Cage out of my mind. In the cheeriest voice I can muster, I say, "Not lately." Then I remember McJogs-A-Lot and can't help but smile. "Well, I almost chased one today, but he got away."

She pats my shoulder affectionately, "Don't worry, you'll find a good man soon."

Cage...

"In Los Angeles?" I scoff. "*Good* men don't exist." Not that I care one way or the other.

She winks, "You just have to kiss more toads."

Been there, done that.

She continues, "There's a prince out there waiting for you."

That's what I thought...

She grins, "I can feel it in my old bones."

I do my best to sweep the pieces of my broken heart back into the secret compartment inside me. I force a smile, "You're not old, Mrs. Mueller."

"Older than you," she grins and reaches into her purse, pulling out four twenties for my tip. Nobody tips as big as Mrs. Mueller, but this is a lot even for her.

"Oh, Mrs. Mueller, I can't take that. It's too much."

She presses the money into my hand with a grin, "I don't need it."

"Thank you so much, Mrs. Mueller," I smile.

"Just make sure you put it to good use. Take a nice young man out to dinner. If he doesn't like the idea of you paying for his meal, you'll know he's a toad without the bother of kissing him."

"I thought the men were supposed to pay."

She snaps her purse shut with authority, "Maybe in my day. But this is the twenty-first century, young lady. Strong women like you and I can hold our own."

I nod appreciatively, "You're right," I cheer. "Strong women like us don't need men to pay our way!"

She waves goodbye and walks out of the room.

I almost tell her that maybe we don't even need men, but I stop myself when I think about—

Cage...

Thinking about him only makes me feel weak and sad. If women didn't need men, then why does their absence make us so miserable sometimes?

I sigh.

Cage...

When is the pain going to fade?

Wow, I really need to step outside for a breath of fresh air so I can clear my head before my next client.

Chapter 5

RIVER

The storm clouds shadowing my mood still haven't cleared by the time I finish changing the linens on the massage table.

Cage...

The California sun beckons me through the glowing window blinds. A stroll around the hotel pool might help brighten my mood.

I walk toward the massage room door. When I reach for the doorknob, the door blows open in my face, nearly knocking me down.

"Hey!" I shout as I jump back. "You almost killed me!!!"

A huge guy in a dark tailored suit fills the doorway. He's incredibly handsome.

Hello, sunshine.

He has short cropped raven black hair, flawless skin, ice blue eyes, and chiseled features. He ignores my comment about my brush with death but his eyes sweep over me with heated intensity.

He's sunshine, all right. My body warms under his piercing gaze quite nicely.

From the look on his face, I can't decide if he's mad at me or wants to eat me. Or do other things that predators do when they aren't hunting or sleeping. You know, the thing that usually comes right before sleeping? And involves coming? Yeah, that part. Purr.

I don't know why, but I'm super horny today. It must be my hormones. Am I ovulating? Or is this guy doing it to me? No, McJogs did it too. I'm blaming the hormones.

Cage...

Should I feel guilty that I'm going guy crazy today? Or does my horniness mean I'm ready to start dating again? I'm voting for dating. Because seriously, who needs to be depressed about an ex when it's raining angels today? Well, this suit guy looks like more of a devil, but you know what I mean.

Speaking of devils, I almost forgot what a clumsy oaf this guy is. Almost. I don't care how hot he is. An oaf is an oaf. By now, a gentleman would've apologized for nearly knocking my block off.

I smirk and grumble sarcastically, "Can I help you?"

"I need massage," he says with an accent.

"You have to have an appointment," I say confidently but with noticeable tease. I can't help myself. He's too hot. At least I'm not batting my eyelashes. "Did you talk to Jocelyn at the front desk when you came in?"

It takes him a moment to process what I said. Does he not know English?

Eventually, he answers, "Is no one there." He glances around the room. "And is no one here. You massage me." He closes the door behind him and slides his suit jacket off.

Okay, hot or not, he's way too rude and demanding. And if English *is* his second language, he could still be more polite. Isn't 'please' one of the first words you learn in any language, along with 'thank you'?

Yeah, this oafish jerk in a suit can wait for his massage until later. Or tomorrow. Or never. So what if I'm not busy at the moment. "I'm sorry, but you'll have to wait. I was about to go on my break." It's a lie, but he doesn't need to know. "Maybe you should book an appointment with Jocelyn at the front desk?"

"I no wait."

Wow, this guy is beyond rude. I frown and fold my arms across my chest, "I'm sorry, but you'll have to wait." Why does it always feel so good to say no to jerks?

He says, "I pay double."

Does he think money makes up for his bad behavior? I shake my head.

He pulls a wallet out of his back pocket and offers me three hundred dollar bills.

The spa only charges $150 for a forty-five minute massage. This is Beverly Hills. Stuff is expensive. Anyway, who am I to say no to good fortune? I snatch the money out of his hands, ignoring the fact that my principles disappeared the second the money appeared. What can I say? I'm poor and this is my job.

Without missing a beat, I say, "It's three hundred for the massage. Double is six hundred." Because demanding jerks pay extra. I sort of hope he doesn't have the money and goes away. Then I get my principles back.

He pulls out three more bills and hands them to me without a thought.

My principles are nowhere in sight. Like I said, this *is* my job.

Okay, I don't have to love or even like all my clients. Besides, it's not like I'm ruining the environment or cutting down rain forests. I massage people so they feel better. Even rich jerks need to feel better. I bet if more rich jerks got massages, they'd be less jerky, and the world would be a better place.

My conscience clear, I fold the bills into my purse and put it under the sink. When I turn around, he's unknotting his tie.

I motion toward the Japanese screen, "You can change back there."

He glances at it absently while unbuttoning his shirt.

Is he going to undress in front of me?

I clear my throat, "Ahem. The screen?"

He ignores me and hangs his shirt over the chair with his jacket. "You have hanger? For suit?"

First, how is it that his question manages to sound like a demanding command? This guy is way too entitled for his own good. Second, I'm surprised an oaf like him bothers to hang his clothes. Maybe oaf is the wrong word. I always thought oafs were ugly. This guy is way too handsome to be an oaf. What's the word for handsome oafs? Hoafs? Maybe not. I'll have to ask Finch. She'll know.

"Hanger?" he question-commands. "For suit?"

"Yeah, yeah," I frown as I walk to the small closet in the corner. I pull out two wooden hangers and jam them in his face.

"You hang," he says.

I bark, "I'm not your mother! Hang your own clothes."

He cocks his head toward his suit jacket on the chair then glances at the hangers in my hand. Then he pins his eyes on mine. He arches a demanding eyebrow expectantly.

Is that supposed to be a silent command? Does he expect me to obey? If he does, he's totally got the wrong girl. I arch my own eyebrow rebelliously. Two can play at this game. I say nothing.

We end up playing eyeball tennis for at least a minute, our gazes bouncing from the suit jacket to the hangers and back to each other's eyes, over and over again.

Until now, his face has been an inscrutable mask. But I swear I see the slightest hint of amusement crinkle his eyes.

"You hang," he grunts.

I was wrong. That's not a look of amusement. It's a look of assholery. What a total prick. He gives rich people a bad name. Mrs. Mueller is rich, and she's a sweetheart.

I drop the wood hangers at his feet and they clatter on the tiled floor. I turn my back and wash my hands in the sink because I can't think of anything else to make it look like I'm busy. While wiping my hands on a fresh towel, I can't help but notice that he has hung his suit on the hanger and put it in the closet.

I also notice he's down to boxer briefs.

The rest of him is slabs of rugged muscles.

Holy crap.

This guy has an incredible body. His black boxer briefs do little to disguise the bold bulge hidden within. The word 'bulge' in lower case doesn't do it justice. We're talking:

Bah-*BULGE*!!!

No wonder he's such a jerk. He's clearly rich, he's incredibly handsome, his body is picture perfect, and he's packing salami in his pants. To my surprise, I think that this suit jerk is actually hotter than McJogs.

I pull a large towel off the stack in the cupboard beneath the bonsai tree on the counter. Suit Jerk will need something to wrap around his waist. When I turn to face him, he's completely naked.

He's got a salami all right.

Bah-*BULGE*!!!

I jump and blurt, "Ohmygod!" I cover my eyes and hold out the towel. "Put this on!" I can't help but peek through my fingers, but only enough so I can see his smug face.

He's smirking. He knows what he's doing. He probably does this sort of thing to unsuspecting masseuses all the time.

I growl, "Take the towel!" I shake it.

He doesn't grab it. He just stands there, no doubt gloating.

I throw the towel at him and turn around. Normally, if a client acted like this, I'd walk out and tell Luciana, the spa manager, to call security. She'd send the boys here in no time, and Suit Jerk would be tossed out on his ass. But he already paid me $600 cash. I'm morally obligated to follow through on the massage. See? I have some principles left. I'll just have to pretend this man's assitude isn't as off the charts as his hotness.

I warn, "I'm not turning around until you put that towel on."

"Ok. I put towel on," he chuckles.

Still not looking at him, I notice how masculine his voice is. Rich, resonant, and manly. He could probably be a voiceover guy and do movie trailers. I imagine the gravelly movie trailer voice guy saying, "*In a world filled with assholes, one ass hovers above them all...*" I giggle to myself while imagining a giant towering asshole hovering above the Empire State Building.

"What is funny?" Suit Jerk asks.

"Nothing," I deny. "Is your towel on?"

"Yes. Is on."

I turn around.

He has the towel draped over one shoulder. He stands with one fist planted on a cocked hip. His biggus dickus winks back at me. Well, maybe not a *wink*. More of a wave. Is there a breeze in here?

I turn away and shriek, "That is not on! Wrap it around your waist!"

"My English not so good," he chuckles. He's totally lying. If he knows enough about the world to wear a suit, he knows to cover his ding dong when he gets a massage. This is the Beverly Hills Resort, not a whorehouse in Bangkok or wherever.

No more Miss Nice Girl. I growl, "Put the towel around your waist or we're done. And I'm keeping your money."

He chuckles to himself. The towel rustles.

I demand, "Is it covered?"

"I need bigger towel."

I bark, "Make it work." The towel I threw him is big enough for a rhinoceros *and* a rhinoceros dong. Wer-GEEK! Oh, wait. That's a wooly mammoth call. I stifle a giggle.

Suit Jerk chuckles and I hear more rustling.

Wer-GEEK!

I stifle my own laugh, but I smile to myself. I'm glad he can't see me. What a prick. Yes, without a doubt. His prick was truly impressive. I mean, what an ass. But I'm sure his ass is as nice as his cock. Wait, why am I thinking about man buns? I meant ass*hole*. This guy is the part of the ass that shoots poop. I shake my head. My cheeks heat. I'm totally blushing.

What is this guy doing to me?

I take a deep breath and turn around slowly, prepared for more nonsense.

Nope, the towel is wrapped around his narrow hips. He wears it rather low, showcasing his prize winning abs and a V better than McJogs-A-Lot's. Suit Jerk is also taller and probably a tad more muscular.

I expected an assknot like this to wear way too much cologne, but I don't smell any. However, I do detect a faint but pleasant scent of man. I resist the urge to inhale deeply.

Is it a rule that guys this hot have to be jerks? Or do they end up jerks because so many women throw themselves at them? I don't know, but there's no way I'm throwing myself at Suit Jerk and bloating this ass balloon's ego even further.

"Lie down," I point to the table.

"You join?" He raises an inviting eyebrow and cocks his head toward the massage table.

It takes a moment for his words to register. Join? As in, me and him? I repress a shiver. My cheeks glow. I really need to work on my tan so guys like this can't read me like a trashy romance novel.

I cough, "No, um, just you. On the table."

He winks and lies down face up on the sturdy massage table without breaking eye contact the entire time. That was kind of weird. I wonder why he did that? I don't know why I'm asking. This guy has been weird since he walked in.

The table creaks beneath him and he shifts around to get comfortable. How much does this guy weigh? With all that muscle on his huge frame, and his huge other parts, he must weigh a ton.

Wer-GEEK!

I titter before asking, "Can you turn over? So I can start with your back?"

"Start with front. Is good."

Is not good. I have a process. "We should really start with your back. The spine is the root of everything else." He better not tell me to start by massaging his front root.

"Start with front root," he says with finality.

No he didn't.

I don't know if he intended any innuendo, but I ignore it if he did. "Sorry, that's not how I work." I fold my arms across my chest and cock my hip.

"Start with front. I watch and make sure you do good job."

I wrinkle my nose, "Nobody watches a massage. You're supposed to relax and feel it."

"I watch. You very beautiful. You eyes relax me."

Did he just say "you eyes?" Anyway, awww. That was actually really sweet. I smile at him.

For the first time, his face relaxes. I didn't realize it until now, but this guy is incredibly tense. Before, his handsome face was tight, controlled, and nearly frozen. Like an angry stone mask. Now it eases into something soft and open. Not what I was expecting from a jerk like him.

I have to admit, I'm a sucker for tough guys who can show their vulnerability now and then. I relent, "Okay. We start with the front."

"Good," he nods.

I start with his neck. Everyone has tense necks. I stand at the head of the table and slide my hands under his head and begin dragging my palms upward in a repetitive motion.

He stares up at me.

I smile briefly but glance away. I don't like to make eye contact with my clients because it's distracting to me and them. Especially when it's a guy. That's why I start on their backs. By the time I turn them over, they're so relaxed, they almost always have their eyes closed. Not today. I can feel this guy's eyes all over me.

Not that I mind.

Then I realize he can see right up my nose. Not the most flattering angle for any woman. I turn away and tuck my chin into my chest, hoping to hide my nostrils. I hope I don't have any boogers. Not that I check often, but you never know. The last thing you want is a hot guy seeing your nose nasties.

"Show me you eyes please." His clumsy words run together.

What? Did he actually say please? Sure, it still sounded sort of like a command. But it's progress. Maybe he's not a total prick. Just a partial prick.

Why do I keep thinking about pricks around this guy? Maybe because his is the first one I've seen in forever, and it's like having a third person in the room.

Duh.

Wer-GEEK!

He sighs heavily, relaxing into the massage as I continue to stroke his neck. "For small girl, you have strong hand. Is good."

Girl? I remind myself it's just this guy's limited English skills. Otherwise, I'd have to school him. Get Mrs. Mueller in here with me to teach him a thing or two about feminism and the English language. Maybe next time. I shake my head, but I smile, "Thank you?" I say uncertainly.

"Is good," he smiles back at me.

He really has beautiful eyes. Even upside down, I feel like I could literally fall into them. They're wide open and reveal a side to him I suspect he rarely shows anybody.

A pleasant sensation thrills its way out from my stomach in fluttery waves.

Connection.

I feel it.

Between me and this man. Something profound.

I shouldn't be feeling a connection because we barely know each other. But I am.

Those eyes of his are doing something to me. They're penetrating my own defenses, whispering right past my own barriers, the ones I keep in place when I work with clients. That's the thing about massages. Although they're very intimate, you have to maintain a certain distance from your clients. Otherwise, it gets way too confusing.

Like right now.

My entire awareness has condensed down to the glowing blue eyes of this strange man gazing up at me. I feel our hearts communicating in a clear yet indecipherable language. I don't know what is being said, but I feel it.

And I see that he feels it too.

He's as mesmerized as I am.

This is way too weird.

It's never happened to me before. Never. Not with a client, not with a boyfriend, nobody. But it's amazingly wonderful and pleasantly intoxicating.

I can't think of a good way to describe it other than flow.

Flow.

Something flows between us.

And it feels incredible. It feels peaceful. It feels like home. Like essence.

I'm only half aware that I've stopped massaging him. My hands lovingly cup the back of his neck and I find myself leaning toward his face ever so slightly. Like I want to kiss him.

Whoa, that's way beyond weird.

Weirder is the fact that I swear his eyes are starting to water.

He blinks repeatedly and scrubs his forearm across his brow. He's trying to hide whatever feelings are straining to come out. He sniffs harshly, as if pulling his emotions back inside, then smears his fingers down his face like he can wipe away his feelings. He sniffs again and adjusts his jaw, wiggling it around, opening and closing it a few times. He clears his throat several times.

I know what he's doing. He's putting his armor back on. I can see it in his face, which is now tense and stoic. Stone.

He avoids my eyes entirely. He stares off into space like I'm not even there. He grumbles, "Is okay. You massage. Please."

That fluttery feeling I had is gone. It's replaced by a sense of emptiness in my chest. It sounds stupid, but it's almost like that feeling you get when you have great sex with a guy, but afterward he hops out of bed for one reason or another.

Abandonment.

Cage...

I heave a deep breath in and out.

I'm here to massage this guy. Not develop feelings for him.

Back to business.

Time to do my job and earn my paycheck.

That's all this is.

A job.

Chapter 6

RIVER

I remind myself that the big oaf with the English impairment on my massage table is just a physiological problem to be solved, not a man whose heart needs healing.

I run through the standard questions in my head. Where is the client most tense? Which muscles are locked and need release? How best to bring about long-term relief?

Those eyes... That essence... That flow...

No, this is just a mechanical problem with an answer. After mulling things over for a moment, a solution presents itself.

I shift my stance and go to work on his trapezius muscles on the top of his shoulders. Working the entire neck is much easier when someone is on their back, and the reason I start there, but I can improvise. I use my fists to knead the big trapezius muscles. Geesh, his muscles feel like inch-thick Tug Of War ropes. He must be incredibly strong. And incredibly stressed to be this chronically tense.

No wonder he came in for a massage.

I kind of feel sorry for him.

Those eyes...

I block all of that out. This guy's a client. I'm doing a job.

There's no way I'm going to release all the kinks in his neck today, so I go to work on his chest. Big muscle guys always have tight pecs.

I shift around to his right side and lean my palms on the front of his deltoid, pushing his entire shoulder blade into the table. This should help relax his chest. After a minute of that, I run both hands down the length of his arms, smoothing the muscles out, trying to elongate them. Something about the idea of elongating stirs my hormones.

I can't help it.

None of my clients are this physically flawless. Everyone knows there's an undeniable power in physical beauty. I'm not immune.

Massage, massage, massage. I'm just doing my job.

Yeah, right.

It's sort of like I'm caressing his arm, but I swear I'm just working his muscles. Very clinical. Not erotic. Nope.

Stroke, stroke, stroke.

I mean, 'Elongate the fascial tissue by applying even and continuous pressure.' I read that in a massage textbook at some point.

Who am I kidding?

I'm totally stroking.

Stroke, stroke, stroke…

Am I enjoying running my hands all over this guy's smooth skin?

Maybe just a bit.

Does that make me a pervert because I'm copping a feel?

No, it just means I enjoy my job. If I recall, he was the one who told me to touch him. In fact, he ordered it. I'm totally not a perv.

I notice his body is very hot to the touch. I'm not surprised with a guy like him. He must work out all the time to keep muscles this big.

Mmmm, big muscles…

Are they turning me on?

A better question is, are my panties getting wet?

Err, I mean, ahh…you know what I mean.

I walk around the table and go to work on his other arm.

He moans out a breathy sigh, "Is good. Is very good." He smiles up at me.

Phew, I'm totally working up a sweat. Not because of his hot body. Well, sort of because of his hot body. But mainly because I use my whole body when giving a massage, and it takes a lot of extra effort to knead this guy's heavy muscles. He's just so damn big.

In every way imaginable.

Wer-GEEK!

On that thought, I happen to look up and notice the growing bulge beneath his towel.

Yes, it's an occupational hazard. He's not the first guy to get an erection while I'm giving a massage. The easiest thing to do is pretend I don't notice.

In this case, it's difficult. He's uncoiling beneath his towel like a waking python. Soon, it will be tenting the towel. Unless it drills a hole through first.

Like I said, I pretend it's not there. I just keep massaging. No erect dicks for miles. Tents are for camping only. They provide shelter from the rain and giant snakes.

Since I've already massaged his neck, I shift down to his feet. Everybody likes a good foot massage. And it's further away from his tent built for two. Or in his case, ten. As in, inches.

I'm just estimating, of course.

I knead the sole of his foot and work the ankle in circles. All while staring at the ceiling. I would whistle if I knew how.

Did I mention this guy has beautiful feet? I'm only noticing his feet. That's it. He doesn't exist above the ankles.

Wow, I'm totally sweating now. Or is that just my panties dripping?

Okay, maybe I'm enjoying this more than is professionally appropriate.

"Ahhh," he moans in his deep voice. "Is good..."

"Is good?" I nearly moan the words myself, parroting his pet phrase without realizing it. I clear my throat and say in an authoritative tone, "I mean, is my work satisfactory? Does it meet your expectations? I mean, uh..." I don't know what I mean. But I do know that I'm losing my mind.

He chuckles softly, "Is good." His face eases into a wide post-orgasmic smile.

I've seen this look on my clients many times. Not everybody knows that a good massage is a lot like a good orgasm. It's all about the release. A massage isn't as sudden and explosive as sex, but the afterglow can be just as intense. Often, the afterglow of a good massage rivals the afterglow of sex. It's true.

"Today I see funny thing," He says lazily, a half grin easing onto his mouth.

Now I'm curious. He doesn't seem like the humorous type. "What?" I ask flirtatiously. Of course I want to know. Right now, I want to know everything on this guy's mind. Especially what he knows about sexual afterglows. Cough. I mean, his funny story.

"I drive here, I see, uh..." his brows knit. "I not know word."

"Can you describe it? The word, I mean?"

"Dee-*describe*?"

"What you saw? Tell me what you saw. Describe it." While he processes what I said, I work my hands up his ankle, but I won't go any higher than his calf muscles, which are plenty stiff. I don't want to get too close to his…ahhh…other stiff parts. Cuz now his towel is fully tented. There's enough room under it for an entire army platoon. Not that I'm looking. I just notice it in my peripheral vision.

Wer-GEEK!

"What I saw is car. Funny car."

"Funny car?" I'm not sure what that means.

His eyes search mine. His are very hypnotizing. And at this moment, surprisingly playful and curious. I suspect maybe this big bad man is a softie underneath his armored exterior.

He says, "Is shashek car."

"Shashek?" I have no idea what a shashek is.

He snaps his fingers several times. Is he summoning a servant or something? It's now obvious that being commanding is second nature for him. I wonder if he grew up super rich? With maids and butlers and stuff?

"How you say…" his brows knit together, "klaun?"

Then something clicks. "Do you mean clown?"

"Yes!" He smiles. "Clown car! I see clown car today. When I drive hotel!"

"You drove a hotel?" I giggle.

He shakes his head, "*To* hotel. Sorry, my English very bad." He sounds apologetic. Like he's embarrassed by his bad grammar.

I don't mind. The way he speaks is actually kind of cute. "It's okay," I grin. I kind of like that he has some humility. Maybe this guy is more than just a cocky bastard with a hot body and a thick wallet.

And thick hard cock.

Wer-GEEK!

Amazingly, he's still erect. How can he still be erect talking about clown cars? Not that I'm paying ANY attention to what's going on underneath his towel. Ahem. "So, um, you saw a clown car today?" Why does that sound familiar?

"Yes," he smiles. "Has big eyes and hat on top! Hat with pro-*propeller*!"

For a moment, I'm surprised he knows the word propeller. Before I can ponder that any further, it falls into place. I grin, "You saw the Pink Dot delivery car!" I'm not really surprised. Anyone who drives around Hollywood often enough is bound to see one.

"Pink Dot?" he asks uncertainly.

"Yeah! Pink Dot is a grocery store in Hollywood. Their delivery cars are blue VWs with pink polka dots and pink eyes for headlights! And they have giant plastic beanies on the roof! With a propeller on top!"

His face looks vacant for a moment. I remember he's processing all the words I threw at him. Then recognition settles in. "Yes! Propeller car! Funny Volkswagen!"

"You saw that too!"

"When I drive to hotel! In Vest Hollywood!"

"Vest? Oh! You mean West Hollywood."

He watches me speaking closely then nods, "Yes. Wuh-*West* Hollywood."

It's so cute watching him try to pronounce the word correctly. His cocky attitude is completely gone. I could learn to like this guy. And I don't even know his name.

His smile widens and he says, "Clown car almost hit me!"

My stomach suddenly clenches. The puzzle pieces snowfall into position with alarming speed. "The Pink Dot car almost hit you?" I ask flatly.

"Ano. I mean, yes."

My eyes narrow. "Were you driving on Santa Monica Boulevard?"

"An—yes."

I nod and a hint of irritation creeps into my voice, "Was it near the IHOP by Barney's Beanery?"

"American pancake!" His eyes widen with glee. "You saw?"

The puzzle is nearly complete. One last piece to place. "Do you drive a red Lamborghini or whatever?"

"You saw! Is my car!"

Uh huh. "Yeah," I say sarcastically, "I saw you run a red light and—"

He cuts me off with a loud donkey cackle, "Funny car make funny sound! OO-GAH! OO-GAH! OO-GAH!" He laughs and grins like a fool, completely unaware that he is a complete and total asshole. No, he's worse than that. This guy is not fit for the bottom of a toilet.

I purse my lips while he enjoys his sick joke. When his laughs fade to chuckling, I grumble, "You nearly ran into me today."

"Ran? I ran with you?"

He's not getting it. I shake my head. "Your car? You almost killed me? Causing me to almost kill the woman at the bus stop?"

His face slackens again. He's processing my words.

I switch to hand gestures. I hold up one hand and say, "My car." I hold up my other hand. "Your car." I slide my hands forward and swerve one hand toward the other, just like how his car nearly slammed into mine. Then I make the hand representing my car swerve like it's going off the road. I make a screeching tire noise. "Eeeck!" Then I smash both hands together before exploding my fingers apart. "Boom!"

"I hit you car?" He cocks his head to the side and shakes it. "I not hit car today."

Not technically. And maybe not today. But driving like that, he will sooner or later. And sure, mine didn't explode when I ran up the sidewalk, but I nearly killed that woman. There's no way I'm going to explain the finer points of his insane driving habits with our language barrier. I should fish this guys wallet out of his suit and cut up his driver's license. If he even has one. A lunatic like him shouldn't be on the road.

Speaking of wallets, that reminds me. I grab my purse out of the cupboard beneath the sink and fish out the $600 he paid me. I fling the bills onto his chest. I don't want this guy's money. I don't want anything to do with him. "Get out." I shoot a stiff arm toward the door and point.

"But I pay you." He's clearly confused.

"I don't care. Keep your money." I secretly smile to myself when I realize my principles aren't as cheap as I thought.

He sits up on the table. The towel falls to the floor, revealing his fading erection. It curls into his lap, chastised, looking as slump shouldered as he does. He has no idea what's going on. If it wasn't for the language barrier, he would totally know. But now I couldn't care less about this dangerous jerk.

"Out," I growl. "*Now.*"

He stands up and steps toward me. His dick droops between his dickish legs. Because right now, every part of him is dickish. He towers over me.

I glare at him and say sarcastically, "You understand goodbye?"

He narrows his ice blue eyes. They're cold and metallic.

"Go!" I shout. "That way!" I jam my finger at the door. "Out!"

His face hardens. The grim stone mask is back, hardening all the muscles in his cheeks, jaw and lips. His eyes glint like glass beneath his furrowed brow. He takes a step toward me.

I can't help but take a step back. He really knows how to intimidate people when he wants to. And he's barely trying. I hate to think what this guy acts like when he lets his anger out.

I don't plan on finding out.

In a low voice, he growls through clenched teeth, "My clothes?"

Damn it. I can't make him walk out of here naked.

"Fine," I spit. "Get dressed and get out. I have another client in a few minutes." I storm past him and yank the door open. I don't look back when I slam it behind me.

What an asshole.

Chapter 7

RIVER

"Oh my god," I hiss, "I am so PISSED!!"

Finch wrinkles her nose, "Did Mr. Skelton make you massage his nasty old feet again?"

"Worse." I grimace.

We stand in the lobby near the concierge desk.

Finch asks, "Did Mrs. Ragsdale make you finger her bunions?"

I frown, "What's a bunion?"

"I don't know, but I hear they need to be fingered," she snickers. "What's up?"

"I had the biggest douche come in just now and demand a massage."

"What happened?"

I huff, "The guy was a supreme jerk. He kept bossing me around. He didn't even have an appointment."

"How rude," Finch scoffs.

"I know, right? Anyway, he didn't bother to cover up and his dong was all over the place!"

Finch winces, "Gross!!"

I can only wonder what she's imagining. Probably old and frail Mr. Skelton's wrinkly peanut dong, not Suit Jerk's hot bod and hot salami. Wait, I need to rephrase that. Make that: Suit Jerk's rotten body and rotten sausage. No one who is that big of an ass can be considered appealing in any way, shape, or form.

Finch says sympathetically, "I hope he was a good tipper."

"That's the thing. I didn't take his money because it turns out he ran me off the road on the way to work this—"

"Wait, wait, wait," Finch interrupts and whispers in a low voice, "Hold up. Hottie alert." Her eyes gleam as she stares over my shoulder at someone behind me. I'm about to turn around to look when she blurts, "Don't look! He'll see!"

Now I'm curious. I whip around and follow her gaze. For a second, I don't see anyone in the lobby. Then Suit Jerk emerges from behind a large column.

I groan and roll my eyes, "That's him."

"Who, my future husband?" Finch jokes. Her eyes are glued to Suit Jerk as he struts across the high-ceilinged lobby with purpose.

"No, wiseass. That's the douche I had to massage!"

"And you're complaining?" Finch huffs. "I should be so lucky. Look at his ass! He can sure fill out a suit. I'm in the wrong line of work. All I do is carry people's bags."

"Trust me, that's all that guy is. A douchebag."

Finch winks, "I'd totally carry his douchebags."

I frown, "What does that even mean?"

"I don't know," Finch giggles, "but his wish is my command. Now be quiet while I take a mental snapshot of his ass."

"You can't even see it under his suit jacket," I scoff.

"I have X-Ray vision. Now shut up. I need some material for my bedtime date with B.O.B. tonight." She bites the corner of her mouth and lifts her hand to make a motion.

I quickly grab her wrist and in a low voice growl, "If you make cat claws and say 'Rawr!', we are officially no longer friends."

"Jealous, are we?" Finch grins.

"No!" I bark. "I'm not jealous at all! That guy is a jerk! See that red Lamborghini he's climbing into?"

We both watch the valet lift the door of the Lamborghini upward instead of out, unlike on a regular car.

"Nice car," Finch purrs.

"Yeah, so nice he ran me off the road on the way to work! He made me almost hit a woman who was waiting for the bus!"

Outside, Suit Jerk slides into the car with a satisfied smirk on his face. He probably cares more about that car than his own mother. Boys and their stupid toys.

Finch asks, "Do you think he'd take me for a ride in that car? You know the kind of ride I'm talking about," she winks.

"Have you listened to a single word I've said?" I huff.

Finch cocks her hip and smirks, "Yeah. You told me you're totally into this guy and you got to see his dick when you massaged him."

I scowl, "That's not what I said!"

"Yeah it is," she says confidently. "Wait!" Her eyes pop open. "You saw Lamborghini guy's cock?"

"Yeah."

She gawks, "Oh my god, girl! Why didn't you tell me it was *his* cock! I was picturing a shriveled earthworm or a dehydrated toadstool or something!"

"Gross," I grimace and consider stamping my foot on her toes to break the spell that Suit Jerk has inadvertently cast on her, but instead I just stamp the floor. "And, I am NOT into him."

She nods. "Uh huh. And my name isn't Finch Barksdale. I'll tell you one thing, Riv. That guy must be hot shit based on the way I saw Mr. Duchamps kissing his hot ass when he drove up earlier."

"You saw this guy drive up?"

"Yup. It was like the president had arrived or something. Duchamps was bowing and scraping the whole time."

"Do you know who he is?"

Finch gives me a shrewd look, "Why do you want to know? I thought you said he was a douchebag?"

I open my mouth to object but clamp it closed. After a moment's thought, I say, "Sure, he's hot. But he's an ass who nearly killed me, which makes him a horrible person. And, I hate him. It's that simple."

Finch looks at me seriously for a moment. Then she breaks into a smile and nods, "Yeah, that's what I thought." She taunts me schoolyard style, "Riv likes the douchebag! Riv likes the douchebag!"

I shake my head, "When did you become my frenemy, Finch? I thought we were besties?"

She arches an eyebrow, "Well, when you quit lying to me about liking that guy, we'll be friends again, cross my heart," she grins and X's her finger over her chest.

I fold my arms and whine, "You're such a bitch, Finch." I turn and walk back toward the spa.

"That's why you love me," she hollers mirthfully. "Cuz I know how to treat a bitch!"

Did she not hear the part where Suit Jerk almost killed me and caused me to kill someone else? Since the lobby is still empty, I turn and stick my tongue out at her and sneer.

Finch hollers, "Is that any way to treat your pimp?"

I flip her off while sneering.

She giggles, "You know you love me!"

Her good humor is infectious. I shake my head and grin as I walk into the long hallway that leads back to the spa. Finch definitely makes work way more fun. Even if she is off about me and Suit Jerk.

I totally don't like the guy.

Who would?

He's dumb and dangerous.

I'm totally going to steer clear of him.

Chapter 8

RIVER

When I squeeze my way through L.A. traffic after work that day, I discover there is now something wrong with my steering. My Chevy keeps drifting to the left.

"What's wrong, girl?"

She doesn't answer. Poor thing.

Damn it! Sheena wasn't limping to the left before I hit the curb this morning.

Stupid Suit Jerk! It's all his fault!

Mr. "Is Good!"

More like Mr. "No Good!"

I should've kept his money, *then* thrown him out. Instead of going easy on him.

What was I thinking?

Not only did I earn every penny of that $600, but he already *owed* me for whatever it's gonna cost to fix Sheena! Stupid me. That's the last time I throw away money on principle. Pride always has a price. I read that in a book.

On the way home, I spot an old Auto Repair garage that looks halfway reputable. I pull over to the sidewalk and check my smart phone. They've got good reviews on Yelp. I circle around the block and pull into the old building.

Thirty minutes later, a mechanic with greasy hair and an equally greasy gray jump suit says, "Your leading arm is bent, the control arm is cracked, and the trailing arm is twisted up to the bolt."

Who knew cars had arms? And so many of them? I guess Suit Jerk isn't the only one who doesn't know English. Feeling stupid, I wince as I say, "Can you translate that?"

The mechanic smirks, "A bunch of stuff is broken. You need to fix it."

"What's it gonna cost?"

He hikes his eyebrows and blows out a stream of air that smells vaguely like motor oil. From the look of his teeth, he probably drinks it by the glass. He says, "Oh, I'd say with parts and labor, it's gonna run you about nineteen seventy five."

"$1,975!!" I blurt. I don't have that kind of money. I don't even have that much room on my credit card. Not even close.

I. Am. Fucked.

Yes, now is one of those times when swearing is appropriate, even for me.

"You wanna make an appointment to fix the car?" the mechanic asks casually.

"I don't have the money. Is it drivable?"

"For now. But you're gonna make things a lot worse if you don't fix it soon."

"But I need my car for work!" I blurt without thinking. I'm just complaining out loud.

"My advice?"

"What?" I ask hopefully.

"Take the bus," he says flatly.

Great. Not my Plan A by a long shot.

Nope, I wasn't nearly hard enough on that stupid Suit Jerk!

If I ever see him again, I'm demanding my six hundred bucks back, plus fourteen hundred more!

Argh!!!

Chapter 9

RIVER

I'm in a shitty mood when I drive down the dark alley behind my apartment building and park in the small lot in back.

I don't know where I'm going to find the money to fix my car. At least it's drivable. For now.

The good news is I'm home and don't have to worry about it until tomorrow.

Tonight, I get to worry about homework for my classes at Los Angeles City College. That's the official name but everybody calls it LACC. I'm halfway through my Associates in Business Management, which is what my counselor told me I should get if I want to learn how to run a small business. While I like working at the Beverly Hills Resort as a masseuse, I'd rather work for myself. But, between work and school, I haven't made much progress on building my own massage business.

I could, if I had the motivation. But I don't.

Why?

Cage...

Yeah, him.

I haven't exactly been highly motivated lately. The emotional fallout after his mysterious bail out has been draining.

That's why I'm looking forward to bed tonight.

With any luck, I'll jump into slumberland and find McJogs waiting for me. I'll marry him and he'll turn out to be the coolest guy ever with a fun yet dependable job he loves, and we'll make babies and live happily ever after.

Time to get my slumber party started. But first, I have to get out of my car, eat some dinner, and do my homework.

I haul myself out of my seat and close Sheena's door with a rusty squeal. I pat her hood, "Sorry about the arms, girl. I promise I'll fix you as soon as I can."

Silently, she says, *"Don't worry about me, hun. I'm Queen of the Jungle."*

I smile to myself as I walk out from between the cars.

Why is it so dark? Oh yeah. The security light in the parking lot is still out. My landlord is a total slumlord. I hope no prowlers are waiting in the dark, ready to pounce.

After today, I don't really care.

Pounce away, prowlers.

When I walk past the row of small bungalows toward mine, I notice something rustle in the bushes. I reach into my purse and grip my canister of pepper spray. I hope whoever is waiting to pounce likes extra hot, cuz I'm all out of mild.

The bushes rustle again.

I yank out my pepper spray and point.

I wait until I see the whites of his eyes.

The bushes rustle as he comes out of hiding.

Unfortunately, the only thing white about him are the two fat stripes running from the top of his head to the tip of his bushy tail.

Skunk!!!!

I gasp.

He sniffs the air and looks at me as if to say, "You think your pepper spray is better than mine, ésa?" Most of the people in my neighborhood are working class Mexicans, and they all speak to their cats and chihuahuas in Spanish, so I assume all the wild neighborhood animals speak Spanish too. Cuz they talk to the cats and stuff.

I decide it's best not to have a stench showdown with Señor Skunk, because his pepper spray is extra, extra, extra hot.

I spin and run back to my car, my pepper spray in one hand and my jingling purse in the other. I lock myself inside Sheena and wait until I think it's safe to come out.

Right as I'm about to open my car door, Señor Skunk waddles by with his nose in the air and waves his tail.

We both know who is *el jefe* of this neighborhood.

He disappears under a ratty wooden fence between the parking lot and the big apartment building next door.

When I'm sure he's long gone, I exit my car and walk casually back to my door. This time, the bushes don't rustle and I'm not even thinking about my pepper spray when I notice a tall shadowy figure hovering by my front door.

Twice in ten minutes? Come on! This time, I actually hope it is a skunk as every muscle in my body contracts in expectation of a confrontation.

Adrenalin races through my body.

Where is Señor Skunk when I need him? Shouldn't he have my back, since we're from the same hood? Skunks. Can't trust 'em.

In a low voice, the shadowed man says, "I've been waiting for you..."

For a split second, I wonder if I'm gonna die on my own doorstep.

Then recognition sets in.

It's been a long time since I've heard that voice. My body reacts instantly and I'm shaking twice as much as I was when it was just the adrenalin. Emotions are way more powerful. At the moment, I think I'd rather die than have a conversation with this man.

"Cage," I sigh, not in relief. "What are you doing here?"

He steps out of the shadows. The soft warm glow of the city lights faintly illuminates his handsome face. It's not fair that he gets the sexy mood lighting. Not after what he did. Where are those harsh accusatory interrogation lights?

I want to ask him, "Why did you do it, Cage? Why?"

Since I don't ask him out loud, he doesn't answer. Instead, he stands there looking handsome. He wears a stylish V-neck sweater rolled up to reveal his muscled forearms, frayed jeans, and flip flops. He always exudes this Matthew McConaughey hippie artist thing with the Magic Mike era body.

His handsomeness is just one of the reasons I hate him so much.

I growl, "What do you want?"

He reaches up and smoothes back a lock of my hair like he always used to. "You're as beautiful as ever."

I roll my eyes, "You don't get to say nice things to me, Cage. You lost your privileges." I pull back, even though he's not touching me anymore. "And don't touch me." Part of me wants him to keep touching me. To touch me like that ten times a day every day until forever. That part of me wishes he never stopped touching me like that. But he did. That's why the other part of me reminds me that Cage is a total ass. "What do you want?" I demand huffily.

His smile curls into that cute grin of his. "I wanted to see you, Riv."

The touch-starved part of me loves that he calls me Riv. The other part hates that he does, and hates that cute grin. Because now it's a lie. It didn't use to be. But now it's the enemy. Even so, it's endearing and cute. I force myself to look away. "Okay, you've seen me," I say sarcastically. "Now you can go."

"Ouch," he drawls softly. "I guess I deserved that."

I knot my brows and glare at him, "You deserve that and a thousand times worse."

"Would it help if I said I'm sorry?"

What is he doing? I don't like this at all. I blurt, "No."

He leans over and lowers his head until he finds my eyes with his. "Not even a little bit?"

I look away and fold my arms across my breasts, "Not even one tenth of a little bit."

He softly grazes my cheek with the backs of his fingers. He knows how sensitive I am to his touch.

My cheek heats and I want to shiver and melt into his touch. I want the last six months to never have happened. But they did. I pull away, "Don't, Cage."

He slowly lowers his hand, "I'm sorry."

"Seriously, Cage, why are you here?" I search his eyes. His beautiful mahogany eyes. I really do want to fall into his gaze, but I know better. I'm not going through hell twice.

He slides his hands into his jeans' pockets and shrugs his broad shoulders. "I don't have a speech prepared or anything…"

Speech? Oh no. He's not going to rekindle what he burned down, is he? I cut in, "Then maybe you need to go home and write it all out first so you can think about what you did to me."

He grins his wide, pleasant grin, the one that I fell for in the beginning.

I try to remind myself that it's just a facade, that he may act nice, but his actions often weren't. Not in any overt way. More like his lack of action.

That's why it's so hard to hate him right now, which is what I *should* be doing. But that smile of his melts my resistance like I'm a piece of chocolate in his mouth, all sweet and delicious, and he wants to devour me.

I hate Cage.

I opposite of hate Cage.

Talking to him is a terrible idea. I need to run away. Maybe if I find Señor Skunk, I can explain everything and he'll chase off Cage as a favor for a homie. I glance around, looking for the Señor.

"Why are you so nervous?" Cage asks in his smooth slow-motion voice. "I'm not going to hurt you."

Maybe not physically. But the fresh wounds on my heart have reopened like I haven't moved on a single inch from Cage. Who was I kidding watching McJogs this morning? I can't even think about guys right now. My heart still belongs to Cage.

If I'd known in the beginning what I know now, I never would've given it to him.

Then again, it's not like I had a choice. He is impossible to resist.

In a soft voice, Cage says, "Can we talk? Inside?"

I'm about to say yes when my bungalow door whips opens and light pours out.

"What are you doing here, Cage?" my brother demands. "I thought I told you to get the fuck out of here and never come back."

Saved.

Chapter 10

RIVER

"What's up, Stone," Cage drawls while he grins at my brother.

"Wipe that smirk off your face, Cage," Stone barks. "I stopped buying your brand of bullshit the day you broke my sister's heart."

My brother rocks. I'm so glad we're roommates. I suppress a giggle.

Stone wears a sleeveless Affliction T-shirt and running shorts. His left arm is covered in a tattoo sleeve from wrist to shoulder. My brother is usually working out every waking minute he's not at his job as a security guard. He steps out of the apartment and bumps his chest against Cage's. Cage is several inches taller than my brother, but my brother isn't scared of anybody. He does MMA, and he's a total badass.

"Easy, Stone," Cage says casually. "I'm just here to talk to your sister." Cage doesn't act afraid, but he should.

When things ended between me and Cage, Stone was as mad as I was sad. He told me every day if he ever saw Cage again, he'd knock him out or whatever. Normally, I like to think I can fight my own battles. But it's nice to know that Stone has always had my back, and always will.

Like right now.

I squeeze past my brother and go inside.

"Whoa buddy," my brother says to Cage.

I turn and Stone has planted his palm on Cage's chest. Cage stares down at Stone's hand with amusement.

Stone chuckles at him, "You're not coming inside."

"I need to talk to your sister."

"No you don't," Stone grins. It's not a friendly grin.

Go, Stone.

Cage leans around my brother and says, "Riv, we should really talk."

I smirk, "If you have something to say, Cage, then say it."

Cage hikes his eyebrows and darts his eyes at my brother, "In private?"

"What?" I demand, "You don't want Stone to hear more of your patented bullshit?" Now I'm mad. Mostly at myself, because I was a millimeter away from letting myself fall into Cage's arms like the last six months had never happened.

"It's not bullshit," Cage says. "I was a total ass, and I want to apologize. But there's some things that maybe you don't understand. Things I never told you. I fucked up. I admit it. But it's, well, it's complicated." He glances at Stone again.

My heart swells at Cage's words. I want to sit down and hear him out. But that would be emotional suicide. I know it. I know better. I shake my head, "You had your chance, Cage. Now it's too late."

I watch Cage sigh. "Maybe it is. But I'm not giving up, Riv. I love you."

Why did he have to say that? My heart races in my chest. Tears are going to seep over my eyelids any second.

Even Stone doesn't know what to do. He turns his head and gives me this pleading look that Cage can't see because of the angle.

As nice as it is to think other people will fight your battles for you, in the end, I know you have to fight your own. The only one who can get me out of this is me. "Go away, Cage." I mumble and turn away.

I walk down the hallway and into the bungalow's lone bathroom. I close the door and lock it before collapsing on the floor against the tub. I wrap my arms around my knees and weep softly.

The only light in the dark bathroom is the thin line of muted yellow coming in beneath the door.

I hear harsh words from Stone, but I can't make them out. I tense up, afraid of what he might do to Cage now that they're alone. A second later, the front door thuds closed and soft footfalls approach the bathroom. I relax, knowing Stone didn't do something rash.

There's a gentle knock on the bathroom door. "You okay, sis?"

I sniff, "Yeah."

"I sent him packing."

"What'd you tell him?"

"I told him I'll kill him if he breaks your heart again."

I chuff a gurgley laugh, "Thanks, Stone. If you do kill him, can you only half kill him? I want him left alive so he can contemplate the error of his ways."

Stone chuckles, "Yeah, okay." After a pause, he says softly, "Do you need anything?"

"No, thanks."

"Okay. I'll leave you alone. But if you do, just holler. I'll be in my room working my kettle bells."

"Okay."

After another pause, he says, "I love you, River. Don't let that prick back into your life. It's a bad idea. Just sayin'."

I smile though my tears, "I love you too, Stone."

I know he's waiting for me to agree with him that more Cage in my life is a bad idea. But I can't.

After a moment, I hear him walk away.

As much as I wish I could wall Cage out of my life forever, I don't know how.

He still lives in my heart like he never left.

Although the bathroom is dark, the light coming in under the door is just enough to cast a faint gray glow across the tiles.

Right now, I want to escape everything. Escape my feelings, thoughts of Cage, my broken car. All of it. I want the entire world to go away. I need to block it out.

Just for a few minutes.

I need peace.

I tip onto my side and wrap my arms around my knees. I close my eyes tight.

All is soothing darkness.

I hear Stone in his room grunting quietly as he lifts his weights. There's a soft thump as he sets them down and pads out of his room toward the kitchen.

All is quiet.

For a moment, I float in nothingness.

Then I see eyes.

Ice blue eyes.

Haunted eyes.

They glow like two full moons.

They stare into my heart and pry away the barriers around my soul.

My heart opens, yielding willingly.

I step off an internal ledge and fall into those eyes that are consuming my thoughts and it feels like flying into the silence of space.

Chapter 11

RIVER

My Chevy barrels toward the woman waiting for the bus on Santa Monica Boulevard.

A red Lamborghini with white polka dots and comical cartoon eyes for headlights rockets past me. Its hood is open and filled with teeth and a fat red tongue. The engine roars with insane laughter, mocking me.

I try to turn Sheena's steering wheel, but it spins around uselessly, somehow sabotaged by the laughing Lamborghini.

I notice Cage is driving the Lamborghini, but he doesn't own one. I don't question it. Somehow, it makes perfect sense that he's driving the evil car. As it passes, I notice the license plate reads, "MANMOBILE."

It figures.

Before I can wonder about it further, the woman waiting for the bus screams. Nauseating horror blooms in my stomach when I realize that the woman is my mom.

My bumper is going to crunch into her and crush her to death. I'm going to kill my own mother...

I slam on the brakes at the last second. I can't look. I clamp my eyelids shut—

Tires screech—

SCREECH!! SCREECH!! SCREECH!!

My alarm clock tears me out of the terrible dream. I've never been happier to be woken up in my entire life. That was easily the worst dream I've ever had.

I switch off my alarm and stare at the ceiling.

I should call in sick today. I'm not sick, but after that dream, I'm definitely suffering from some form of mental illness. To make matters worse, I slept like crap. I feel so tired, I doubt I'll be any good at work if I go in.

Last night, I tried to go to bed early, hoping sleep would make me feel better after my long day. It was hopeless. I should've known better. I laid in bed for hours running a million different 'what if' scenarios through my head about getting back together with Cage. I considered calling him a hundred times. Thankfully, I didn't. At some point, I was so exhausted, I fell asleep. That's when the nightmares started.

I don't remember any of them except the last one, but the painful nightmare feelings are still crystal clear.

Jagged raw betrayal, as powerful as the day Cage left.

The terror of yesterday's close call in my car.

I tell myself that Cage is my past, that I didn't hit that woman waiting for the bus. But the dream police question my convictions.

I take in the surroundings of my bedroom, hoping that concentrating on the real world will wash away the eerie certainty that my nightmare actually happened.

Southern California sun glows through my blinds, filling my small bedroom with soft white light.

Today is a bright new day.

Today will be better than yesterday and all the dark days before it.

I hope.

Chapter 12

RIVER

When I pass IHOP on the drive to work, I briefly consider parking and waiting for McJogs.

Who am I kidding? I'm not in the mood to flirt with any guys today. Mopey sad people don't flirt well. It's common knowledge.

If I'm in a better mood tomorrow, maybe I'll wait for him then. Or at the very least, tell myself I will.

Maybe I need to go back to taking the short way to work and forget all about McJogs. And guys in general. I'm so not ready for men right now.

Relief washes over me when I pull into work and the only car in the roundabout out front is a black Town Car picking up a middle aged couple. I didn't realize I'd been worried, but I guess I was. It makes sense. The last thing I wanted to see today was—

Those blue eyes...

—that Red Lamborghini.

I drive into the parking garage beneath the hotel and look for a space. That's when I notice the red Lamborghini parked in the chained-off valet section.

I groan audibly. Please tell me that's not the same one. This is Beverly Hills, and there's quite a few Lamborghinis driving around. Best not to think about it.

I take the elevator to the hotel lobby and the first person I see is Finch.

She beams when she sees me and jogs across the marble floor of the lobby, "Guess who's back!" she squeals.

My stomach lurches. I know where this is going.

She practically gasps, "Remember that hot guy from yesterday?"

"Unfortunately," I groan.

"He's staying at the hotel!"

"Yay," I mutter sarcastically.

Those eyes...

"I helped cart all his bags to his suite this morning. I think he's going to be staying here for a while!"

I shake my head and acid bubbles in my stomach. Is it reasonable to hope that he won't want another massage after I threw his money in his face?

Finch scrutinizes me and frowns, "Are you okay?"

"I'm not feeling well."

She looks at me with concern, "You're not sick, are you?"

"I am now," I smile sourly, dreading—

anticipating...

—the possibility of bumping into Suit Jerk during his long stay.

"You don't look sick. Am I missing something?"

I really don't want to talk to her about Suit Jerk. To Finch, he walks on water. But he's only half my problem. I say, "Cage came by my apartment last night."

"What!" Finch's eyes pop. "What did he say?" Finch knows the whole story about Cage. She was right by my side through the entire thing.

I grimace, "I think he wants to get back together."

"Do you?" she asks.

I don't answer right away.

She squeezes my arm affectionately. Then her face gets serious, "Don't do it, Riv. If he bailed once for no reason, he'll bail again. Right when it hurts the most. He was probably chasing after some other woman anyway," she says sourly.

"How do you always know what I'm thinking?" I scoff.

She smiles and shakes her head, "It's my only talent. Besides carrying people's baggage."

"Which baggage are we talking about?" I half joke. "I could use some help with mine."

She quips, "Oh, I'm not carrying your emotional baggage. Especially not if you get back together with Cage. If you do that, you'll have more bags to carry than Lady Gaga's roadies. If he broke your heart once, he'll do it a second time."

"You really think he can't change?"

"Nobody ever changes, River," she says bitterly. "They say they will, but it never happens." Finch has had her own share of man troubles.

I feel my cheeks quivering as she looks at me sympathetically. My tears brim as I ask, "If guys never change, then why do I still want Cage back?"

She squeezes my arm again, "Because you're lonely and sad, Riv. Not because he's some great guy. Don't re-open your heart to him. He had his chance and he blew it."

I wish I had her conviction.

She plants her fists on her hips and says emphatically, "Be done with him, sistah! Kick his ass to the curb! Don't let him hurt you again!"

"Maybe you're right," I sigh heavily. "I wish I didn't feel so weak. Why can't I woman up and get over him?"

"Because 'womaning up' means pretending the feelings aren't there, even when they are. That never solves anything. It's a band-aid. What you need is a distraction."

"How is a distraction any different from a band-aid?" I ask doubtfully.

"It's different because it's real. Go find a different man and make some new feelings for someone else to replace the ones you have for Cage."

I try to picture McJogs in my mind. "I don't think I'm ready for a random hookup with—"

Those ice blue eyes...

"—some random guy."

"So take up skydiving! Or learn how to juggle chainsaws."

"Chainsaws?" I grin skeptically.

She huffs and flings her fingers, "It doesn't have to be chainsaws. Or even juggling. It doesn't matter what you do. But you need a distraction, or you'll be thinking about Cage 24/7 until you do something stupid like call him. If that happens, don't come crying to me when he screws you over again."

"Yeah," I say absently.

I hear men's dress shoes click across the lobby behind me. I'm suddenly afraid it's Suit Jerk.

Finch says to whoever it is, "Hey, Mr. Duchamps."

Semi-relief washes over me. Mr. Duchamps is the general manager of the Beverly Hills Resort. He's not Suit Jerk, but he is wearing a suit, tends to be a jerk himself, and it's never easy to stay on his good side. But I'm glad it's him and not Suit Jerk.

I hope Mr. Duchamps doesn't think Finch and I were goofing off.

"Ladies," Mr. Duchamps says snootily. He's bald and has a thin mustache that looks like someone drew it on with a grease pencil, but the rumor is that it's real. Not that anyone has ever asked. Mr. Duchamps isn't a very sociable guy with the staff. He snoots, "Do you two have nothing to do?"

Finch and I exchange a nervous glance. When Finch doesn't answer, I speak up, "I was on my way into the spa. But I was asking Finch if—"

"Did you only now arrive, Miss Freeman?" Mr. Duchamps checks his watch. He's such a tyrant about people being late.

"Yeah, but—"

"I believe that makes you late, Miss Freeman."

I'm immediately on the defensive, "I'm sorry, there was traffic, and—"

Mr. Duchamps' grease pencil lip curls into a sneer, "This is Los

Angeles, Miss Freeman. There is traffic *every* day. Or have you not learned that by now?"

"Yes, Mr. Duchamps," I say apologetically. "But it was worse than usual and—"

He cuts me off with an arch of his eyebrow and a bitter look, "Then plan for it next time, if you please."

"Yes, Mr. Duchamps," I nod nervously.

I'm pretty sure that someone shoved a broomstick up Mr. Duchamps' ass when he was a kid, and it's never been removed. It was probably put there by his mother, who is most likely a warty old witch. So it's a magical broomstick that gives Mr. Duchamps special powers to irritate, unnerve, and annoy.

"Miss Barksdale," he says to Finch, "Don't you have anything to do?" He draws out the word "do" like "dyooooo."

"Yeah, um," she says nervously, "Someone on four needs towels."

"Then make it happen, Miss Barksdale." He walks away without looking back.

When he's at the edge of the lobby and too far away to hear us, Finch whispers, "Have you ever noticed that Mr. Duchamps' name rhymes with douche?"

We both start tittering. After a moment, our tittering is on the verge of erupting into loud laughter. Finch nudges me toward the hallway that leads to the spa before it gets any worse.

"Go!" she whispers. "You're gonna get us in trouble!"

"Me?" I hiss irritably.

"You're the trouble maker! Now go! Jet! Bounce! Audi five thoudie!" She shoos me with her hands.

I stroll casually across the lobby, no longer in a hurry. I'm so grateful for Finch. Without her, today would be way worse than it is.

That's when Mr. Duchamps reappears and says across the empty lobby, "Miss Freeman, what are you still doing in the lobby? You have a client waiting for you."

Why is he telling me? Mr. Duchamps never has any idea who is on the spa schedule. That's Luciana's job. Unless it's someone super important.

Someone who receives presidential treatment.

My stomach sinks again.

Mr. Duchamps says, "Are you waiting for an invitation, Miss Freeman? Hop to!"

I hurry out of the lobby and down the hallway to the spa.

Something tells me I should be hurrying back to my car.

I really should've called in sick.

Chapter 13

RIVER

Suit Jerk sits in one of the designer chairs in the waiting area for the spa, reading something on his smart phone.

I stumble to a stop before he sees me.

He can read. I'm surprised. Oafs are usually illiterate. The mere sight of him makes me grimace. All I can think about is how rude he is and how he almost caused me to kill someone with my car yesterday.

I want nothing to do with—

Those ice blue eyes...

—a total asstard like him.

What to do? If I turn and run, maybe he won't notice, then I can go home and spend the day in bed.

Jocelyn Reason, the girl who works the front desk, is busy on her computer. She hasn't noticed me yet. The second she does, I'm sure she'll say hello, then it'll be too late for me to bail without being seen.

Wait, why does Jocelyn keep stealing glances at Suit Jerk? She's typing away on her keyboard, *clickity clickity clickity*, then she secretly gawks at him for a moment while twirling her hair. Then more *clickity, clickity, clickity*. Gawk. Twirl.

Clickity, clickity, clickity.

Gawk.

Twirl.

Wow, that is *really* annoying.

Why? Who knows.

But I want to yell at her, "Would you STOP staring already?! Before you start drooling on yourself?! It's totally rude!!"

I'm going crazy. I blame my sleep deprivation. That's it. I'm going home to bed.

I spin on my heel and bump right into Luciana, the spa manager.

"There you are," she says. "I've been looking all over for you."

I have no doubt I look like a deer in headlights. I bite my lower lip.

Luciana is a gorgeous woman of indeterminate age. Although she's obviously over forty, she could be as old as seventy. There's no way to know for sure. I think it's a combination of good genes and a pampered lifestyle. Her husband Giovanni is some kind of multi-millionaire movie producer, and she only works here to have something to do. Stress is not a factor in her life, and she has plenty of money to Botox or get daily facials or robot replacement parts or who knows what else.

She smiles her fake business smile, "River, you have a special guest. We don't want to keep him waiting too long, do we?"

I want to say, "Yes, I totally want to keep him waiting. He can wait until doomsday, for all I care." Instead, I just nod.

On her four inch heels, Luciana is really tall and can easily see over my head to the waiting area. "Ah, there he is!" She leads me by the elbow up to Suit Jerk, who is sliding his smart phone into his dark suit jacket.

He stands up and towers over both of us.

Even in her heels, Luciana is looking up at him.

"Good morning," Suit Jerk smiles, pinning his ice blue eyes on mine. They flicker like stars under his dark brow.

Do I detect a sparkling warmth in those eyes that wasn't there the first time I saw them? Or the last time, when I kicked his ass out? Indeed I do.

Luciana purrs, "Here she is, as you requested."

She's always flirty with the upscale male clientele, but this morning I notice an extra note of flirtation in her tone. Usually, it doesn't bother me. It's good for business. But today, it's totally irritating. I think I'm just annoyed because hot guys like Suit Jerk make women behave like idiots.

Yeah, that's all it is.

Luciana smiles her wax museum smile, "River is one of our best masseuses. She always does an excellent job."

Although Luciana is complimenting me, it's obvious from the way she's drooling that she's just trying to flirt with Suit Jerk.

I do my best not to scowl openly. Not that it matters. I think as far as Luciana is concerned, I disappeared the moment she laid eyes on Suit Jerk.

To my surprise, Suit Jerk ignores Luciana.

His eyes are locked on mine.

Those eyes…

Chapter 14

DRAKKEN

The intentions of the woman managing the spa are obvious and boorish. I know her kind well. I have been around people like her my entire life. She smells my money and power, and she is drawn to it like the drunkard to drink.

She is easily ignored.

The young angel with the soothing hands and mesmerizing aqua blue eyes is not. She captivates my attention with ease, yet she makes no effort to do so.

Her presence alone enchants me.

Everything that is not her fades from my awareness.

I want to tell her that she is the most beautiful creature in the entire universe, that her eyes hypnotize me and steal my breath away, that her bright smile vaporizes the stone walls around my heart, washing away all my pain and years of dark—

(...)

—memories with the light of her happiness, as if my past never existed.

There is only now. Sweet, joyful now.

But I can't tell this angel any of these things.

All that comes out of my mouth are the words of a clumsy man.

"Is good."

I sound like an idiot.

I don't have the English vocabulary or grammar to show her who I am inside this verbally stunted exterior.

Chapter 15

RIVER

Suit Jerk nods. "Is good." He's not looking at Luciana. His ice blue eyes are locked on mine. They aren't cold at all.

They're inviting.

I tear my eyes away before I start blushing. I stare at the floor, hiding my confusion. I shouldn't be feeling this way about Suit Jerk. I should be righteously pissed right now. Not blissfully bashful.

What's wrong with me?

I need to find out if Mr. Duchamps will lend me that magic broomstick up his ass so I can fly out of here. It's the only escape plan I can think of. Even if Mr. Duchamps *were* here, I know he'd refuse. Partially because he doesn't go anywhere without his magic ass-broomstick, and partially because his motto is: What the hotel guests want, they get.

Especially when they're getting the royal treatment like Suit Jerk.

"We massage now?" Suit Jerk asks me.

Luciana laughs throatily, "Mr. Skalakova, your English is so endearing."

"Thank you," he smiles at her oddly.

I almost laugh, but stop myself.

Skalawhatsis? Is that Suit Jerk's name? It sounds like a hacking cough or a sneeze. Is he Russian Mafia? He totally seems like a criminal, based on how he manages to steal the good sense of every woman who lays eyes on him.

And wait a second, did he just say "Thank you" to Luciana? He never thanked me yesterday at any point during our massage. Nor did he apologize for nearly killing me.

My lip curls sourly.

Luciana is still laughing her come-hither laugh. She leans forward, offering up extra artificially youthful cleavage for Suit Jerk while she twirls the pearl necklace dangling between her artificially enhanced boobs. She may as well be saying, "You can shoot your load right here, Mr. Skala-kackala-cacka. Right on my necklace." Then she'd have a metaphorical pearl necklace to go with her real one.

Why am I being so catty? I meant it when I told Finch that I'm totally not interested in Suit Jerk.

But Luciana clearly is.

I have no idea if she's faithful to her husband or not, but based on her behavior right now, I suspect she won't be much longer.

"We massage now?" Suit Jerk asks me again.

Luciana grins like the Cheshire Cat. "It's okay, River. I'm sure Mr. Skalakova doesn't bite. Or do you?" She winks at him and brushes her fingers across the lapel of his suit.

Gag. She doesn't know him very well. Hasn't she learned that other people's looks can be as deceiving as hers? And, could she be any more obvious? I give her five seconds before she starts unbuttoning her blouse.

Without thinking, I say, "Why don't you massage him, Luciana? You're always telling me how much you miss the hands-on work."

The tiniest hint of irritation flashes across Luciana's face. Luciana doesn't actually do massages. She never has.

Why did I say that?

I hope she's not pissed.

Luciana laughs her warbling socialite laugh and brushes her nails across my arm, "Oh, River. You know I'm not half the masseuse you are, my dear."

I want to say she's none of the masseuse I am, but I don't. I'm not at all surprised she rolled with my lie for the sake of appearances. If she is pissed, she'll chastise me later in private.

Suit Jerk is doing his best to follow what Luciana and I are saying. After a moment, he says, "I like Riv—*River* for massage." He frowns, "You name River? Like water?"

He's doing that earnest 'learning English' thing again. Admittedly, it makes him more endearing. I smirk, "Yes, like water."

"Is good," he nods. He clenches his fist in front of him and says, "In my country, river is strong word." He says it with a great deal of pride. He winks at me, "You strong girl. You make good massage." It's a statement of approval and, dare I say it, respect?

I smile and nearly giggle, "Yeah." My grasp of the English language has dwindled to near nothing all of a sudden. I guess it's catching.

Luciana takes a step back and surveys the two of us. Her smile is wide and perfect. Perfectly devious. She bristles with obvious but restrained tension.

If this guy is as important as Luciana and everyone else is leading me to believe, it would explain her tension. Whatever the explanation, I'm sure I'll find out later.

I glance at Suit Jerk. I mean, Mr. Skala-kackala-cacka or whatever his name is.

His eyes survey Luciana intently.

Now that his attention isn't on me, I realize that despite his crippled English, this guy is really smart. He's assessing Luciana like he's reading her mind.

"We massage now?" he asks me and nods in the direction of the massage rooms.

I detect a distinct twinkle in his eye. Is that twinkle for me? He didn't twinkle for Luciana.

Not that I care.

He offers me his hand, almost like a prince at a fashionable ball.

I take it.

"Same room?" he asks.

"Yes," I nod.

Luciana's eyebrows suddenly tense. The change in her expression is nearly imperceptible, but I caught it.

I hear her robot super computer brain beeping and blorping at top speed.

What's that about?

Luciana says in a faux-friendly voice, "Enjoy the massage, Mr. Skalakova." She's really good at covering up her anger in front of customers.

But I know better.

I smell trouble.

And it smells like Luciana's expensive perfume. I'm sure she has hers brewed from the tears of enslaved children who work in factories in fourth world countries, factories no doubt owned by her rich husband.

Oh shizz. It suddenly hits me. Did Luciana figure out that I gave Mr. Suit Jerk a massage yesterday without collecting any money?

No time to worry about it now.

Mr. Skala-whatever leads me out of the waiting area.

Clickity, clickity, pause. Jocelyn looks up and openly gawks at his ass while twirling her hair.

Luciana also gawks, but without the hair twirl. She would never muss her hair over any man.

I smile at both of them.

Suck on this, bitches! He's with me.

Those weren't my thoughts. They were the thoughts of some nympho who has taken over my brain.

Chapter 16

RIVER

Mr. Skally-waggs leads me into the massage room and I close the door behind us.

There's something deliciously ominous about the sound of the door latching.

Clit!

I mean, *Click!*

The doorknob totally did not say, *Clit!*

It said, *Click!*

Click! Click! Clit!

Okay, enough of that.

But on the topic of doors and locks, I consider locking this one. Why? Who knows.

But I have this sneaking suspicion that Luciana would find out. We're not supposed to lock the door when a client is in the room. It's a liability thing with the fire department or the police or whatever. I'm sure it has something to do with making sure this isn't a whorehouse. Or in case a hot guy sets my panties on fire.

Mr. Chaka Khaka unknots his tie in front of me. Is he going to disrobe in full view again? If so, someone needs to call the fire department.

Good thing I left the door unlocked.

He smiles at me. That same knowing and intelligent smile I saw in the hallway.

"Mr., Ah…" I don't bother making an attempt at his last name because I will slaughter it like baby lambs wandering into a saw mill.

"Skalakova," he says instantly.

"Mr. Skala—" I hesitate because I still don't have the hang of it.

"Kova," he says warmly. "Skala-kova."

"Skala…"

"Say with me," he commands. "Skala…"

"Skala," I repeat.

"Koooo-va."

"Kova."

"Skalakova."

I grin, "Skalakova!" I don't know why I'm having such a hard time with his name.

"Is good," he smiles. "You call me Drakken."

I raise my eyebrows. Did he just try to hack up some phlegm, or is that an actual name? "Uhh…"

"Drakken. In my country, is word for dragon."

"Your name means dragon?"

He nods, "Yes. Drakken. Two K's."

"That's a cool name. I don't know anybody named Dragon."

"Now you know me. But is Drakken. Two K's and E."

"Drakken?"

He smiles, "Is good. You have hanger?"

I pause. It's almost a command, but not as overt as the last time he was in here. At least he's asking. I let it slide and grab hangers from the closet.

"Thank you," he smiles and loops the tie around the top of the hanger.

I'm shocked. That's the first 'thank you' he's given me. Maybe he's not a complete jerk. "Hey," I blurt, "in your country, which is a stronger word, River or Drakken?"

He chuckles, "Both word strong."

"Yeah, but which is stronger?" I press.

"Depend."

"Depends on what," I grin.

"Depend on person." He sets the hanger down on a chair and steps in front of me until his chest is inches from my face. He gazes down at me with amusement in his eyes.

I shoot a gaze back up at him, even though he's taller than a ten story building. I'm not backing down.

He suddenly grasps me firmly by my upper arms with both his hands. Is he going to rip my arms off or something?

"Hey," I say nervously, "what are you doing?"

"This." He smirks, lifts me off the ground, and sets me to the side like I weigh zero pounds. "Excuse, I go to closet." He grins and picks up the hanger, slides his suit jacket onto it and hangs everything in the closet.

"Ha. Ha," I smirk. "Are you saying your name is stronger than mine?"

He shrugs while removing his gold cufflinks. "Name? Hard to say. Arm? Yes." He winks.

He has a point. But I don't admit defeat. "Hey, how do you say 'river' in your language?"

"Reka." It comes out sounding almost like Shreka, which makes me think of Shrek.

I'm not a model by anyone's stretch of the imagination, but in no way do I resemble a sloppy green ogre. And what's with all the K's? His language is a bit too harsh for my taste. Sort of like what I know of him. I smile politely, "I'll stick with River. It's easier to say."

"Okay," he smiles while unbuttoning his expensive dress shirt.

I stare as he unveils his muscles. I can't help myself. He's way less of a jerk than last time, so ogling him is okay. But I'll totally stop if he reverts to jerk.

He slides out of the knit shirt and puts it on another hanger. His muscles dance impressively when he does the littlest thing.

Wow, this guy is a serious piece of hot couture. I mean haute. I think his flexing abs have got me all mixed up. Either way, he sizzles in all states of dress. He might even be a mirage generated by the heat waves pouring out the neck of my spa uniform top.

"Oh," he smiles, "I forget." He reaches into the pocket of his suit jacket and pulls out his wallet. He counts out $600 and offers it to me. "For last time."

I stare at the money and debate about taking it. This is the money I threw in his face on principle the last time. If I take it, does it mean I'm selling out my principles for the almighty dollar? Or do I consider this the money he owes me for driving my car off the road and screwing up my alignment? I'm going with owes. Even principles have bills to pay.

And now I'm angry again. But I hide my anger and take the money, "Thank you, Mr. Skalakova." I put the money in my purse and stash it under the sink. When I turn around, he's scrutinizing me. "What?" I frown.

"You mad."

I thought I was hiding it.

"Why you mad?"

A better question is, why is he doing this? Is he trying to get me worked up? Or does he just work me up without effort? Neither is good.

"You tell," he commands.

How to word it? You drive like you're insane? Erm, does he know the word insane? How about cuckoo? Is cuckoo universal? This language barrier thing is annoying me at the moment. I really want to vent about him running me off the road and messing up my alignment. But what are the chances he knows what alignment means? I'm guessing zero. I barely know myself. I'll never be able to explain it.

So I stick to the basics. "Remember last time? You ran me off the road? By the clown car?" My irritation is obvious.

He smiles pleasantly, "Oh, yes! Clown car! Is very funny." He nods his head.

"It's *not* funny," I fume.

He frowns, "Clown car is very funny. Little propeller?" He spins his finger round and round in the air. "And big eye?" He blinks comically. "And oo-gah, oo-gah?" He chuckles to himself.

I think he expects me to laugh.

Okay, I'm pissed. I shake my head, "Not the *car*. You. *You* are not funny. You drove me off the road that day. I almost hit that woman! Thankfully, I didn't. She's okay. But my car is not! You *broke* my car!!" I can't think of a simpler way to say it.

"I broke you car?" he asks innocently.

His bad grammar is now an obstacle I can't seem to clear. Or is he toying with me? I can't tell. I suspect he is, and that infuriates me further. I bark, "Your! You say, 'I broke *your* car!'"

Confused, he says, "No one break *my* car."

"Oh!" I groan. I know he's not this dumb. He's totally fucking with me. In the annoying way. I lose it. "You broke *my* car and you broke *your* words! Not *you* words! YOUR words!! You say, 'I broke *your* car!' That's how you're supposed to say it!!!!"

He's studying my face raptly, watching my mouth in particular. "Say again."

"What?! Say *what* again?!" I growl.

"Say again. I watch you...*you*-ruh face." His eyes are locked on my lips. It sort of makes me nervous but I can tell he's not thinking about licking them or kissing them or whatever. Not that I would let him. He's waiting for me to speak.

Since when did I become this guy's English teacher?

"Say again. Please. You-ruh."

He said please. My anger subsides slightly. I roll my eyes and sigh. "Your." I draw out the words, "YOOUUR. Say it. *Your*."

His lips tremble and he tentatively speaks, "You-ruh. You-or-uh. *Your*. Your!" His eyes light up. "Your! I broke YOUR car! I broke it!"

I cock my hip and put a fist on it dubiously. We're still not supposed to be happy about my broken car.

"*Your* good teacher," he says proudly.

I almost correct him again, but I don't have the energy to explain to him the difference between *your* and *you're*.

"Thanks," I smile thinly.

"Teach more. I pay you."

"Now?" I shake my head. "What about *your* massage?" I grin when I say your.

He grins too. "Not now. Later. I pay you good. Okay?"

"Uhh...maybe?" I want to scratch my head. How did we end up here? I'm not sure I want a reason to see this guy regularly.

"Oh, uh, I need ah, ah, ah-*pologize* for you."

"Huh? Apologize for *me*? What'd I do?" I frown.

"Uhh...is wrong word. Apologize *to* you."

I'm shocked. "Why?" I can think of a thousand things for him to apologize about, but I don't even know where to begin.

"For *your* car," he smiles, obviously happy about using the correct word.

"What do you mean?"

"When I drive Lamborghini and break *your* car. Is mistake."

"Oh?"

"Lamborghini is new car. I drive yesterday in morning first time. When I see you and clown car."

"Okay," I smile uncertainly. Is this supposed to be an apology?

"Ahh..." his eyes dart around uncertainly, "Lamborghini has auto assist? Yes?"

I nod, not sure what he's talking about.

"Auto assist is like...computer assist? Make easier to drive car? Hard to lose control?"

"Yeah?"

"Is turned off, but I not know, yes? When I drive, and see you, car in front slow down fast, yes? I push brake, but foot push gas and brake same time. I have big feet. Gas and brake are small and..." he holds his hands close together.

I nod understanding.

"Yes? I press brake and gas same time. Lamborghini have strong engine. Very strong. Car go very fast. I must..." he swerves his hand in the air.

"Swerve?" I prompt.

His eyes light up and he points at me, "Yes! I swerve to not hit car in front!"

"Is that when you ran me off the road!"

"Yes! I very sorry! Very bad car. You understand?"

"I think so? So like, you had to swerve around the car in front of you to avoid hitting it? And that's when you swerved into my lane and made me almost hit the woman waiting for the bus?"

"Yes! I sorry. Ten times sorry. I do very bad. I very sorry for bad."

I want to ask why he was following so close or going too fast or whatever, but I don't. Do I take his word for it? I search his eyes.

His hardened stone mask is gone, his eyes have that boyish innocence. He wants me to believe him. He cares what I think, which is way different from his attitude when he walked in yesterday.

Thinking back, I remember clearly what happened *after* he swerved into my lane, but not before. Before I was thinking all about McJogs. Maybe Drakken is telling the truth. And in the end, nobody got hurt. Except Sheena the Chevy, but she can be fixed.

Reluctantly, I chose to believe his version of events. Besides, he apologized. I never thought he was the type. Drakken struck me as the sort of guy who blamed everyone else for his problems.

His boyish innocence still glows on his face. "How much for you, uh, *your* car? For break? To fix?"

"Oh, uh, it's gonna cost me $1,975."

"I pay." He pulls out his wallet and hands me $2,100 in hundreds. This guys carries way too much cash.

"Oh, no, I can't take that. You already gave me $600."

"$600 is for massage last time. $2,100 for fix your car."

"What? No, I said $1,975."

"$125 is for bad day," he smiles. "You sad because I break you, *your*, car. Take money. Take."

I look at the bills in his hand uncertainly. I hate taking money from people for free. But he did run my car into the sidewalk, even if it was just an accident. And, this way, I can give Luciana the money for yesterday's massage, so she'll have nothing to complain about. Problems solved.

He arches his eyebrows hopefully, "You take."

I take the money from him, but hand back $100. "$25 for bad day," I grin. "That's more than enough."

He frowns, "No, no, no. $125 not enough." He hands me the hundred. "Take. For you."

Reluctantly, I take the bills and fold them in my hand, "Thank you so much, Drakken," I smile.

"Thank you, Reka."

I wince slightly when I hear the pronunciation. The Shreka thing isn't working for me.

He corrects himself, "I mean, River."

I smile while I put the money in my purse.

This strange man never ceases to amaze me.

Unfortunately, I worry that that's a bad thing.

Chapter 17

RIVER

"Massage now?"

I nod absently, "Yeah. Yes. Take off your pants and lie down."

He cocks a grin at me and unbuckles his belt right in front of me.

My heart races. "Wait! Behind the screen!" I point at the shoji in the corner, then grab a towel.

Before I hand it to him, he's already unzipping his slacks.

"Stop! Go behind the screen!"

"You no like? Is no good?" He grins, flicking his eyes down at his body.

He towers over me. His slacks hang loose on his narrow hips. Every inch of him from his V to his abs to his chest and muscled shoulders looks priceless.

I smirk, "Is okay."

He feigns hurt, "*Okay*? Is no good?"

I giggle. "Nope. No good."

"*No* good? No more okay?"

I shake my head and smile, "Take your pants off."

He slides them down to his ankles without removing his shoes.

"Behind the screen!!" I point.

He shuffles across the room with his slacks around his ankles.

I can't help it. I literally bend over and belly laugh. He looks hilarious.

He winks at me as he shuffles behind the screen. He's so tall, his entire head pokes over the top. He smiles and glances briefly down at his screened-off body. "You want to see? Is very good," he chuckles.

I shake my head and grin. "No!"

"Okay. Towel? Please?"

I drape it over the screen.

A moment later he walks out in the towel and lies down on his back. "I ready now."

"Um, can you turn over? I'd really like to start with your back." Last time, he wouldn't let me touch it. What was up with that?

His face hardens into his familiar stoney mask.

Did I say something wrong?

His icy blue eyes search mine.

Those eyes seemed so soothing a second ago. Now they've hardened. Yet I'm struck by their crystalline beauty. They're nearly luminous in contrast to his darkened brow and remind me of twin aurora orbs over an Arctic night sky. There's something magical about them and I have the distinct feeling he's reading my mind like he did the other day.

My heart accelerates and I feel him crawling inside me. I've never felt so naked, and I'm the one who's dressed.

How does he do that?

After a moment, he nods quietly, "Is okay. You good person." He slowly turns over and I see his back.

An elaborate and intricate tattoo covers every inch of skin from his neck to his hips, and the backs of his arms to the elbows. How had I missed it?

That's when I realize he totally hid his back from me last time. Whether he was standing up or lying down, he never allowed me to see it. But why? It's a tattoo. Everyone has tattoos nowadays.

Is he embarrassed by it?

I gaze at the image. I'm not quite sure what it is at first. It's sort of abstract, yet incredibly beautiful and intricate. I could imagine him wanting to hide it if it looked terrible. But this is a work of art. Leonardo da Vinci would be proud to have drawn this.

I marvel at it, trying to figure out what it represents. Before I realize it, I'm lost in the hypnotizing design, trapped in the lines like the wall of a maze, at the center of which lies this man's heart.

Where did that thought come from?

"Massage now?" he asks, startling me from me trance.

"Oh, um, yeah. Sorry. I just need some massage oil." I grab the bottle from the counter and rub some into my palms, still staring at the tattoo. That's when it clicks.

It's a dragon. A huge chaotic dragon with thousands of scales and an infinitely looping tail that coils around the base of his spine and ends with the head just below the line of his shirt collar. The dragon's wings extend down the backs of his arms. When he's dressed, it's completely hidden. Like a dark, shameful secret.

But a dragon?

I don't get it.

Why would a dragon be shameful?

It can't be the tattoo.

"Massage now," he growls, his face nearly buried in the cushion of the massage table. There's something almost demonic about his voice. Just a hint, but it's unmistakeable, and nothing at all like his boyish innocence thing, or his abrasive cocky thing. This is far worse.

This is the voice of darkness.

It's more than a bit frightening.

I push away my concern and focus on the task at hand. I walk around the table so I'm standing near his hips.

I swear the dragon tattoo is moving. Like, the coils are coiling and uncoiling.

I blink my eyes and tell myself it's just an optical illusion. He was flexing his muscles and I was moving at the same time, which made it appear yada, yada, yada.

So, muscles and massage. That's why I'm here. I think I'll start with his lower back. I rest my palm on his skin carefully.

Just in case that dragon actually *was* moving.

He winces and jerks beneath my touch.

I pull my hand away abruptly. That's weird. Big strong guys like him always pretend they don't feel pain. "Um, do you have a back injury or something?"

He shakes his head. "No."

I glide my fingertips gently across his skin, reluctant to continue. That's when I notice the flesh beneath his tattoo is rough and—

"Stop!" He grunts and flips onto his back. "Massage front." His face is the hardened stone mask and his brows are clenched in anger.

"I'm sorry, did I hurt you?" I don't know how I could have. I barely touched him.

"No. Is not you."

What does that mean? Did someone else hurt him? I'm not really sure what's going on.

"Massage front. Like other time. Is good." The look on his face is nowhere close to good.

I arch my eyebrows, "Are you sure?"

He nods confidently, "Is good. Massage please."

I stare at his eyes for a long time. They are metallic shields, blocking out my attempt to see what lies within him. For a moment, I feel like I'm staring at the mechanical eyes of a robot. A lifeless, soulless machine.

It makes me sad.

Like magic, those metallic shields flicker for a fraction of a second and I see behind them. I see into him. It sounds corny, but for that half second, I see into his soul. I can't explain how, but I do. And I know with chilling certainty that he's hiding something terrible.

Scratch that. He's hiding *everything*.

He's not just hiding his bad parts, he's hiding the good parts too. Who he *really* is, what he *really* feels, what he *really* wants out of life. Everything he presents to the world is fake. An act. That's the only way this man knows how to live.

His true self is hidden behind layer after layer of emotional armor. It lives hidden within. Trapped inside with a monster, struggling to survive.

I shudder at the thought.

Fortunately for me and everyone else within striking distance of this man, the monster can't come out.

At least that's what I tell myself.

I can't begin to imagine the specifics of what Drakken lived through, and I can't imagine the burden he lives *with* every single day.

My heart swells with sympathy for him.

Chapter 18

RIVER

One of the weird things about massage is that it can release long-trapped emotions. But that usually happens after multiple sessions, when I've had a chance to work over an area that is chronically tight and defended. Not after a single touch.

Unless touching Drakken's back is some kind of trigger for him?

That's the obvious answer.

And, he obviously knows his back is a trigger. I mean, he wouldn't even let me see it yesterday. So why did he agree to let me touch it today?

Does he trust me?

Already?

But I threw his money in his face and kicked his ass out of here barely twenty four hours ago. And now he's opening up? None of this makes any sense. But it makes my heart race all the same.

"Massage now? Please?" he asks, not in his demon voice. It's a plaintive, vulnerable voice I can't refuse.

"Uh, yeah. Sorry."

Since he's on his back again, I start working on his neck like last time. Like before, his neck muscles feel like they're made of steel cables. The tension this man carries is more than any man ever should.

I have new sympathy for him.

I work quietly on him for a while, doing my best to massage away his tension.

At the moment, I'm working the same knot in his chest I found last time. I really need to get around to the back of his shoulder blade. Since he won't turn over, I improvise and hook both my arms around his until I have a good grip. Then I gently tug on his entire arm, asking the shoulder muscles to relax.

All his muscles make his arm weigh a ton.

The next thing I know, I'm leaning into it. Each time I tug, my boob bumps his bicep.

Sure, I'm wearing my white spa uniform and a bra underneath. But it's my boob touching him.

Normally, I can get through an entire massage without my boobs getting involved. Normally, my clients let me massage their backs, so it isn't an issue.

When I'm working on a female client, some boob involvement is no big whoop. But generally it's a bad idea when massaging a man.

Maybe Drakken won't notice.

His eyes flicker open. "Is good," he sighs.

I hope he means the massage and not the boob contact. Either way, I pretend that all boobs have ceased to exist.

The growing bulge beneath Drakken's towel spears my fantasy through the core, popping it like a boob balloon.

Men are so predictable.

Like yesterday, I ignore it.

Ignoring is easier this time because I'm really focused on getting his shoulder to relax. I do my best to keep my face passive. Also, I shift my grip so my boob is no longer touching him. It puts more strain on my back, but I can handle it. I don't want him getting any ideas.

Clearly, my strategy is failing miserably, because I see full tent in the corner of my vision. And a confident smirk on his face.

He watches me closely.

I want to snicker, but that might sound like flirting. I knit my brows, hoping that a serious face will put him off my scent.

But the blush spreading to my cheeks is a dead giveaway.

I don't know why I'm having such a hard time ignoring his arousal. Err, maybe hard is the wrong word. Drakken has the hard part covered. What I mean is, I've ignored countless erections since I started doing massage therapy a few years ago. I've had numerous offers from guys for happy endings or something "not on the menu." But I don't do hand job massages. Period. No matter how hot the guy might be. Because it's a great way to get fired. And I'm not a hooker.

"Is good," he moans. His eyes open halfway. A dreamy smile spread across his face. He reaches up and gently skims his thumb across my cheek.

Golden flowers of light bloom where he touches me. Normally, if a guy touched me like this during a massage, I'd jump back and tell him to keep his hands to himself or I would end the massage. Instead, I murmur, "Is good."

His dreamy smile grows wider.

I'm getting really hot now. The combination of my effort working his arm and that touch has my skin broiling. I need some distance. Time to switch to the other end.

I focus on massaging his feet for a while. Like last time, it doesn't do anything to reduce his erection, but it's the best I can do.

His cock stands proudly beneath his huge army tent, which makes me think of that famous statue of the U.S soldiers planting the flag at Iwo Jima during World War II. It would take at least that many men to handle Drakken's flagpole right now.

I stifle a snicker.

"What is funny?" Drakken asks in his baritone voice, which sounds drunk with relaxation and mellow arousal.

"Nothing," I say, now working on his calves. I realize he's got tons of tension in his quads, like most muscular guys, so I go to work on his upper legs. That's when I notice the towel is sort of in my way. I push it up and pool it between his legs, giving me better access to his upper thighs.

I lean my forearm on his quad and push down with all my body weight, dragging the muscle down toward the kneecap. I do this several times.

I can't help but notice that the motion causes his cock to bounce slightly. Each time I glide down to the knee and release, it goes *boing*.

Drag, *boing*. Drag, *boing*. Drag, *boing*.

The motion is hypnotic.

Am I drooling? Maybe. But I'm not going to wipe my chin. It would be a dead giveaway.

I finish with this leg and walk around the table. I start on his other leg, same technique.

Drag, *boing*. Drag, *boing*. Drag, *boing*.

I squeeze my knees together because all the boinging is getting to me. I'm also intimately aware of the texture of my panties, which have decided now is the best time to caress me. Funny how you never notice your panties 99% of the time. But when a huge cock is bouncing inches from your face, all of a sudden your panties have something to say.

Mmmm. Oh! Look at THAT! It's so BIG!! Is it just me, or is the roof leaking?

I do my best to ignore the comments.

That's when I realize, on maybe the twelfth drag and boing, that

Drakken's towel has slipped downward. The tent pole is no longer centered. The towel is now precariously close to sliding entirely off.

If I keep working his quad with the drag and boing, I'm going to see full cock.

I remind myself I saw it last time when he got undressed.

I also remind myself it wasn't erect, and I was eight feet away.

This is an entirely different situation.

But I can still feel knots in his quad. And massaging him is way easier than addressing the issue of the slippage.

Drag, *boing*. Drag, *boing*. Drag—

The towel is a quarter inch from slipping entirely off.

—*boing*.

And the towel slips.

It falls in slow motion.

Without a thought, I grab for it.

Caught it!

Not the towel.

It.

His cock.

Because I was a moment too slow, even in slow motion.

Time pretty much stops.

I wince and hike my eyebrows.

I'm holding his cock.

He lifts his head from the table and peers down at me.

My eyebrows are now literally floating in the air above my face, much like a cartoon character who is extra surprised.

Not that I'm aware, but I'm still gripping his cock. It's a very firm grip, which is appropriate for a very firm cock.

Drakken arches an eyebrow of his own. Unlike mine, it's still attached to his forehead. He mutters casually, "Is good?"

I explode with laughter and my face falls onto his muscular thigh where I do my best to bury my cackling laughter. While nearly weeping with glee, I say, "Is good."

"You massage him too?" Drakken asks innocently.

This sends me into fresh hysterics and I'm literally spitting laughter between pursed lips. I'm gonna need to blow my nose in a second. But I can't lift my face. I'm too embarrassed.

And I'm still holding Drakken's cock.

All I can think is that the camper in his pants is going to be sleeping under the stars without a tent tonight. I snicker again.

Drakken drops his head back to the padded table and chuckles, "Is good."

I'm not letting go of his cock yet.

I don't know why.

Wait, I totally know why. I have a magnificent cock in my hands. Why would I *want* to let go? The pressing question is: what am I going to do about it?

Hmmm. Hard cock in hand? It's a tough decision. On the one hand, I have no intention of breaking my 'no hand release' rule. I'm a masseuse. Not a hooker. On the other hand, the one currently holding a cock, I sort of *want* to give him a hand job. Because what woman doesn't want to play with a beautiful cock attached to a hot body like Drakken's?

This woman does.

I pump his cock once, experimentally.

I pause, waiting to see what he says.

He's silent.

I pump a second time.

I pause again.

In a low, choked voice, he grunts, "Is good."

So I choke his cock some more. It helps that my hands are already slick from massage oil. It's easy to slide and glide up and down his silken monument. I realize my fingers aren't long enough to wrap all the way around his girth. Wow. But they can work the thick tip just fine. I caress the purple head, working circles, squeezing and releasing.

You never really appreciate how big a big cock is until it's in your hands.

I am *so* bad.

"Is good," he whispers hoarsely.

Well, they do say that bad is the new good, and I'm pretty good at hand jobs.

It's all my massage experience.

His heavy cock strains in my hand. I can feel it twitching. Holy shit, he's not going to come already, is he?

Don't tell me Drakken is a Minute Man?

His cock twitches again.

I can't believe I'm doing this.

I'm giving a hand job to a total stranger on my massage table. I remind myself he's not a *total* stranger. I know his name, first and last. We're acquaintances. That's not whorish, right?

But is giving a hand job at work—in the spa, with the door unlocked, meaning anyone could potentially walk in at any moment, even my boss Luciana—is that whorish?

No, because I *want* to be doing it. As a favor. Drakken is tense. He deserves an orgasm. I'm just helping him out. It's not like we're standing in Times Square in front of a crowd. That would be performance art, because it's Manhattan, but I digress.

The huge cock in my hands has turned a deep red. I increase my tempo as it strains inside the grip of my fingers.

Up, work the tip, slide down to the root, up, work the tip, slide down to the root…

Faster, faster…

Faster…

Fastest…

Top speed…

Pedal to the metal…

Drakken's back arches, he hisses through his teeth and grunts, "Reka!"

We have lift off!

Hot cum shoots straight up.

It's a white foam geyser.

I've never visited Old Faithful in Yellowstone National Park, but this is the next best thing.

SPURT!!!!

Drakken makes a *lot* of cum.

Spurt!!

Splash after splash touches down on his hips in creamy white ropes.

Spurt!

I keep working my hand while he bucks on the table. He's not shouting or anything, but the sound of the massage table creaking on the tiled floor is pretty damn loud.

Spurt.

I really hope nobody outside decides now is the time to walk through the door.

As his orgasm fades, hot cum continues to burble out the tip of his manhood, soaking my hand in a sticky white glove.

This is a huge mess.

Part of me wants to clean up the crime scene before Luciana barges in, because at this point it seems inevitable.

But I don't want to abandon him at such a sensitive moment.

I slow my hand motions with each stroke until I come to rest, my hand lax around his slackening cock.

What did I just do?

I blame Finch. She told me to find something to distract me.

Distraction found.

Holy shizzle.

I am *so* dirty.

And I think I like it.

"Is good," he sighs.

Again, I drop my forehead to his thigh to stifle my giggles.

Chapter 19

RIVER

I lift my head and look at Drakken. For some weird reason, I feel like I'm in trouble. Part of me wants Drakken to reprimand me with rigid authority. You know what I mean.

At the moment, he's not exactly rigid.

You also know what I mean.

But that's not it.

I've never done anything like this and I'm embarrassed.

I say quietly, "I should clean you up. Stay right there."

He grins sleepily, "Okay."

I grab fresh towels and wipe him down.

He watches me closely. "Is very good."

"Was it?" I smile.

He nods, "Very, very good. You do again?"

"Drakken!" I hiss.

He chuckles.

To my surprise, his soft cock seems to be filling with blood again. Is that even possible? Maybe he's more than one kind of Minute Man.

Needless to say, that's all he's gonna get. This was totally a one time deal for me. I was glad to do it, but once is enough for my bucket list of naughty accomplishments.

When I finish wiping him clean with fresh towels, I stuff the dirty towels in the bottom of the laundry bin in the cupboard. I really hope nobody discovers the cum soaked towels. I'm pretty sure the maids and the laundry people can spot cum stains from a mile away. I really don't want this getting back to me.

Why do I feel so guilty?

Oh yeah. Because I'm not supposed to sex up my clients on the clock.

I remove the big towel pooled around Drakken's waist and drape a fresh one over his lap. "So, um, how long was your appointment for today?"

"Ninety minute." He glances at the clock on the wall. "More time, yes?"

"Yeah. Are you sure you don't want me to massage your back?"

His face dances through a series of conflicted looks. "Thank you, no. Next time?"

I shrug my shoulders, "Okay. But I could do a lot more if I could work on your back. There's not much left to do on your front. Today, anyway."

"I massage you?"

"What?!" That's definitely not allowed. Who am I kidding? I just gave him a hand job! "I really shouldn't."

He sits up on the table. His towel remains in place, but it is seriously tented. He really does recover fast.

"You like?"

He totally caught me looking at his cock. "Um…"

"You like," he grins confidently.

I roll my eyes because of his cockiness. And his cock. "No," I deny, shaking my head.

He chuckles, "You like."

"Drakken," I gush. "Stop!" But I rest my fingers on his forearm.

"You lie down. I massage you." He slides off the table and stands. His towel falls to the floor. Before I have time to react, he scoops me up and lays me on the table. "You relax, okay?"

Now I'm totally nervous. Someone could seriously walk in at any moment. Not that anyone ever does. But with the door unlocked, they easily could.

"Uh," I mumble, "hold on a second." I jump off the table and twist the door lock before lying back down.

"Is good," Drakken grins.

Okay then. I'm going to get a massage from a hot guy. While I'm at work. Right after I gave him a hand job.

Why not?

I'm not flirting with disaster.

Nope, not me.

Besides, it's just a massage. It'll be fun. And it'll certainly keep me from thinking about an ex-boyfriend with bad timing whose name I've forgotten for the moment.

I wonder fleetingly if I should disrobe so Drakken can give me a proper massage. No, that really would be flirting with disaster. You can totally massage people while they're dressed. It's not as good, but it's good enough.

Speaking of which, I wonder if Drakken knows what he's doing.

I flip onto my stomach. "Can you massage my neck?"

"Yes. Is good."

His powerful hands squeeze the tops of my shoulders and begin to knead. Oh, wow. I'm instantly melting. I forget how tense I can get. Just because my clients walk out of my massage room feeling relaxed and buttery doesn't mean I do.

"Oh…" I moan. "Right there."

His hands squeeze and release, push and pull, slide and stretch up and down my neck and shoulders until I'm a floppy mess.

It feels incredible.

"Where the hell did you learn how to massage like this?"

"I have many massage. I remember what is good, what is bad. I give you good."

"I'll say," I moan. He must've had a shizz ton of massages over the years if he's this good. If he grew up rich, it makes sense. Rich people go through massages like candy.

I'm so relaxed when he starts running his hands down my ass, I don't even think about it. I just go with it.

Hot guy massaging my ass.

My pelvis is on fire.

In a good way.

Panties say, *Yeah, the roof is leaking.*

I can feel that afterglow thing coming on.

And I haven't even had sex.

But I feel like I'm on the verge of a mellow orgasm of some kind.

My core is tingling with need right now.

I try to think about relaxing, but all I can see in my mind is a spurting cock. Hard, hot, throbbing.

I'm hot and throbbing too.

I hope he doesn't notice.

He leans his hands downward on the backs of my thighs. Every time he presses down and slides, my knees creep slightly apart.

I can't tell if he's doing it, or if I'm doing it.

Mainly, I don't care.

I just want to open.

I've been so closed for so long, all I want to do is open. Wide.

And daydream about hard cocks.

Whew, I'm flushing from head to toe. My spa uniform feels *really* hot right now. I'm going to sweat right through it at this rate. I want to fan my face, but I'm so relaxed, I really don't want to move.

But one thing is for sure. My panties are soaked.

"You like?" Drakken asks thoughtfully.

I nod and groan, "Yes. Is good," I giggle.

I hear him grin, "Is good."

Do I need an excuse to strip my clothes off? Would that be too forward?

The next thing I know, Drakken is slipping my shoes off. He says, "I massage feet."

I feel his strong thumb work into the sole of my foot. "Oh god," I sigh. "Keep doing that."

He does.

Feet are usually not a focus for me during sex, but they are totally an erogenous zone.

Every time he slides his thumb from my heel to the ball of my foot, it sends a pulse straight between my legs.

Okay, I'm dying right now.

I haven't been this horny since forever.

When he finishes with my feet, he walks back toward my hips and squeezes my ass again.

He slides his thick fingers right down the crack of my ass and cups my womanhood through my uniform pants.

I totally let him.

Wow, he's bold.

I feel pressure against my wet folds.

"Your hot," he states boldly.

I don't notice his incorrect usage of 'your' because I'm too busy being used. And loving it.

"Ahhh," I moan. I've lost the power of formal speech.

His fingers throb between my legs. "Very hot. I take off your pants."

Yeah, I pretty much have forgotten where I am. I don't really care. He can do whatever he wants with me. "Uh huh."

He manages to turn me gently over without any help on my part.

I gaze up at him.

His face is warm, inviting, and ravenous. He unsnaps my pants and slides them down over my ankles.

Cool air caresses my wetness.

My panties are still on, but not for long, I'm guessing.

He slides fingers across my thighs. "Your legs beautiful." He leans down and kisses his way up one leg, lifts my uniform shirt so he can kiss my taut stomach, then kisses back down my other leg. He stands up and looks at me longingly. "You very wet."

I nod and grin, "What are you gonna do about it?"

He chuckles softly, "Make you very wet. Make you scream."

"Really," I tease. I've totally forgotten that screaming in the massage room is the worst idea ever. But I've forgotten it, so I don't object.

He slides my panties down my legs. Then he smells them deeply. "Is good."

Works for me.

"I keep," he says and walks toward the closet. He opens it and stuffs my panties into his suit jacket.

Also works for me.

I'm not thinking rationally at this point.

He returns to the table and slides his strong finger inside my hot tunnel. "Is very wet." His thumb glides across my clit and I quiver.

"Oh, guh-god."

Pleasure fireworks up into my body as his second finger enters me.

His thumb circles round and round while his two fingers go in and out.

The sweet tension builds and I'm floating in clouds of ecstasy.

"You like," he says with assurance.

"I like," I moan. "Is good…" My entire core seems to be breathing. Inhale pleasure, exhale tension. Inhale pleasure, exhale tension. He is emptying all of my stress out of my body and replacing it with pure ecstasy. It's wonderful. I don't remember hand jobs being this good.

"Yes…" I sigh. It's the only word I know anymore. My eyes roll into my head as a strong wave of warmth washes up my body. I feel a huge orgasm on the horizon. It's going to blow me away when it finally gets here. I already know it.

A pleasant desert wind billows across my body, increasing the pleasure. I'm basking on some tropical beach, kissed by the sun. Sunshine drizzles between my legs and my wetness heats with need.

Then I realize the hot wind is Drakken going down on me. I'm vaguely aware that his face is buried between my legs. Everything has blended into a haze of hot sensations, but I have a vague awareness of his tongue lapping and teasing, plowing through my folds and slickening my clitoris.

The heat storm builds, and tropical storm clouds churn inside me.

He lifts his face away from my core just enough to whisper, "Is good, Rivka. You come." Then his greedy tongue plunders my wetness.

"Come," he growls into my folds. "Come for Drakken."

I have no choice but to obey his command.

My stomach seizes first as the storm waves crash inside me. Explosions of ecstasy thunder outward from there, reaching the far shores of every cell in my body. My stomach gives way to the pounding between my legs and my back arches, lifting me off the table. I gasp sharp shallow breaths, struggling for air and whimpering, "Uh, uh, uh, uh, uh, uh, uh…"

I'm nearly paralyzed with pleasure.

"Is good, Rivka," he hisses. "Is good."

I explode with final orgasmic cataclysm.

The storm tears me apart and sinks me into the warm depths of heaven as the ocean gods claim me.

Chapter 20

RIVER

"River?" Luciana asks through the massage room door. "Is everything okay in there? Your next client is waiting."

Oh shit!!

I totally lost track of time. I'm lying on the massage table, my pants and panties gone, with Drakken gently caressing my forehead and gazing down at me with his magical eyes.

Too bad Luciana had to break the spell.

Now I'm in a panic.

I jump off the massage table and look for my clothes.

Drakken hands me my pants, a cocky smile on his face. He has way too much cock for his own good.

I whip my head from side to side, looking for my panties, then I remember he put them in his suit.

Okay then.

I yank my pants on, left leg first. That goes on fine. But yanking on the right nearly knocks me on my ass.

Drakken catches me in his arms, narrowly averting me from breaking my butt bone.

"Thanks," I whisper. "Lie down on the table! Like I'm massaging you!"

He does, and wraps the towel around his waist before lying on his back.

Luciana knocks on the door again.

I dash across the room and unlock it. "What's up?" I smooth a lock of hair behind my ear.

I think she's trying to frown, but all the Botox she uses makes it impossible. In a low voice she says, "You locked the door." The odd look on her face translates as: Why the fuck is this door locked?

I mutter, "Ahh..."

She ignores me and says, "Mrs. Mueller is waiting for you. You should have finished with Mr. Skalakova ten minutes ago. Is everything okay?"

"I massaged Mrs. Mueller yesterday. Is she back again?"

"She most certainly is."

"Oh, uh..." I suddenly realize I'm not wearing my shoes or socks. This is highly incriminating. We're not supposed to take our shoes off for a massage. I pin my eyes on Luciana's, trying to hold hers in place with the force of my own.

She blinks, as if trying to break free of my eye-locking hold. But she can't do it. Or at least that's what I'm telling myself. And I'm not giving up. She will not notice my bare feet!

I concentrate really hard.

I don't know how long I can keep this up. I've never done it before. But it seems to be working.

"Is my fault," Drakken says, sitting up on the table.

Still holding Luciana's eyes on mine, I smile nervously and mumble through clenched teeth, "His fault."

I don't know why I'm throwing Drakken under the bus, I just am. Oh yeah, cuz he can't get fired. Sorry, buddy.

Luciana's eyes finally flick past mine.

She's stronger than I thought.

Her eyes land on Drakken.

He's now sitting up and smiling at Luciana.

Her face melts with naked desire.

Drakken says, "I ask River to massage, uh, twice." He reaches behind him and plants his palm on his lower back. He arches his torso and winces, "Back very stiff."

Something about him was stiff, but it wasn't his back. And now it's completely relaxed between his legs. No tents in sight.

Luciana smiles her wax museum smile again, "Certainly, Mr. Skalakova. Your well being is our number one priority." She turns to me, "Shall I tell Mrs. Mueller that you're unavailable? Or shall I arrange another masseuse for her?" Her eyebrow arches sharply.

"Oh, uh, I think we're done now. Don't you, Drah—I mean, Mr. Skalakova?"

He purses his lips and nods, "Is good. I dress and go, okay?"

"Fantastic, Mr. Skalakova," Luciana says. "I trust that Ms. Freeman gave you our usual five star service?"

I stifle a giggle.

Drakken nods, "Is very good. Many stars. I count five hundred. Maybe five thousand."

I'm going to burst out laughing. I try to hold it in.

"Excellent," Luciana grins. "I'll leave you two alone." In a low voice for my ears only, she says, "Please don't dawdle, River. We can't keep Mrs. Mueller waiting. It sends the wrong impression to our other guests."

I nod, "Totally. I'll finish right up."

Luciana still hasn't seen my bare feet yet. I think it helps that I have one covering the other. One bare foot is less obvious than two.

I really want to push the door closed and force Luciana out of the room, but I don't.

Is she going to go, or just stare at me?

Her eyes finally flick downward as she pulls the door closed. She stops half way.

Sighing shizz.

"Your shoes…" she says absently.

"Uh…"

She drills me with a hard glare, "You can explain later. The door?"

I realize I'm gripping the doorknob with white knuckles. "Oh, sorry." I release it.

Luciana pulls the door closed behind her as she leaves.

If there's one thing I know about Luciana, she's not going to forget this. We will definitely be having a discussion later.

And I thought I'd gotten away with an on-the-job orgasm.

Damn that bucket list.

Naughtiness never turns out nice.

But it was totally worth it.

If I don't get fired on sex charges.

Is it illegal to have sex in the work place?

I think only if you get paid.

I turn and Drakken is pulling his wallet out of his suit jacket. "How much?"

Why does that sound so wrong all of a sudden?

"Oh, you can pay Jocelyn in the waiting room. If you want, you can bill it to your room." I really don't want to exchange any money at this exact moment.

"Okay. And tip? I pay you tip, yes? For cash?"

"Ahh…this one's on me?"

"On you?"

"Well, um, you gave me all that money for last time, and for my car, and it's more than enough. Really. You've been more than generous."

"You sure?" He holds out a stack of bills. "I have more money. Is good," he smiles.

I wave my hands, "No, really. It's on the house."

"Okay. If you change mind, tell me, yes? I stay at hotel. In Sunset Suite. Twentieth floor. You say hello any time, okay?"

"Okay," I grin despite my unease. This is all super weird right now.

"I go?" he asks.

I nod. I feel like I'm doing the walk of shame, and I'm standing in place. "Yeah," I say nervously.

"I dress now, okay?"

"Okay."

While Drakken changes, I go about changing the linens on the table and prepping the room for Mrs. Mueller.

Drakken takes forever behind the shoji screen, but eventually he walks out wearing his suit. He looks seriously sexy all dressed up. Panty dropping sexy. I mean that literally, and from recent experience. He also has my panties in his pocket. He can keep them. Men always like trophies.

Drakken cups my cheek and brushes his thumb across it. "Thank you, Rivka."

I pause, "I thought it was Shreka?"

He frowns, "Shreka?"

"Or however you say 'river' in your language."

"Oh, Reka," he grins.

"Yeah, what happened to that?"

"You not like. I change to Rivka. Your name in English, but like, ah, pet name?"

"Like a nickname?"

"Yes," he smiles. "Rivka is nickname. For you. Okay?"

Um, I'm not entirely comfortable with him nicknaming me all of a sudden. Then again, I gave him a hand job and he ate me out. Maybe we're on a nickname basis now. There's worse things.

And I kind of like the sound of it.

He takes a sudden step toward me and I'm intimately aware of his intensely male scent. It makes me dizzy in a good way. I think the post-massage and post-orgasm afterglow that is still permeating my body makes the effect of his scent more intense. I have a strong desire to tear his clothes back off.

Before I can, he leans into me. I think he's going to kiss me on the mouth. Instead, he kisses one cheek, then the other. "Thank you, Rivka."

Oh. I sort of wanted him to kiss me.

But he has already pulled away.

"You're welcome, Drakkenka," I snicker at my made up nickname.

He wrinkles his nose and shakes his head, "Drakkenka? No, is no good. For easy, maybe, uh, Drakka? Or Drakkozsha, but is hard."

I grin, "I like Drakka. Fewer Z's in it."

He chuckles, "Drakka is good. Okay, bye now." He walks out of the massage room.

Now we have pet names for each other?

Holy crap.

This is way more than a simple distraction.

My life just got complicated.

I'm not sure how I feel about that.

Well, if this never happens again, I don't have to worry about it.

Drakken stops in the hallway and turns to face me. "One thing."

"Yeah?"

"Close eyes."

"Why?"

"Close eyes," he smiles.

"Okay." I close them.

"Now give hand. I give you gift."

I know what he's going to do. I whisper so no one can hear us out in the hallway, "I told you, Drakka, I can't take your money today." I'm somewhat unnerved that I used his nickname without a thought.

"Is not money. Is gift. I promise."

"Okay," I sigh and raise my open hand.

I feel something sharp edged set on my palm. He closes my fingers over it. It feels like paper, but it sure isn't money.

"Goodbye," he mutters.

Before I can open my eyes, he kisses my lips.

I'm so surprised I forget about whatever is in my hand.

Drakken breaks the kiss after only a second.

I watch him stroll casually away.

Mrs. Mueller passes him in the hallway. Her eyes goggle and she looks him up and down. "Oh my goodness," she whispers to herself, looking completely discombobulated.

I smile at her. "Good morning, Mrs. Mueller. Ready for a massage?"

She gasps, "Who was that dashing stranger?"

I lick my lips unconsciously, "That was Drakken Skalakova."

I close the door behind us.

Mrs. Mueller chuckles, "I hope he asked for your phone number or your Facebook, or whatever it is you young people do nowadays. You don't want a man like that getting away if you can help it."

"Oh, he's staying here at the resort. In the Sunset Suite."

"When are you seeing him again?"

"I have no idea," I say dreamily.

"Soon, I expect, based on the ear to ear grin I saw on his face in the hallway."

My heart hums at the thought.

"I'll change," Mrs. Mueller says as she walks behind the shoji.

That's when I remember the paper thing in my hand. I open my fingers.

Resting on my palm is a paper butterfly.

Folded out of a hundred dollar bill.

What the WHAT?

Did Drakken just fold this for me? While he changed a few minutes ago?

No frickin' way.

It's beautiful.

But I told him no money!

Okay, this totally doesn't count as payment for services rendered. It's totally an origami butterfly or whatever you call it. And that makes it a gift as long as I don't unfold it.

Wow.

Drakken is a man of a thousand mysteries.

I wonder what else I'm going to find out about him?

Whatever it is, I have a feeling it's going to be good.

And, oh yeah: Cage who?

Finch was so right.

Now I don't have to take up chainsaw juggling. I like my fingers way too much to lose them. They're really good at grabbing things.

Like cocks.

Drip.

And I'm not even wearing any panties.

Chapter 21

DRAKKEN

What an angel.

While I ride the elevator, I consider pulling Rivka's panties out of my pocket to smell them. But that's not necessary. I can smell her all over my face.

The smell is exquisite.

The elevator dings at the twentieth floor.

I walk down the carpeted hallway toward my suite, lost in wonderful thoughts.

Back in that massage room, with Rivka, I felt something.

Something profound.

Something truthful.

Something I have not felt since…

(…)

Blind rage explodes inside me.

Fire and anger consume me, every muscle in my body tensing.

I stumble once as I walk along the hallway.

(…)

No.

I will not allow myself to think about the past.

The past is set in stone. The past cannot be changed.

The past only brings pain.

Infinite and indescribable pain.

(…)

I slam the door on my past and hammer it shut. The familiar stone wall cements into place on my face. I am good at building walls. I have many, many years of practice.

As I walk stiffly around a turn in the hallway, I grimace and clench my jaw, blocking out all emotion, deadening my thoughts.

To my surprise, an image emerges from the gray haze in my mind, floating to the surface.

Those eyes.

Rivka's liquid blue eyes.

My face softens as I remember her hands, her touch, her smile. Her scent, her taste. Her moans…

Every single detail about her washes away the gray haze I know so well, and takes with it all my rage and hatred, cleansing my soul to the marrow.

My mind is a vibrant summer garden, drenched in color and pleasant sensation.

I had forgotten what this feels like.

Ease had become alien to me.

As if for the first time, I feel it meandering through my veins in a slow delicious flow.

For once, I am truly happy.

My stone face relaxes. I smile from ear to ear.

Today is a perfect day.

I reach into my suit to pull out Rivka's panties. I am going to hold them to my face and inhale their scent with great joy.

My fingers touch the silky material at the exact moment my phone rings. I suddenly tense as if the panties themselves came to life. I smile at my foolish thought and retrieve my phone.

I tell myself it's probably my assistant calling. She calls fifty-one times a day. I have a faint smile on my lips when I look at the number.

313 999 561-666

It's not my assistant.

It's an international number.

I know it by heart.

No one else in the world knows this number.

Except me.

My smile is crushed to dust by a falling wall of stone.

The mask is back.

I squeeze the metal case of my phone so hard, the glass screen splinters into a spiderweb of cracks.

I am ready to fight. To punch, to pound, to kill with my bare hands. Whenever I see that number, I am always ready to fight.

But I am in Los Angeles, California. I am far, far away from my past.

I force myself to relax.

I push back the anger.

(fear)

I punch the IGNORE CALL button on the phone with my finger. I faintly feel the sting of the fractured glass as it separates flesh.

A drop of blood smears across the screen, seeping into the cracked glass.

Tomorrow, I'll buy a new phone with a new number. Again.

(safe)

((for now))

Book 2

Chapter 1

DRAKKEN

Age 6.

I run through the garden as fast as I can.

"Drakken!" she laughs and runs behind me. "Wait for me!"

The sun is bright yellow and warm.

I love the sun because the sun loves everybody. He loves the green grass and the blue sky and the white clouds. He loves cats and dogs and birds and boys like me. And he loves her.

"Drakken!"

But he doesn't love her as much as I do.

Nobody loves her as much as I do.

Not even the sun.

I'm going to marry her some day.

I slow down so she can catch up. "Let's be birds!" I smile as big as I can.

"Okay!" she smiles too.

We flap our arms and run as fast as we can. We laugh and laugh and laugh. The grass and the wind laugh too.

"I'm flying, Drakka! I'm flying!"

Right now, I am happier than all the toys in the world.

"Look at those clouds!" she shouts. "They look like candy!"

"Maybe we can eat them!"

"Yeah!"

We jump as high as we can and try to catch the closest clouds.

"They're too high!" she laughs.

"Jump higher!" I giggle. "Higher!"

"Almost got it!" she smiles.

"Jump as high as you can!"

We jump, and jump, and jump.

We flap and laugh and flap and laugh forever.

We get tired and slow down.

"I can't reach the clouds, Drakken. They're too tall." She is sad.

"I'll help." I hug her and pick her up as high as I can. "Grab it! The one on the bottom!"

She reaches up. She laughs. "I got it, I got it!" She bites the cloud and chews on it.

She's too heavy and we both fall down in the grass and roll down the hill, laughing and giggling and somersaulting in the sunshine all the way to the bottom.

We stop with our arms and legs wide, smiling up at the sun.

He shines on us, smiling back.

We hold hands.

I smile at her.

She smiles at me.

I love her.

I love her more than anything ever.

I even love her more than Mommy and Daddy. I know it's naughty to say that. But it's true.

I love her.

Her...

Chapter 2

DRAKKEN

Now.

I wake up in a luxurious king-sized bed.

The room is nightmare black.

Despite the darkness, I know I'm in the Sunset Suite of The Beverly Hills Resort.

I was dreaming of birds and blue sky and sunshine.

I was dreaming of her.

Her...

Being awake is the real nightmare.

I want to die.

I squeeze my eyes shut as hard as I can, grimacing as the pain tears me apart. With all my heart, I want to leave this waking nightmare behind.

It's useless.

My summer dream of colors and love is smashed by blackness.

She's gone.

She's always gone.

The blackness consumes me.

The blackness takes everything.

Everything.

My heart stops.

I welcome sudden death.

Liquid blue eyes fill my mind.

Rivka...

For the first time in a decade, I sit up in bed, set my feet on the floor, and stand up with a smile on my face.

Those aqua blue eyes...

I don't want to die.

Rivka...

Chapter 3

RIVER

"Damn it, Cage. Why are you here?" I growl at him. I was just saying goodbye to my client Mr. Skelton when Cage walked into the spa's waiting area holding a bouquet of roses.

Cage flashes his mahogany eyes and drawls charmingly, "I needed to see you, Riv."

I smirk, "I didn't need to see you."

Why did Cage have to pick now to show up and start meddling? Do men have a sixth sense for knowing when to step in and best mess things up?

Probably.

"Awww, come on, girl," he chuckles. "You know you're happy to see me," he grins casually, sliding his thumb down my arm.

"No I'm not," I hiss, yanking my arm away.

Despite my irritation, I know objectively that nine women out of ten would melt the second a man like Cage slid his thumb down their arm.

Women like Jocelyn, for example. She is totally eavesdropping behind her desk, hanging on Cage's every word like he's the star of her own personal soap opera.

Unfortunately for me, this mess is real, and I have to deal with it.

My next client, Mrs. Ragsdale, sits in a waiting room chair flipping through a magazine. Her lips are pursed and she keeps eye daggering me. She hates having to wait.

I need to make this thing with Cage quick. I can't have him loitering around.

I guide Cage to the hallway leading out of the spa. I whisper growl, "My day was perfect until you showed up. And why the hell did you come to the resort? This is my job, Cage. I sort of need to keep it," I say sarcastically.

"I really need to talk with you, Riv. We didn't have a chance the other night. Stone *sure* didn't want me talking to you," he chuckles like there's no sensible reason why my brother would've objected.

"Gee, Cage, I can't imagine why," I growl. Wow, when did I get so confident around Cage? The night he stopped by my bungalow, I was a puddle of emotions. I guess a great orgasm from a hot guy is a sure cure for all kinds of things. I bet a Drakken induced orgasm could cure the common cold.

I've been so uncharacteristically peppy and upbeat for the past week, Finch commented on it. Daily. But I haven't told her about Drakken. Not yet. I'm savoring the memory. And I'm kind of worried about getting in trouble. Not that Finch would tattle, but what I did with Drakken is a big deal. I mean, I sexed a client on spa premises. During a paid massage, no less.

That never looks good no matter how you spin it.

"Can't we talk, Riv?" Cage drawls. He gives me his usual puppy dog smile, the one he used to use whenever he'd been bad and wanted to make up. It always worked on me in the past. Who knew that cute puppies could be so manipulative? Cage totally gives puppies a bad name. But his puppy charm isn't gonna work on me today.

Neither are the roses, which I have yet to acknowledge. Currently, they droop at his side.

As they should.

I huff, "You need to go, Cage. Mrs. Ragsdale doesn't like to wait. Her bunions take forever."

"She has bunions?"

Finch made it up, but it sounds like a good excuse. "Yeah," I whisper. "I need to finger them or she gets really mad."

Cage frowns. "All right. I don't want to keep you from your...*job*."

Why does he say it like an insult? Whatever. "Yes, my *job*. Some people have them."

"What happened to you starting your own business?"

I roll my eyes, "I can't afford to. I have to finish my Associates degree first. And I have bills to pay. Remember?"

"I can help you with that, you know." Cage is a very successful sculptor. He has a lot of rich clients all over Los Angeles who feel that a life-size portrait painting is too twentieth century. There's nothing like having a life-size marble *statue* of yourself to tell your guests that you're disgustingly rich.

I shake my head, "You said you could help me build my business back when. Then you bailed. Why is now any different?"

"Because I've changed. I've seen the error of my ways. And I brought roses." He holds up the bouquet.

"Are we doing this now?" I demand.

He lifts an eyebrow. "If you want."

I glance at Mrs. Ragsdale. I only see the back of her head, but based on the way she's practically ripping the magazine pages out every time she turns them makes me think she's tired of waiting.

Screw her and her fictional bunions.

She can wait another thirty seconds, magazine pages be damned.

I hiss, "Cage, you left *me*. Remember? For no good reason. Remember?"

"Let me explain..." he drawls, "...and let me apologize. There was a good reason."

Apologize? That's news.

His mahogany eyes catch the light in the hallway just right. His grin is seductive, and he is undeniably handsome.

This isn't his puppy dog thing.

This is Cage being irresistible Cage. The Cage who stole my heart years ago with his gorgeous looks and easy going demeanor.

I sigh with frustration.

The look on his face says that he knows he's wearing me down. I know the look well. I've seen it a thousand times.

I hate that he's so handsome right now. I hate that he brought roses. I hate that he wants to apologize. More than anything, I hate that I'm even listening.

But I can't help it.

I still love him.

Chapter 4

DRAKKEN

I slide my new phone into my suit jacket as I step into the elevator on the twentieth floor. My fingers brush against the silken panties in the jacket pocket.

Rivka.

I've kept her panties with me every day since I removed them from her beautiful body. I take great pleasure in knowing she never asked for them back. Each morning, I transfer them from yesterday's suit to today's.

Since I'm alone, I pull the panties out and hold them to my nose. I inhale deeply as the elevator descends. Sadly, the scent is fading. I suspect because I've sniffed it all out. I grin and chuckle to myself as I inhale again.

I can still smell her on the smooth silk.

Rivka.

She of the aqua blue eyes.

I have been so busy with business meetings since our illicit rendezvous, I haven't seen her since. But I've missed her smile, her touch, her eyes.

Her soothing liquid blue eyes.

I need to see those eyes.

I slide the panties back into my jacket.

The elevator dings and the doors open. I walk across the marbled floor of the lobby and suddenly stop.

A young man carrying a bouquet of roses walks toward the long hallway that leads to the spa. He is quite handsome, and about my age. Perhaps a year or two younger. His destination is obvious. The Beverly Hills Resort has but one masseuse that a man as handsome as this one would buy roses for.

Rivka.

The handsome man walks with purpose.

This won't do.

I glance around, searching for a solution.

The young blonde woman at the concierge desk in the uniform is watching the man with the roses intently. Her face knots with concern and she takes several steps in his direction, then stops.

She knows him.

Does she know Rivka?

The look on her face says that she knows far more about this situation than I do.

Sometimes, the best strategy is to collect more information.

I am a patient man.

I walk up to the concierge desk and ask the petite blonde, "You know man? With flower?" I nod in his direction.

Her faces jumbles with uncertainty. She doesn't know me. But we've spoken a number of times since I moved into the Resort, and I am always polite. It pays to know the help and gain their confidence.

"Yeah, why?" she asks.

"Who is flower man?"

"Just a guy I know."

My poor English is always a hinderance when subtlety is required. Fortunately, subtlety isn't always necessary. "Is he friend to River?"

The young woman's eyes flicker and she smiles knowingly. Her lips purse, clearly holding back information. "Yeah, he's her, uh, friend. Why do you ask?" She already knows the spirit of my question without me having to ask it.

"Is he *very* good friend for her?" *I arch my eyebrow suggestively.*

"Maybe…" she grins. "Maybe not."

I pull out my wallet and hand her a twenty dollar bill. "How good?"

She palms the money and slides it into her pocket. "They *used* to be *very* good friends," *she says obliquely.* "The best kind of friend a girl can have…"

The amused grin on my face is once again pulverized by a wall of stone. My good mood is shattered.

If he was Rivka's lover, he has certainly brought roses to win her back.

That is not acceptable.

The blonde says, "They haven't been—"

I don't hear the rest of her sentence because I'm already striding with hot purpose down the hallway toward the spa. My vision soaks red with rage.

I will break that handsome suitor's arms and batter his face into shattered bone and pulpy red flesh until it's as red as the bouquet of roses he carries…

My body is on fire as I storm along the hallway.

Before I reach the entrance to the spa, I hear Rivka's voice, "Damn it, Cage. Why are you here?"

I slow my steps.

Her suitor mumbles inaudibly, then Rivka speaks again, "I didn't need to see *you*."

I stop in my tracks, just short of being seen.

I back up a step and listen closely.

Rivka is clearly irritated with this man.

I wait, needing certainty.

"Sir?"

Someone tugs the back of my suit jacket.

I flinch and nearly shout in surprise. I'm on the verge of whipping around to strike whoever grabbed me, intent on shattering their nose with the back of my elbow. Fortunately, I stop myself before hurting a perfect stranger. I turn around calmly.

The blonde concierge looks up nervously and asks, "What are you doing, sir?"

I grab her upper arm gently but firmly, then guide her back up the hallway.

"Sir, if you—"

"Shhh. No say," *I hiss.*

"What?!"

"No say!" *Damn, I can't remember the right word. Then it comes to me.* "No speak!"

"Okay, okay," she whines.

When we arrive at the concierge desk in the lobby, I release her arm and say, "Very sorry." *I pull more money out of my wallet and hand it to her. One hundred dollars.*

"Wow, thanks."

"No say to Rivka, okay?"

"Rivka?" *she says elaborately.*

I shake my head, "River. No *speak* this to her. Please."

The blonde smiles a hungry cat's grin. "You like her, don't you?" *Apparently, she is as clever as a cat as well.*

I don't bother denying it. To do so would serve only to confirm her suspicion. "Yes. You no speak. Okay?"

"To River?"

I nod, "Yes." *I hand her another hundred.* "Okay?"

She takes it and adds it to the treasure trove in her uniform pocket.

Greed is a wonderful source of leverage.

I say, "What is you, *your,* name?"

"I'm Finch."

"Say again, please?"

"Finch."

I watch her mouth closely. "Finch…" *I say the word experimentally. I extend my hand,* "Finch, my name is Drakken."

She shakes it.

I hold her hand firmly, "You my friend, yes?"

"I guess so."

"You no speak this," *I gesture back and forth across the lobby, hoping she'll understand what I mean.*

I don't care that Rivka knows I have feelings for her. I have no doubt she senses it already. She is very intuitive. Nor do I care that her friend Finch knows. But my short temper is most embarrassing. It's a sign of weakness. I can't tolerate any weakness…

(…)

Weakness is dangerous.

My weakness is the source of all the pain and regret I've ever felt…

(…her…)

The blonde says, "You mean don't tell her I saw you chase after that guy just now?"

My mask is in place, but I don't wear the stone mask. I wear the liar's mask because this situation requires flattery and delicacy.

I smile my own cat's grin, "Yes. No tell her. And no tell people. No people. Okay?"

"I can't make any promises," *she grins mischievously.*

If they're friends, sharing this tidbit of gossip will be irresistible. If not with Rivka, then perhaps with others. I can't allow that to happen. I need to convince this Finch. I feign a hurt look, "We friend, yes?"

"I wouldn't go that far," *she chuckles.*

Time to revise my strategy. I smile and pull two more hundred dollar bills from my wallet. I hold them out for her.

She reaches for them, but I snatch them away.

"Hey!" *she whines.*

"You no tell River, okay? One week, no tell. One week, I give you money. Okay?"

She crinkles the corner of her mouth. "Three hundred. Three hundred and I won't say anything for a week."

If you let them think they have you, they win. "No. No money. You tell. Is okay." *I fold the money into my wallet.*

"Okay. One hundred now, and one hundred in a week."

She is a clever one. But her greed is her weakness. I shake my head. "No. One week, you no tell River. One week, I give you money. And, no tell people. Deal?"

"You mean, don't tell *any* other people? Keep it a secret? From everyone?"

"Yes."

"Fine," *she rolls her eyes impertinently.* "Deal. For one week. But you better pay up. I know where you sleep. And I have the master key..." *She winks and holds up a keycard.*

I think I catch the gist of her words. "You no tell, I pay. One week." *I nod for emphasis.*

"My lips are sealed."

Chapter 5

RIVER

I'm about to ask Cage to explain himself so I can hear his apology in detail when a series of images flash through my mind, bright and hard.

Those ice blue eyes...

That rock hard cock...

Drakken's face buried between my legs...

A subtle and profound sensation passes through me. I remember that inexplicable flow that passed between Drakken and I when I was massaging him. That sense of pure emotional connection beyond all words...

I shiver.

Cage grins at me, his face now confident and cocky. He probably thinks

I'm thinking about *his* cock.

Wrong cock, buddy.

Fresh confidence courses through me and I say forcefully, "You had your chance to talk, Cage." I fold my arms across my chest.

"When? Last week?" Frustration strains his voice. "Stone practically ran me off like I was a rabid wolf! That wasn't what I'd call a chance to talk, Riv."

"I'm not talking about last week, Cage. I'm talking about *every* night for the last six months. You could've explained yourself a hundred times. But you didn't. You disappeared, Cage. You *abandoned* me."

"I didn't *abandon* you."

I huff, "You may as well have. You just up and left."

"I said goodbye, didn't I?"

He's trying to suck me back in.

I won't let him.

I picture Drakken's ice blue eyes.

That's all it takes.

I snort a laugh and shake my head. "Leave, Cage. I'm not talking about this. I have work to do. And take your roses with you." I turn around and walk away.

Wow, that felt really, really good. I stifle a smile as I walk confidently toward Mrs. Ragsdale.

"I'll call you later, okay?" Cage says hopefully behind me.

I ignore him.

I hope he likes how it feels.

Chapter 6

RIVER

The setting sun reflects off the marble tiled floor of the hotel's main lobby when I walk through it on my way home at the end of the day.

A delivery truck is parked in the roundabout outside. Several guys wearing matching dark green shirts and jeans are unloading huge bouquets of roses onto the cement beside the van. There's a ton of bouquets. Someone must be having an event here at the resort in one of the meeting rooms or whatever.

Finch hurries across the lobby, a look of high drama on her face. "I saw Cage come in earlier with a bunch of roses!" She grabs my elbow and pleads, "What happened? *Please* tell me you didn't get back together with that douche!"

"No way! He totally wanted to talk but I gave him the boot." My car keys jingle in my hand as I gesture like I'm tossing out a piece of trash.

"That's my girl," Finch nods. "If you'd said yes, I'd have to beat some sense into you." She holds up her small fists. "I haven't given anyone an ass whuppin' in a while. But I'll totally do it."

"I give you permission to beat Cage's ass the next time you see him. I sort of wish you'd beaten his ass today so I wouldn't have to talk to him." I joke, "What kind of bodyguard are you, Finch? You totally didn't have my back today!"

An odd look crosses her face.

"What?" I ask.

"Nothing." She shakes her head and grins uncertainly. "Hey, what's with the roses?" Finch points behind me.

I turn to see what she's talking about.

One of the flower guys walks into the lobby with a huge red rose bouquet in each hand. He stops at the check-in desk and sets the bouquets down while he chats with the woman behind the counter.

I turn back to Finch "I don't know. Probably an event in the ballroom or something. Anyway, quit trying to distract me. What are you holding back?"

"Nothing!" she insists.

"Come on, Finch. When I gave you permission to beat Cage, you got all weird on me. What aren't you telling me?"

Her face twists with strained agony. She pretends to weep and sniffle, "I'm just heartbroken, *sniff*, you think I'd abandon you, *sniff*, in your time of, *sniff*, need. *Sniff*."

I swat her arm, "Forget about it already. But next time, make sure you have my back, okay?"

She frowns, "Are you throwing down the gauntlet, Riv?"

"Consider it thrown," I grin.

"All right. Cage is officially banished from the resort. Forbidden. If he wants to come through those doors—" she points toward the front of the lobby where another flower guy walks in with more bouquets, "—he will be doing it over my dead body."

I gasp, "You would lay down your real life to save my love life?"

She winks, "If you had one."

I laugh, "Oh, snap!" I pause, then blurt suggestively, "How do you know I don't? Maybe I met a guy."

She scowls, "When?" She says it like it's a total impossibility.

I shrug, "Last week."

"You did not," she chuckles dismissively.

I frown, "Way to show support, Finch."

"What? You haven't even looked at another guy since Cage."

"Maybe I've done *more* than look…" I giggle suggestively.

"No way!" Finch's eyes goggle. "I never thought you would!"

I shrug, "You were right when you told me I needed a distraction."

Yet another flower guy carries rose bouquets into the lobby and sets them down at the check-in desk with the others.

Finch snaps her fingers in my face, "Riv! Over here!"

"Sorry. What?"

"Did you, you know…" She gestures frantically and whispers, "Did you have S-E-X with Mr. New Guy?"

"It wasn't sex," I titter nervously.

"Okay. So, who was it with?"

"Nobody you know," I lie. I'm not quite ready to tell her it's Drakken. I don't want to jinx things with him. Especially not with Cage sniffing around while I'm still partially vulnerable to his charms. I definitely need Drakken to continue being my distraction.

Two of the flower guys walk back to the delivery van to pick up more rose bouquets. It's gonna take forever for them to move all of them.

"Hey," I say to Finch, "Maybe we should help those guys with all those roses?"

Finch eyes them dismissively then glares at me, "Don't try to distract me! I was asking who you hooked up with! It wasn't one of your clients, was it?"

I frown. How the heck did she guess? I bite my lower lip.

She gasps and her mouth O's. "Shut UP!" She squeaks in disbelief. "You hooked up with one of your *clients*?"

Wow, she can *always* read my mind. I don't respond, because anything I say will totally convict me.

She looks concerned, "It wasn't here in the spa, was it?"

Against my will, I blush.

"Ohmygod, Riv! You're such a slut! When you said you met a guy, I assumed you meant like at a bar or wherever!"

I glance around the lobby to make sure neither Mr. Duchamps nor Luciana are about to walk into the middle of my confessional session with Finch. I don't see either of them. But I do notice that there are now so many bouquets in front of the check-in desk it looks like a field of roses.

Finch tugs my arm and hisses, "Riv, tell me! I need deets! What dirty deed did you do with the dude in the spa?"

"How do you know it was a dude?" I quip.

"Because you're not a dyke! Quit stalling and spill, bitch!"

I giggle and raise my hand to my mouth to hide my words, "It was just a—" then I silently mouth the words, *"hand job."*

Finch's eyes bulge. She hisses, "WHAT?! I thought you never did that to clients!"

"I didn't do it for money," I say insistently. "It just sort of… happened." I don't bother to explain the financial arrangement between me and Drakken, or the origami butterfly. Money and sex never look good together.

"I hope it was a cute guy and not Mr. Skelton," she snickers.

I growl, "Of course it was a cute guy."

"What else did you guys do?" Finch demands.

I frown, embarrassed.

The flower guys are now carrying the rose bouquets down the long hallway toward the spa.

That's weird. All the meeting rooms and the big ballroom are the other way, in the South Wing of the main building.

"Hey, A.D.D.!" Finch barks, startling me. "What aren't *you* telling *me*, Riv? Did your mystery man give you finger play? Did he flick your jumping bean? You know, the one that makes all women jump for joy?"

My eyes pop and I swat my palm at her, "Shut up, Finch!"

"What else happened, Riv?" she begs. "I need to know!" She giggles and jiggles my shoulder.

I yank my arm out of her hand and titter, "No you don't!"

She cocks her hip and plants her fist. "Really? *Really?* When was the last time I had a date? My love life hangs by a thread. As of this moment, you've had way more action in recent history than me. I'm a young woman crawling across a sexless desert. You sit in a sex crazed oasis, sipping margaritas, surrounded by hot shirtless guys with abs who fan you with giant palm fronds like you're the Cleopatra of Sex. Meanwhile, I'm so far removed from your sexual paradise, I can't even feel the breeze of those palm fronds. I'm desperate for a sip of your sexual nectar. So pour me a glass already, bitch."

I grin, "How do you know it's nectar? Maybe it's only sexual tap water or whatever, and it has zero nutritional value."

She slaps my arm, "It's life-giving nectar and you know it. So quit hogging and share a glass already!"

I consider. Tingles tickle my skin, sizzling out from my sex as I remember what happened with Drakken. I think my sexual afterglow is still lingering a week later, because it's lighting up my cheeks right now. "Um…" I blush, "Well, he started by giving me a massage."

Her jaw drops, "He gave *you* a massage?"

I nod. "And he sort of… ahhh… " Again, I silently mouth the

important part, *"Went down on me."*

Her brows knit together. "Wait, what? My lip reading skills are a bit rusty."

I whisper, "He went down on me..."

She slaps her hand across her mouth and her eyes headlight. "What?! No WAY!"

I nod, "Yes way."

She shakes her head, "You are LYING!"

"I'm totally not."

She practically laughs when she says, "You WHORE! Who was it?" She whips her head around as if my mystery man is standing in the lobby.

"He's not here."

"Have I seen him? With my own two eyes?" she asks and literally points both index fingers at her eyes,

"Uhhh..." Of course she has. "Remember that guy with the red Lamborghini?"

"Wait, you hooked up with *that* guy?" She frowns, "The one you hated? The one you said hit your car? Didn't you tell me his license should be revoked and he should be forced to take the bus until his dying day?" She looks at me pointedly and her eyes twinkle.

Why are her eyes twinkling?

She demands, "It was *him*?"

The sound of high heels pistoling off the marble floor of the lobby catches my attention.

Crack! Crack! Crack!

I turn and see Luciana scissoring toward me with a look of pleasant murder on her face

"There you are, River," Luciana smiles sweetly. Of course, it's her antifreeze smile, which is sweet but also highly poisonous, and one more piece of evidence that Luciana is in fact a cyborg robot, and therefore requires antifreeze for her radiator or whatever.

Finch whispers in my ear, "I think I have to help someone with their luggage." She scurries off.

"Coward!" I hiss.

Luciana stops in front of me and folds her hands in front of her waist. It's obvious she wants to wring her hands together, but she resists the urge. Instead, steam comes out of her ears. Invisible steam. I can see it, but no one else can.

"River, would you please follow me?"

"What's up, Luciana?"

Her robot eyes flicker, "Please follow me." She spins on one foot and scissors back toward the spa.

I follow.

Two of the flower delivery guys pass us in the hallway.

When we arrive in the waiting room, Luciana says, "Can you do something with *these*? They're disturbing my feng shui."

'These' are the garden of red roses covering up the spa's front desk. There are so many bouquets, the desk is a blanket of red petals, and more are on the floor.

"Are these for me?" I ask doubtfully.

"They're certainly not for me," Luciana says with noticeable jealousy.

"No, seriously, these are for me?" I ask in disbelief.

"That's what one of the delivery men told me," she rattles.

A flower guy pushes a cart covered with yet more bouquets into the waiting room.

"More?" Luciana groans.

The guy shrugs and unloads the roses, setting them next to the rest of the garden on the floor.

Luciana rolls her eyes in disgust. I've never seen her so irritated.

"Who sent them?" I ask her.

"I have no idea. Please remove them. I don't want them here cluttering things up in the morning." Luciana clacks her way up the hallway.

I plant my hands on my hips, looking at all the roses.

Did Cage send them?

I bet he did. He probably thought his one bouquet earlier wasn't enough to get my attention, so he decided to try more.

When in doubt, go big.

If he was here, I'd tell him that throwing money at me isn't going to change a thing. Heck, he could walk in with a mariachi band playing I Will Always Love You by Whitney Houston while he serenaded me, and I'd still tell him it's not going to work. I'd be laughing the entire time, but I'd still have to say no. Err, maybe. I'd have to say maybe because you gotta give a guy credit if he tries to sing a Whitney Houston song accompanied by a mariachi band. And buys you a million roses.

"Excuse me," I ask the flower guy, who is still taking bouquets off the cart and setting them on the floor.

"Yeah?"

"Do you know who sent all these roses?"

He stands up straight and reaches into his back pocket. "Let me check the receipt." He pulls out a stack of receipts and flips through them. "Here it is. Let's see..." He scans the paper, "Not that I can see. Looks like whoever it was paid cash. Didn't give a name."

"Wow. How many bouquets are there altogether?"

"Twelve dozen."

"Wait, did you say twelve *dozen*?"

"Yeah. Twelve dozen bouquets of roses. I guess your mystery man likes you a lot," he grins. "You got over five thousand bucks worth of flowers here. It took the gals at the shop all day to assemble everything."

This definitely sounds like the sort of thing Cage would do. He may not be a millionaire, but I know he has enough money to burn on a romantic gesture like this. Cage's hand-carved marble portrait sculptures are all the rage.

Maybe I was too hard on him when he came in this morning. Maybe I should've heard him out instead of shoving him out the door. He did try to apologize, after all. But I was being quite the little bitch. Maybe I owe him a call.

I mean, a million roses deserves at least a single phone call, right? Even people arrested for murder get that much.

But I have to know for sure before I make the call to Cage.

I ask the flower guy, "Um, isn't there some way you can find out who sent them?"

He scratches his chin, "Maybe Bethanie back at the shop knows. I could ask her."

"Could you?" I ask earnestly.

"Sure," he smiles. He makes a call on his phone. "Hey, Carol. Is Bethanie still in? ... She went home? ... Okay. Hey, do you know who sent the twelve dozen roses out to the Beverly Hills Resort? ... Uh huh... Yeah... Uh huh... Okay, thanks, Carol. Talk to you later." He ends the call.

"Well?" I ask hopefully.

"Sorry. Guy didn't leave a name," he smiles politely. "Anyway, I got more of your roses to unload."

"More?"

He chuckles, "I told ya, it was twelve dozen. I'll be right back."

The guy pushes the empty cart past Finch on his way out.

"Damn!" Finch gasps. "Don't tell me these are all for you?"

"Yup," I grin.

"Who sent them?"

"I'm not sure," I sigh.

"Is there a card?"

"Maybe? Will you help me look?"

"Totally."

We search through the individual bouquets.

"Finch, what the eff am I gonna do with a million red roses? Luciana says she wants them outta here by morning because they disturb her feng shui."

"Tell her she can feng shove-it-up-her-butt," Finch smirks. "They're *roses*, not an eyesore."

I chuckle, "I wish I could."

"Who knew love could be such a pain in the ass? Oh wait! I know! Anyone who has ever been in a long term relationship."

"True that," I snicker. "Sometimes you gotta take the good with the bad."

"Found it!" Finch holds up a fancy envelope and starts to open it.

"Hey!" I yank it out of her hand. "That's mine!"

"Come on, Riv. Share the love," she jokes.

"It's my love," I giggle greedily.

"I think there's more than enough to go around," she says sarcastically, motioning at all the roses.

I nod agreement as I open the card.

It's a fancy white piece of textured stationary embossed with roses around the border. In gold ink, a single word is written in elegant cursive script:

"Rivka"

Holy Shizz.

I guess Drakken liked his hand job.

Chapter 7

RIVER

Luciana smiles at me archly from across her desk the next morning.

Maybe smile is the wrong word.

What's that look called that cobras get when they're trying to hypnotize a mouse? I can't remember, but that's the look Luciana wears right now.

She says, "I notice you managed to dispose of those roses last night. Thank you for that."

It took Finch and I nearly two hours to give away 142 of the bouquets to various guests and staff at the resort, all of whom were grateful to receive them. Finch kept one for herself and I brought the last one home and put it on my dresser. Problem solved. Love shared.

"No worries," I smile at Luciana, knowing full well she's trying to set me at ease before she strikes. I remain on my guard.

Clear blue sky fills the windows behind Luciana. The stylish decor of her small office matches the rest of the spa. I sit in one of the minimalist dark wood chairs facing her desk. On the desk, a bonsai tree rests beside a quietly bubbling zen fountain. Gentle Japanese koto music drifts from hidden speakers.

I think the music and the fountain are supposed to lull unsuspecting mice into a false sense of security.

In a voice rich with honey—or whatever mice like to eat for dessert—Luciana continues, "For some strange reason, those roses have got me thinking."

"Oh?" I ask nervously.

"Jocelyn happened to mention that a young man named Cage had brought roses for you yesterday morning?"

Jocelyn. The spa's receptionist. That gossipy bitch. "She did?" I ask, trying to buy myself time to think.

"Yes. And I couldn't help but wonder, was Cage also the one who sent you that garden of roses last night?" Her voice is melodious and hypnotic.

Cobras are very charming when they're hungry for mice.

I shift in my seat nervously, "Okay?" I don't know where she's going with this.

"May I ask, were all those roses from Cage as well?"

"Uhhh…" I suddenly feel trapped and very much like a mouse. Do I answer yes or no? Or run away before the snake eats me?

"Well?"

"Yes," I lie. I hope that was the right answer.

She nods and smiles. "Is that so?"

I think her forked tongue goes *thip, thip, thip*.

Everybody knows snakes smell with their tongues, and I'm pretty sure snakes can smell when the mice are lying. The thing is, you don't need to be a snake to smell bullshizz.

Luciana totally knows I'm lying.

The only choice I have is to shovel on more fertilizer and hopefully bury this snake in a mountain of brown. "Yes. It's *very* so," I say confidently.

"Hmmm. They weren't from someone else? Perhaps a wealthy suitor of yours?"

"Suit—" cough, "*suitor*?" Drakken wears suits every time I see him.

"Yesssss." She nods thoughtfully for a while. "Do you know why I ask?"

Thip, thip, thip.

I'm not saying a thing. I shrug, too frightened to speak.

She smiles, "I ask because the image of you standing shoeless in your massage room while you were with Mr. Skalakova a week ago has been plaguing me like a bad nightmare ever since."

Spoonful of shizz.

I was hoping she'd forgotten about my bare feet. Why didn't I work up a cover story earlier? I knew Luciana would confront me sooner or later.

She continues, "For a week now, I've been asking myself, 'Why would River have her shoes off during a client massage?' Unless something unseemly was going on…"

Cupful of shizz.

Luciana coils a finger through her beloved pearl necklace. The pearls emit little clicks as they constrict around her index finger like a shimmering snake subduing its unsuspecting prey.

The office suddenly seems dreadfully silent. All I hear is the ominous click of the tightening pearls.

Tick. Tick. Tick.

Luciana offers a friendly frown, "Is there something else you'd like to tell me about Mr. Skalakova's exorbitantly elongated ninety minute massage that I witnessed last week?"

Thip, thip, thip, goes her tongue.

"Wuh—*witnessed*?" I quiver.

"Yes," she hisses.

Bucket full of shizz.

The phrase 'exorbitantly elongated' describes Drakken's manhood to a T. Don't tell me Luciana *saw* us exchanging oral favors. Does this place have hidden security cameras I don't know about? It could. It *totally* could. Mr. Duchamps and Luciana *are* both sticklers for every single detail.

Dump truck full of Shizz.

Tick, tick, tick, go the pearls.

I'm finding it really hard to breathe at the moment. That pearl necklace may as well be wrapped around my neck.

I'm on the verge of panic.

Part of me wants to blurt out the truth and beg Luciana's forgiveness. I'll apologize profusely and promise never to do it again. The other part of me says, No! Get a hold of yourself! If you lose your head and panic now, she's going to fire your ass for being a prostitute! Then you'll have to become a prostitute to pay your bills! It's lose-lose! Don't do it!

I try hard to concentrate and remain calm. I need to buy myself some time.

"Uhhh…" I stammer.

Luckily, playing dumb is just as good as playing dead. Cuz that's all I've got at the moment.

Like the frightened mouse I've become, I start tittering and chittering nervously, "Well, uh, you see, uh, the thing is, uh…"

Luciana arches her eyebrows expectantly, still fingering her pearl necklace.

Tick. Tick. Tick.

Thip, thip, thip.

She gives me that cobra look again, "You do have an answer, don't you, River?"

Nope.

Wait a second…

Inspiration strikes.

I said inspiration. Not the cobra.

Like most snakes, Luciana doesn't realize that it's easy to mistake a mouse for a mongoose.

I'm not anybody's mouse.

I'm a frickin' mongoose.

I eat snakes for breakfast.

I smile indulgently, "Have you ever had a Thai massage?"

She chuckles throatily, "I don't like the sound of where this is going…."

I'm sure she's picturing brothels in Bangkok and live sex shows. I press, "Have you?"

"I can't say that I have," she smirks with irritation.

"Well," I smile, "the cool thing about Thai massage is that the masseuses often stand on you as part of the massage process. It's really very smart, you see, because it uses their body weight instead of elbow grease. You know what I mean?"

"I'm not following," she glowers.

"It's simple. Mr. Skalakova is a very muscular man."

Her irritation eases slightly, replaced by an indulgent smile. She says wistfully, "True."

"And it takes a lot of force to work the kinks out of manly muscles like his."

"I can imagine," she sighs and stares off into space. Yeah, you know she's imagining Drakken naked. At this point, her hand relaxes on her necklace and her index finger falls free of the pearls.

See that? The mongoose escaped.

"So anyway," I say. "I decided the best way to work out some of his kinks was to walk on his, uh, legs. His thighs are *very* muscular…"

She looks surprised. And curious. "Do tell."

"And I can't do that with shoes on."

She smiles and nods appreciatively, "That's ingenious, River. What will you think of next?" She chuckles. "I knew there was a reason why so many of our clients request your services."

Take that, snake. Chomp, chomp.

"So, we're good?" I smile like a mongoose with a full belly.

"For now," she says ominously. "But if I find out that you have done anything *untoward* with one of our clients *anywhere* on resort premises, we will have a problem. A *serious* problem. This is not a brothel, Miss Freeman. This is *The* Beverly Hills Resort. Am I making myself clear?"

Oh, snap.

Sneaky snake!

This mongoose suddenly has indigestion.

Gurgle.

Chapter 8

RIVER

I open the door of Luciana's office and smash right into Drakken.

"Rivka," he grins. "Is you massage now?"

I blurt, "Drakken! I mean, Mr. Skalakova!" I sound as guilty as a kid with both hands and both feet in four different cookie jars.

"Good morning, Mr. Skalakova," Luciana says, having slithered up silently, just like the sneaky snake she is. "How can we help you today?"

Drakken takes a moment to assess the situation. I hope he picks up on my nerves. He already called me Rivka. I hope Luciana didn't notice.

Drakken smiles politely, looking between us. After a moment, he asks, "I buy Riv—uh, *River* now?"

I wince. Eek. Did he have to use the word 'buy'?

"For massage," he adds quickly. "I buy her for massage."

He's making it worse. If I had the shizz shovel I was using earlier to bury the truth about what Drakken and I were doing in the massage room the last time, I'd use it right now to bash him over the head and knock him out before he makes me look even more guilty. Not only are my hands and feet in the cookie jar, my face is totally covered in Cookies & Cum. I mean cream. Cookies & Cream. Same difference.

Luciana smiles charmingly at Drakken, "Of course, Mr. Skalakova. River would be happy to—" she stabs me with a pointed look, "—*massage* you. You do remember where the room is?"

Oh, god. She totally knows.

Drakken glances down the hallway toward the door. "Yes. Is that." He points. "Come, River. We massage now. Okay?"

Why did he have to say we? Where's that shovel?

"Uh, yeah. Sure," I mutter.

Drakken walks toward the room.

I turn to follow him, but Luciana grabs my arm.

Her face is a plastic mask of phony pleasantry. "Remember what we talked about?"

I muster my mongoose courage and say casually, "What do you mean?" For once, playing dumb is the winningest strategy.

Her phony smile stretches tighter. "Behave yourself. Or else."

Shizz.

I turn and walk calmly away.

I don't know what happened, but all my mongoose courage is completely gone. I'm right back to being a frightened mouse. Luciana really did a number on me. Although I'm ecstatic to see Drakken, I'm scared to death we'll do something that will get me fired the second I walk into that massage room and close the door behind me.

Chapter 9

RIVER

Drakken unbuttons his dress shirt. His jacket and tie already hang in the closet. His face is relaxed, inviting, and wide open. None of his usual tension is there. His ice blue eyes are locked on mine. They send hot thrilling chills down my chest that dribble right down to my sex.

He rips his shirt off.

Oh, shizz.

Every single muscle from his arms to his shoulders to his chest to his abs flex and release. Flex, twist, flex. Flex, flex, flex.

This man is a work of art.

He's more defined than the anatomy charts I studied in massage school to learn all the muscles. The ones that have the skinless guy so you can see the muscles better. Whoever makes those anatomy charts should just take photos of Drakken and use them instead.

Drakken tosses his shirt onto the chair in the corner. The grin on his face says he's going to do dirty things to me.

I like dirty.

I feel my sex flutter between my legs. I'm already wet.

Drakken strolls toward me like he owns the universe.

He certainly owns my universe at the moment. I can't even think a single rational thought. My mind is a jumble of arousal and pent up need.

"You are wet for me." He says it like it's a foregone conclusion, which it totally is.

All I can do is whimper.

I need this man inside me.

The thought surprises me out of my sexual fugue.

I haven't had that thought in so many months, I'd almost forgotten the words.

But I remember them now.

I need Drakken and his rock hard cock inside me.

Drakken grins, "You are wet." He knows it without me having to answer. He toes his loafers off and unbuckles his slacks.

I'm paralyzed with desire. All I can do is stand here in my white spa uniform while I drench my panties and watch his beautiful body move with hypnotic perfection. I am going to let this gorgeous man do *anything* he wants with me. I have no doubt it will involve mind-bending orgasms that stop my heart.

He slides his slacks off his muscular legs and hangs them over the chair back. He peels his boxers off and tosses them onto the chair.

And there it is.

Right out in the open.

Drakken's cock.

It's hard and erect and pulsating with fiery need. Both he and his cock stand tall and proud.

My entire body shakes with need.

I'm going to fall to my knees and devour that hot cock of his. Then I'm going to beg him to put it inside me, *deep* inside me, and fuck me until my body explodes with ecstasy. He's going to make me scream so loud, I'm going to shatter all the windows in the room.

Behave yourself. Or else.

SLAM.

Luciana's words destroy my moment.

I can't do this.

The massage room door isn't even locked.

What if Luciana were to walk in right now?

I can't have sex with Drakken in the massage room. Even if I did lock the door. What if we're too loud? What if Luciana knocks? Am I going to wrap a towel around myself and answer the door like I've just stepped out of the shower and everything is cazh? No. She'd never believe it.

Shizz.

I can't do it.

I *want* to do it.

I want to be the free-spirited girl I used to be. The one who was full of laughter and life before Cage left and I turned into a dreary shell of myself. I don't want to go back to being her.

Behave yourself. Or else.

I have a job. I have responsiblities.

I can't have sex with the hottest man I've ever seen in my entire life, in the middle of the massage room of *The* Beverly Hills Resort, no matter how badly I want to do just that.

This adult thing *really* sucks.

Chapter 10

DRAKKEN

"I can't do this, Drakken," *Rivka mutters.*

"No?"

I was about to tell her that she doesn't have any choice, that I am going to tear her white uniform to shreds and fuck her senseless.

Sadly, I wouldn't be able to say it that directly. It would come out clumsily. Something like, "I sex you now. I sex you very good." *But she would understand the intent. And that's all that matters.*

I have been blessed with an incredible sense of smell. At this moment, I can literally smell the musky scent of desire dripping between her legs. I know it well. I've inhaled it from her panties so many times, I have it memorized. It's the sweetest scent I've ever known.

She shakes her head, "No."

She means it.

She isn't playing a game meant to tease. She doesn't want to say no and pretend to resist while I overpower her, heightening her arousal by fighting each other.

She means no.

Something is wrong.

"You are sad, Rivka?" *I say it gently, compassionately.*

Her face shakes with indecision.

Mine begins to lock down. The stone wall is about to fall. I endeavor to prevent it. I will myself to relax. I want to remain open to her. I want to know what she's feeling, what's bothering her. That can't happen if I close down myself.

"Say to me, Rivka. Okay?"

She nibbles her lips like a frightened mouse. What has come over her so suddenly?

Whatever it is, I too am frightened. I'm not accustomed to interacting without my stone face in place. This is very hard. If only I could explain to her what I'm feeling.

"I can't do this, Drakken. I'm sorry." *Her regret strikes me across the mouth like a hard slap.*

"No?"

She shakes her head rapidly. She radiates fear, waiting for me to speak.

I don't know where to begin.

Did I cause this shift in her mood? Was I too bold? Was I being too presumptuous taking my clothes off without asking permission? No, that can't be it. I smell her desire.

I chastise myself. Just because a woman is aroused, doesn't mean she necessarily wants to have sex right at that moment. She may be considering it, but consideration and decisive action are not the same thing.

Women are complicated creatures, and I respect that. She is welcome to change her mind. In truth, men are no different, and often as mercurial.

I am an ingrate. I was far too hasty. Rivka is bold, but that doesn't mean she is ready to have sex with me whenever the whim strikes me.

"Rivka, I..." *don't have the damned words.*

"Let me *nonsense*, Drakken." *She speaks rapidly,* "You see, I was just— *nonsense nonsense nonsense* Luciana. *Nonsense nonsense, nonsense nonsense nonsense,* and I was *nonsense nonsense, nonsense nonsense nonsense.* Does that make any *nonsense*?"

"No?" *I say with utter puzzlement.*

She spoke so quickly, her words have all jumbled together in my head. I do my best to comprehend the intent of what she said despite my inability to make sense of the individual words. One thing is clear, she doesn't want to have sex. But I can't decide if she means now, here in this room, or ever?

Before I can collect my thoughts and try to pare them down to simpler words, she continues.

"*Nonsense nonsense nonsense.* And she said *nonsense nonsense nonsense nonsense, nonsense nonsense. Nonsense nonsense nonsense nonsense, nonsense nonsense* roses. So I can't *nonsense nonsense nonsense* with you. Not *nonsense nonsense nonsense.* Or *nonsense nonsense nonsense nonsense.*"

Damn it. I have no idea what she just said.

I can't follow her words.

But I did catch one. Roses.

Damn. Were the roses too much? Did I overwhelm her with them? Perhaps twelve dozen was over doing it. I curse myself. I should've ordered one large arrangement, not the entire flower shop. But that handsome lover of hers was intent on winning her back. I lost control. I couldn't help myself.

"Is rose bad?"

She shakes her head, "No. It wasn't the roses." *Her face shines with pain, brightening her fear.*

My own fear seizes me.

My face solidifies into stone.

Did her friend Finch *inform her about my rash behavior? Despite my bribery, I would hope that her loyalty to Rivka could not be purchased for a mere pittance. I certainly wouldn't hold it against* Finch *if she had broken my trust in favor of telling Rivka the truth. The way I stormed after Rivka's ex-lover, intent on decisive violence, was most embarrassing and well beneath me. Perhaps Rivka feels the same way about my volcanic temper. It would certainly explain her heightened degree of fear right now.*

I need to address this. "What make you sad?" *I plead,* "Please say, okay?"

Sensing her continued discomfort, I grab one of the folded towels off the counter top and wrap it around my waist. My erection is completely gone, which is for the best. Now is not the time.

There's a knock at the door.

"Sorry," *Rivka says.* "Hold on a *nonsense.*" *She turns away from me to open the door.*

The boorish manager of the spa leans her head through the door. Her eyes dart suspiciously between Rivka and myself. She says, "River, can I speak with you for a *nonsense?*"

"Nonsense," *Rivka says.*

The two of them step outside.

The door pulls shut. I rush to it and place my ear against it.

It's hard to make out what they're saying. With my weak English, I can't make any sense of the few fragments I discern.

A minute later, the door opens.

A young woman I've never met before stands beside Rivka and the spa manager.

The manager says, "Mr. Skalakova, this is Serenity. She's one of our *nonsense* masseuses. She will *nonsense* you with the utmost *nonsense.*"

The young woman has lustrous blonde hair and an hourglass figure. Her bosom is as believable as an automobile salesman on a slow day.

Why is she here?

Why is she replacing Rivka?

Rivka's face is strained with immense sadness and tremendous regret. "Sorry, Drak—I mean, Mr. Skalakova. I'm really sorry." *She is near tears.*

What did I do?

Rivka turns and walks away. She visibly shakes as she walks, nearly broken by sadness as she disappears around the corner in the spa's hallway.

The spa manager smiles at me pleasantly, her hands clasped beneath her breasts. She resembles an authoritative nun, the keeper of chastity and virtue.

Did Rivka tell her that I had been too bold and taken my clothes off like an entitled heathen? Did Rivka ask for this young woman to serve as her replacement? She must have.

Did I cause this? I must have.

My temper. My insolence. My bravado.

The roses.

Too many cursed roses!

It all adds up.

Rivka believes I'm a terrible man, nothing but a spoiled child.

It's the only explanation.

Damn it, what have I done?

Chapter 11

RIVER

I can't believe Luciana pulled me out of there and replaced me with Serenity. Serenity sucks at massage. She has limp hands and doesn't know what she's doing. I think Luciana only keeps her around because she's so beautiful and helps bring in more male clients, and because her big tits get her big tips. Luciana probably makes her split the money 80-20. Serenity wouldn't even have a job here if not for her tip-worthy tits.

But the *real* reason Luciana made the switch is obvious. She thinks I was going to fool around with Drakken.

Well, she was wrong.

I wasn't.

I have self control.

I know better. Once was an experience I'll treasure until my dying day. But I wasn't about to do it again. Not after her warning.

So she pulled me out of there for no reason. She's never done that before. It makes me look incompetent and it makes me furious.

"Something wrong" Jocelyn asks. She sits at the spa's reception desk.

"Uh, nothing," I say absently. I can't talk to her right now. She probably saw what happened and just wants to hear the latest gossipy office drama.

I'm so angry at Luciana, I'm ready to scream. I need some air. I go out the back door of the spa. It opens on a cement pathway that leads out to the pool and the tennis courts.

At least it's sunny outside.

The huge pool behind the main building sparkles blue. A few guests are already out in colorful swimsuits, basking on the loungers and soaking up the rays. I keep walking, trying to burn off my anger. I make it past the tennis courts, and all the way out to the golf course. My anger is nowhere close to subsiding.

I pace back and forth at one end of the driving range, watching men and women in colorful checkered and striped clothes hitting ball after ball into the green.

I can only imagine what Drakken is thinking right now. He looked heartbroken when I told him we couldn't fool around in the spa. He looked confused when I tried to explain that Luciana was watching me and her warning was the *only* reason I didn't want him right that second. Worst of all, when Luciana told him that Serenity was going to replace me, he looked absolutely miserable. It was written all over his face.

But there was nothing I could do.

Luciana is my boss. She gave me a direct order. I didn't have a choice.

I stop in my tracks.

Fear squeezes my chest and I gasp to myself.

What if Drakken thinks I didn't *want* to massage him? What if he thinks I resisted his advances because I wasn't into him anymore?

Oh no!

I just now realize that I didn't thank him for all those wonderful roses. I didn't have time. I was too busy trying to explain how the roses and my bare feet had made Luciana suspicious. But I never thanked him for the roses! Not once! I probably sounded like a total ass! Like I didn't even care about his roses.

Drakken probably thinks I hate him right now. He had that hard stone face going when I left. He probably thinks I have zero interest in him.

Stupid Luciana!

Now Drakken is in that massage room, *my* massage room, and Serenity has her hands all over him. What if she tries to give him a hand job? I could totally see her doing that. It would help explain all the tips she gets. And what if Drakken lets her?

Clink!

The guy closest to the fence just smacked his ball way out over the green. I watch the ball arc up higher and higher, then fall, fall, fall.

Just like my hopes.

I have to stop Serenity.

I run back toward the main building.

I don't know what I'm going to do, but I'm going to do something.

Chapter 12

RIVER

"Are you okay, Riv?" Finch asks as I storm past the tennis courts.

Several games are in progress. A bunch of older couples wearing tennis whites and sun visors smack the day-glow green balls around in the warm sunshine.

"Hey, Finch. Can't talk now."

She falls into step beside me, "You look like you're going to murder somebody. Do I need to intervene?"

"Huh? No. I won't murder her. But I might pop her fake tits with a pin."

Finch chuckles, "Do you have a tit pin handy?"

"No. Do you?"

"Sorry. I'm fresh out of tit pins."

I smirk and roll my eyes.

"Seriously, Riv, where are you going in such a hurry?"

I explain everything in brief while we walk quickly.

Finch grabs my arm and stops me short. "Riv, do you seriously think he bought you a million roses only to accept a hand job from the next pair of over-inflated tit balloons that floats along?"

I snicker and wrinkle my nose, "Uh, when you put it that way..."

She nods with confidence, "Of course he won't. He was probably just confused by the whole situation. Didn't you say it was weird how Luciana totally surprised you guys with Serenity?"

"Yeah?"

"I'm sure Drakken thought it was weird too."

A tennis ball flies over the fence and bounces toward us. Mrs. Mueller waves through the fence, "River, would you please be a dear and toss me that ball?"

Before I can respond, Finch scrambles after it and lobs the ball back over the fence.

"Thank you, dear!" Mrs. Mueller calls.

Finch dusts off her hands. "Anyway, Riv, don't worry about it. Just talk to Drakken about it later. I'm sure he'll tell you that Serenity gave him a plain vanilla massage. Heck, I bet he'll be so bored he falls asleep. Or Serenity will be so bad he asks her to stop."

"You think?"

"Of course. That guy only has eyes for you, Riv."

"How do you know?"

She looks around nervously then shrugs, "I don't know. I just do. That hot hunk of man meat is all yours. You're all he thinks about. I'm sure of it."

"Maybe you're right. Maybe I was jumping to conclusions."

"It's okay. That's why I'm here. To stop the jumpers. No more crazy thoughts, okay?"

I sigh, feeling way more relaxed than I was before Finch stopped me and talked some sense into me. Who knows what I would've done if she hadn't. Stormed into Luciana's office and yelled at her? Barged into the massage room so I could yank Serenity out by her hair? Neither scenario would've helped me keep my job.

"You're right, Finch. I got carried away. Thanks."

"Any time, Riv." She reaches out and gives me a quick hug, rubbing my back vigorously. "It's all good, girl."

I nod. "I should get back to the spa. Luciana is probably wondering where I went. Laters." I turn and walk back toward the pool and the main building.

"Trust me, Riv," Finch hollers, "The only thing Drakken wants is more of your patented handiwork!"

"My what?"

She smirks and holds up her forearm, which she strokes repeatedly from elbow to wrist with her other hand. Like she's giving a giant hand job.

A white-haired couple heading toward the tennis courts passes me. Indignant horror pains the old woman's face as she watches Finch hand-jobbing her arm.

The old man stares with obvious interest.

The old woman yanks his arm, "Stop staring, Walter."

I giggle, "You're crazy, Finch."

Finch wiggles her fingers while continuing to stroke herself.

"Are you waving goodbye," I holler, "Or suggesting Drakken's thing has fingers?"

Finch bends over and belly laughs. "Now I finally know what a French tickler is!!!"

"I don't think he's French," I giggle.

Finch falls to her knees then rolls onto her ass, gasping with laughter.

The old woman with Walter grimaces, "Children." She spits the word with disgust.

I chuckle and stroll back to the spa, feeling much better.

Chapter 13

RIVER

Deciding to trust Finch's conviction, I take some time to enjoy the sunshine before going back into the main building. I'm going to trust that Drakken isn't doing anything with Serenity I should be worried about.

Wow, do I have feelings for this guy already?

I guess I do.

When I finally walk back into the spa, Jocelyn goggles at me from the reception desk.

"Where'd you go?" she asks. "Luciana is looking all over for you."

Shizz.

"Why?" I ask. "Didn't Serenity handle my client for me?" I say it with more sarcasm than I wanted to. I should've said it innocently, like I don't care. Then maybe Jocelyn would be more apt to drop some gossip about what happened with Drakken.

"Oh, she took care of him," Jocelyn says suggestively. Her eyes search my face.

Jocelyn isn't stupid. She's toying with me.

I nod, trying to cover my irritation. "That's cool," I sigh casually, looking around the spa like I'm bored. Meanwhile, my heart starts racing in my chest. I want to fish for information, but that would be a dead giveaway. "What did Luciana want?"

"You were supposed to take Serenity's client an hour ago."

Oh, shizz.

I totally forgot.

Luciana literally told me I was supposed to massage picky Mr. Sharp for Serenity while Serenity massaged Drakken. I was so pissed off and freaked out, I completely spaced it.

I gasp, "Is he still here?"

Jocelyn relaxes into her chair and smirks, "Who, Mr. Skalakova?" she asks knowingly.

"No! Mr. Sharp!" Don't tell me Jocelyn knows about me and Drakken too. Did Luciana tell her, or did she figure it out herself?

"Mr. Sharp had a doctor's appointment, so he couldn't wait."

Holy shizz.

Luciana probably thinks I'm the most irresponsible and unreliable employee of all time. I have to find her and make amends.

I knock on her office door.

"Enter," Luciana calls through the door.

I open it.

Luciana sits at her desk.

Mr. Duchamps, the general manager of *The* Beverly Hills Resort, sits in the chair across from Luciana. His mouth disappears into a white line beneath the black line of his grease pencil mustache.

"Miss Freeman," he says sourly. "We were wondering where you went."

Unholy shizz.

Chapter 14

RIVER

"Don't let it happen again, Miss Freeman," Mr. Duchamps says tersely as he stands up from the chair.

I just spent the last five minutes listening to him lecture me while I stood here like an obedient child and sucked it up. All I did was nod a lot and say "Yes, sir," and "No, sir," a thousand times.

He sniffs once, "I have more important things to attend to. Do your job," he snaps. He grasps the bottom of his suit jacket and tugs it sharply before walking out of Luciana's office.

When the door closes, Luciana smiles pleasantly, "I did not enjoy that one bit, River. Did you?" She asks it so nicely, she sounds like a sociable hostess asking what I thought of her fruit torte or her new hairdo.

"No, ma'am."

"Would you care to explain yourself?"

No? "Ahh…"

"You know how much Mr. Sharp hates to be kept waiting."

"Yes, ma'am."

"He was so irritated, he decided to speak directly to Mr. Duchamps about it."

"He did?" That's not good. Mr. Duchamps is way too busy to worry about something as small as this.

"He did," Luciana smiles again with her 'have some more fruit torte' smile. "How do you think that makes *me* look?"

With that smile on her face, I'd say like a two-faced bitch. "Not good?" I offer.

"Not good at all."

She's totally making me feel like I'm sitting in the principal's office because I skipped school or stole the answers to the math test or whatever. I'm sure she's going to tell me this is all going on my permanent record. I thought I'd left this shizz behind when I graduated high school. This sucks.

"You disobeyed me, River."

"Sorry," I sigh. I feel like an idiot. "It won't happen again, ma'am."

"Please stop calling me ma'am. It makes me feel old."

She wants me to do her favors now? If it wasn't for her, this never would've happened. Serenity would've massaged Mr. Sharp, I would've massaged Drakken, and everything would be golden.

"Yes, ma'am," I say obediently.

She cringes.

"I'm mean, Luciana. Sorry," I wince. "So, should we like, give Mr. Sharp a free massage or whatever?"

"Perhaps next time. Now I believe that Mrs. Ragsdale is waiting for you. Again. You know how much she hates to wait."

I do my best not to roll my eyes. If she hadn't been lecturing me, I'd already be massaging Mrs. Ragsdale.

I walk toward the door and grab the knob.

"That's twice, River."

"Twice what?"

She smiles her fruit torte smile, "Twice you've erred."

Who says 'erred' anymore? The fruit-faced bitch, that's who.

Luciana coils her fingers around her pearl necklace.

Tick, tick, tick go the pearls.

She's doing that snake thing again. Like she wants to eat the mouse. She asks, "Do you know what happens after the third time?"

"Isn't the third time the charm or whatever?" I try not to grin sarcastically when I say it. I'm all mongoose at the moment.

She smirks, "No. The third time is when convicted felons go to prison and never come out. Or, in your case, never come back to your job here at *The* Beverly Hills Resort. Follow?"

"Yes, ma'am," I say quickly. "Sorry, I mean, yes, Luciana."

Now I'm all mouse.

Luciana is totally to blame for all of this. If she'd just have let me massage Drakken, none of this would've happened.

I mean, it's not like I gave one of my clients a hand job and he gave me oral sex, then paid me a huge amount of money afterward, all in the middle of *The* Beverly Hills Resort, and Luciana caught me with my shoes off.

No, nothing *remotely* like that *ever* happened.

Luciana is *entirely* at fault.

Stupid bitch.

I hate the fruit-faced snakes more than any other kind.

Chapter 15

RIVER

Fortunately, I'm busy with clients the rest of the day. I kick ass and take names. Or should I say, I massage ass and take tips, because everyone is super happy with my work.

I'm good at my job. My clients love me.

Except when Luciana interferes.

Whatever.

With any luck, all of this will blow over. I just need to talk to Drakken and explain I can't give him any more massages at the spa. And maybe ask what happened during his massage from Serenity. Only cuz I'm curious.

At the end of my work day, I walk out of the spa and bump into Finch pushing an empty bellman's cart into the lobby from one of the elevators.

She smiles, "What up, Riv?"

"Hey, Finch," I sigh.

She stops in place and holds up her arm so she can give it another elbow-to-wrist hand job. "How were things with Drakken," she winks, totally exaggerating the wink with her mouth wide open and tongue hanging out.

"Stop!" I giggle.

She wiggles her fingers like last time, "Was there any French tickling?"

"He's not French! I'm not French either! There was no French anything!"

"Not even kissing?"

"No," I sigh. "He was long gone when I got back to the spa. Luciana *and* Mr. Duchamps totally chewed me out for walking off on the job."

"Lame," Finch rolls her eyes.

"Now I'm all worried Luciana is trying to find a reason to fire me."

"What's up with that mummified bitch? That woman *reeks* of formaldehyde," Finch grimaces, wrinkling her nose.

I snicker, "That would explain why she looks so good for her age."

"She's probably, like, a thousand years old."

"Two thousand," I giggle.

A black limo drives up outside in the roundabout catching my attention. I ignore it. We see limos here every day.

"Well, I should probably go," I sigh. "I'm super tired from massaging all day, and I have a ton of homework tonight."

"Totes," she smiles. "See you tomorrow." She wheels the bellman's cart across the lobby.

I wave and I'm about to punch the down button for the elevators when I notice a red Lamborghini drive up behind the limousine.

A valet runs around to the driver's side of the Lamborghini and Drakken steps out.

My heart soars. He's wearing a dark suit and looks like a million bucks. A huge smile beams from his face. I totally need to go thank him right now for the roses and apologize for what happened in the spa this morning. I'm sure if I explain things slowly and simply, he'll totally get it. It'll all turn out to be no big deal. Then Drakken and I can *finally* pick up from where we left off the day I gave him that hand job and he rocked my world in the best, yummiest, most orgasmic way possible.

Drakken chats with the valet then walks to the back door of the limousine. That's weird. Does he know whoever is in the limo? Drakken opens the door of the limo himself and a porcelain white hand reaches out. Drakken takes it and helps a gorgeous supermodel in a business suit step out.

She stands in front of Drakken, looking up at him, a sly smile on her face. She smoothes Drakken's lapels and fixes his tie.

Drakken smiles from ear to ear.

The supermodel tiptoes up and kisses Drakken right on the mouth.

Right. On. The mouth.

I'm beyond shocked.

I stumble behind a column that has a potted plant next to it so I can watch in secret. But I *can't* watch. I'm suddenly too nauseous. I grimace and look for a place to barf. Good thing I'm standing behind this potted plant. I peel back a few of the big leaves near the bottom and find a barf target in the potted dirt. Good to go.

After a moment, I realize I'm not *actually* going to barf. But I sure feel nauseous. I do my best to get my emotions under control.

Drakken and the suited supermodel walk across the lobby. The supermodel leans into Drakken, arms hooked around his elbow. She looks happier than any woman in the history of happiness.

I don't know who this new nobody happens to be, but Drakken obviously knows her *very* well.

I notice the limo driver and the valet outside are busy unloading luggage from the trunk of the limo. The supermodel is probably staying at the resort. But I don't think she's getting her own room because she and Drakken walk right past the check-in desk and go straight to the main elevators.

Drakken presses the up button.

Gee, I wonder where they're going?

Drakken's room, perhaps?

I'm close enough that I can hear their conversation, but they aren't speaking English, so I can't understand a word they're saying.

While they wait for the elevator, Drakken speaks with uncharacteristic ease and animation. The words flow from him like spun silk or threads of gold.

The supermodel giggles continuously, clearly entertained by whatever he's saying.

Although I don't understand a single word, I can imagine what they're saying.

Drakken: *"I've missed you, mon amour. I have counted the days since our last rendezvous. Each one has weighed on my heart like a stone. Now that you are once again in my arms, my heart is free to soar to the heavens, and I will never let you go..."*

He's not speaking French, but whatever he's saying sounds super romantic. You get the idea.

Superbimbo: *"I've missed you too, my love. Let's go up to your suite and fuck like minks."*

Drakken: *"Hells yeah, babe."*

Or something like that.

The elevator dings and they walk inside.

As the elevator soars up to the top floor, my mood plummets down to the basement.

For all her encouragement, I guess Finch was totally wrong about Drakken. Those roses didn't mean a thing. I'm sure he's rich enough to buy a million roses for every woman in town. He'll probably buy a bunch for whoever this supermodel play toy happens to be. I wouldn't be surprised if he also buys a bunch for Serenity and sends them to the spa this evening. I wonder if Luciana will make me clean those up too.

Drakken is a total playbum billionaire.

What a cliché.

My irritation doesn't stop my heart from falling to pieces like a bag of marbles spilled all over the marble floor of the lobby. Marbles everywhere.

I run down the stairs instead of waiting for an elevator to the parking garage because I'm about to explode into tears. I jump inside Sheena and slam her door so I can ugly cry in private.

I am such an idiot.

Chapter 16

RIVER

"I totally need a drink," I groan in Julietta's ear as I drag her through the noisy crowd inside Bar 454.

"The 'drown your sorrows' round is on me, sistah," she smiles.

Julietta Fabiano is my next door neighbor and a super cool chick. She's an aspiring actress, just like 90% of the women under 30 living in L.A. With her mane of wavy black hair, tanned olive skin, long legs and triple-strap skin-tight black dress, the guys' eyes are all over her everywhere she goes. Especially at a crowded bar like Bar 454. Julietta doesn't seem to notice.

I don't care that all the attention is on her. Between Drakken and Cage, I have too many men coming in and out of my life already.

Julietta and I order Cosmos from the cute bartender with the tight button-down black shirt and flexing forearms. He flirts with Julietta. She flirts back, but doesn't follow through. Before we got here, I made her promise that tonight would be sisters before misters. She joked that she could make an exception for one night.

Julietta tips the bartender after he slides our drinks across the bar and we go look for a couch.

Bar 454 has over a dozen different themed sections with furniture to match. Tropical Resort, Old Time Library, Jungle Safari, and a bunch of others. Julietta and I pick Art Deco and sit on a rectangular red couch.

I tell Julietta all about Drakken, from him driving me off the road almost a month ago, to our X-rated massage, to the flowers, to him kissing that supermodel the other day. I also catch her up to speed about Cage.

Julietta sips her Cosmo. "So, wait, Cage brought you a bouquet of roses?"

"Yup," I groan, "Can you believe he came back now? Why not six months ago? Or even six weeks ago?"

Julietta chuckles, "Girl, when it comes to Cage, I can believe anything. That guy is as random as the lottery numbers. And as dependable."

"Wait. It gets worse. This week he came into the spa *again*. Twice. He brought me See's chocolates, probably because he knows how much I love them and wouldn't be able to resist."

Julietta grins, "See's are totally the bomb."

"Totally. Anyway, then it was these super expensive vintage boots I pointed out *one* time at Jet Rag, like, nine months ago! I can't believe he remembered! Heck, I can't believe Jet Rag still had those same boots!"

"Did you keep the boots?" she asks curiously.

"No! He can return them or whatever. But I kept the See's," I grin. "Only because you can't return the hand-picked boxes. I had no choice but to eat them."

"Totes," Julietta winks. "Wait, how come you didn't share any with me?!"

"I've still got half a box. I'll give you some when we get home."

She narrows her eyes, "You better."

We clink glasses and share a giggle.

Julietta says, "Cage sure is trying hard to win you back."

"I know, right? What do you think I should do?"

"That's easy. Wait him out and see how long it takes him to run out of gas. If he gives up too easily, then you know he wasn't serious about winning you back. He has to prove he's not going to run away again."

I nod, "For sure." I swirl my Cosmo and take another sip.

"So, what's the sitch with this Dragon guy?"

I roll my eyes and set my drink down on the boxy coffee table. "I don't know. I haven't seen him in a week. He's probably sleeping with that supermodel right now," I say sourly.

"Do you see them together a lot at the resort? Like, sitting by the pool or whatever?"

"No. I haven't seen either of them."

"And you're still obsessing about him? Maybe he's not that into you."

Feeling guilty, I pick up my Cosmo and take another sip. "But he bought me all those roses."

"So? Guys buy me flowers all the time. It doesn't mean anything."

"But a million? It was a *ton* of roses, Jay."

She shrugs, "Rich guys do weird shit like that all the time. They think their money makes up for bad behavior. Trust me, it doesn't." She glances around the crowded bar. "Maybe you should pick one of the cute guys here tonight who're all staring at you and go home with one of them. Then you'll forget all about Dragon *and* Cage."

"It's Drakken. Two K's and an E. Anyway, you know I'm not like that, Jay. I can't go home with a random stranger."

"I know, I know," she rolls her eyes impatiently. "I just think it would help clear your head *and* your heart."

Julietta and I have argued back and forth about the merits of short term flings versus long term relationships since the day we met. We learned a while ago that we have to agree to disagree.

She says, "So, what's so special about this Drakken guy anyway?"

Thinking about the answer to her question makes my heart stutter. I can't think about Drakken and what we did and that magical flow we shared without getting warm all over and a little bit sad that I never get to see the guy.

I set my glass down and muse, "I feel like Drakken and I had this weird and intense connection when I massaged him."

"Of course you did," Julietta scoffs. "You had your hands all over a super hot guy's cock! It's called lust, girl."

I roll my eyes, "I'm not talking about the sex. I'm talking about *before* the sex. I felt something, Jay. Something, I don't know, *important*, something *special*."

Julietta looks at me sideways, "You're in *love*, girlfriend." She flicks her tongue on the L in the word love.

"I can't help it," I say defensively. "I really like this guy. Ever since I saw him kiss that supermodel, I've been miserable."

Julietta nods thoughtfully. "Are you sure you're not reading too much into their kiss?" she encourages, "Maybe it was just a L.A. hello kiss."

"I don't know," I sigh uncertainly. "Maybe it was, maybe it wasn't."

"Did he like, *kiss* her kiss her? I mean, was there tongue? Did she wrap her arms around his neck? Did he squeeze her ass or anything like that?"

I try to picture the moment in my mind. It makes me sick to think about it, but I play through the memory anyway. "If I'm being honest, probably not. I really couldn't watch for very long. But what I saw seemed *really* friendly."

"What you *watched*?" She chuckles, "How much did you actually see?"

"The first two seconds?"

"Two seconds?!" She scoffs and shakes her head, "Don't be cray-cray. He was probably just kissing her hello. The hello kiss is totes norm in L.A. You should see him again. But take things slow. It's way too soon to be in love with this guy."

"Slow? You're the cray-cray one, Jay. I gave him a hand job!"

"Do you know how many guys I've given hand jobs to?" she asks proudly.

"No."

"I don't either," she giggles, "and that's my point. It's the twenty-first century, Riv. A hand job is hardly more than a handshake these days."

"What?!" I scoff. "Since when?"

She smirks confidently, "Since I said so."

"Okay," I challenge, "then I dare you to go up to a random guy in this bar and shake his dick!"

Julietta sets her glass down, "You think I won't?" She stands and smoothes her tight black dress. "Given the right dick, I'll grab it for free."

"Oh, wait! You're planning on grabbing a *hot* guy's dick."

"So?" she snickers.

"So, that's too easy. We need to make this more of a challenge." I glance around at the guys in the bar. "I need to find the right specimen..."

"He better not be heinous," she grimaces. "No trolls."

"You're not chicken, are you? I thought a dick shake and a handshake were the same?"

"Not when you're the one picking the dick," she winks. "Your taste in dicks is currently open for debate." She plops down onto the couch.

"You're not backing down, are you?"

"Hells no! But if you get to pick the dick, we need to sweeten the deal." She sips her Cosmo.

"Okay. How about I buy your drinks all night if you shake the dick of my choosing. If not, you're buying mine."

"Nuh uh. We need a real bet. I can get guys to buy me drinks all night long." She flicks her lustrous black hair over her shoulder. Knowing Julietta, she totally could. She looks dangerously sexy tonight, like she could chew her way through every man in the room.

I say, "Okay, what do you suggest?"

She taps her chin thoughtfully, "How about, whoever loses has to do the other person's laundry for a month."

Since I get to pick the guy, I'm feeling confident. "You're on."

We shake on it.

Julietta taunts, "You know you're gonna lose. The guys here tonight are pretty cute. I sort of like that bartender..."

"There's no way I'm picking him!" I tease as I search the room for the perfect candidate.

We spend the next half hour arguing over which guy to pick. They're all either way too cute, making it too easy, or way too heinous for Julietta's tastes.

"This isn't working," I sigh and shrug my shoulders. "We should go to another bar and find a better selection of dicks for you to shake," I quip.

"Works for me. I can grab dicks anywhere," she laughs.

When we walk out the front door, Julietta suddenly reaches down like a ninja and grabs the crotch of the cute bouncer. He wears a tight Bar 454 T-shirt and has intricate tattoo sleeves on both muscular arms. He also has a short Channing Tatum haircut. Surprised, he jumps and grunts, "What the fuck?!?"

Julietta winks at him.

When he gets a good look at her, he drawls, "Heeeey, girl. What's your name?"

Julietta and I both cackle gleefully but keep walking.

Julietta leans into me and grabs my elbow as we saunter down the sidewalk, "You owe me laundry for a month, bitch!" She laughs merrily.

"No way! He's totally too cute. And you totally didn't shake his dick! At best, that was a grab. No actual shaking occurred!"

"Okay, two weeks, *and* you have to iron all my audition outfits. I need to look my best for the camera."

"I'm not ironing anything! There was no shake!"

Our buoyant laughter floats up into the Los Angeles night sky.

Chapter 17

RIVER

On my way to work a few days later, I notice that Sheena the Chevy is suddenly drifting to the left much worse than before.

Whenever I make a right turn, something in her right front wheel rattles *really* loudly.

GUGGA-GUGGA-GUGGA!!

Poor Sheena.

If she gets any worse, I'll have to have someone drive me to work. Or start taking the bus. Since Stone and Julietta both work nights and sleep late, it'll probably be the bus.

This is such a groaner.

I should've listened to the mechanic and fixed Sheena as soon as I had the money. But Stone was short on cash for rent this month and I had to cover his half. Rent in L.A. is crazy expensive, even for our crappy bungalow. Now I don't have enough money to fix Sheena, and no room on my credit card to cover the difference.

Fan-fucking-tastic.

I'll have to deal with it after work.

I park beneath *The* Beverly Hills Resort and trudge across the underground parking lot toward the elevators.

Maybe I need to hit Drakken up for a loan. He has cash coming out his butt. Too bad I can never find the guy. He's quite the enigma.

Oh well, I'm used to dealing with things myself anyway. I'll figure it out.

Somehow.

With any luck, I'll make a bunch of big tips today.

Nope. No tips.

Today turns out to be super slow for everyone at the resort. None of my regular clients come in like they're supposed to. I must've jinxed myself hoping for tips.

Okay, tomorrow, NO TIPS!

(*Which secretly means I'll make tips. Fingers crossed secretly.*)

Eight hours later, I trudge back to the parking garage and climb inside Sheena. I pat her steering wheel gently.

"Hold together, girl. I promise I'll fix you as soon as I can."

I start the car and back out of the space.

Chapter 18

DRAKKEN

The subterranean parking garage beneath the Beverly Hills Resort rumbles as I drive my Lamborghini down the ramp.

After a long and drudgerous work day like today, I don't bother using the valet. I've shaken so many hands and flashed my business smile so many times, I don't care to look at another person even if it meant saving my life. I just want to be alone.

A comforting image flashes through my mind.

Those liquid blue eyes…

Despite my anti-social mood at the moment, there is one person on this planet I would be more than happy to see.

Rivka.

But I haven't had a single spare minute to seek her out. My business obligations are continuous and intense. Everything rides on them.

Everything.

(…)

But I desperately want to see Rivka and apologize profusely, both for my frequent absences, but also my buffoonish behavior.

She deserves an explanation.

Perhaps I need to pry Rivka's phone number out of that young woman Finch. I suspect she'd understand that my intentions are noble. If she's on hand in the lobby, I'll ask her straightaway.

I park in the space reserved for me in the valet area and walk groggily toward the elevators.

On the sloped parking level below mine, the engine of a compact sedan revs and the white tail lights shine as the car backs out of its space.

I watch the car absently through the gap in the cement columns.

When the car curves backward into the lane, a loud noise rattles from the front wheel well. This car is clearly in need of a major repair. I hope whoever owns it takes it to a mechanic immediately. It doesn't sound safe to drive.

As the car drives up the ramp and circles around the column at the end, the wheel rattles again.

I can't let this person drive this car, whoever they may be. I'll have the valet send for a cab and pay the fare myself.

I step into the middle of the lane between all the parked cars and wave casually until the car rolls to a stop. With its headlights shining, I can't see the driver.

The driver's window cranks down with an audible squeal. This car hasn't seen better days in more than a decade.

"Drakken?" *Rivka asks, leaning her head out the window.*

My exhaustion evaporates like the mist at the bottom of a waterfall on a hot day. My mood elevates instantly.

"Rivka," *I sigh.* "Is very good for see you." *I feel myself smile with pure joy, like the young boy I once was.*

She steers her car toward the side of the lane and parks beside a BMW. She steps out and closes the car door, which creaks rustily.

How old is her car? I doubt it's safe to drive for many reasons, not merely the problem with the steering.

Rivka stands near her car. An air of uncertainty restrains her. "Hey," *she says softly.*

"Is you, *your*, car?"

She frowns, "Yeah. Why?"

"Is make bad sound in wheel. Very bad."

"Oh, uh, yeah. I was gonna get that fixed."

"I so sorry for I break. I need give you more money?"

She shakes her head, "No, you gave me plenty."

"Why you no fix? Is no good for drive broke car."

She smiles politely, "It's fine."

"Fine? What is 'fine'?"

"Um, fine is like 'okay'. My car is okay to drive. She's seen worse."

"She is car?" *I ask dubiously.*

Rivka grins, "Yeah. Her name is Sheena." *She pats the front fender affectionately.* "Sheena always makes sure I'm safe, don't you girl?" *She smiles at her car like it's a living thing. For her, perhaps it is.*

I smile back, touched by her childlike nature. "Your friend need hospital very bad."

Rivka grins, "Should we call an ambulance? You know, woo, woo,

woo!" *She mimics an ambulance siren while giggling.*

I grin as well, "Yes, I call hospital on phone." *I pull my smart phone out of my suit jacket and pretend to dial.* "Hello? Hospital? Is Rivka's car. She is very sick. Yes. Send ambulance, please." *I put my phone in my suit.* "They come in five minute. I wait with you, okay?"

"Okay," *Rivka smiles.*

Her smile melts my heart. It melts the armor that is always there, and it melts away the haze that has muddled my brain for the last two hours. Driving in Los Angeles traffic is a mind numbing affair. I swear, I spent half my day in traffic. I think I'll hire a car and driver for myself. Perhaps it will improve my general mood.

"Thank you for the roses, by the way," *Rivka smiles bashfully.*

"Oh, yes! Roses! I so sorry. Is too much?"

She chuckles, "Sort of. I mean, don't get me wrong. They were amazing. But it was *way* too many. I couldn't take them all home, even though I wanted to. But I kept one bouquet for myself and gave the rest away to a bunch of people at the resort who were really happy to get them."

I mostly follow her words, but the intention is clear. I am relieved. It wasn't the debacle I feared. I nod, "Is good."

"Too bad my boss Luciana was mad."

"Oh?" *I wince, regretting once again the sheer volume of roses I purchased. It occurs to me that I never thought my actions through with any clarity. I responded to the appearance of her ex-lover with impulsive haste. I should've known better. I should've demonstrated restraint.*

"It's okay," *she soothes, sensing my anxiety.* "They were really nice roses."

I smile apologetically, "Is Luciana mad for roses? Is why she take you from massage?"

"Huh? You mean why she replaced me with Serenity?"

"Serenity?"

"Yeah. Serenity is the name of the girl who replaced me. The girl who gave you a massage when I left."

I frown. I never paid any attention to the woman's name. "Is Serenity big girl?"

"Big?" *She looks up thoughtfully.* "No, she's only an inch taller than I am."

I hold my hands in front of my chest as if I'm supporting two large watermelons growing from my body.

"Oh. Duh," *Rivka chuckles with obvious humor.* "Yeah, that's Serenity. How was your massage with her?"

I sense Rivka's fear. Fortunately, I can honestly lay it to rest. "I no massage with her. I go look for you."

"What?"

"After you go, I try for find you in hotel. I look in lobby, in front, outside, but you are no there."

"You did?"

"Yes, very much," *I say earnestly. I can't possibly convey the desperation with which I searched for her that day. I even tried to track down her friend* Finch, *who seems to know everything that goes on at the resort, but she too was absent.* "Is make me sad I no see you."

"It did?"

"Yes. Very sad."

"Awww," *she smiles warmly.* "Well, I was very sad I didn't get to massage you."

"Is true?" *I ask hopefully.*

"Is true," *she grins.*

Relief washes over me. "That day, I think you no want to massage. I think you mad for roses, and for—" *I stop myself. I can't tell her about seeing her ex-lover. She'll likely think me a jealous child. A strong woman like Rivka doesn't want to indulge the fragile temper of a weak child.*

"For what?"

It's exceedingly difficult to bend the truth when one is being vulnerable and honest. Fortunately, I have another truth that I can utter with absolute sincerity. "For, uh, for sex in massage?"

Rivka's eyes shine with alarm.

"I sorry," *I say hastily. Perhaps I was too blunt. But I didn't know how else to say it.*

She steps toward me and whispers nervously, "Not here!"

Fabulous. Now she thinks I'm asking for sex right this instant! I knew I was too bold. We made love in her workplace, for gods' sake! I am far too rash for my own good and hers. I blurt, "No! No here!" *I touch her elbow timidly, hoping to offer mild reassurance that I'm not about to ravish her in the parking garage, in plain view no less. I've already done more than enough to jeopardize her job here at the resort. I should've known better.*

But I couldn't help myself.

Although Rivka steals my good sense with ease, I take full responsibility for my actions. At nearly thirty years of age, I should be able to control my own erections by now.

"I sorry, Rivka! Very sorry! For massage. For we do, uh, *bad* during massage, okay? Very bad, and I very sorry. Okay?"

"You don't have to apologize for *that*," *she giggles. Her face reddens with embarrassment.*

Mine does too. Truly, I am no more than a buffoon.

She leans into me affectionately.

The proximity of her body paralyzes me with my own pent up desire. I can't be so close to this amazing woman without yearning to tear her clothes off. But I'm not about to tell her that now. Later, at a more appropriate time, and hopefully in a more appropriate fashion.

"How about later?" she mutters into my chest.

My heart stops.

I was not expecting her to say that, of all things.

Then my phone rings.

Right in Rivka's ear.

She pulls away abruptly, "Ow! That's really loud," she giggles.

Flustered, I pull out my phone, intent on silencing it. I hope I didn't deafen Rivka permanently.

313 999 561-666

(fear)

That number...

My awareness shrinks down to nothing.

(rage)

All I can think about is that number on the phone.

How did HE find me so quickly?

((no escape))

I changed phones and changed numbers, yet HE found me.

(((...HIM...)))

My heart pounds in my chest. My body burns with rage. The stone mask falls into place and I start to shake.

I see HIS face.

I want to kill.

"Drakken? Are you okay?"

Rivka.

Her voice is like the proverbial light at the end of the tunnel.

Sanctuary.

Her aqua blue eyes beam into mine.

At first, the sensation is torturous. My desire to remain open to her wars with my need to protect myself from...

HIM.

"Rivka, I..." I can barely choke out the words.

"What's wrong, Drakken?"

I can't tell her. I can't even speak of it. The pain is overwhelming. The memories are lethal. I can't, I can't, I can't.

I break her gaze and stare at my phone.

313 999 561-666

Rivka's fingers slide over the screen of my phone, blocking out the number, breaking its hold on me.

Staring at her strong yet delicate hand, I feel immediate peace.

I don't know how she does it, but she does. No one else in the world can set me at ease like Rivka.

"What is it?" *she asks softly.*

I want to tell her. But I can't. It would blow me apart like a fallen star. Some other time. At the moment, I'm profoundly grateful that she has taken away my rage, a feat that normally requires days.

She did it in an instant.

I have to thank her.

Somehow.

"I fix your car," *I say clumsily.*

"My car?" *she asks, confused.*

I nod insistently, "Yes. Your car. Is very bad. I fix." *I want to do something for her to show my appreciation.*

She crinkles her nose, "It's fine. Sheena is a badass. She won't break down on me, will you, Sheena?" *She turns toward the car, still holding my hand.*

I don't want to let go of Rivka's hand.

It is my lifeline at the moment.

(fear)

I block out the memories.

"No, I fix. She is bad. Sheena need doctor," *I grin forcefully.*

She eyes me uncertainly. "It's totally okay, Drakken. My car is fine. She made it this far. I'll get Sheena fixed. I'll make a doctor's appointment first thing tomorrow," *she winks confidently.* "If I have to, I can always take the bus."

"The bus?" *I shake my head.* "No bus. Bus is slow. Bus is dirty," *I frown with obvious disgust.*

She snickers, "The bus isn't *dirty*. Plus, I can do homework on the bus."

"Home work? Is like, uh, clean toilet or wash clothes? How you make home work on bus?"

"No," *she giggles.* "You're talking about *house* work. I have *school* work. I can totally do school work on the bus."

I picture her struggling to write a jittery line in a notebook while the bus bounces over every bump. "You need desk for school work."

"I can do my reading. I have a *ton* of reading."

"Ton?"

"Uh, very much reading," *she winks.*

I nod. "I fix car for you, okay?"

"Drakken!" *She laughs,* "I'll be fine. Don't worry about me. Seriously."

She is insistent and confident. "You are strong girl, Rivka," *I smile proudly.* "Very strong."

"Thanks, Drakken. You are too."

"I am strong girl?" *I joke.*

She laughs, "You're the strongest girl I've ever known."

"I very strong girl." *I hold up my hands again like I have watermelons growing from my chest.* "Strong here. Strong like, uh, rocks!"

"Rocks?" *she giggles.*

"Yes, rocks. Massage girl has rocks here," *I shake my hands in front of my chest,* "And rock here," *I squeeze my head with both hands.* "One big rock in head!"

Rivka laughs with abandoned happiness. "Yes! Serenity totally has rocks for brains *and* boobs! I swear, her chest is chiseled from stone! They *never* move! Not even when she jumps up and down!"

I don't entirely follow her words, but I get that she's commenting on the massage girl's breast implants. Rivka's laughter is so infectious, I laugh right along with her, equally amused.

My phone rings again, slicing through our laughter.

"Don't," *Rivka warns.*

I glance at the screen. I sigh with relief. It's only Charles. "Is business. Is okay. I need to speak, okay?"

"Oh, okay. I should probably go. I have, um, school work." *She smiles.*

"Okay. We talk soon, okay?"

She bites her lower lip. It's the cutest look I've ever seen. I have no desire to take Charles' call. I want nothing more than to nibble on Rivka's lower lip for her. But Charles and his substantial bank account will not wait for anyone. Without his investment money, my plans will never come to fruition. I have no choice.

She smiles sympathetically and touches my wrist with her electric fingers, "Answer your phone. I'm sure it's important. We'll talk soon."

Regrettably, I answer it.

Rivka climbs into her car and starts the engine.

"Hello, Charles," *I say to the phone.*

While he and I speak, I can't help but watch Rivka drive out of the parking garage alone.

I think about how strong she is.

I think about how independent she is.

I think about her dilapidated car.

More than all these things, I wonder when I will next be so fortunate as to be in her presence.

Chapter 19

RIVER

"Oh boy!" I yawn, my mouth wide open. I'm leaning my elbows against the concierge desk in the lobby the next afternoon. "I stayed up way too late last night studying. Who knew Marketing was so interesting?" I yawn again.

"I can see your tonsils," Finch quips. She points her finger toward my mouth until it's almost *inside* my mouth.

"Stop!" I swat her hand away and pull my head back.

She grins, "What do they call that little fleshy punching bag that hangs from the back of your throat?"

"Your uvula?"

"Yeah, that thing. You know some people get that shit pierced?"

"That's weird."

"I was thinking I should get *my* uvula pierced."

"Totally," I say sarcastically, stifling another yawn. "I need a nap."

"Do you think a uvula piercing is extreme enough? Or should I do something *more* extreme?"

"You could pierce your lady parts."

Finch waves her hand dismissively, "Nah. People do that all the time. I want something epically extreme."

I smirk, "How about you pierce your brain?"

Her eyes light up. "That would be AWESOME!!" She feels around on her head with her fingers. "But where would I put it?"

I roll my eyes and we both chuckle.

Finch glances up and her eyes narrow. "Hey, isn't that your car?"

I turn around and look outside through the glass wall at the front of the lobby. "Where?"

"Hanging from that tow truck?"

"What?! Oh shit! That's my car! Sheena!!!" Panic contracts every muscle in my body and adrenalin pours through my veins. I run across the lobby, through the revolving door, and across the covered roundabout. Now I'm sprinting full speed. "Stop! That's my car! Bring back my Sheena!!!!"

The tow truck driver doesn't hear me.

That doesn't stop me from trying to save Sheena. "Come back!" I shout. "You're kidnapping my car!" I run full tilt after the tow truck.

The main driveway leading up to the resort is downhill and the slope helps me run. I turn my legs over as fast as I can. I'm gaining on the tow truck. Luckily, the truck will have to slow down at the bottom of the driveway where it connects to the street. If there's cross traffic, he'll have to wait and maybe I can stop him.

I run as fast as I can.

The truck slows near the bottom.

Almost there.

A wave of cross traffic breezes by. The tow truck is forced to stop.

I'm gonna make it. I'm gonna save Sheena!

I pump my legs as hard as I can.

The traffic clears and the tow truck motor revs up.

"Wait! Stop!"

I'm only a few feet away when the tow truck pulls forward and turns onto the street.

"STOP!!!!" I scream.

When I transition from running down the downhill driveway to turning up the uphill street, my body weighs down suddenly. I nearly trip face first onto the pavement, but manage to keep my legs underneath me. My feet slap asphalt. *Slap, slap, slap!*

"STOOOPPPP!!!"

The tow truck accelerates at a reasonable pace, but it's going way faster than I could ever run.

I slow to a jog and watch my car disappear into the distance.

I'm surrounded by the plush green shrubbery along the road, and the numerous luxe mansions adjacent to *The* Beverly Hills Resort. I'm distinctly aware of the contrast between all this richness and my cheap ass car, which is now long gone.

The only explanation I can think of is that the city of Beverly Hills towed my rust bucket because it's an eyesore.

Someone runs up behind me.

"What happened?" Finch asks, breathless.

I'm heaving huge gulps of air in and out. "I don't know, I don't know." I lean over, hands on my knees as I recover from my all-out sprint.

"I'm so sorry, Riv," she comforts, rubbing my back.

When I recover enough to speak, I stand up and start thinking out loud. "Did you see the phone number on the tow truck?"

Finch shakes her head, "No. But I did see the name. It was something like Ralph's Auto or Raoul's or something like that."

"Okay, that's good. I'll check online and see if I can find them. They have to be close to Beverly Hills, right?"

"Probably. You didn't miss a car payment or anything , did you?"

"No. I'm never late on a payment. I can't tell you how many pairs of shoes I have NOT bought so I would never miss a car payment," I scowl.

"That's good. So they didn't repossess it."

"No," I shake my head, still breathing hard.

"Maybe we can ask the guys in the parking garage. Maybe they'll know."

"Yeah. Good idea." I nod hopefully and start walking up the access road in long strides.

Finch trots behind me, catching up.

"This is fucked up, Finch," I say forcefully. "Someone kidnapped my car."

"At least no one kidnapped you," she quips.

"Not funny, Finch."

"I'm sorry, Riv. I really am. If you need a ride to work, let me know. I'm totally there for you."

"Thanks."

We walk up the long curving shrubbery-lined driveway. It's long enough to be called a road, and it's way longer uphill after you've used every drop of adrenalin in your body.

A flatbed tow truck passes us, going up the hill. Its big motor revs loudly because it's weighed down by a shiny blue convertible sports car chained to the bed.

"What's that about?" Finch asks, referring to the car.

"I have no idea. But isn't it ironic that when my crappy old car gets *stolen*, someone else is getting a brand new one delivered to their frickin' *hotel*? It must be nice to be rich."

Finch says, "I bet some rich socialite is having her sweet sixteen at the resort and it's a present from Daddy."

"Probably," I grouse. I don't know anyone personally who has ever received a brand new car for a present. That shizz only happens in movies and on reality shows.

When we reach the top of the hill, the tow truck with the blue sports car is parked in the roundabout. The driver climbs out of the cab with a clipboard in hand. He spots me and Finch.

I'm in my spa whites and Finch is in her concierge uniform as always.

"Hey," he calls out, "Do you guys know who I should talk to about delivering this car?"

Finch says, "Yeah, just go inside to the front desk. They have a list of all the resort guests."

"It's not for a guest."

"Oh?" Finch asks while leading us over toward the guy.

He's got the standard grease monkey auto shop navy jump suit on, he's really tan, has a mess of bleached blonde surfer hair, and he's pretty darn cute. Now I know why Finch wanted to stop and chat.

"Hey, Finch," I say quietly, "I'm gonna go talk to the guys in the garage and ask them about my car."

"Okay," she smiles absently, her eyes glued to the handsome surfer tow-truck driver.

I hear them talking behind me, but I don't pay attention to what they're saying. I'm too focused on figuring out how to pay the ransom for Sheena.

"Riv."

If I can't find the tow truck company, I'm never gonna get my car back.

"Riv!"

My car insurance isn't gonna cover the cost of a new car, because Sheena wasn't new when I bought her. I'm sure they'll give me a few bucks for a bucket like her, but I doubt it will be enough for something reliable. Damn, I was *so* close to paying off Sheena! Yes, I had payments on my used car. Now I'll have more. I guess it's back to five more years of no new shoes.

"RIV!!" Finch yells.

I jump and turn around, my heart pounding in my chest, "What?"

Finch grins, "My friend Cooper here is looking for River Freeman. Do you know where we can find her?"

Cooper is smiling too, his white teeth flashing in the sun.

I'm struck by the fact that Cooper and Finch look good together. Then I blurt, "What?"

"Come *here!*" Finch barks, pointing agitatedly at the ground right in front of her while she hops excitedly from foot to foot.

I walk over to her and Cooper.

Cooper grins, "Are you River Freeman?"

"Yeah. Why?"

"This Audi is for you. But I need to see your ID before I hand it over."

"What?" I laugh.

Finch yanks on my arm, "It's for you, Riv!"

I shake my head. None of this makes any sense. "I'm sorry, could you repeat that?"

Cooper turns the clipboard so I can see it. There's a stack of official looking forms with all kinds of official stuff printed on them, but the hand written message in the middle of the top page reads clearly:

"*Deliver to River Freeman, The Beverly Hills Resort, spa employee.*"

I blink and gasp, "What the eff?"

Cooper raises his blond eyebrows, "If you're River Freeman, this car is yours." He pops open the switchblade style key and holds it up.

It finally sets in. I laugh, "No way. This isn't mine."

"It's yours if you want it," Cooper smiles. "Just show me your ID."

I frown, "I can't take this car."

"Sure you can," Cooper says with good humor.

"Where's your driver's license, Riv?" Finch demands.

"Inside," I say absently. "In the spa."

"I'll go get it." Finch turns to run.

"Wait!" I shout.

She stops in her tracks.

I ask Cooper, "Does it say who sent the car."

Cooper looks at the clipboard, "Drack, Drakken Skah—" He holds the clipboard close to his face, "Skalakoo-koo?" He smiles casually and drops the clipboard to his side. "Something like that."

No way.

Why am I not surprised? Drakken was super insistent last night about fixing my car. I guess he really meant it. I totally have to thank him. I can't believe this. It almost makes me forget about Sheena getting carnapped.

Cooper continues, "Anyway, my boss said that this Dookie guy said this Audi is a loaner for you. We already took your Chevy. I guess it needs some front end work?"

I ask, "*You* guys took Sheena?"

"Who?" he frowns.

"My Chevy Cavalier. I call her Sheena."

"Oh," he grins. "Yeah. One of the other guys picked her up. I guess no one told you?"

"No." When I finally put everything together, my eyes light up. "This is so *stupid*!" I smile.

"That's what I said," Cooper jokes. "Anyway, get your ID, sign the papers, and I'll unload the Audi for ya."

Finch eases into a grin, "I'll go get your license."

"Wait. It's in my purse, in the cupboard. I better go get it."

"Even better," Finch grins, "I'll keep Cooper company while you're gone."

I run into the hotel and jog across the lobby.

"Please *walk*, Miss Freeman," Mr. Duchamps hollers at my back.

"Yes sir!" I say obediently and walk quickly to the spa to get my purse. When I return to the roundabout outside, Finch and Cooper are yucking it up.

The blue convertible is already on the ground.

"What kind of car is this again?" I ask.

"Audi TT-RS," Cooper replies. "Great set of wheels. You'll love it."

"I don't know…" I flash a glance at Finch.

She smirks, "Don't be *that* girl, Riv."

I frown, "Which girl?"

"The one who is so uptight she can't accept a gift. It's a *loaner*. Drakken was the one who screwed up your car in the first place, right? He's fixing it for you. Don't be an Uptight Ursula. Take. The. Audi."

"What about insurance?" I wince. "Isn't insurance for a sports car way high?"

Cooper says, "It's insured already. I've got the forms right here. It's some private company. You just gotta sign it."

Finch whispers, "Do it, Riv. All the cool kids are. The first one is always free. It's just the tip, you won't get pregnant. Marijuana is *not* a gateway drug. You drive better drunk than you do sober..." She has an evil impish grin on her face.

I grimace, "Are you possessed?"

"Yes," her eyes pop open in a crazy evil expression, "And my head will spin around and round and I'll projectile vomit all over your ass if you don't sign those papers. Right NOW!!!"

Cooper chuckles.

I give him a final skeptical look and take the clipboard. I giggle, "Okay, I guess I don't have a choice." I'm mad with glee as I scribble my signature on all the lines Cooper points at. I hand him the clipboard when I'm done.

He says, "We'll have your Chevy fixed in a few days. Shop's number is on the paperwork." He detaches pink copies of all the forms and hands them to me.

Finch quips, "Don't fix it too fast, Cooper. My friend Riv needs some time to enjoy her Audi." She grins at me.

Cooper chuckles, "Gotcha." He winks and says humorously, "Turns out the shop's got a backlog a mile long. It could be weeks until your alignment's done."

This is unbelievable. I totally have to thank Drakken the second I see him.

Chapter 20

RIVER

I'm all smiles driving home after work that night in the blue Audi. The top is down and the air is in my hair.

Because it's L.A., I spend a lot of time at traffic lights, surrounded by cars. A bunch of different guys check me out, flashing smiles and shooting flirtatious looks or outright asking for my number. I smile politely but don't respond to any of them.

I don't remember guys ever checking me out this much in the past. It must be the car. It's fun to be the center of attention for once.

Before I left work, I tried to find Drakken so I could thank him for the

Audi, but he wasn't anywhere at the resort. Neither was his Lamborghini.

When I get home, I park in the lot behind the bungalows. I climb out of the car and beep the alarm.

"What the fuck?" Stone asks, standing behind the Audi. He's shirtless, his arms are folded across his chest, and his muscles bulge and twitch. "Where's Sheena?"

"Long story?" I haven't told him anything about Drakken.

"I've got time," my brother says, sounding vaguely parental.

"It's a loaner. Sheena is in the shop." I figure telling mostly the truth will set him at ease. I just have to leave the more exciting parts out if I don't want him freaking out.

"What? Why?"

"Uh, I sort of hit a curb a few weeks ago and messed up my alignment."

"What?" he barks. "How'd you hit a curb?"

"It was on the way to work. Some guy—" I stop myself short.

Stone eyes me shrewdly, "Some guy what?"

I slump my shoulders and groan, "Some guy swerved into my lane or whatever. So I ran into the sidewalk trying to get out of the way."

"What?" he barks, concerned. "Why didn't you tell me?"

"I'm fine, Stone. Don't worry about it. It's ancient history."

I always appreciate that my brother cares as much as he does, even though it can be irritating at times. Times when I'm trying to hide aspects of the truth I don't want him knowing about. Truths like giving a rich guy a hand job at work and getting a new Audi in return.

Stone nods, "Okay. What happened to your Chevy?"

"A bunch of the arms are broken."

"What?"

"I don't remember. The mechanic guy said the arms needed to be fixed."

"Control arms?"

I walk toward the bungalows, hoping to draw Stone away from the Audi so he'll stop asking about it. "Something like that." I pull out my house keys out of habit, but the door to our bungalow is open.

Stone follows me inside. "And what's the deal with the Audi? You said it's a *loaner*?"

My plan to distract Stone didn't work. Strategy is not my strong suit. I should probably stick to playing dumb. That seems to work well most of the time. But this is my brother. He won't fall for it. "Yeah. The repair shop loaned me the Audi," I say it like it's no big deal.

Stone blusters, "Nobody gives an Audi convertible for a loaner. That car costs like fifty K."

"No it doesn't," I deny petulantly. Not that I know one way or the other.

Stone smirks, "What do you know about cars, Sis?"

"A lot," I say defiantly.

"Really," he snickers.

I cock my hip, "Yeah, wise guy. I know how they have control arms for the front wheels and, and… control *legs* for the back wheels!" I say it with an air of superiority as I flick my hand in the air.

Stone chuckles, "Control legs? Ha! How did you *really* end up with the Audi?"

I sigh, "I've had a really long day, Stone, and I'm super tired. I need a shower and I need dinner. Can we talk about this later?"

"Sure," Stone smirks. The look in his eyes says, "I will grill you later."

I take my time in the shower. It's a woman's privilege. I hop out just before the hot water runs out. The tiny bathroom is a sauna and the fog cuts visibility down to a foot. When I finally open the bathroom door, cool air buffets my face and the jungle air pours out into the hallway

The smell of tomato sauce tickles my nose. I walk barefoot out of the bathroom into the kitchen, a towel wrapped around me.

Stone is at the stove, stirring a saucepan of bubbling red meat sauce. A colander of cooked spaghetti sits in the sink. Two salads on plates rest on the counter top.

Stone quips, "You owe me a story. Nobody gets an Audi for a loaner."

"Are you trying to bribe me with dinner?"

He chuckles, "It doesn't count as a bribe when I already cook you dinner all the time."

"It's not like I make you cook," I grin.

"Riv, you consider protein a condiment. If you put more meat in your dishes, I'd happily let you cook every night of the week. Hey wait a second," he says thoughtfully. He narrows his eyes, "You leave out the protein on purpose, don't you, Sis? So I'll do all the cooking?"

"Oh," I pout. "You figured it out."

"You suck, Riv." He serves the salads and the steaming spaghetti on our little breakfast table.

"I'll be right back," I say.

"You better not be planning on jumping out your bedroom window to avoid telling me about the Audi."

"I need a bathrobe!" I holler. I return to the kitchen a minute later, my hair wrapped in my towel, belting the terrycloth robe around my waist.

"Have a seat," Stone says, motioning with his fork, which has a wad of spaghetti wrapped around it.

"Aren't you supposed to pull the chair out for a lady?"

He stuffs his forkful of spaghetti into his mouth, "I'm eating. And I'm your brother, not your boyfriend."

"I'm not sitting until you pull my chair out," I twinkle.

Stone glowers hatefully at me.

I arch an eyebrow expectantly, "I thought you wanted to hear about the Audi?"

He sighs and heaves himself to his feet and slides my chair out.

I sit down. "You're gonna push my chair in, right?"

"Fuck," he hisses, and pushes my chair forward harshly with his thigh.

"Hey!" I blurt in a surprised giggle.

He drops into his chair and stabs a forkful of salad.

"Was that so hard?" I tease.

He frowns at me for a second with pure hatred. Then he opens his mouth wide, showing me a chewed up slaughter of spaghetti and mangled salad.

"Oh, gross!" I turn away, wincing.

He chuckles.

"I think I'm gonna hurl," I force out a fake gagging cough. "Yeah," *gag*, "I'm gonna hurl." I lean over, pretending I'm about to puke on his plate. "Gack!"

Stone swipes his plate off the table and holds it high in the air, "Hey! Not on my dinner!"

I giggle and spear some salad onto my fork.

Stone lowers his plate toward the table cautiously.

When the plate is an inch from the table, I suddenly lean toward it and fake a puke, "Bleeeeh!"

"Would you fucking stop?!" Stone whines.

I giggle, "When did you get so sensitive, tough guy?"

"You know how I feel about my food. My body is my temple."

I roll my eyes and chew on my salad.

He says, "So, wanna tell me about the Audi?"

"No."

"Come on, Sis. Nobody loans out a brand new Audi. Unless you brought in a Ferrari to the dealership to get it fixed."

"Maybe I flirted with the mechanic."

"*You* flirt? You *never* flirt." He winds more spaghetti around his fork.

"What can I say? I'm trying new things. I flirted with the mechanic and he loaned me the Audi."

"That's it?" He doesn't sound like he believes me.

"That's it," I smile calmly.

Stone nods shrewdly for a while, staring at me. "I'm watching you, Sis." He hooks two fingers toward his eyes, then hooks them toward mine.

"Like a hawk."

"Yeah, okay. Whatever," I say dismissively. I dig into my spaghetti.

"Like a hawk," he says seriously.

"With bad eyesight" I quip.

"I can see fine," he grunts.

I roll my eyes. Older brothers are all the same. No guy is ever good enough for their sister, and he has no frickin' idea what's really going on.

I plan on keeping it that way.

For the time being, Drakken will be my dirty little secret.

All mine!

Chapter 21

RIVER

Between work and going out with Julietta on a semi-regular basis, I've been falling behind on my Management classes at LACC.

Why have I been going out so much when I have homework, you ask?

Men.

Or, lack thereof.

Isn't that always the reason for self-medicating?

For the past several weeks, I haven't seen a sign of Drakken *or* Cage. Neither Julietta nor I were surprised that Cage disappeared so quickly. But Drakken's disappearance is a bit of a mystery. I never had a chance to thank him for the blue Audi. If I don't see him soon, I'm going to pin a thank you note on the door to his room and call it good.

Anyway, I realized last week that I needed to start hitting the books instead of the bars. So, I cut back completely on going out and I've been studying like crazy every night, trying to catch up. The only down side is that I'm not going to bump into any men—Drakken, Cage, or otherwise—while studying in my room.

Since I would really like to thank Drakken in person for the blue Audi, I hatch a plan to catch him *and* get my homework done. I will catch two birds with one plan. I never liked the idea of stoning birds to death, so I just trap them.

After eating a quick breakfast in the morning, I pack my crappy laptop in my bag. My plan is to do my studying at the resort's main bar after I finish work tonight. The main bar has a clear view of the lobby and the main elevators. If Drakken comes or goes from the resort, I will definitely see him.

When I arrive in the underground garage, I notice Drakken's red Lamborghini is parked in the valet area. It's the first time I've seen it there in days. I know because lately, I've been checking for it. Not in a stalkery way. Just a casual, "*Oh, would you look at that? There happens to be a red Lamborghini in the valet area. It might be Drakken's, or it might not. Not that I care either way.*"

Yeah, yeah, yeah, you say skeptically.

Sure, it totally *looks* like I've been stalking him. But that's not it at all. I really want to thank him for loaning me the blue Audi.

I already had Finch check the resort computer to confirm that Drakken is still staying in the Sunset Suite, in case I need to pin that thank you note on his door. He is. It's the best room in the building. No surprise there.

I considered leaving a thank you message for his room at the front desk, but I wasn't sure if he bothered to check his messages, and I felt that a fancy gift like the Audi deserved a face-to-face thank you.

I mean, it's a *huge* gift.

Even if it is a loaner.

I take the elevator straight to the twentieth floor and head to the Sunset Suite. To thank, not stalk. I raise my hand to knock on the double doors.

I pause.

What if he answers and that suited supermodel is hanging off him? I'd almost completely forgotten about her. What if she's like, wearing just his shirt or whatever, and he's like, shirtless, and they both have bed head hair?

Do I really want to see that?

No.

Then again, maybe it's best to find out now so I can stop stalking him. I mean thanking.

My heart starts pounding.

I knock.

And wait.

No answer.

I knock again.

Sigh. He's not here. Or he's having shower sex with the supermodel.

I don't wanna think about it.

Whatevs.

I have work anyway. I take the elevator back to the lobby.

"Hey, Riv!" Finch smiles.

I walk over to the concierge desk. "Hey, Finch. Did you see Drakken this morning? His car is in the valet but I knocked on his door and he didn't answer."

"Wow," She smirks, "When did you become such a stalker?"

"I'm not a stalker!" I frown. "I'm a thanker."

"A what?"

"A *thanker*. Thanking is not stalking. Anyway," I say pointedly, "have you seen him?"

"Yeah. Some limo picked him up earlier."

"Oh. So he's not in his room?"

"Not unless he snuck back in here."

"Was he by himself?"

"Yeah. Why?"

"Oh, nothing," I deny.

Finch never saw the suited supermodel. At least, not when I saw the woman that one time. Maybe she was a one night stand for Drakken? She could easily have flown out the next morning to go shoe shopping in Paris or whatever. Or so I tell myself. The idea certainly makes me feel better.

"Nothing?" Finch smirks. "We both know a woman only asks if a guy was alone because she suspects he was with *another* woman. Duh."

"Well, was he?" I say indignantly.

"I told you, no."

"Then shut up, Finch," I snap.

"Oooh, sensitive," she chuckles.

"So?" I whine.

"I'm just kidding," she smiles.

I roll my eyes, trying to let go of my irritation. "If you do see him, *please* tell me. Okay?"

"Totally. And if I see him with any women at all, I'll yank out all their hair and claw out their eyes. Even if it's some old woman who looks like she's Mr. Steamy-kova's grandmother."

"Finch!" I blurt.

She laughs. "Don't worry. I'll just keep an eye out and tell you if I see anything."

"Thanks, Finch." I smile and walk down the hallway toward the spa.

My entire work day passes without word from Finch. I'm bummed she never saw Drakken come in, but I remain optimistic he'll show up while I'm studying in the main bar with my laptop.

This morning, I considered bringing a change of clothes so I'd look nice for Drakken, but I realized he'll be more likely to spot me if I'm in my white spa uniform, which I'm wearing now.

I pick a table with a good view of the lobby, order a chicken salad, and start studying. Tonight's topic is Marketing, which is my favorite class by far. The entire time I jot down notes about how I can market my own massage business whenever I get around to starting it.

I barely notice the time pass.

The next thing I know, the bar is full of people and it's dark outside. But no sign of Drakken. I'll stick it out awhile longer. I still have Management homework anyway.

Around 9:30pm, I glance up from my laptop. Still no sign of Drakken. Maybe I better go home. I can already tell I'll be tired by the time I climb into bed as it is.

Disappointed, I pack up my laptop and slog across the lobby toward the elevators.

A limo pulls up in the roundabout outside.

Excitement energizes me. Could it be Drakken?

A valet opens the back door of the limo.

A leggy blonde steps out in a red dress.

An equally leggy brunette steps out in a blue dress.

A gorgeous redhead steps out in a yellow dress.

The three of them giggle drunkenly.

Looks like a bachelorette party to me.

So much for Drakken. I sigh and turn toward the elevators—right as Drakken steps out of the limo in a charcoal gray suit that looks amazing on him.

The three women in the red, blue, and yellow dresses surround Drakken like primary colored bees buzzing around the honey pot.

I smirk.

The four of them stumble into the lobby.

I duck behind a column and spy. Spying is not stalking. Stalking means you're obsessed with someone you have romantic feelings for. Spying is when you're collecting information about the enemy.

Drakken is obviously the enemy.

I don't know why I got my hopes up. I'm sure he loans primary colored Audis to every drunken bimbo that comes along in a primary colored dress.

I continue spying, despite my irritation.

That's when I realize the colorful honeybimbos are doing all the buzzing. Drakken seems to be indulging their attention but he's not basking in it.

A tall handsome man with short silver hair and a silver goatee walks past me in the bar area and steps into the lobby. He's wearing a silver gray suit. I think I saw him come into the bar earlier. He greets Drakken and the buzzing bimbo bees. The bimbees buzz around the silver-haired man as readily as they did Drakken.

What's that about?

Then the brunette in the blue dress leans up and kisses Drakken on the corner of the mouth.

Okay, I've seen enough. I turn and skulk across the lobby like a proper spy.

"Rivka?"

Shizz.

He saw me.

I freeze in my tracks and hunch over, hoping he won't see me if I remain still. Standing in the open. Like an idiot.

I turn to face Drakken as he strolls toward me, a huge grin on his face.

I'm sure he's grinning because of the bimbees. They probably had a primary colored four-way in the limo on the drive over.

"You here very late," Drakken says.

"Uh, yeah," I wince.

He pulls a handkerchief out of his suit jacket and wipes the bright red smear of lipstick off the corner of his mouth. Frustration knots his face as he smudges and smudges until the smear is clear.

"Is gone?" he asks.

"What?"

He points at his cheek. "Is gone?"

"Oh, uh…" I lean forward for a closer look. I'm just trying to be polite. "Yeah. It's clean."

He's about to stuff the handkerchief back in his suit jacket, then he stops and slides it into a pocket in his slacks. He smiles at me, his frustration gone, "I happy to see you, Rivka." He grins foolishly.

He's a fool, all right.

I smirk, "Don't you need to get back to your lady friends?"

"Who?" He's totally confused.

"The three women you came in with?"

Has he forgotten them already?

He shakes his head, "Is no my friend. Woman are, uh, *kurva*?"

"What's a kurva?"

He chuckles, "Sorry, I no know English word. Woman are *prostitutka*?"

Disgust drags my face into a scowl. I guess prostitute is the same word in every language. I seriously need to leave right now.

"Is you mad, Rivka?"

Is it that obvious? Of *course* it's that obvious. "No, I'm not mad. Just disgusted."

His brows knit, "What is dis, dis-*guh*, dis-*gusted*?" He says it with great effort.

Wow, do I have to explain right now? I hate this language barrier thing.

His ice blue eyes flash at me hopefully. He sincerely wants to know. His face is doing that open innocent thing.

It would be rude for me to walk away without at least answering his question.

I roll my eyes and huff, "Disgust is what I'm feeling right now because I watched those three whores, I mean *prostitutes*, hanging all over you."

His brow knits as he concentrates on my words. He nods and smiles indulgently. "*Kurva* for Charles."

"What?" I ask impatiently.

"*Prostitutka* for Charles. No for me."

"Who's Charles?" I blurt.

Drakken turns back toward the main bar, "Charles is tall man with three girl."

Sure enough, the tall silver-haired guy is at the bar, surrounded by the three bimbees. He's having the time of his life. The redhead in the yellow dress is on the barstool to his left. The blonde in the red dress sits to his right, and the brunette in the blue dress stands between his knees and leans into him while she strokes her fingers across his cheek.

Drakken says, "Charles ask for many pretty girl. I buy for him."

I don't know if that's *more* disgusting or less disgusting.

"Why?" I blurt.

"For business. To make deal. Is how big business work. Is how..." he trails off. "I no has word to say." His frustration is obvious.

I fold my arms across my chest and frown. I don't want to have this conversation right now. I'm sure whatever the explanation is, I don't want to know.

"Is no for me, okay? I no pay for *prostitutka*. No time. Uh, zero time."

"Zero times? You've never paid for a prostitute?" I chuckle skeptically. "Not once? Not even tonight?"

"Me pay?" he smirks cockily. "No, I no pay."

Okay, that just made it worse.

I can't decide if he's insinuating that he doesn't have to pay for sex because he's so good looking, or if he gets his prostitutes for free because he's so rich, and like all rich people, he gets free stuff all the time.

Either makes him sound like a total tool.

Chapter 22

DRAKKEN

I know what Rivka is thinking.

She thinks I'm a spoiled playboy with a taste for high-class whores.

It's a reasonable assumption. Rich business men are notorious for hiring prostitutes, or keeping mistresses, or simply bedding every pretty young thing in sight.

I did my best to explain that such things are not my style, but I doubt she took my meaning. I imagine the only thing she took away from my bumbling explanation is that my intelligence is on par with that of a rather unintelligent talking parrot.

If only I could explain to her that the three prostitutes I hired are a necessary entertainment for Charles. I would never expect to close our pending ninety million dollar deal without showing the man a good time first.

I have already paid the three women handsomely. They are here of their own free will.

I know for a fact that Charles is trustworthy and his tastes are unremarkable. He will shower these women with attention and buy them drinks for the evening. I'm sure he'll decide to hire one or more of them for constant companionship while he's in Los Angeles. He may have sex with them, or he may not. But that is entirely his affair.

Although highly ambitious, Charles is essentially a kind man, but he doesn't know how to interact with women in an intimate way. So he purchases their affection.

I can't hold that against him. In his own glorious way, he is rather pathetic. But if these women can elevate his mood, so much the better for everyone involved.

I can't explain any of this to Rivka.

I can barely explain to her that I have never hired a prostitute for my own indulgence in my entire life, nor will I.

"Prostitutka *is no good for me, Rivka"* I say passionately. *I don't know how else to say it in English.*

Her face is still strained. She doesn't yet understand.

"You is good for me, Rivka," *I plead. I find that if I don't have the words, an honest emotion conveys more than a substantial vocabulary.* "Please, Rivka. You good for me. Okay?"

She radiates discomfort. "I don't know what you're trying to say, Drakken."

I sigh heavily. I hate this. My mind is crippled by ignorance. "What is word…" *I gesture frantically. Such a simple word, yet I don't know it. My own frustration gets the best of me. I clench my fists and grunt. Like a caveman. If Rivka only knew how embarrassing this is for me.*

But I need to explain myself. I need for her to understand.

"What is word?!" *I growl.* "What is word?!"

My aggravation escalates.

It permeates this awkward exchange.

Rivka grows increasingly nervous as I seek that one word that conveys my feelings accurately. I float in an ocean of meaningless words, the words of my native tongue, none of which Rivka can understand. I flail madly, trying to grasp that one simple English word that I so badly need. I know that I know it, but I can't remember it. It drifts just out of reach. I won't give up. I grab like a madman, clutching desperately for that life preserver of a word, slowly sinking amidst all these unbreathable words...

Why can't I remember this one damn word? I know it! Damn it, I know it! What is it!!!

"Like!!" *I blurt victoriously.* "Like, like, like!" *I smile from ear to ear and breathe a sigh of relief.* "I no like pretty girl, Rivka. I like you!"

She frowns.

That came out wrong. I point toward Charles and the women at the bar. "I no like three pretty girl. For Charles. I like you, Rivka. You. Pretty Rivka. I like pretty Rivka," *I grin, feeling like a boy who has just discovered girls.*

(...)

A shock jolts through me.

Sadness and hatred explode through my body in a fiery storm.

My face hardens instantly.

Rivka gives me a strange and distrustful look.

I am the stone faced man.

No!! Not now!

Not now.

I struggle to relax. I breathe deeply, trying to let it go.

(...)

I inhale again.

This is so difficult.

The emotions blaze through me like wildfire decimating a tinder-laden forest.

I gaze into Rivka's eyes, tortured by my painful memories. I beam my desperation through my eyes, hoping she'll understand. Hoping she'll see the man I am inside the clumsy shell.

Her aqua blue eyes embrace mine.

I feel it.

That profound connection we shared in the spa. I feel it wash through me in a cooling flood of compassion.

A steady rainfall begins to patter down on the wildfire inside my heart. The flames subside, fading in strength, quieting, shrinking, hissing out of existence.

I look down and notice her fingertips resting on my wrist.

The clenched fist hanging at the end of my arm like a stranger relaxes. I will my other fist to release. Reluctantly, it does.

"I like you, Rivka. Only you."

Chapter 23

RIVER

I'm totally confused.

Three thoughts knock against each other in my head as I watch the emotional battle subsiding on Drakken's softening face.

One, what was with his total meltdown just now? I feel bad for him because he's obviously in some kind of terrible pain. But I have no idea why.

Two, why did him telling me he likes me freak *him* out? *I like you, Rivka. Only you.* It totally freaked me out too. The anguish in his voice reminded me of how the serial killers always sound after they have the girl locked up in a sex bunker somewhere in the middle of a remote forest and they tell the girls how much they "love" them. The thought gives me shivers.

Three, what's up with Drakken and the hookers? I'm not sure how I feel about how casual he is about buying hookers for his business deal.

Speaking of which, what kind of business deal is he making anyway? I have no idea what Drakken does for a living. For all I know, he could be an international drug czar. Or an international pimp. Who knows. The only thing I really know about him is that he's super rich. Criminals are often rich. The smart ones, anyway. Drakken could *easily* be a criminal, and a smart one at that. He's more than mysterious enough to qualify.

This whole thing is seriously weirding me out.

I blurt, "Are you a pimp, Drakken?"

He blinks, "Pimp? What is pimp?"

I roll my eyes. I can't give any more language lessons tonight. I'm tired, it's late, and this is way too complicated to hash out in five minutes.

"Never mind," I sigh with obvious exhaustion.

"Please tell. What is pimp?"

I shake my head, "Drakken, I need to go home and sleep." I hope those words are simple enough.

He looks hurt.

I feel like a jerk.

He nods, "Okay. You sleep. Sleep is good. I drive you, okay? No sleep and drive." He mimes holding a steering wheel in both hands then closes his eyes sleepily and pretends to snore. He suddenly makes a smashing noise, "Krrrck!" and his eyes pop open comically.

I roll my eyes and smile against my will.

He grins, "No break Audi, okay? And no break you."

"That's sweet."

Well, he obviously cares about me. Whether in a serial killer way or a healthy way is yet to be determined. But more importantly, I'm so tired and confused, I nearly forgot the whole point of my staying here so late. The thanking. Not the stalking. "Oh, Drakken, I really wanted to thank you for loaning me the car. It really means a lot."

"Is okay," he smiles. "I break you, *your* car, so I make good. Okay? I told you I fix your girl at doctor," he says proudly.

I smile, "Yes, thank you. That was very kind of you. I'll call the, uh, doctor's office tomorrow." I wink. "I'm sure they've fixed Sheena by now. Then I can return your Audi."

He nods, concentrating. "No, no. Is good. Keep Audi. Okay?"

I don't argue.

He smiles hopefully, "I drive you now, okay?"

"Oh, no, Drakken. You don't need to do that. I live close and traffic is light this late. I'll be fine. Besides, how would I get to work tomorrow?"

"I send car."

"What, the Audi?"

"No. Limo."

I shake my head, "Thank you, but that's way too much." I don't want to explain that being dropped off at my house by Drakken means Stone might see him, and I'm not letting that happen tonight. I need sleep, not Stone drama. My brother would freak. The first thing he'd ask is what a rich guy like Drakken does for a living. Considering I haven't resolved the pimp question myself, I don't want to find out in front of Stone.

Drakken says hopefully, "I drive you, okay?"

"What about your friend Charles?"

Drakken glances at the bar. "Is okay. He like three girl very good."

Charles doesn't seem to be wondering where Drakken went. He seems quite content with the colorful bimbees.

"I drive, okay?"

I sigh a smile, "Fine."

"Where is Audi?"

"In the garage, this way." I lead him to the elevators.

While we wait for one, I glance at Drakken from the corner of my eye. He sure looks dashing in that suit. Then again, pimps always look good and drive flashy cars, from what I understand.

The elevator dings and we take it to the underground garage. At the Audi, Drakken opens the passenger door for me.

"For lady, okay?" he smiles.

"Such a gentlemen," I grin and sit in the car. He walks around to the driver's side. Two minutes later, we're at the bottom of the resort's long driveway.

"Which way?"

I point, "That way."

While we drive through Beverly Hills, Drakken glances at me repeatedly. He smiles every time.

It's making me blush. "Watch the road!" I giggle. "Or you're going to hit some girl driving a Chevy and break *her* car."

He chuckles, "I no hit car. Audi have small engine."

I instruct him to take Sunset Boulevard, which is quicker at this hour. We pass by The Cobra Lounge. On the marquee, the red letters spell out 'L.A. Gunslingers'. Then we pass all the guitar stores, including the huge Guitar Central building and Big Momma's Guitars.

True to his word, we make it all the way back to my neighborhood on the east side of town without hitting anybody.

I instruct Drakken to park around the corner from my bungalow. This late at night, all the spaces on the street are filled with parked cars.

"Pull over into that red zone," I say. "By the stop sign."

It's the only place for him to stop without double parking.

"Okay." He parks the car and turns the engine off.

The warm streetlights cast an orange glow on Drakken. Even in this horrid lighting, he's incredibly handsome.

His ice blue eyes search mine.

I feel that flow.

Despite our lack of a common language, we communicate effortlessly.

My heart starts to pound in my chest. I'm hyper aware of every sensation. The cool night air. The heat pouring off Drakken's hand, which rests on the console near my knee. The smell of the new leather inside the Audi. The smell of Drakken's manliness. The tickling pops of the leather as I squirm in my seat. The tightening of my panties. The shrinking of my bra.

Drakken leans toward me, his eyes pinned on my lips.

A car rolls up to the stop sign beside the Audi. I'm so focused on Drakken, I barely notice.

Drakken's lips are an inch from mine…

"River? Is that you, girl?"

Drakken's lips are a millimeter from mine…

"Oh my god, girl!" The voice laughs.

My consciousness finally stirs and I realize that Julietta is staring at us through the rolled down passenger window of her old Toyota Corolla.

Drakken turns to look at Julietta.

Julietta gawks, "Oh my god, he is HOT! You didn't tell me Dragon was this hot!"

Drakken looks at me and frowns, "Who is crazy girl?"

I smirk and say loud enough for Julietta to hear, "My nosey neighbor."

"Nosey?" she scowls. "I thought we were besties, Riv?"

"Not right this minute, we're not," I singsong.

"Okay, okay," She rolls her eyes. "I'll leave you two alone."

She drives off.

I imagine that Stone will come out when Julietta parks, thinking it's me. Then he'll ask Julietta if she's seen me, and she'll probably spill the beans. Then Stone will come grill Drakken for half an hour about being a pimp or whatever.

As much as I want to kiss Drakken right now, it's probably safest for him to leave.

Remember that thing I said about how being a mature adult sucks?

Yeah, still sucks.

"I should go," I sigh.

Drakken smiles, "You sleep, yes?"

I nod, "Yeah, I'm really tired."

"I walk you to house, okay? For no bad to you."

The only bad I'm worried about in my neighborhood is Stone seeing Drakken, and that scares the shizz out of me. I shake my head, trying to hide my alarm at the thought, "No! That's okay! I'll be fine. It's just around the corner."

"Okay. I drive you."

"No!" I unbuckle my seatbelt and open the door.

Stone could be here any second.

I turn to Drakken.

Those ice blue eyes...

That flow...

I really want to kiss him.

Other than one quick peck at the spa, which was not much more than an L.A. goodbye kiss, we have *never* kissed, and that was *weeks* ago. Sure, I've shaken his dick vigorously, and he kissed my kitty with plenty of tongue, or however Julietta might say it, but we haven't had a real kiss.

A *kiss* kiss.

Isn't it about time for the real deal?

Those ice blue eyes...

And that soft vulnerable face filled with a desperate yearning that he seems to only ever show me.

Those full lips...

I've never wanted a kiss so badly in my entire life.

Every cell in my body screams, "Jump him!"

I throw myself at him and his mouth claims me. The heat between us is instant and intense. His hand strokes the back of my neck while his tongue plows into my mouth, filling me.

His hunger is potent and lulls me into peaceful surrender.

He devours me.

I forget everything else.

"Where is she?" Stone shouts.

Shizz!

I yank back from Drakken. "I have to go! You have to go!" I jump out of the car and slam the door. "Go!"

Drakken is confused.

"It's my brother!" I hiss. "Go!"

"Your brother?"

"He's very protective. Uh, he..." I don't know how to explain this in less then three seconds. "Just go!"

"Okay," Drakken says uncertainly.

"Please go," I beg.

"Okay." Frowning, he starts the Audi.

"Which way?" Stone hollers from around the corner. His voice echoes loudly off all the tightly packed apartment buildings.

I'm sure the neighbors are already at their windows to watch the show. Great.

I hear Julietta plead, "She's fine, Stone!"

I point back down the street and say to Drakken, "Go that way! Quick!"

"Is okay?" he asks uncertainly.

"Yes!" I hiss. "It's just my brother!"

"Is bad brother," Drakken chuckles nervously, obviously worried.

"No, he's good! I promise. Just go! Please!"

"Okay," he nods and does a U-turn.

I run around the corner to intercept Stone.

His shirt is off, he's all pumped up like usual, and looks furious. "Are you okay, Riv?" He grabs me by the arms.

"I'm fine, Stone," I grumble. "I stayed at the resort to study in the bar. I wanted a change of scenery." I'm hoping the explanation will soothe him.

"Who drove you here?"

Shizz. I don't have an explanation ready. "A guy from the hotel."

Julietta trots up beside him

"Which guy?" Stone demands. "Where's your car?"

He's asking questions so quick, I can't think of a good cover story. "One of the valets!" I fish for a name. "Jason. I—I was really tired and he offered to drive. He, uh, said he'd pick me up for work tomorrow morning."

"You let some dude named Jason drive the Audi? The fifty thousand dollar loaner?"

"Yeah, why?"

"What if he wrecks it? How well do you know this dude?" Stone demands.

I roll my eyes. "I know him well. Okay? I see him every day before I go home. We chat all the time." I've spoken to Jason all of once.

Stone looks super suspicious. He nods a lot and looks me over.

I hold out my arms, which are bare up to the short sleeves of my white spa uniform. "See? No cuts, no bruises. No track marks."

Julietta says, "She's fine, Stone. I told you."

I notice people are staring at us from their balconies.

I turn and say to everyone, "Nothing to see here! Show's over!"

Stone looks around, finally aware of his surroundings. He waves at a guy across the street who is walking a German Shepherd. "Hey," Stone smiles with embarrassed amusement. "She's my sister. Just making sure she's okay."

The guy with the German Shepherd frowns uncertainly, "Are you okay, buddy? You sound like you're off your meds."

Stone chuckles, red faced and clearly feeling like an idiot. "Yeah, yeah. It's cool. We're cool. I'm cool. She's cool." He throws up his arms. "Everybody's cool! Your dog's cool!"

The guy hikes his eyebrows and says to his dog, "Let's go, Pedro. I think that guy has lost his marbles." Pedro chuffs agreement and the two of them walk around the corner.

Stone scowls and chuckles in a low voice, "Who names a German Shepherd 'Pedro'?" He says it like it's the dumbest thing ever, or at the very least, dumber than he's acting right now.

Julietta and I both roll our eyes at Stone.

"What?" Stone gawks at both of us, trying to act cool. "He should name his dog something like Rex or Thor, not fucking *Pedro*." He spits out the name with comic disgust. He chuckles. Chuckles again. Puts his hands on his hips. Tries to act casual. He glances between Julietta and I several times. "What?"

"Are you finished?" I ask, barely containing my giggles.

Stone shrugs his shoulders, "Yeah, whatever. Let's go inside."

The three of us walk quietly toward our bungalows. Stone leads the way.

Julietta makes a kissy face at me behind Stone's back.

I swat her arm and glare daggers at her.

Stone doesn't notice. He shakes his head and mutters, "Pedro. Pfft."

Julietta and I exchange a look before erupting into loud laughter. I can tell our laughter is heightened by the fading tension of the moment.

I giggle, "Stone, don't you know all the neighborhood animals speak Spanish?"

"Spanish?" he scoffs. "They don't speak *Spanish*."

"Oh yeah?" I challenge. "What language *do* they speak, smart guy?"

He chuckles, "Everybody knows animals speak, uh, Animalish."

Julietta giggles, "You're an idiot, Stone."

He rolls his eyes, "I may act like an idiot, but it doesn't mean I'm fucking stupid."

"You sure?" Julietta chuckles doubtfully.

Stone says to me, "You really oughta put a leash on your friend. She's getting too big for her britches."

Julietta barks harshly, "Are you saying I have a fat ass, Stone?"

Stone winces, "No! You do not have a fat ass!"

Julietta glares at him.

"Tell her, Riv!" he pleads. "She doesn't have a fat ass!"

"You don't have to keep saying it," Julietta groans.

"It's not fat!" he whines. "It's really nice, all heart-shaped and shit!"

"Stone!" I chastise.

"What?! It's a great ass! Is that so bad for me to say? Julietta has a great ass!" Stone says earnestly.

I shoot Julietta a look and we both burst out laughing again.

Stone frowns, "You guys are dicks."

"Awww," I coo. "Poor Stone."

Stone wraps his muscled arms around Julietta and I. "If you guys weren't girls, I'd kick both your asses."

Julietta says to me in a conspiratorial whisper that Stone can totally hear, "He's just saying that cuz he knows he *can't* kick our asses."

I grin, "I know, right?"

Julietta follows Stone and I inside our bungalow. Stone feeds us, and we all chat until Julietta goes home super late.

The next morning, I'm pleasantly surprised to find a limousine waiting to take me to work. Drakken isn't inside, which is a bummer. But hey, I'm getting driven to work in a frickin' limo!

Now I have to thank him for yet another thing.

I hope I can find him when I get to the resort.

I really want to thank him with the rest of the kiss that Stone so rudely interrupted.

Chapter 24

RIVER

While I massage Mrs. Mueller in the spa, I yawn for the hundredth time today and the thousandth time this week.

"Excuse me," I yawn into the back of my hand.

"It's okay dear, I'm sleepy too."

Last night was the fourth straight night in a row that I couldn't sleep because I was tossing and turning and thinking about kissing Drakken until dark o'clock in the morning.

Sadly, our brief but passionate late-night kiss in the Audi was days ago. More sadly, the memory of it is starting to fade.

Whenever I go looking for Drakken at the resort, I can never find him. Although his Lamborghini is in the garage, Finch told me he now gets picked up by a limo super early every morning. I'm starting to think he isn't a pimp. Pimps are night owls, from what I understand, and they sleep late.

But I hear that the most successful drug czars are the ones who get up super early.

"All done," I say to Mrs. Mueller.

Mrs. Mueller pulls her towel tightly around herself as she sits up. "That was fabulous, River. Simply fabulous. I do believe your massages are adding years to my life," she beams. "I don't remember ever feeling *this* good. Not even when I was your age." She stretches her arms over her head as she walks behind the shoji screen to dress.

"Aww, thanks, Mrs. Mueller."

I change the linens while she dresses.

When she comes out, she says, "You need to go out and round up some young men. You've had nothing new to report for weeks."

I sigh, "Believe me, I'm trying. But all the men in my life seem to have disappeared."

She pulls five twenty dollar bills out of her purse, "Maybe this will help."

"Wow! Thank you, Mrs. Mueller. This is really generous of you. Are you sure?"

"It's no bother," she waves dismissively. "Just make sure you spend it on some nice new shoes, or a fancy dress, or whatever honey you think will attract the most men."

I smile, "I totally will. I just don't know if it'll actually help bring in the men. I've had the worst luck lately." I'm thinking of Drakken. A new dress won't do any good if he never sees me in it.

She frowns compassionately, "Don't you worry, River," she winks. "A good man is *bound* to find a pretty girl like you."

"You're so sweet, Mrs. Mueller. Thank you so much." I give her a big hug.

"Oh, piffle," she chuckles, returning the hug warmly and patting my back.

I walk her to the waiting room and wave goodbye as she walks out of the spa.

Jocelyn sits behind the reception desk. She wears the same white spa uniform I do, even though she isn't a masseuse, but she fills out her uniform much better than me. Her hair is always up in a fancy do, her makeup is perfect, and she always has a different pair of flashy earrings. She leans forward and whispers, even though the waiting room is empty, "Whatever happened to that guy who was bringing you roses and stuff?"

"You mean Cage?"

"Yeah, him. The one with the dreamy brown eyes who kind of looks like a young Matthew McConaughey, but like the hippie artist version. Isn't he your boyfriend?"

"*Ex*-boyfriend."

"I knew that," she nods.

No she didn't. At least, I never told her. I don't talk to Jocelyn much. She always struck me as catty, a bit of a backstabber, and too smart for her own good.

"Cage is totally hot," she muses.

I roll my eyes. "So is a volcano, but you should never jump into one."

Why does it bother me that Jocelyn is lusting after my ex? I mean, it shouldn't, right? It's not like I have plans to get back together with Cage. I mean, not any *serious* plans. I'm following Julietta's advice of playing 'wait and see'.

Jocelyn sighs. "My last ex was a volcano."

"What do you mean?"

"He was an alcoholic. The angry kind. I thought I could fix him. Then I wised up and realized it was never gonna happen and left his drunk ass. He was hot though. The sex was volcanic in the beginning." Jocelyn folds her arms across her breasty uniform top and nibbles on her French-manicured pinky nail and gazes glassily off into the distance. "Mmmm. Yeah, sex with the volcano was super awesome. Except when he was sloppy drunk. Then he couldn't get it up. Such a waste of a good cock. Totally tragic."

I can't decide if she means it's tragic that her ex is an alcoholic, or that she didn't get more of his high quality cock before she left him.

Jocelyn is *so* weird.

Why am I talking to her again?

"Yeah," I say absently. "That's sad." I can't decide if I mean her ex is sad or she is. Probably both.

She looks at me thoughtfully. "Remember that hot guy you massaged awhile back?"

I play dumb, because it has been working really well for me lately, "Which one?"

"The one Luciana wouldn't let you massage anymore?"

I wince. Anymore? Does she know something I don't? What the eff? If Luciana made some rule that I can't massage Drakken anymore, I'll totally lose it right this second.

Jocelyn watches me carefully.

I pull myself together, but I can tell my cheeks are burning. I say as casually as possible, "What about him?"

Jocelyn examines her nails. She says without looking at me, "I was wondering if you, you *know*, fucked him."

WHAM!

That's the sound of me falling flat on my back and busting my head wide open on the floor. Or the sound of me busting Jocelyn's head wide open with a sledgehammer. Take your pick.

I clamp my mouth shut because I seriously want to scream.

Jocelyn's eyes are now boring into mine.

I stare right back. Bore away, bitch. I'm not saying a thing.

"If you *didn't* fuck him," she says thoughtfully, "You *should* have. I know I would."

"Okaaay…" I say, my discomfort obvious.

"I bet you saw his cock. A guy like that probably loves to show it off…" she chuckles wistfully. "Did he get hard when you massaged him? I bet his cock was big and thick…"

Gulp.

Is she trying to bait me into saying something so she can go tell Luciana? I'm not biting. The best thing to do when you're guilty and you want to throw someone off your scent is to go on the offensive. "T.M.I, Jocelyn. What you do behind closed doors should stay behind closed doors."

Jocelyn smirks, "Don't act all high and mighty, River. You would totally fuck him. Any woman alive would fuck a guy that hot. I bet you *wanted* to fuck him. Knowing you, I bet you were too scared to do anything."

She doesn't know me. She might be right, but she doesn't *know* me.

I'm dying to tell her what actually happened. I'm not the frightened little prude she thinks I am. But there's no way I'm going to tell her and risk it getting back to Luciana.

I look away, otherwise I'm going to glare at Jocelyn until I say something stupid.

"Yeah," Jocelyn's tone drips with obvious judgment, "you're too straight to do something crazy like that. You're waiting for your ex-boyfriend to apologize enough times before you let him fuck you again. Just to be safe. Because that's the kind of girl you are. I bet Cage was your first real love. I bet he made you cry when you came and cuddled you after. I bet you thought he was going to be your forever. He broke up with you, didn't he?"

"No," I lie.

She nods knowingly, "He totally did. Probably chased after some other girl who was way more down to fuck than you ever will be, but it didn't work out."

I don't know if that's true or not, but I sure don't like the sound of it.

Jocelyn continues, "Now Cage is begging to come back. I bet when he left, you stayed up nights crying over him, wishing he would come back, because you're dying to kiss and make up so the two of you can walk down the aisle one day and get married and have kids and live happily ever after like a stupid fairy tale." She chuckles to herself. "But you're gonna make Cage beg first. I see the way you blow him off every time he comes in here. You pretend you hate him, but secretly you love that he comes in. You're gonna make him beg and beg until you break him. You want that control over him. Because you think if you can control him, if you can make him *beg,* he won't leave you a second time. It's the only way you'll feel safe."

I roll my eyes, pretending that she's nowhere close to the truth even though she's standing right on top of it. I swallow hard, but try to hide it. My throat clicks anyway.

She is totally wrong. I don't want to control anybody. Cage has to want to come back on his own. I mean, he has to really, *really* want to come back for the long haul. He has to do more than come by the spa with gifts and slick apologies every now and then. He has to show that he *really* means it, like Julietta said.

Wait a second…

Jocelyn sniffs with superiority, "You need to live a little, little girl. Find a volcano who rocks your world. A volcano you can't control. One that will blow your mind. Then you'll forget all about Cage. Go fuck a guy like the one you massaged, but were too scared to fuck. What was his name again? Skala-something? Go fuck him. He'll teach you a thing or ten about how to live. Then you'll finally get over Cage."

I feel myself shaking. I fist my hands at my sides and gear up to say something fierce and equally cutting about Jocelyn being a selfish slut, but I realize her words ring true. A huge cathedral bell bongs in my head and my heart.

Bong! Bong! Bong!

Damn it. I'll have to think about what she said. But not in front of her. I won't give her that satisfaction. Sound advice from annoying people is the *worst* kind.

The reception desk phone rings, breaking the tension. Saved by the bell. Not the bonging cathedral kind. The phone kind.

Jocelyn answers in a sing-song voice, like she wasn't just stomping up and down on my self esteem a second ago, "Resort spa, how can I help you? Uh huh... Yes... I'll have to check the schedule." She holds the phone against her ample chest and says to me, "Guess who wants an in-room massage?"

Sometimes the resort guests want a massage in their room. It's no big deal.

I shake my head, "I don't know, who?"

She smirks, "Now's your chance to find out what it's like to fuck a real man. Mr. Skala-whatever wants a private in the Sunset Suite."

This is a big deal.

My heart pounds in my chest. I feel my entire face flush red. There's no way Jocelyn's missing that.

Jocelyn taunts me with her smirky smile. She whispers and winks, "Go fuck him, River. It'll totally be worth it."

I don't think I've been subjected to peer pressure like this in my entire life. This is insane. Part of me wants to say no so I can shove it in Jocelyn's face. The other part of me is desperate to see Drakken. Any excuse will do. It's not like we *have* to have sex. I can give him a private massage in his room and it can totally be platonic or whatever. But at least I'll get to see him.

"Fine," I blurt. "I'll do it."

Jocelyn's smirky smile widens. She says to the phone, "What time, sir?" She covers the receiver with her palm and says to me, "Now?"

I chew my lip, "Yeah, fine."

Jocelyn says to the phone, "Yes, River is available right now. I'll have her come right up." She sets the phone receiver in the cradle. She smiles at me, "Go fuck him, River. If you don't, I will."

I feel myself starting to grimace in disgust, but I turn away before Jocelyn sees it.

She says to my back, "Don't worry, I won't tell Luciana that you're the one giving him the massage. I'll put it down in the computer as Serenity. It'll be our little secret." She nibbles her lower lip suggestively and winks at me.

Oh, shizz.

I totally forgot about that part.

Do I trust Jocelyn not to turn me in?

No.

But do I want to see Drakken so badly my thighs are quivering and I already feel myself getting wet?

Yes.

I grab a little massage kit and a portable massage table from the back of the spa and haul everything to the elevator. I look for Finch in the lobby, but I don't see her. I really need one of her patented pep talks after Jocelyn dissected my heart and left it lying on the operating table.

thump-THUMP.

thump-THUMP.

thump-THUMP.

It doesn't help any that Jocelyn knows I'm doing this. She is *so* evil.

But I'm not letting that stop me.

I am *so* doing this.

And not because Jocelyn said I should. I'm doing it for me.

I just hope I don't end up regretting it.

Chapter 25

RIVER

A few minutes later, I'm on the twentieth floor, knocking on one of the Sunset Suite's elaborate double doors.

Alarm bells clang in my head. My heart goes hummingbird. I'm about to pass out.

What is going to happen when Drakken opens this door? Is he going to be standing here naked, gorgeous as ever, already sporting a hard on? Will he sweep me off my feet, carry me inside, and teach me things about sex that I never knew existed? Will he rock my world and make me forget that Cage ever existed?

I don't know, but I desperately want to find out.

I knock again.

What is taking so long?

If we *do* end up having sex, will Jocelyn find out? Will she tell Luciana? Will I get fired?

Do I even care? Knowing the only thing between me and Drakken is this thin door, I don't know that I do.

Sometimes, the risk is worth the consequences.

The sound of someone twisting the knob from the other side startles me.

I shake with anticipation.

The door opens and…

The suited supermodel stands in front of me.

Wait, did I come to the wrong room? I thought she was gone. Didn't she fly back to Paris or something? I haven't seen her in weeks.

She belts the sash of a super short silk robe around her waist. Her nipples point through the purple silk. Her legs are *really* long and slender. She arches an eyebrow, "Yes?"

I'm not sure what to say.

The door suddenly opens the rest of the way. Drakken stands behind the supermodel. He wears only black boxer-briefs.

I almost drop my little massage kit and the portable massage table and run back down the hallway while sobbing like a child.

I don't.

Because I'm paralyzed. My heart no longer works. I can no longer breathe. I just stand there.

Drakken offers a sleepy, post-orgasmic smile, "Hello, Rivka."

I almost shout, "Don't Rivka me, you douchebag! You obviously just fucked this supermodel!! And now you want a massage?! What, is it going to be a three way?! Because one woman clearly isn't enough for you, you brainless ass balloon?!"

But I don't.

I still can't even speak.

"Rivka, please to meet Svetlana," Drakken smiles. "Svetlana, she is Rivka."

I hate that he keeps calling me Rivka. Each time he says it is a slap in my face.

Svetlana offers me her delicate hand and a smug yet icy glare.

Could she be any more obvious? Her look is the eyeball equivalent of peeing on something to mark your territory.

I stare at her hand absently. I can tell that a horrid scowl is slowly twisting my face into a trollish mask. I'm probably also turning green, based on the nausea I'm feeling. There's no way I'm shaking her hand.

Svetlana drops her arm to her side. She turns to Drakken and says something rapid fire in that foreign language again.

Drakken nods, "Okay."

Svetlana slides back into the suite and pads barefoot across the carpet. Her silk robe is so short I can practically see her ass cheeks when she walks away.

I hear a door close somewhere inside the suite.

Drakken smiles at me, "You here for give massage?"

Hells no.

He strokes the side of my cheek.

I want to cringe away, but I can't move.

He takes the massage table out of my hand and pulls me gently into the room.

Why can't I resist? The only explanation is that my heart is broken and has ceased pumping blood, therefore, I'm a walking corpse. That may not be technically true. But one thing's for sure. I no longer have the will to live.

I'm vaguely aware of the Sunset Suite as I enter the room. It's huge and luxurious with high ceilings. There's a sitting area with three plush couches and several comfy chairs surrounding a dark hardwood coffee table that features a huge arrangement of fresh flowers. There are a number of doors off the main room, and the setting sun is visible through the floor-to-ceiling windows as it drifts toward the Pacific Ocean.

I guess Julietta was all wrong about the L.A. Hello Kiss between Drakken and this Svetlana bimbo. I'm also thinking that she's been doing plenty of dick shaking with Drakken as recently as the last five minutes.

"Where should I make table?" Drakken asks.

There's so much free space in the room, the table could go anywhere. But I don't have the ability to answer. Not that I want to.

I'm thinking it would be a very good idea for me to leave. Not only would it save my heart from further hammering, it would also mean Jocelyn won't have any dirt on me about massaging Drakken against Luciana's orders. Neither reason is enough to get my legs moving or break whatever spell is numbing my brain.

Drakken sets the table down by the window and unfolds it like a pro. "Here is good. Oh," he smiles, "I remembers, how is limousine? You like?"

He may as well be speaking a foreign language.

I don't even blink a response. My eyes are vacant.

One of the doors inside the suite opens and Svetlana walks out fully dressed. She wears a totally luxe sequin mesh V-neck dress that is as short as her silk robe. She looks like she's going out clubbing, but it's still afternoon. Her long dark hair cascades over her shoulders in lustrous waves. Her eyebrows look professionally tweezed. Her makeup is light, but she doesn't need much with her natural beauty. In her strappy stilettos, her legs are truly incredible. She is so good looking, I feel embarrassed standing in the same room with her.

I probably look like a rat turd by comparison. I certainly feel like one.

Svetlana carries a small clutch purse. She pecks Drakken on the cheek, "I will see you later. I'm going shopping on Rodeo. We will have dinner when I return, yes?" Despite her faint accent, her English is impeccable and precise.

He smirks at her, "No buy very much on shopping, okay?"

She grins and swats his arm with her clutch. "I spend however much I want." She tosses her hair and spins on her toe before strutting toward the main doors.

Drakken rolls his eyes for my benefit.

It doesn't benefit me at all.

I want to curl into a ball and die.

Svetlana walks out of the suite and pulls the door shut behind her.

I need to gather my strength and get out of here.

"We massage now?" he winks suggestively.

I'm on the verge of throwing up. For real. I can't believe he thinks I'm going to give him another hand job or even touch his horrid skin after the way he just shoved Svetlana in my face. I mean, he could've at least *waited* until she was gone and denied her existence. Even that would be better than watching her parade around half naked.

I can't take this. Time to woman up. "Why don't you have your *girlfriend* massage you," I spit venomously.

"Girlfriend?" He looks around uncertainly. "I no have girlfriend."

"Huh?" I blurt in total disbelief. Was he on some other planet until just now? "Svetlana?"

He snickers, "She is no girlfriend."

"What, is she your fuck buddy?" I scoff.

"What is fuck buddy? Is bad word, yes?"

I shake my head and groan. I'm not explaining it.

"Why you mad today, Rivka?"

Because you're a liar? Well, not technically. I never asked him if he had a girlfriend. Or a fuck buddy. I guess I should have. Serves me right.

"I'm not mad," I lie. I'm furious, but I'm not telling him.

"Yes, I see in your eyes. Your mad."

Like always, his grammar is wrong. There's nothing cute about it now. It's as ugly as he is and it infuriates me. "It's *you're* mad. You *are*. *You're mad*," I growl.

"*You're* mad." He nods thoughtfully and his eyes narrow. "So, why you're mad, Rivka?" He grins and shakes his head, "You're? Is not sound right."

"Does it even matter?" I groan.

"Is matter to me."

Why the eff does grammar matter at a time like this? Some men are entirely clueless. Maybe Drakken really is as dumb as he sounds.

He says earnestly, "I no want mad massage."

Oh. He wasn't talking about the grammar.

He smiles, "We talk about your mad first, then massage. Okay?"

He can't be serious. I chuckle, "You're not getting a massage from me."

"No?"

"Hell no," I grimace.

"Why?" he asks innocently.

"Uh, Svetlana," I suggest with great irritation. "Duh?"

"Svetlana? I no understand."

Do the men in his country have a lot of mistresses or something? So this is totally normal for him?

I roll my eyes impatiently. I'm not going to tell him my feelings are hurt because he's clearly forgotten about the special connection we shared the last time I gave him a massage, and everything else that happened between us. The hand job. The oral sex. The most amazing orgasm I've ever—

I stop myself. I don't even want to think about it. I want to forget about it. Forget I ever met Drakken. Put all this behind me. Maybe put men behind me forever. Yeah, I'll become a lesbian. No, I'll become a spinster because I don't *ever* want to feel the heartbreak I'm feeling right now ever again.

"I need to go," I sigh.

Concern weighs on Drakken's face. "You sad, Rivka. Tell me why you sad." He lifts my hand from my side and squeezes it gently between both of his.

I try to pull my hand away, but I can't.

Not because he won't let go. Because I instantly feel that same magical flow I felt with Drakken the very first time I massaged him. That overwhelming soul to soul connection through our eyes. And I'm not even looking into his eyes.

Those ice blue eyes...

I tilt my head up and look at them now.

The sense of flow between us increases a million times. The feeling is wonderful. I never want it to stop.

Flow.

But it's a lie.

I shake my head, trying to block out the feelings.

Drakken was just with that Svetlana whore, or whatever she is to him. They probably just had sex.

My bottom lip starts to quiver.

In a soft voice he says, "Why you sad, Rivka? Say to me, please?"

A tear spills down my cheek and rolls across my lips. I sniff against my will and smudge the tear away with my free hand. Why am I crying? I should be hating.

"What is make you sad, Rivka?"

My voice quivers as I ask, "Are you having sex with Svetlana?"

"Svetlana?" He chuckles as if it's the craziest question he has ever heard. He shakes his head vigorously, "No. She is, ahh..." he trails off uncertainly. He huffs and frowns, looking around the room. "Is, ahh... is, uh..."

Is he hiding something?

The flow says...maybe. I don't know for sure.

His face struggles with whatever he's trying to say, "She is, uh, uh, ass?"

"She's your *ass*?" I ask uncertainly.

He nods, "Yes, ass. Uhh... ass..."

"Ass playmate?" I giggle. It was the first thing that popped into my head.

He considers for a moment, "No, is not that. I no know word. Is ass, ass, assi*stant*!" His eyes light up with joy. "She is *assistant*!" He snaps his finger and points at me victoriously.

"Your *assistant*? She works for you?"

"Yes, she work very much for me. For every day. For business."

"Why is she staying with you in your room?" It's the obvious question.

"You mean, sleep here in room?"

I nod nervously, afraid of what he might say. Just because she's his assistant doesn't mean they're not sleeping together. Bosses sleep with their assistants all the time. Especially when they look like supermodels.

He nods knowingly and walks toward the door that Svetlana had walked out of earlier when she was all dressed up. He points into the room, "Her bed."

I see a huge bed that is all made up. A mountain of girlie luggage stands in the corner.

He walks to another door and opens it. "My bed." The covers on this bed are all messed up. "I am in bed from sleep when I call for massage. Is why I no has clothes. Svetlana is in her room when you are here. She open door. I no tell her is you."

"Wait, so you guys have separate rooms? And you were still in bed after waking up from your nap when you called the spa for a massage?"

"Nap is sleep, yes?"

"Yeah."

"Yes! I is nap, *then* call for massage. Svetlana, she no know."

It all sounds too convenient. I *want* to believe him. But I'm afraid to.

He shakes his head vigorously, "Svetlana, me, no sex. Not one time. Okay?"

I search his eyes.

The flow says he's telling me the truth.

It's weird that she's staying with him because I would imagine someone as rich as Drakken would buy a separate room for his assistant. But I do believe he's not having sex with her. Since we're having this discussion, I decide to clarify everything I can think of, just in case.

I ask nervously. "And you're not having sex with any other women? Or men?"

"No," he smiles. "No sex for woman, no sex for man, no sex for bird, and no sex for cat."

I crinkle my nose, "Birds and cats?"

He nods and grins, "No, uh, *birds*. And no, uh, cats?" he says uncertainly, testing out the words.

"Drakken," I giggle, "That's gross!"

"I say *no* sex with birds!" he chuckles. "And no sex with cats!"

I roll my eyes at his rudimentary joke. It's pretty funny despite the poor grammar and it sets me at ease. I ask, "So, you're telling me you're not having sex with *anyone*?"

He shakes his head, "No. I have no time for sex, okay? You're first in long time."

Oh. That's a surprise. "Really? *Really*?"

"Yes. Is true. I very busy with business. Busy business," he chuckles. "Two word is funny."

"So how did we, I mean, you and I, in the massage room?"

"I no understand."

"You know," I lower my voice, "the *sex*? How did that happen?"

He nods and a cocky look settles onto his face. "*You're* special."

"Special? How?"

"Your eyes. Very kind eyes."

"No one's ever said that to me before," I say bashfully. The day I met Drakken, I never imagined he would be the kind of guy to say something romantic like that. Back then, he struck me as the kind of guy who only notices things like boob size or how tight a girl's ass is or how flat her stomach is. But he has managed to surprise me at every turn.

Without a doubt, he is a very special man.

"Is true," he says. "Your eyes give me happy. Your eyes remembers me…" His face grows thoughtful for a moment. Slowly his smile fades. Then his brow darkens and his features solidify into that hard stone mask I saw the day we met.

I feel all the flow between us cut off like a power blackout. One second, everything is glowing with bright light, the next, all is dark. I have no idea what is flowing through his heart right now or if anything is flowing at all.

He looks… *dead*.

"What?" I say nervously. "Did I say something wrong?"

His head bows, hiding his eyes, but I see his jaw muscles dancing. Anger sweeps through him. His entire head and neck redden with rage.

He is in pain, terrible pain.

I know it.

"I'm sorry, I didn't mean to…" I trail off.

"Is okay," he seethes. "I use bathroom, okay?"

"Okay."

Drakken turns and walks into the master bedroom, heading toward the master bath. His dragon tattoo is fully visible. It comes to life as he walks, the coils of the dragon writhing on his muscular back.

I stand on the threshold of the master bedroom, afraid to cross it, afraid to follow Drakken.

The bathroom door slams behind him. It booms through the suite.

Whoa.

Did I piss him off? What the eff just happened? He was telling me how my eyes made him happy, then he was suddenly holding back earth-shattering rage. That makes zero sense. Shouldn't he be happy because of my eyes?

I consider walking into the master bedroom so I can knock on the bathroom door, but something holds me back. Fear, uncertainty, my own nerves, I don't know.

After a few minutes of tense waiting, I walk toward the big windows and gaze out at the ocean for a while, watching the sun go down, trying to relax my frazzled nerves.

When my feet get tired, I plop onto one of the couches in the sitting area. My exhaustion from all my recent late nights sets in and I sink into the comfy couch cushions. It happens so fast, I don't even notice when I slip into slumberland.

Chapter 26

DRAKKEN

Rivka reminds me of her.

Her...

She reminds me of the happiness that is gone forever.

Every single morning, I bury these memories so I can function. Sometimes, the memories rise from the grave no matter what I do.

That is when the ghosts of my past attack me. Bleak undead memories that eat me alive from the inside.

Each day, I lose another piece of myself to my past. I'm afraid that one day, my memories will consume me and I'll be nothing more than a stone-faced shell, a mere ghost of a man.

Countless times I've tried to let go of the past so that my heart might heal, so that I can live again.

But love never dies unless you die with it.

I don't know how much longer I can carry this burden.

I clutch my face in my hands and squeeze as hard as I can, trying to keep myself from blowing apart from the rage I have because of what HE did.

HE took it all.

HE took everything.

I sit on the edge of the large tub, clenching every muscle in my body, holding myself together until the rage finally subsides.

Chapter 27

RIVER

"Rivka, wake up," Drakken mutters softly. "You're sleep."

I stir, "Huh?" It takes a moment before I realize where I am. My eyes flicker open.

Drakken sits on the couch beside me, wearing only his boxer briefs, gazing at me affectionately, his hand resting on my knee. His hardened angry mask is gone, replaced by an inviting smile.

That's a relief.

I rub my eyes and blink several times, yawning, "Oh my god, was I really asleep?"

He chuckles, "Yes. I am in bathroom long time. Very sorry."

I smile to myself, remembering how I considered Drakken a simple oaf when we first met. But he's not your everyday oaf. He's a gorgeous grammatical oaf. It's sweet. His bad grammar makes him less than perfect, and he's not self-conscious about it at all. It's easy for people to be confident when everything in their lives runs smoothly. Much harder when they barely know what they're doing. Most people I know hate to suck at something in front of strangers. Not Drakken. He is bold and confident in his clumsiness.

"Why you are smile?" he asks.

I grin and shake my head, "Nothing. How long was I asleep?"

He nods his head from side to side, considering. "One hour?"

"An hour! Crap!" I jump to my feet, feeling like an idiot. I've never fallen asleep in the middle of a job before. We should've finished Drakken's massage by now. Jocelyn is going to be super suspicious if I don't check in. For all I know, I might have another client waiting impatiently in the spa for me right now.

"I have to call the spa," I say anxiously. "Can I use your phone?"

"Okay."

I grab the resort phone on the end table next to the couch and call the spa number.

Jocelyn answers, "Resort spa, how can I help you?"

"Hey, Jocelyn. It's River. Do I have any clients waiting for me right now?"

She takes a moment to answer, "Why, are you busy fucking Skala-whatever?" She sounds smarmy and superior.

"I'm not—no, it's not like that. Hold on a second. I'll call you right back." I slam the phone onto the cradle.

Bitch.

"You okay?" Drakken asks, concerned.

"I should probably go," I say apologetically.

"Why? You no massage?"

"Um, it's complicated." I don't want to explain the drama dynamics going on between me and Jocelyn.

"You no massage?"

The way he asks, with his open vulnerable face, makes it impossible for me to say no to him.

"Hold on," I say and dial the spa desk.

"Resort spa, how can I help you?" Jocelyn says.

"Mr. Skalakova would like to extend his massage by an hour."

"I'm sorry," she says, "I need his authorization."

She's just being a bitch. I hand the phone to Drakken. "She needs to talk to you."

He takes the phone, "Yes? … Okay. … Yes. … One hour. Yes. Thanks you."

I grin when he says 'thanks'. I think today is the first time I've heard him use plural words. Even though he's doing it wrong, I like that he's trying and growing.

"We massage?" he asks.

"Yeah."

"I get towel." A minute later, he walks out of the master bedroom wearing only a bath towel. It's so low on his hips, it nearly reveals the bulge at the bottom of his V.

Bah-BOING!

Any doubts I had about being here vanish in an instant.

What's the word for a female boner? Nippler? Clitter? Clinipler? I'm not sure, but whatever the word, I just got one. If I was sleepy when I walked in here, I'm wide awake now.

Drakken looks truly incredible. The angled golden light of the setting sun cuts across his muscled body, enhancing the definition of his chiseled abs and hard arms. He's so incredibly good looking, it's only natural to picture him with a flawless beauty like Svetlana.

I stamp the thought out before it ruins my mood.

I'm here.

Not her.

Drakken steps toward me, stopping a foot away. "Massage now?"

"Uh…" Drool.

His ice blue eyes catch a glint of sunlight, making them glow with a pale blue fire. That cold heat flows into me and my heart zips into overdrive. My cheeks warm, my nipples strain against my bra, which suddenly feels a cup size too small, and my dampening panties feel entirely too tight.

If my eyes make Drakken feel happy, I can safely say his eyes make me feel…alive.

Alive.

That's what it is.

Without thinking, I reach up and place my palm against his cheek. "Drakka, Drakkozsha, your eyes make me feel…alive."

I don't know if he understands the meaning, but I wanted to say it anyway.

His smile, which was already warm and inviting, widens into unabashed joy. "You remembers my pet name, Rivka." His eyes dance and moisten, revealing a sensitivity and depth far beyond what I expected this dashingly handsome oaf would ever have.

My chest tightens as I realize that I know next to nothing about this mysterious man. It's frightening to feel such an intense connection with a total stranger. My heart wants to defend itself, wants to pull the armor more tightly around itself, to protect itself from certain disaster.

But those eyes.

Those ice blue eyes.

They sneak past my emotional armor and lift me up. The emotional lightness I feel right now is undeniable. All because of Drakken's eyes.

I want to cry with joy and laugh with sadness, because all emotions are flowing within me simultaneously. That clogged feeling I've had ever since Cage left is now gone.

I am awake.

I am flow.

Drakken lifts his hand and cups my chin gently.

And I float.

My body weighs nothing.

He murmurs, "Rivka, I..."

My feet are no longer touching the carpeted floor of the Sunset Suite.

I become sunset.

I float on a ray of light as Drakken leans toward me.

"Drakka," I sigh.

His lips touch mine and I fly, soaring my way to freedom.

The kiss is soft, tender, warm, wet, enveloping and all consuming.

We're kissing.

I melt.

Our tongues swirl together like buttery sun rays.

He's melting too. I can feel it.

We're joining, mixing, combining.

Becoming one.

It's just kissing. It's infinitely more than kissing.

It's everything.

And it's volcanic...

Fuck you, Jocelyn.

And fuck me, Drakken.

Fuck me *now*...

Chapter 28

RIVER

A narrow beam of awareness informs me that the physical world still exists. It's a wonderful place of pleasure and connection that calls to me.

Drakken's arms embrace my waist. Mine coil around his neck. The towel knotted around his waist falls away, unraveled by his waking serpent.

He is completely naked while I remain fully clothed in my white uniform.

My back arches, pressing my hips against him. His hungry tongue plunges deeper, and I allow it.

We both moan and sigh. Our hands roam over each other's bodies, caressing, grabbing, clawing, soothing, sliding, needing.

Above all things, needing.

We need each other.

We need.

And we give.

I peel my spa uniform top over my head and drop it on the floor.

Drakken's hands come to rest on the curve of my hips. "You want this, Rivka?"

"I want this." I unhook my bra and shrug it off. It falls away.

His eyes fire when he looks down at my nakedness. He sighs, "Your…"

"Breasts," I offer.

"Your breasts are beau—? I no know word," he shakes his head, embarrassed.

"Beautiful," I say confidently.

"Beautiful. *Very* beautiful. I sorry, I no know more words in English," he says bashfully. "You have very much beautifuls. Very much."

The poetry in his eyes, his tone of voice, and his heart transforms his words into a wonderful thing that I truly cherish.

In his simplicity I discover his honesty, his truth.

I nod at him, "You have very much beautifuls, Drakkozsha. Very much."

He smiles, understanding.

I arch my neck, eyes hooded, mouth hungry for another kiss. He feeds me, fills me with his tongue, his fire. He breathes his burning passion into me and it expands inside my chest.

We press chest to chest, my exposed nipples rubbing against his hard muscles. The sensations tingle, buzz, and dance through my skin, penetrating my body in flickering waves. He pulls me tightly into him, squeezing my breasts against him with savage, ferocious need.

He growls into my mouth, grunting with desire as our tongues clash and battle. His overpowers mine and I yield willingly. Strong hands gouge my ass through the thin material of my uniform pants, pulling me forcefully closer.

I jump up and wrap my legs around his waist, opening myself at the same time.

His thick cock throbs between us, demanding attention. It rubs hot and insistent against my core. I am so wet right now, my panties are literally drenched. But my clothes are in the way, making it impossible for me to cool his fire.

I know how to fix that.

I know how to cool his fire. Women have done it since the beginning of time. My womanly wetness is all it will take. All I have to do is take my clothes off and let nature do the rest.

It's so obvious we both want this.

"Bedroom," I moan.

He responds by squeezing my ass hard and grunting aggressively. His hips thrust upward. He grinds his naked cock against me. Then he turns and carries me into the master bedroom of the Sunset Suite.

We crash into the bed, him weighing down on me like an impossible force. This powerful man is going to take me.

Right here.

Right now.

He leans back suddenly and pulls hard at the waist of my pants with both strong hands. I think he's trying to tear my pants off my body. Seams start to pop. Drakken is more than strong enough to rip my pants to shreds.

I suddenly picture myself walking out of the Sunset Suite wearing torn up pants. If Jocelyn already thinks I'm having sex with Drakken, torn up pants will be hard proof. Can't have that.

"Wait!" I gasp.

He stops. "Is okay?"

I unhook the clasp at my waist and unzip my pants in a frenzy, kicking them and my shoes off at the same time like they're on fire.

Drakken yanks them past my ankles, and I'm down to panties.

He grabs them savagely and this time he literally rips them apart, the fabric popping firecrackers as the waistband splits apart.

Holy shizz!

His passion fuels my own.

The tattered panties are still looped around one leg, so I push them down. Drakken grabs them at my knee and tears them apart before throwing the cotton wreckage across the room.

Never in my life have I been with a man who is so utterly monstrously animalistic. The experience is overwhelmingly erotic.

This man is a beast.

I am his prey.

His mouth dives between my legs and he feeds.

The pleasure is instant and intense.

"Is so wet, Rivka. I drink you. I drink all of you."

His powerful hands pry my legs apart, and I open to him, revealing my most intimate center. His hands hook around my thighs and he jerks me across the mattress, into his chest, trapping me in his grasp.

He feeds.

"I eat you, Rivka. I eat you all."

His hot tongue scorches my clitoris and a burning orgasm explodes between my legs.

My eyelids flutter before clenching shut. I moan loudly, gasping for breath, sucking gulps of air through clenched teeth. My body is hot. Oh, so hot. "Don't stop, Drakka. Don't stop. Don't... Stop... Don't stop..."

Fingers are inside me, pushing, filling, forcing, pistoning into my swollen core.

"Duh, duh, don—don—don't stop!"

A second orgasm shatters through the first, burning through me like wildfire.

Alive.

I am *so* alive.

I scream as my hips buck. It's too much, too much pleasure, too much pain, too much sensation. But it isn't enough, I want more, I need more. I claw at Drakken's head, pulling his face into my wetness. His hair is too short to grip so I clench my fists and pound them into the mattress, pushing my pelvis up into his ravenous mouth.

Every muscle in my body locks as if I'm being electrocuted. I spasm from head to toe. Swirling energy throbs out from my core, whirlpooling inside my skin. My insides have liquified and suddenly all the tension flows outward in a warm rush of release.

I collapse into the bed, overwhelmed, breathing hard, trying to catch my breath. "Ohmy—" *gasp* "ohmy—" *gasp* "ohmy*god*—" *gasp* "ohmygod, Drakken..." *gasp* "That—" *gasp* "that was..." *gasp* "that was *incredible!!!*"

He slithers up my body, guiding his hips between my legs, positioning his manhood against my wet entrance like a hungry serpent. He plants his strong arms on either side of my head, trapping his prey. His head hangs above mine and he gazes down at me.

Pink light from the fading sunset washes across his handsome face. His fiery raging passion suddenly cools into a warm gentle expression. That boyish innocence is back, accompanied by a disarming smile.

"Is good, Rivka?"

I laugh and nod, "Is *soooo* good, Drakka."

He lowers his head and kisses me.

Oh god, his tongue feels so good. I can taste myself on him. I inhale the scent of my passion and wetness combining with his skin and his sweat and his need. Our aromas mingle into a mesmerizing cocktail of sexual satisfaction.

I bask in the afterglow of my release as it warms over me.

He shifts his weight onto one arm and with the other squeezes my breast while licking the nipple.

I didn't think my body could produce any more pleasure at this point, but apparently it can. My full breast sings as he kneads it then twirls the hard nipple with his tongue.

"So soft, Rivka," he murmurs as he squeezes my breast and pinches the nipple between his teeth. "So beautifuls. You are beautifuls woman." He smiles that boyish smile, his face bathed in the last tendrils of the reddening sunset.

He kisses my left cheek, then the right. Then he kisses my mouth softly, tenderly, lovingly. He pulls away slowly and his eyes connect with mine.

Those ice blue eyes...

He is so open, yet he says so little.

In his silence, he says everything.

The urge to weep overcomes me and my eyes water. I blink away tears.

"Are you sad, Rivka?"

I shake my head, "No."

"Is happy tears?" he grins.

I nod, "Yes. Happy tears." I giggle and sniff joyfully. "Happy tears."

He kisses me again.

Drakken's words are so genuine and honest and true. It's as if his limited vocabulary allows for a limitless depth of expression, as if words are no longer in the way of true emotional communication, no longer confusing things. Our feelings rise to the surface, above all things.

This man is like no other I've ever known.

I have feelings for this man.

I don't even know him.

It scares me.

It thrills me.

It makes me feel alive.

I drape my arms around his neck, "You make me feel alive, Drakken. Alive."

"Is good?" he smiles.

"Is good," I grin.

I was all wrong about how volcanos work.

I stepped into this one and it's amazing.

I guess Jocelyn was right.

Whatevs.

You learn something new every day.

Chapter 29

RIVER

"I think it's your turn," I tease.

"My turn?" Drakken doesn't understand.

"To feel alive." I flick my eyes downward and gaze at his hot hard cock. The shaft of it lays heavily against my wetness, twitching with need against my swollen folds.

"Oh, yes," he chuckles. "I alive now. Very alive." He raises himself back up on both arms. His hips thrust gently forward, slowly slide back, forward, back.

His cock slides against my wet sex.

It makes me think of a boat floating in a harbor on gentle waves, swaying rhythmically, calmly, pleasantly. The soft slap… slap… slap… of the water against the smooth hull, hard against wet, rising, falling, lapping, splashing. Hardness. Wetness.

The root of his thick cock is tickling my clit and it feels incredible.

Despite my two orgasms, I'm getting super turned on again. I want Drakken to feel the ecstasy he's just given me.

I run my fingers along his muscled arms, feeling the hard ridges, the deep indentations, the rippling veins. Such a powerful man.

His cock caresses my entrance.

I vaguely realize that he hasn't yet entered me.

He hasn't even tried.

He just slides forward, back, forward, back.

It is totally turning me on.

I want him inside me. It's driving me crazy that he's *not* inside me.

Is he doing this on purpose?

If he is, it's *totally* working for me.

I'm in awe of his self control.

Any other man on the planet would've tried jamming his dick inside me the second he had me naked on the bed. Not Drakken. He's incredibly patient. I've never been with a man like him. Not that I have much experience, but I do have some. And I've heard so many stories from my girlfriends about how impatient guys always are that it's a cliché.

Not Drakken.

He waits. He teases. He heightens.

"Is good?" he asks, still sliding against my wetness.

"Is *crazy* good," I sigh. "Ohhh… Keep doing that…" My clit is buzzing with yumminess.

Drakken could rewrite the book on foreplay. He smiles his cocky smile. "You like?"

"I like *more*," I purr and squeeze his ass, pulling him against me.

But still, he won't enter me.

I'm beginning to think this is a control thing. Whatever it is, it's delicious.

Then he suddenly slows.

I start to worry.

Everything in the room turns upside down.

"Is something wrong?" I ask nervously.

"Ahh… I need more words." The look on his face says that something is clearly bothering him. He rolls off me and lays beside me. "I sorry."

Whoa.

What the eff just happened?

I can feel him withdrawing emotionally. That flow between us is fading.

I want it back.

I'm not sure how to reclaim it, but I'm going to try. I twist and drape my knee over his thigh. I caress his cheek with my hand. "What is it, Drakkozsha?" I murmur, "We'll figure it out. I'll help you with my words." I try to sound as compassionate and patient and loving as I possibly can. Yes, loving. It seems like the only word that fits at a time like this.

"Is, um, what is English word? Kon?" His brows knit and he taps his fist against his forehead. "Konedom?"

I wrinkle my nose, "Condom?"

His eyes light up, "Yes! Condom!"

Oh. Duh. I don't know what I was worried about. Relief washes over me.

"I have no condom!" he says gleefully.

I'm pretty sure he's happy because he said it correctly, not because he's out of condoms. But it's awesome that he's thinking responsibly.

I frown-smile, "Oh, uh, yeah. I see what you mean. You don't want to have sex without a condom, right?"

"Yes!" he points at me. "No condom, no sex, yes?"

I can totally respect that. "Well, I am on the pill."

"On pill?"

"Birth control pill. You know what that is, right?"

He nods, "Yes, birth control pill. For no baby."

"Yes," I grin, "for no baby. So we don't need a condom. I mean, if you don't have any STDs. I don't. You don't, do you?"

"Esteydees? I no know word."

At times like this, the language barrier complicates things. But what's a little extra effort for the right guy? I say, "Sexually transmitted diseases?"

"Oh, yes," he nods thoughtfully. "Like AIDS, yes?"

I nod, "Yes." Just hearing him say the word makes me nervous.

He shakes his head, "No AIDS. I get blood test. Long time back. No STDs. I have no sex after test. No disease. Okay?"

I breathe a sigh of relief.

He says, "And you? No AIDS?"

I shake my head frantically, nearly gasping, "No! No AIDS, no nothing."

He arches an eyebrow, "Is good."

"Is *so* good," I purr as I nip his lips with my teeth.

He returns the kiss, our tongues clashing and fighting for control. Now it's my turn to blow his mind. The best way I can think of is with a good blow job.

I push him onto his back and kiss my way down his body, flicking my tongue across his nipples, biting them gently, licking every inch of his abs. I reach down and grab his cock at the base, squeezing his thickness, feeling the pulsing heat.

He groans as I slide my hand up the shaft and tickle the tip with my circled fingers. I kiss my way down his V and shift my body until I'm straddling his muscular thighs. I cup his balls in one hand and hold his cock aloft with the other as I lick the skin from the base upward, circling under the red ridge of the bell, teasing the sweet spot.

Drakken groans and chuckles, "Is so good, Rivka."

I'm just getting started. He's in for a surprise. I lick the tip and taste the tangy pre-cum. My lips encircle the head and I go down.

All the way down.

I feel him pulsing against the back of my throat. I relax every muscle in my neck, letting him in deeper, then pull back a little so I can exhale and breathe my heat onto his manhood.

He groans again as I slide my mouth up, rubbing my tongue along the underside of his cock, compressing my lips around the ridge of the head as I nearly withdraw, but not quite. My lips still kiss the tip, then back down I go, taking him in.

I establish a slow sliding rhythm. Up and down, up and down.

"Is so good, Rivka," he moans.

"Mmmm," I purr around his cock. He's so large, I can't take him completely in, so I work the base with my other hand, squeezing firmly then releasing, clenching my fingers like kegels while I caress his balls.

"Is... so... good..." He chokes out the words, biting them off, every muscle in his body locked, his entire body shaking with pleasure.

Yeah, I totally know what I'm doing.

I continue for quite awhile. I'm amazed he hasn't come already. I'm not complaining. But I am super turned on at this point, and dying to sit on his hot cock and ride this volcano until it blows.

I lift my mouth up off his length a final time and lick the tip, once again tasting his tangy pre-cum. I thrill at the thought of him shooting all of his cum deep into my core. I lick my lips and grin at him.

He smiles back, "Rivka, your sex is very good."

I chuckle, "Thank you." I lazily stroke his huge cock with one hand. "Would you like to put this inside me?"

Usually, when you ask a question like that in this situation, you receive an immediate yes.

Drakken swallows noticeably. His throat clicks. "Is... uh..."

You can say yes at any time. Don't leave me hanging, D-man. We already went through the pre-flight check list. All systems go. Ready for takeoff.

Drakken drops his head against the mattress and squeezes his fingers against his brow. He sighs heavily.

It sounds like frustration.

I'm not sure why. He's as hard as a rock. I'm wet and ready and willing.

I have no idea what's going on.

He props himself up on his elbows. His face tenses, threatening to lock down into that stony walled-off look I've seen on him so many times. But he's fighting it. Something is really bothering him.

"What's wrong, Drakka?"

"Is hard."

Yeah, it's hard. I'm totally ready to ease myself onto his cock and ride him bareback until his mind is blown.

He sits up and I slide my butt off his thighs, kneeling beside him.

Now he looks...tortured. His face shadows and darkens. "I don't have word," his voice trembles.

"Tell me," I say soothingly. "I'm here, Drakkozsha." I beam every ounce of love in my heart straight into him through my eyes,

He looks away, breaking the connection.

The flow is fading.

I try to hold onto it.

But I can't.

He examines his hands, which he holds up in front of him, fingers hooked into claws that now curl into fists. Every muscle in both his arms tense suddenly, the veins popping out. Blood rushes to his chest and turns the skin red. He grunts, "Acchh, is too much."

Is he getting angry?

Before I can say another word, he jumps off the bed and starts pacing back and forth.

"Is too much!" he shouts. "Is too MUCH!!" His erection is fading. His mind has gone somewhere else. He's not in this bedroom with me. He's thinking about something other than this moment. He has to be.

The sense of flow is completely shut off.

I feel completely alone and a bit scared.

He paces around the bedroom and seethes, "Is too much!" He shakes his fists and hunches over. "Is too MUCH!!"

I try to remain calm and think this through. There's no sane reason why he would be mad at *me* right now. But that doesn't mean I won't get caught in the crossfire if he suddenly turns volatile. Unfortunately, I'm a massage therapist and not a regular therapist. I don't have any training for this.

He starts banging his fists against the sides of his head. "IS TOO MUCH! IS TOO MUCH!"

Watching the agony overtake him is breaking my heart.

I want to soothe him, but I don't want to say or do the wrong thing and make things worse. Fear tingles throughout my body. I'm suddenly afraid to speak or even move. But I do anyway, "Drakken? Are you okay?"

He jumps as if he had been alone in the room and I suddenly appeared in a puff of smoke. He stares at me like I'm a complete stranger.

Without realizing it, I drag my arm across my chest and cover my breasts defensively.

In a desperately pleading voice, a frightened and small voice, he squeals, "Is too much!" His face is red and strained with tearful rage.

"What, Drakken, what's wrong?" I'm on the verge of tears myself. I feel his pain projecting off of him in waves, but I don't understand it. My heart pounds in my chest. I can't move.

"Go!" he shouts! "GO!!" He points out the door. "GO!!!!"

His command shakes me to the core. The feeling of rejection and abandonment is immediate and powerful. It hurts so badly I want to start sobbing.

"GO!!!!" His entire body tenses when he yells. He is a raging giant.

Now I'm afraid. Whatever courage I had before is completely gone.

The negative emotions storming in this room are so powerful, I have to block them out, or I'm going to collapse into a ball of fear and tears.

I try to think as logically as possible about this situation and look for my best exit strategy. I'm naked. My panties are torn to pieces. My clothes are scattered around the suite. "My clothes," I mutter carefully. "I'll just get my clothes..." I slide cautiously off the bed.

Drakken spins on his feet and struts across the room, moving away from me. When he nears the far wall, he spins, and struts toward me. He looks like a caged monster that wants to run, to escape, to flee.

But he can't.

He's trapped.

The monster growls a long string of harsh words in the same language he uses with Svetlana, pouring them out as if he's speaking to someone not in this room. He's raging at someone inside his own head.

That much is obvious.

But I don't know if he's raging at himself or someone else. There's no way to tell.

I take a tentative step toward him. Then another and another.

He still paces and rages.

I feel like if I could just touch him, lay a soothing hand on him, I could ease his suffering. It's what I do as a masseuse. I heal. Drakken needs healing. I know it in my heart.

"Drakken?" I mutter. "Drakkozsha? Baby? Talk to me. Please, Drakka. Tell me what's wrong."

I'm a few feet away from him when he spins violently and BOOM!

He has just punched a hole in the wall, burying his arm halfway to his elbow.

"GO!!!!" He shouts with pure rage and yanks his arm out. White plaster dust billows out of the hole in a thick puff. He faces me, staring me down, every muscle in his body vibrating with volcanic rage.

I freeze in my tracks.

Maybe I *was* right about volcanos.

What was I thinking jumping into this one?

Now I'm *totally* afraid for my safety.

Drakken's other fists smashes a second hole in the wall.

BOOM!!!

I tell myself over and over, *I am not afraid, I am not afraid, I am not afraid...*

I take a step closer.

Drakken lunges sideways and picks up a vanity chair that sits in the corner and hurls it against the vanity mirror, shattering the glass. The chair and the mirror topple to the floor in shards of wood and glass.

"GOOOO!!!!!!!!"

Okay, this is bad.

I need to get out of here. Now.

I back up slowly, pretending I'm invisible.

Drakken locks his rage-filled eyes on mine.

Shit.

I'm in trouble.

I back up another step.

Drakken falls to his knees. His body begins to shake. Tears drip down his cheeks. "Is too much!" he wails hoarsely, barely able to get the words out. "Is... too... much!!" He folds at the waist and hammers his fists into the carpeted floor.

The floor beneath my feet ripples from the heavy blows. It feels like he's going to bring the building down.

This volcano is about to explode.

"IS TOO MUCH!!" he shouts and pounds the floor again, shaking the room. He remains on his knees, folded over, outstretched arms resting in front of him, fists clenching and shaking, knuckles white, his face buried in the carpet and his head rolling side to side, his body quivering with silent sobs.

It's the saddest thing I've ever seen.

I take a step toward him.

I'm completely naked, only a few feet away from an insane monster. But I'm not afraid.

Not afraid...

I take another step, expecting the monster to strike like a coiled rattlesnake. But he doesn't.

He sobs.

I kneel beside him and reach out to touch him...

He's going to attack me...

I am not afraid.

He shakes, his fists clenching and unclenching like he's going to grab things and crush them in his powerful fingers.

I am not afraid...

He sobs.

He's not a monster.

I lower my hand toward his back.

His tattoo covered back.

The elaborate dragon tattoo shakes as Drakken sobs. His skin radiates heat, burning like dragon fire.

My hand is an inch from his skin.

I'm suddenly afraid that the heat pouring off of him will literally burn me if I touch him. But that's just an illusion.

I rest my palm on his back as gently as I can.

I feel scars.

Oh my god…

His back is covered with scars.

That's when I realize that the intricate tattooed dragon is a disguise, camouflage for the numerous puckered and ragged scars criss-crossing his back in long jagged gashes. The scars are the reason he hides his back.

The scars…

They feel like *gouges* in his flesh.

What happened to this poor man?

Did somebody *whip* him?

Oh. My. God.

Sadness overtakes me.

Chapter 30

RIVER

Some time later, after my own tears have subsided, Drakken's phone vibrates on the night table next to the bed.

Drakken doesn't seem to notice.

It buzzes and buzzes on the wood. After the fourth buzz, it stops. A moment later, it buzzes again and again. Then stops. Then buzzes again.

Maybe it's an emergency or something. I reach over to pick up the phone and look at the screen.

There's no name, just a number.

313 999 561-666

For some reason, it seems familiar. I can't remember why. Either way, it doesn't even look like a real phone number. It's probably one of those scam phone numbers where they're phishing for your personal information.

I set the phone back on the night table.

There's a knock at the main door of the suite.

Shizz

I'm naked.

I'm kneeling next to Drakken, who is also naked and sobbing in a ruined heap in the master bedroom of the Sunset Suite of *The* Beverly Hills Hotel. This does not look good.

Luciana.

What if Jocelyn sent Luciana up here on purpose so she would catch me in the act?

No, no, no!

Panic sets in.

My chest locks down and I can't breathe. I pray that whoever it is will go away.

There's another knock at the door.

Fuck.

I can't open that door. It *might* not be Luciana. It could be Jocelyn for all I know, or someone on the resort staff. I have no idea.

Whoever it is knocks again.

Volcanic shizz.

Anyone with a brain can see I basically had sex with my client during a private massage. Not technically, but close enough. And worse, there are two holes punched in the wall, a broken chair, and a shattered vanity mirror all over the floor.

This place looks like a crime scene.

There's even a lifeless body on the floor. Except Drakken isn't actually dead. At least that much is good news.

I grab my pants and shoes and socks off the floor. My panties are around here somewhere.

If Mr. Duchamps finds out about this, I will totally get fired. It doesn't have to be Luciana or Jocelyn standing outside that door. It could be anyone on the resort staff. I'm sure whoever it is will mention this to *somebody*. I mean, they have to fix everything. Word will get around. I might even get accused of being a prostitute. Mr. Duchamps strikes me as the kind of analhole who would totally prosecute my ass for sullying the reputation of his fine establishment. And Luciana will stand right beside him the entire time, nodding with self-righteous agreement.

This is beyond bad.

I'm fucked and I didn't even get fucked.

There's another knock at the door.

Where the hell are my panties? I can't leave evidence behind. Then again, it's not like I can jump out the twentieth story window and escape unnoticed. The only way out is through the front door and past whoever is standing outside.

Maybe I can wait for them to go away? The doorknob rattles and whoever it is knocks again. Nope, waiting isn't going to work. I need to get dressed.

Where are my damn panties!!

Fuck it.

Nobody'll know they're mine. If I recall, they're torn to shreds anyway. I turn toward the door of the master bedroom. That's when I see my panties hooked around a lamp shade on the desk beside the doorframe. That doesn't look good. I grab them and nearly yank the lamp to the floor. I catch the lamp at the last second in both hands and set it upright.

I dash into the sitting room and grab my shirt and bra off the rug and now I have all my clothes wadded in my hands.

But I'm still naked.

The doorknob rattles again.

Maybe if I grab a towel from the bathroom, I can pretend I'm a guest of the resort and pass it off. No one will ever know. Unless it's Jocelyn or Luciana or Mr. Duchamps or anyone else who works here.

I dart toward the door to check the peephole.

A woman's voice drifts through the doors, "Drakken? My keycard is not working."

Svetlana.

She's going to open this door any second.

Do I really want to be standing in front of it completely naked, holding my wadded up clothes? Probably not.

I dart back into the master bedroom.

Drakken is still comatose.

No help there.

As quick as I can, I clip my bra around my waist then twist it into place with shaking hands and slip my arms through the straps without bothering to adjust myself in the cups. My right breast hangs halfway out of the cup. I'm not worrying about it now.

"Drakken? Are you there?"

I jam one leg into my pants but stumble forward when I try to jam the other one in. I throw my hands forward to break my fall. Luckily, the bed is there to catch me. I land on my chest and twist onto my ass into a sit-up position and yank my pants past my knees. I stand up frantically, about to pull my pants all the way up when—

The front door opens and Svetlana walks into the suite.

So much for luck.

I freeze.

The master bedroom door is open. If I slam it, she won't see me. But she'll know I'm here and I'm sure she'll start knocking. I decide pulling my pants up is the smart choice.

Too bad I decide after Svetlana walks into view. She holds two shopping bags in one hand. She stops short. Her eyes goggle, "What is going on?" she demands.

I lock eyes with her.

My face knots with guilt and surprise.

Why guilt?

Because I'm not wearing my shirt and one boob hangs out of my bra. My uniform pants are not quite half way up my thighs and I wear no panties. My woman parts are pretty much fully on display. At least I waxed recently, so I know I look good down south.

I wonder what Svetlana is going to think about all this drama.

Her sculpted brows knit together. Her eyes flick past me. She has a clear line of sight to Drakken on the master bedroom floor. She trots past me and drops her shopping bags as if she's forgotten them and falls to the carpet beside Drakken.

Finally, my paralysis breaks and I pull my pants all the way up.

Svetlana utters a steady stream of words in that same foreign language she and Drakken use. She sounds alarmed and very concerned about Drakken's well being. Judging by the fear straining her voice, I'm guessing she thinks something terrible has happened to him.

Only one of the words that Svetlana says is recognizable to me.

"Drakkozsha!"

She says it over and over while she shakes Drakken gently and tries to get him to respond.

Wait, why is she using his pet name? I thought pet names were for lovers only? I thought she was his assistant? Was he lying to me?! What the eff is going on?!

"Drakkozsha!" she wails.

Drakken doesn't respond. He appears lifeless. A crumpled broken heap on the floor.

Svetlana daggers me with a hateful glare. "What did you do to him?!" Her voice seethes with anger, fear, and worry. "What did you do to Drakken?!" She says it like I murdered him. "Drakkozsha! Wake up!" She slaps his face lightly. "Drakkozsha? Are you okay?"

He groans faintly.

He's obviously not dead.

"What did you do to him?" she hisses at me with pure hatred.

"I don't know! I didn't do anything! He just, he just..."

I don't even know where to start.

But I do know that there's no way I'm getting out of this room without anyone noticing.

I'm screwed.

In a bad way.

Drakken's phone buzzes on his night table, catching Svetlana's attention. She picks up the phone without hesitation and looks at the number.

I wonder if it's that same phishing number that called before Svetlana walked in?

"Oh, no..." she mutters, her voice tight with fear. She stares at the phone and worry withers her face. She moans:

"It's *HIM*..."

Book 3

Chapter 1

DRAKKEN

Age 12.
Every day after school, we meet by the airfield.
I like to watch the planes take off and land.
She likes it because nobody comes out here except us.
This is the only place we get to hang out anymore.
We sit side by side on the dirt with our backs against a big rock near the edge of the woods. Our bicycles lean against a tree.
When we were little, we played together every single day. Ever since we started going to different schools, we hardly see each other anymore. I hate that we see so little of each other now.
It's all my parents' fault.
My parents are rich. Hers aren't. Mine don't want us hanging out together because she's poor. Hers think my parents are assholes.
All the kids in my school are rich. I don't like them. They're assholes too. They think I'm a dumbass because I hang out with someone poor. They say she's trash because she's poor. I'm old enough to know that there's more to life than money and being poor doesn't make someone trash.
Even though she doesn't have any money, she's the richest person I know.
You can't buy nice.
The more money people have, the meaner they are. If you don't believe me, try hanging out with the kids where I go to school. I pretend to like them because I have to see them every day. But I don't.
The only person I really want to see every day is her. I can't imagine life without her.
Her.
Everyone else in my life is an asshole.
Without her, I think I'd kill myself.
BOOM!!!!!
A fighter jet streaks by overhead, punching a hole in the sky, making a sonic boom. It's loud, loud, loud.
I love it.
And I love her.
"Did you see how fast that one was going?!" I shout and laugh, pointing at the empty sky. The fighter jet is long gone. "That's gonna be me some day flying that plane!"

"No it's not, it's gonna be me!" she grins. "You'll be on the ground fixing my planes!"

"Only cause you break them," I joke.

"That's stupid!" she shouts. "You're the one always dying on Air Combat on your PlayStation, not me. I have all the highest scores."

"Only cause I let you win." I bump her with my shoulder and she falls over, rolling onto her back.

"Hey!" she laughs and lunges at me.

The next thing I know, we're wrestling. She's really strong for a girl, but she's still a girl. So I let her win, just like on PlayStation, but not without putting up a fight.

After a while, we're both covered in dust and dirt. I'm on my back and she sits on my stomach, trying to tickle me. I lock my elbows at my sides so she can't get my armpits.

"I'm gonna tickle you, Drakken!" she giggles.

"Stop!" I don't want her to stop. I hate being tickled, but it's okay when she's doing it.

"You're such a baby!" she laughs, tickling like crazy.

I twist my hips and she tips over. I coil around her and a second later I'm on top of her, sitting on her stomach. I grab her wrists and pin her arms to the ground above her head. "No more tickling!" I laugh.

She grins, "Are you going to tickle me, Drakken?" She sounds like she wants me to.

I don't think I've tickled her in years. I thought we grew out of that. I thought tickling was for kids in primary school.

"Well?" she asks in a really weird way.

I've known her all my life, but not once has she had this weird look on her face. I suddenly feel really weird too.

In a good way.

Maybe the best way ever.

Probably because she's the prettiest girl I've ever seen. Prettier than all the girls in school, and all the girls on all the American TV shows and in all the American movies. I never noticed how pretty she was until recently. Now I want to marry her even more than I did when we were little.

"What?" she smiles.

"I don't know." I do know, but I don't want to tell her.

"Do you want to kiss me, Drakken?"

I croak like a frog, "Yes." I want to kiss her so bad it hurts.

She closes her eyes. She licks her lips. They glisten.

I've never kissed her before. I don't know how to do it. I hope I don't screw it up. Then she'll hate me.

She giggles shyly, "Kiss me, Drakken."

I lean forward and kiss her on the lips.

BOOM!!!!!

High overhead, another fighter jet cracks the sky in two.

"How was that?" I ask.

She giggles, blushing.

"Did I do it wrong?" I ask, nervous.

"No," she smiles bashfully.

"Does this mean you're my girlfriend?" I ask hopefully. Please say yes, please say yes, please say yes. I don't know why it matters, but it really does.

"I've always been your girlfriend, Drakken."

Wow! That's better than a million yesses! I want to jump up and cheer, but I don't want to be away from her. I don't want to stop touching her body with mine.

Sitting on top of her, my nose one inch from hers, is better than beating her at Air Combat. It's better than watching the fighter jets break the sound barrier and arguing about who'll be a better fighter pilot when we grow up. It's better than everything I ever imagined.

"Why are you smiling so much?" she asks.

"Because I want to kiss you again."

"You can. If you want."

She licks her lips. Her eyes are half open.

They're the most beautiful eyes ever. I want to see her eyes every day for the rest of my life.

"Hey faggot!" someone shouts from behind me.

I look up and see three of the rich assholes from my school. Slavoj, Oleg, and Igor. They all wear Fila track suits and Adidas shoes. They're trying to look like the players on our national World Cup football team.

"What are you fairies doing out here?" the tallest kid asks. His name is Slavoj, and he's a year older than me. Slavoj's dad owns a computer company that does something with cellular telephones. His dad boasts that one day he'll be the richest man in the whole country. Not that it matters. It just means he and Slavoj are both gigantic assholes.

"Shut up, Slavoj," I growl.

"I see you're slumming with your trash girlfriend again," Oleg says. He makes it sound like a bad thing.

I slide off of her stomach and she sits up next to me.

She whispers into my ear, "We should go, Drakken."

"Okay," I whisper to her.

Slavoj, Oleg, and Igor stand between us and our bicycles. We both stand up and try to walk around the three boys. She holds my hand.

"Not so fast," Slavoj says, stepping in front of us.

"Get out of the way, Slavoj," I warn.

"Or what?"

"Or I'll kill you." I mean it.

Slavoj laughs like I told a joke. "Did you hear this guy?"

The three of them circle around the two of us. All three of them are taller than me and her.

Oleg and Igor laugh like hyenas.

Slavoj stands between us and our bikes.

I push forward, pulling her with me.

Slavoj grabs my arm and smiles a fake smile, "Where do you think you're going?"

"Let go of me," I grunt.

"Why should I?"

"Because I said so," I warn.

"You think you're special because of your dad?" Slavoj asks.

"No." I mean it. "I just think you're an asshole."

She giggles at my comment, but stops herself.

I squeeze her hand, letting her know it's okay.

Slavoj snarls at her, "Don't laugh at me, bitch. You're nothing. You're shit. You're trash. Poor, no good trash."

"Shut up, Slavoj," I growl. "Don't talk to her like that."

Slavoj sneers, "I can talk to her any way I want. She's nothing. She's garbage."

"No I'm not," she says proudly. "Having money doesn't make you special, Slavoj."

"Yes it does," he says confidently.

Oleg and Igor chuckle in agreement.

Slavoj smiles, "My family hires people like your family to clean our toilets and shovel horse shit in our stables."

She smirks, "Is that because you and your family are all animals with no manners and no brains and you need people to clean up after you?"

I snicker openly. I'm proud of her for standing up for herself.

Slavoj frowns. "Shut your mouth, bitch."

Igor and Oleg press in around me and her.

I shoulder past Slavoj and pull her with me.

"Not so fast," Oleg growls.

"Drakken!" she blurts.

I twist around.

Oleg has both hands around her arm.

"Let go!" I bark.

"Drakken!" she screams.

Oleg is really strong. I know because I've wrestled him before in school. He won't let go of her.

Igor grabs the back of her neck.

"Drakken!" She's afraid. She struggles, but Igor and Oleg are older and bigger than her. She can't escape.

Before I can respond, she stomps on Igor's toes.

"Ow! Stupid bitch!" Igor shouts and lets go of her neck.

"Shouldn't a done that," Oleg chuckles and yanks her in a circle by the arm.

She squeals and spins away and stumbles into the dirt.

Oleg lumbers toward her.

I pump my legs and missile at his back. My shoulder hits his kidney.

Oleg falls down face first with a grunt.

I go down with him, but I'm on top of him in an instant. I grab his head with both hands and slam his face into the dirt.

"Get him off me!" Oleg screams.

Igor kicks me in the side of my head.

BOOM!!!!!

I can't see anything except flashing white lights.

"Drakken!" she screams.

"Dog!" Igor kicks my shoulder.

I roll away.

Igor tries to stomp me two more times, but he misses and yelps suddenly, "Get off me, bitch!"

I can see again.

She claws at Igor's cheek with her nails.

Igor waves his arms around, trying to protect himself.

She claws like crazy.

Slavoj slams into me, knocking me back down to the ground.

I start punching as hard as I can. I hit his stomach and his ribs.

Slavoj wheezes out all his air.

I think I knocked the wind out of him.

Oleg hovers over me. His face is covered in dirt. "You're gonna pay for that." He sounds really mad.

Since I'm still on the ground, I punch him in the jewels.

Oleg's eyes roll up into the back of his head and he sinks to his knees. His face goes gray.

Igor is on top of her. Somehow, he knocked her down while I was fighting Slavoj.

"Get off her!" I yell. I jump to my feet and run right into him, knocking him over.

Now it's my turn to do the kicking.

I kick Igor in the face as hard as I can. I hear a snap as his head flies backward.

He crumples to the ground.

I turn to her. I'm so scared right now. "Are you okay?"

"I think I'm okay." She's crying. "Drakken, watch out!"

I spin around and Slavoj slashes at me with a knife. It cuts my shirt open. If he cut me, I can't feel it.

He slashes again.

I jump back.

"Stop it!" she yells.

Slavoj slashes again and again.

I don't know what to do. I know how to wrestle. Not fight someone with a knife. I dance from side to side. I can barely avoid the knife. He's going to cut me if I don't do something—

Whack!

Slavoj stumbles, confused. "What did you do?"

"Put the knife down," she warns. She holds a rock in her hand.

Slavoj touches his forehead and looks at his bloody fingers. "You threw a rock at me." He says it like he's not sure it actually happened.

"Put the knife down," she hisses, "or I'll throw another one."

I kick Slavoj in the wrist and the knife flies out of his hand.

Now Slavoj is pissed. "You threw a rock at me, bitch! You can't throw a rock at me!" At least he doesn't have the knife. "You bitch! I'm bleeding!" He shouts it. "I'M BLEEDING!!" He runs right at her.

I tackle him before he hits her and land on top of him really hard.

"Get off me, asshole!" he screams. "I'm gonna kill you!"

He writhes beneath me. I try to pin him down to make him stop, but he's going crazy.

Oleg stands up and grunts, "You're gonna pay for that, Drakken."

Igor holds Slavoj's knife. When did he pick up the knife? I have no idea. Blood runs from his nose and he looks pissed as hell.

I can't defend myself against both of them if I'm on the ground with Slavoj. I jump to my feet, releasing Slavoj.

He spins around in the dirt, his arm underneath his shirt.

BOOM!!!!!

Everybody jumps.

Who has a gun?

I whip my head around, wondering if I'm going to see a bloody bullet hole in my stomach. Or in her stomach. Oleg and Igor look startled. I glance at Slavoj, expecting to see a gun pointing at my heart.

Or hers.

But Slavoj is just cradling his hand to his stomach like it's hurt.

Everyone is frozen in place.

A second later, I realize the boom was just another fighter jet overhead.

"Let's go, Drakken," she whines in fear and pulls on me.

We run to our bicycles and jump on.

"Come back here!" Slavoj shouts.

"Go!" I hiss at her.

We both pedal as hard as we can.

Oleg and Igor lumber after us, but they're too slow because they're both all beat up.

"I'm gonna kill you!" Slavoj shouts from where he slumps. "I'm never gonna forget this, Drakken! Do you hear me?! I'm gonna kill both of you! I'll tell my dad to hire a hit man, and he'll shoot you when you're asleep! He'll sneak into your houses and he'll kill you both!"

Chapter 2

RIVER

The main pool at the Beverly Hills Resort is called the Sunset Pool. Its invisible Infinity edge faces the Pacific Ocean and it's up on a hillside, so resort guests can relax in the water at either of the two poolside bars and watch the sun go down every evening while sipping cocktails.

It's pretty darn romantic.

If you're with someone.

At the moment, the calm water in the blue pool is smooth and glassy. No guests are using it and no one is on the deck except me.

Whenever I'm mopey, which is just about every day for the past several weeks, I come out here between clients.

Alone.

I reach into my pocket and pull out the origami butterfly Drakken made for me out of a hundred dollar bill way back when. I examine it in the palm of my hand. It sits motionless, unable to fly. I slide it back into my pocket for safe keeping.

It's the only token I have from Drakken, aside from the wilted bouquet of roses. I planned on saving them, but when Drakken disappeared, having dying roses around felt too ominously symbolic, so I got rid of them.

As always, the balcony of the Sunset Suite way up on the twentieth floor is empty.

Like my heart.

I haven't seen Drakken a single time since he freaked out that day. I don't have the courage to go up to his room and knock. I'm afraid he'll open the door and shout in my face like before.

"GO!!!!"

I couldn't deal with that a second time.

I'm pretty sure he's still staying at the hotel because his red Lamborghini is always parked in the valet section of the underground garage.

But I never see *him*.

He's become a ghost.

I feel like I've become a ghost too. I'm back to being the half-dead version of myself that I was post-Cage and pre-Drakken.

It feels awful.

Like something wonderful was taken away from me. Something essential.

I'm barely studying for my classes at LACC, and the last thing on my mind is building my own massage business whenever I finish my Associates Degree. It takes everything I have just to get out of bed every morning and drag my ass through my work day.

But I do.

Like I did when Cage walked out.

I keep going.

Because I don't know what else to do.

"There you are!" Finch hollers from the far side of the pool. She strides across the smooth cement. "I should've guessed you'd be out here." She stands beside me, hands folded behind her back, looking up at the windows of the Sunset Suite. She says thoughtfully, "Do you ever feel like you're some peasant woman staring up at the castle tower, hoping the prince will notice you and come down?"

"Huh?" I frown, "What are you talking about?"

"Nothing," she grins. "How are you feeling today?"

"Like crap," I groan.

"Maybe this'll help," Finch grins and holds out a small white box tied with a shiny white ribbon.

"Awww, that's sweet, Finch. Did you get me a present?"

"*I* didn't. Someone dropped it off at the concierge desk this morning before I got here. Based on the card, I'd say it's from Mr. Steamy-kova."

Hearing his name makes my skin tingle. I frantically slide the white card out from under the ribbon. It has a silver pinstripe border around exacting hand-written script that reads:

"Rivka"

My heart thumps noticeably in my chest. That ghostly feeling I've had for weeks evaporates instantly, burned away by the bright light of hope.

"What do you think it is?" I ask Finch nervously.

"I have no idea," she smirks, "but I bet if you open it, you'll find out."

"Duh. I'm just afraid it's going to be a goodbye note or something.

Maybe I shouldn't open it."

Finch rolls her eyes, "Open the box, Pandora. I'm sure whatever it is won't be the end of the world."

"Maybe not for you," I frown.

"Like I said," she grins sarcastically. "I'll stand a few feet away in case it's a letter bomb or whatever."

I untie the ribbon and open the box. Inside, lying on a tiny white satin pillow, is a red rose bud in half bloom. "Ooh," I coo, "This is beautiful." I lift the flower out of the box and examine it, twirling the short stem in my fingers.

"Is that a real rose?" she asks curiously.

I rub one of the petals carefully between my thumb and forefinger. "Oh my god," I mutter, "I think it's made out of paper." I hold it up close and inspect it. The intricately folded red and green paper is so finely crafted, it looks almost completely real.

"Wow," Finch marvels, "that's amazing."

I glance inside the box and notice a small hand-written note resting on the satin pillow. It reads:

"Very sorry for bad day. I make rose for you. I hope one is no too much. —Drakka."

Whoa.

I can't believe I thought he'd forgotten me. The chasm of disconnect between us has been bridged by this gift.

Now if I could only find the man.

Chapter 3

RIVER

Over the course of the work day, I try calling Drakken's room numerous times while my hope still burns bright. He never answers. I desperately want to thank him for the origami rose and apologize for whatever I did that freaked him out in the Sunset Suite.

Sadly, Drakken is a man who does not want to be found.

By the end of the day, my hope has been snuffed out. I trudge toward the elevators, heading home. Maybe I'll see Drakken tomorrow.

Or next week.

Or never.

Sigh.

While I wait for the elevator, I notice the commotion of dozens of voices echoing across the lobby from the hallway that leads to the south wing of the resort.

That's where the ballroom and the private meeting rooms are located. I wonder what's going on. The Beverly Hills Resort often hosts really cool movie and music industry events. I've seen famous actors and musicians wandering the halls here plenty of times.

Hmmm.

I'm not exactly looking forward to doing my Finance and Accounting homework tonight, and I would be remiss if I didn't at least peek at the action in the south wing. I mean, what if it's a wrap party for the final season of Sons Of Anarchy and Charlie Hunnam is there?

I'd hate to miss that.

Sounds like a valid reason to procrastinate. I stroll across the lobby and down the hallway to investigate.

Only one of the large meeting rooms in the south wing is in use tonight.

The Rodeo Room.

Waiters in black and white formal outfits come and go through the double doors carrying trays of hors d'oeuvres and glasses of champagne. Someone is celebrating something.

A number of men and women in tuxedos and stylish evening gowns mill around the entrance. More people chat and drink inside.

I recognize one of the passing waitresses. "Psst! Melanie! Come here a second." I wave her over to where I stand across from the doors.

She smiles, "Oh, hey River! What's up?"

"What's going on in there? It sounds like a huge party."

"Totally," she rolls her eyes. "Some of the men are super grabby. I've got pinch marks on my ass," she winks.

"Any movie stars or whatever?"

"No. It's some big deal business thing. But some of the guys are pretty cute, and the guy who is paying for everything is super hot." she grins.

"Really?"

"Yeah. But good luck getting a minute with him. I tried to chat him up, but it seems like every woman in the room is vying for his attention."

"He must be pretty hot," I smile.

"I have scorch marks on my panties just from looking at him," Melanie winks.

I picture her vagina shooting flames out of it like a blow torch that burns right through her panties. I stifle a giggle.

"What?" Melanie asks, confused.

"Nothing," I giggle again and shake my head.

She shrugs her shoulders, "Anyway, I gotta get back to the kitchen. Catch you later." She walks back up the hallway.

Curious about Mr. Panty Scorcher, I edge my way toward the meeting room's crowded entrance. I do my best not to be too obvious, but my white spa uniform makes me stick out like a sore thumb.

But I can still look.

The Rodeo Room is set up for a fancy banquet and the room is packed with people. A large projection screen hangs above a podium. On the screen is a huge logo that has a tilted ellipse looping around the words: Gravity Unlimited.

A crowd of gorgeous and expensively dressed women stand off to the side of the podium. There's a lot of hair tossing and boob thrusting. My guess is they're all talking to Mr. Panty Scorcher. Whoever he is, I hope he's wearing a fire retardant tuxedo. He's got enough vaginal fire power surrounding him to burn down the building.

I snicker to myself at the image.

"Good evening, ladies and gentlemen," a woman says on the microphone attached to the podium. "Thank you all so much for being here tonight to celebrate this special occasion."

I realize the woman is Svetlana. Drakken's assistant. If she's here, maybe that means...

Svetlana continues, "I'm sure you are all excited to hear a word from our guest of honor. Drakken, would you like to say a few words?"

Everyone in the room begins clapping enthusiastically.

Drakken emerges from the crowd of gorgeous women to the side of the podium with a huge grin on his face. He's wearing a tuxedo but he looks like a kid who just walked out of a candy store carrying an armload of candy-headed bimbos.

What happened to Freaked Out Drakken? What happened to wall punching Drakken? What happened to *"Is too much!"* Drakken? Right now he looks like *"Is not enough bimbos!"* Drakken.

My mouth sours and my stomach knots as I think about it.

I am so dense.

No wonder I haven't seen Drakken in weeks. He's probably been busy with all these bimbos and a hundred others. I wouldn't be surprised if he's been seeing ten different bimbos a day. Maybe he really is a pimp or a drug czar. Or maybe he's in the boob job business. That would explain all the boob jobs in the room *and* the logo on the projection screen. Gravity Unlimited sounds like a breast implant manufacturing company to me.

Men are all alike.

They prioritize the bimbos.

Drakken leans over the microphone, which squeals momentarily before he speaks, "Hi, everybody. I happy to see you tonight."

Everyone in the room claps and claps for Drakken.

He grins from ear to ear. He's the happiest man ever. He doesn't seem sad or mopey. Based on how he's acting, I doubt it bothers him in the slightest that he hasn't seen or heard from me in forever.

He motions for the crowd to quiet and says, "Is good, is good." He chuckles, "You—*you're,*" he corrects himself, "very nice. Thank you. Is good," he laughs, overcome by the warm reception.

I wince, remembering how I taught him the difference between 'you' and 'your' and 'you're'. He offered to pay me for English lessons that day. But it seems like he's forgotten all about his offer and anything to do with me.

Do I need to totally re-evaluate my taste in men? I seem to always have a thing for the unavailable ones.

I roll my eyes at myself and they start to water.

It's not like I pick who I fall for.

Those ice blue eyes…

No matter how much I hate Drakken right now, he made me feel alive. For the first time since Cage left, Drakken made me feel like everything was going to be okay. Better than okay. Amazing, in fact.

That flow…

That's why I want to stay right where I'm standing. This is obviously an important event. I want to be here for Drakken. He doesn't look like he needs me right this second, but watching him at the podium, talking to this crowd, somehow I sense that he needs me. It's foolish, but it's what I feel. At the same time, the uncertainty and the doubt and the overwhelming memories are twisting my heart and stomach into a knotted mess.

IS TOO MUCH!!!

I can't deal with this right now. I need some space and some time to think.

I turn to go.

"Rivka?"

That one word hangs in the sudden silence. That one word is all it takes to erase weeks worth of gloominess. That one word is enough to ease the knot in my stomach and give me wings. That one word lifts me up and my heart soars.

I suddenly feel intensely alive, as if I'm waking from some kind of dismal emotional hibernation.

I whip back to face the doors to the Rodeo Room.

Two men in tuxedos close them in my face.

On each door hangs a placard that reads:

PRIVATE EVENT

I stand in the south wing lobby, totally alone.

My heart plummets.

If that wasn't an omen, I don't know what is. The world is trying to tell me loud and clear that Drakken is not going to be a part of my life.

Maybe I need to start listening.

Chapter 4

RIVER

My head hangs while I trudge toward the main lobby.

I'm done.

I'm going home.

My heart has been yanked all over the place today. I need my bed, I need a good ugly cry, and I need sleep. I can't wait for this dreary day to be over forever.

It's the worst day I've ever had in my entire twenty three years of life.

My purse hangs on my sagging shoulder like it weighs a ton. It slides off and I catch the strap in my hand. It literally drags along the carpeted hallway. I feel like I can barely stand up, let alone put one foot in front of the other. Any second I'm going to collapse onto the carpet and curl into the fetal position and sob right in the middle of *The* Beverly Hills Resort.

I'm sure no one will mind.

I know it's stupid I feel this heartbroken. It's probably just hormones.

I try to reason with myself. Drakken and I don't have any sort of relationship. We haven't even gone out on an official date. He doesn't owe me anything. Not even an explanation. Sure, we hooked up. But people hook up all the time without things going anywhere. Maybe Drakken and I aren't any different. Usually, people are okay with it. For whatever reason, I'm not.

This feels like the end of my world.

Maybe I just need to grow up and quit acting like a hormonal teenager.

Easier said than done.

"Rivka?"

My heart ignites with shining hope when I hear his voice. I'm instantly wide awake and energized.

I slowly turn.

Drakken stands behind me in the empty hallway. He looks completely at home in his stylish tuxedo. Up close, the combination of confidence and elegance is destructively dashing. No wonder the bimbos in the meeting room were drooling.

I am too.

Now that he's here.

"Hey," I say shyly.

"I very happy to see you, Rivka. I miss you happy—*your* happy eyes." He pauses and grins, "You taught me that."

I can only nod. My heart flies somewhere high above my body.

The distance between us is infinite, farther than the farthest star. His blue eyes shine at me across the vast chasm like ghostly supernovas, bluish pinpricks that seem so small and insignificant when seen from afar. But I know up close those twin blue stars have the power to shatter worlds.

He takes a tentative step toward me. Then another, and another, until he conquers time and space and infinity with ease and grace.

He raises his hand and cups my chin. He murmurs in a soft, boyish voice, "I miss your happy eyes, Rivka. And I miss you." He leans toward me, his eyes dancing across my lips.

I can't speak.

I can't think.

I can't breathe.

But I can kiss.

Our lips touch and his passion burns away all my doubts. His tongue plunges past the border of my lips, invading my mouth with his desperate need. He breathes his desire into me like dragon's fire, his tongue sweeping around violently, attacking mine until I have no choice but to submit to the overwhelming force. I yield willingly, allowing him to consume my own burning desire and make it his own. His vicious invasion has destroyed my defenses and stolen my equilibrium. Up becomes down, black becomes white, and hot becomes cold as the world spins off its axis and time flows in reverse. The entire universe ceases to exist, save Drakken and I.

"Is so good," he murmurs.

"So good," I whisper.

Today is the best day I've ever had in my entire life, and that's not my hormones talking.

Reluctantly, we break the kiss and Drakken leans his head down and kisses the top of mine. His arms wrap around me and I snuggle my cheek against his chest. It's hard beneath the silky smooth material of his tuxedo. His hand caresses my hair gently and I realize his chest isn't the only hard thing about Drakken. His rigid erection is obvious and proud and presses pleasantly against my stomach.

After everything that has happened between us, I should be confused right now. *He* should be confused.

But I'm not. He's not.

We are not.

Everything makes perfect sense.

Everything is in its place.

I bask in the perfection of this moment and hope that it lasts forever.

"Drakken!" Svetlana hisses. "What are you doing?" She stands somewhere behind Drakken. I can't see her but I recognize her evil voice instantly.

I feel Drakken's arms around me loosen slightly.

There went my moment.

I hate Svetlana.

Drakken kisses the top of my head softly and turns to face her. He still has an arm around my waist so I don't feel completely abandoned.

Svetlana fumes, "You can't walk out in the middle of a business dinner like that! Everyone is waiting for you to finish your speech!"

"Is okay," Drakken says dismissively, like it's no big deal.

"It's not okay! These people have certain expectations. You can't act like this. Not if you expect them to take you seriously."

"Svetlana, is..." Drakken switches to his own language. He speaks rapid-fire.

Svetlana responds at length, clearly agitated.

I have no idea what they're talking about. But Drakken's demeanor is calm, collected, rational. Without the hindrance of speaking in English, his extreme confidence and total competence are obvious.

When Drakken finishes, Svetlana sighs and throws her hands in the air, "Okay. It's your business, Drakkozsha, not mine. You do what you want." She shifts her gaze to me and drills me with her eyes while she speaks to Drakken, "But I would hate to see you throw everything away for no good reason, Drakkozsha."

Obviously, I'm the 'no good reason.'

Obviously, she's just jealous. And very possessive when it comes to Drakken. Whatever. And why does she keep calling him Drakkozsha? Is she really just his assistant? Or did they use to date or something? Who knows. Maybe she's still burning a candle for him. I can relate. Whatever the case, she obviously doesn't like me. Not one bit.

She turns and strides back toward the meeting room.

"Sorry for her," Drakken says. He turns to face me and holds both my hands in both of his. "And sorry for me. I am in Long Beach and San Diego for three week. No at hotel. And no massage. Very much business."

It takes me a moment to figure it out. "Do you mean you *were* in Long Beach for three weeks? On business? Until now?"

"Yes, yes," he nods emphatically. "I *were* in Long Beach until three weeks."

I'm still confused when he says 'until', but I'm gonna assume he got the 'were' part correct.

"I miss you ever day, Rivka. Ever night, I think about your eyes. When I sleep, I dream about you. You on my mind ever minute. Is hard for me to work. I think of you, you, you. And me anger, last day I see you. I very sorry for me anger. Is hard for you, yes?"

"It's okay," I soothe. With his hands holding mine, with his starlit eyes shining into me, *everything* is okay.

"On day, I make very mad. I very sorry." His ice blue eyes twinkle wetly and glow bright with hope.

His hope gives me strength. "It's okay, Drakka," I mutter, my voice tight with emotion.

He pauses and chuckles, blinking away tears. One rolls down his cheek and he smears it with the back of his hand while still holding mine. It's like he doesn't want to let go of me. He grins with a mixture of joy and sadness, "I have big business, Rivka. I is big man. Many people look at me for what to do. Before you, I tell people ever day, 'do this,' and 'do that.' Is easy. I all way have answer for ever questions. After I meet you, I have no answer for them!" He smiles, seemingly confused. "I no to tell people, 'I sad about pretty massage girl. I mad to her and now I no see her." He laughs, now with obvious relief. "But I see you now, Rivka. Now I very happy."

"I'm happy too, Drakken." I lean into him and wrap my arms around his back. I snuggle into his chest.

His arms envelope me.

I don't want to be anywhere else except here. I never want to leave his arms. I mutter, "And now you're back?"

"Yes, yes!" he grins that boyish grin like the only thing he cares about is me. "I is back for long time."

"You mean *am* back," I grin.

His brows knit, "*Am* back?"

"Yup. *Am* back. You say, 'I *am* back for *a* long time.'" I giggle as I say it.

"I *am* back for *a* long time." He chuckles, "You *am* very good English teacher, Rivka."

"No," I giggle again, "You say, 'You *are a* very good English teacher, Rivka'"

I can't believe I'm standing in the middle of *The* Beverly Hills Resort, in the arms of the most handsome man on the planet, giving him English lessons. It's too weird. But I love it.

"Oh," he smiles. "Sorry. You *are a* very good English teacher."

"Very good," I grin.

"You teach me more English, okay? I pay."

I wrinkle my nose. "What, now?"

"No," he chuckles. "I have speech. When time is good?"

"Oh, um evenings and weekends, I guess. But I'm pretty busy with school." I don't know when I'll possibly find the time, but for Drakken, I will.

"You with school?" he asks. "For English?"

"No," I snicker. "Business school."

"Oh, I know business very good. You stop school. I teach you business good, for no money. And you teach me English, and I pay."

"I can't quit school!" I laugh.

"Okay, okay," he smiles. "You keep school. But I pay you for English teach. Is good, yes?"

"Okay," I smile. I have no idea where I'm going to find the time to teach him English, but I'll squeeze it in somehow. How could I not?

"What is you—*your* phone number?" He pulls his smart phone out of his tuxedo. I tell him my number and he punches it into his phone. Then he holds his phone to his ear.

My phone rings in my purse. "Is that you calling?"

"Yes," he grins, "is me. Please say hello, okay?"

Even though it's totally corny, I pull my phone out of my purse and answer with a huge grin on my face, "Hello?"

"Hello?" Drakken says. "Is pretty girl Rivka?"

"Yes," I grin up at him from under my eyebrows. This is ridiculous, but I'm totally into it. Not everything I do has to be all grown up and adult.

"You teach me English, okay?"

"I would love to."

"Okay. I call soon and we make time, okay?"

"Okay."

"Bye now, I have speech, okay?"

"Bye," I smile and end the call.

He chuckles and slides his phone into his tux.

I love that this big bad business guy can act like a giddy teenager and share his feelings with me.

"Okay, I go now. I have speech in room. Do you want to come?"

"Oh, um, I should probably go. I have a ton of homework tonight." If I want to give lessons to Drakken, I'll have to get a jump on my own studies or I'll fall behind in no time.

He waves his hand dismissively, "I say I teach you good business, okay?"

"Okay," I grin.

He leans down and kisses me softly.

When he pulls away, his ice blue eyes search mine. "Is good?"

"Is good," I smile. "Everything is good."

Chapter 5

RIVER

The next morning, I take the elevator up to Drakken's room. I've got about five minutes before I need to be in the spa or I'll be late for work, so it's just enough time to see him and say hello.

I hope he doesn't mind.

I knock on the door.

A moment later it opens.

Drakken is dressed in a suit with a tie hanging loose around his neck. His face is hard. When he recognizes me, his stoney expression softens. "Rivka!" he says breathlessly, happily surprised. "I is, uh, *am* late. For meeting."

I suddenly feel like I'm in his way. Maybe I should've waited until he called before barging up here.

He closes the door of the Sunset Suite behind him. "You walk with me?"

"Oh, uh, okay," I say nervously.

He strides down the hallway so quickly, I practically have to jog to keep up.

"I has big meeting in downtown. Traffic very bad. Accident on freeway."

"Sorry," I wince.

When we arrive at the elevator landing, he jams the down button impatiently.

I say, "Maybe I should take the stairs and get out of your hair."

"You are not in my hair," he frowns while knotting his tie with practiced ease.

I chuckle, "It's a saying. I don't want to get in your way."

He grins, "Is okay. Go with me on elevator, okay?" His face softens as he finishes with his tie. "Is all time I has. I need for see you, okay?"

I can't say no to that face. "Okay."

The elevator dings and the doors open. We step inside.

I press the L button.

"Sorry for no time," he sighs heavily. "I want for more."

"It's okay." I rub his back affectionately.

He leans toward the panel, about to press the DOOR CLOSE button. He stops himself and cocks his head to the side and winks at me. "I make more time, okay?" He presses every button on the panel.

"Drakken!" I giggle.

When the door closes, he turns to me, a hot look darkening his brows. He stalks toward me.

"Drakken," I gasp, "what are you doing?"

He backs me into the corner. "I kiss you, okay?"

I nod, "Okay."

The next thing I know, his hot mouth is devouring mine. He slides his hard hand up under my spa uniform, squeezing my breast through my bra as he licks my jaw and kisses my neck and pins me against the mirrored wall.

With mirrors on opposing walls of the elevator, we're surrounded by the reflection of thousands of Drakkens ravaging thousands of willing Rivers. He and I burn with enough real passion for a million imaginary Drakkens and Rivers.

"Oh, Drakkozsha," I moan.

Ding!

The doors of the elevator open on the nineteenth floor. No one is waiting on the landing.

I reach under Drakken's suit jacket and clutch his dress shirt, pulling him into me. My leg wraps around the back of his thigh. I feel his hard erection straining against my pelvis.

The elevators doors close slowly and the descent begins again.

Ding!

Eighteenth floor.

The doors open. No one on the landing.

By now, I am totally turned on.

I grind my hot wet folds against his hardness through the barrier of our clothes, tilting my hips up and down. A wash of electrical pleasure courses through me.

Drakken thrusts into me, oblivious, his sense stolen away by our passion.

Ding!

Seventeen.

Nobody there.

I clasp his head in my hands and lift his face up until we are nose to nose.

His brows are knit in a fury of animalistic desire, his lips torn back across savagely clenched teeth.

I bite my lower lip and narrow my eyes.

Our mouths crash together again. His tongue spears through my lips and he fills me up.

Ding!

Sixteen.

Drakken grabs my ass and pounds his bound up cock between my open legs.

I grab the waist high railing behind me and brace myself while Drakken grinds and grinds.

He lifts me up. I arch my back, still holding the railing as he pulls me away from the wall.

Ding!

Fifteen.

Both my legs are now wrapped around Drakken's waist. He supports my full weight with his powerful hands. I release the railing and we're standing in the center of the elevator. My arms wrap around his neck and we devour each other's mouths.

Ding!

Fourteen.

"Ay dios mio!" one of the hotel maids gasps.

"Shit!' I whisper and duck my head down and bury it against Drakken's neck. He steps toward the panel of buttons and machine guns the DOOR CLOSE button with his finger.

When the doors close, I'm giggling as I release my legs and slide down Drakken until my feet touch the floor. Before I gain my balance, Drakken drives me relentlessly back into the corner.

His hand slides down the front of my uniform pants, under the elastic band of my thong, down the front of my mound, and right inside my waiting wetness.

"Oh..." I sigh. "Oh, oh, oh..."

His finger pumps into me several times before he slides it out and teases my clit.

I grab Drakken's hard cock through his slacks and squeeze it.

He throws his head back and groans. His finger slides back inside me. I squeeze my eyes shut and disappear into intense and pleasurable darkness as we travel past the nonexistent thirteenth floor.

Ding!

Twelve.

"I'm gonna come, Drakka," I gasp. "Don't stop, I'm gonna come."

His thumb swirls around my clit. His forceful hand stretches out the waistband of my uniform pants and pushes them down. They're going to be sagging around my knees by the time we finish.

Ding!

Eleven.

I bite my lip and tilt my chin down, again burying my face in Drakken's chest, trying to silence the pleasure racing through me. "Drakka, oh, Drakka, it's, oh, don't stop, oh god, ohgod, ohgodohgodoh—"

Ding!

Ten.

"Oh my god!" an old woman's voice blurts. "That man is attacking that woman!"

"What?" an old man's voice crackles with fear.

Whoops.

Maybe this was a bad idea.

The doors start to close.

"Stop them, Harry!" the old woman shouts.

I peak over Drakken's shoulder and see the old man raise his cane, rattling it between the elevator doors until they shudder back open.

The old man growls, "Get your hands off her, young man!"

Drakken slowly slides his hand out of my pants and mumbles, "I, uh..."

I peak over Drakken's shoulder.

Harry raises his cane high overhead and shakes it vigorously. "Let her go!"

"Wait!" I shout. "Stop! It's okay! I'm okay! He's not attacking me!"

Harry looks confused.

The elevator doors bump against Harry's shoulders.

"Seriously," I plead, "I'm fine. We were just..." I'm too ashamed to say anything.

The old man and woman look back and forth between themselves and us.

"What's going on, you two?" Harry demands.

Drakken lets out a lazy chuckle. To me he mutters, "You tell. I don't have good words."

"Me?" I argue.

Harry barks, "I want an explanation. On the double!"

I laugh into Drakken's chest. I'm too embarrassed to face the old man.

After a moment, the old woman says, "Leave them alone, Harry. I think it's their honeymoon."

Dumbfounded, Harry says, "I don't remember our honeymoon being like this, Edna."

"We'll wait for the next elevator," Edna says with obvious amusement. "Then you can attack me and make up for lost time," she giggles bashfully.

"Oh!" Harry gasps, embarrassed.

The doors close.

Drakken and I erupt into guilty laughter.

Ding!

Nine.

I lean against the back wall. Drakken stands inches away. I trace my finger lazily across his shirt covered chest.

Ding!

Eight.

"You're still hard," I marvel.

"Is good," he grins.

"I'll say…" I press my palm against it, feeling the heat soaking through his slacks. Can I give him a blowjob and make him come before we reach the lobby? I *want* to. But I don't know if we have time.

I glance up at him and smile.

His hot blue eyes bore into me. His cocky gorgeous smile grows wide and inviting.

Ding!

Seven.

If I'm going to go down on him, I better get going before the elevator goes down all the way.

We're on the seventh floor.

No one is in sight.

You know what they say about lucky sevens.

It's time for Drakken to get lucky.

I push him toward the open doors until he stands between them. I frantically unzip his slacks and undo the buckle of his slim belt.

He braces his hands against the elevator doors.

I grab the waistband of his boxer briefs with both hands and yank down, kneeling in front of him. His cock shoots out, nearly hitting my nose as it springs up.

My mouth dives down and I engulf him with my lips.

"Ahhhhhh!!!" He throws his head back as I work the shaft, the head, all of it at once.

I taste pre-cum and he starts to twitch.

Drakken hasn't been a minute man in the past, but now would be a good time for him to be prompt.

The elevator doors rattle, trying to close, then reopen.

I give Drakken everything I've got.

His cock is hot, hard, and straining against my tongue.

Drakken moans out, "Fuuuuuuuuuhhhhhhccccckkkkk!!! Is so good!!!"

Speaking of fucking, I wonder when he picked up that word. And speaking of fucking, I need him to fuck me. Badly. Before I can ponder whether that's a good idea or not, the sound of people talking echoes up the hallway. They're getting closer.

Shizz!

I shoot to my feet and yank Drakken into the elevator. By the lapels. Not by his man handle. I don't want to hurt him.

Drakken stumbles into the corner of the elevator, his face slack, his eyes rolled back into his head, his knees buckling. His cock reaches skyward. The tip is dark purple. I know what comes next.

Cum.

Laughter from the hallway.

Why aren't the doors closing?

One of the people walking down the hallway exclaims, "I can't believe you called him that!"

They're right around the corner!

Fudge!

I hammer the DOOR CLOSE button.

They finally do.

Any second, Drakken is going to explode and white wash the entire elevator. It'll probably get all over his suit too, and he's as late for work as I am. I can think of only one receptacle that is readily available to prevent a mess.

My mouth.

Oddly, time slows down as I ponder the ridiculousness of this situation. If I don't get to him in time, he's going to paint my face. There's no way I'm walking into the spa covered in money shot. I don't have time for a detour to the ladies room. I lunge at Drakken with my mouth wide open.

I grab his shaft and slam my mouth over the head. Cum fires into the back of my throat. I swallow and moan and grunt in the most unladylike way possible, wanting all of it. Partially because I always finish what I start, and partially because I don't want to leave a mess.

Of course, it never once occurs to me to pull the EMERGENCY STOP button to buy us more time because there is no stopping Drakken's cock. It is *loaded* with cum.

Ding!

Six.

I'm on my knees, deep throating Drakken in the corner.

Thank the stars no one gets on now. The doors close.

Drakken twitches into my mouth. More cum dribbles onto my tongue.

Ding!

Five.

More cum *and* more coming.

Shizz!

How much does he have! I swallow and swallow, taking it all in.

Ding!

Four.

I lick him as clean as I can and stuff his slackening cock into his boxer briefs.

Drakken is finally starting to regain control of his limbs. He tucks in his shirt and starts zipping and buckling.

Ding!

Three.

I smooth my hair and my uniform shirt and dab my tongue at the corners of my mouth, checking for errant cum. "I hope I don't have a client waiting for me in the spa," I mutter.

Drakken buttons his suit jacket and straightens his tie. "Sorry for I make you late."

I grin, "It was totally worth it. I hope you're not too late?"

He checks his expensive gold watch. "Maybe, maybe no. But I go fast, okay? For traffic."

"Okay."

Ding!

Two.

He kisses me briefly. "I call you for Saturday, okay? You teach English, please?"

"I look forward to it," I smile.

Ding!

One.

"Oh! Hey, Riv," Finch smiles, standing in the lobby next to a bellman's cart loaded with designer luggage. Her eyes dance between me and Drakken. She arches her eyebrows with suspicious glee.

I shoot her a "I didn't just give him a blowjob" look.

She grins.

A disheveled but well-dressed Chinese couple stands next to Finch, waiting impatiently. They look like they just flew in from the other side of the globe.

"Excuse us," I say as I squeeze past them and turn toward the spa.

Drakken strolls out of the elevator and turns toward the front doors.

When I reach the spa waiting area, Luciana stands with her hands on her hips. "There you are," she says reproachfully. "I've been looking all over for you. Mrs. Ragsdale wants to know what is taking you so long," she demands. "She's been waiting for over *ten* minutes."

Ooh. Ten whole minutes. Mrs. Ragsdale is *so* annoying. I restrain an eye roll. "Sorry. There was uh…an *explosion* on my way to work."

"An explosion?" Luciana blurts.

"I mean, some pipe burst. You know, one of the really big ones?"

"I'm afraid I don't," Luciana chuckles doubtfully and eyes me suspiciously.

Jocelyn sits behind the reception desk. She chews with amusement on the end of her pen. She has no idea what just happened in the elevator. So why does the look on her face say she does?

So much for being careful at work.

I tap my chin thoughtfully, "What do they call the really big pipes? Oh yeah, a water main," I grin. "That's it. The water main burst and the streets were *flooded*. It was a huge mess. I had to take the long way to get here."

That's my sticky story and I'm sticking to it.

Chapter 6

RIVER

"Can I cream in your coffee?" Drakken asks innocently, holding up the aluminum pitcher of half-and-half.

One of the busy baristas behind the counter makes a face and stifles a giggle when she overhears Drakken's odd question.

We're inside Bean There Done That, my favorite neighborhood coffee shop, about to start our first English lesson, and none too soon.

"Drakken!" I snicker, "You can't offer to *cream* in my coffee! That makes it sound sexual, like you're offering to put—" I lower my voice to a whisper and lean toward him, "—your, um, *cum* in my coffee."

Drakken frowns, confused, "So I say, would you like me to *come* in your coffee?"

The barista's eyes goggle and she blurts a short laugh.

"No, no, no!" I laugh squeakily and mutter, "You don't want to *come* in my coffee either!"

Drakken shakes his head, "I not understand."

"Hold on a second." I don't want to explain the difference between cream, come, and cum within earshot of the baristas and the customers in line, so I grab the pitcher from Drakken, pour my own cream, then cap my caramel macchiato.

"Table by window is open. We sit there, yes?"

"Okay." I follow him to the table and stare at his butt.

It looks perfect in his tight dark blue jeans. He also wears a dark gray cashmere V neck sweater and stylish black leather shoes. This is the first time I've seen Drakken wearing something other than a suit or tuxedo. I imagine he bought the outfit for our English lessons.

Even dressed down, I still feel under dressed in my five dollar fitted Old Navy T-shirt and skinny jeans. What can I say? My wardrobe budget is severely limited. At least I'm not wearing my spa uniform for once.

Drakken pulls out my chair for me, "You look very good today, Rivka."

"Awww, thank you, Drakka," I smile as I sit down.

He drops into the chair across from me. His legs are so long that his knees bump against mine. "I sorry," he smiles.

"No worries," I grin. "So, where were we?"

Drakken frowns, "I not understand word 'come'. Come is mean to go to here or there, yes?"

With a smile on my face, I sip my caramel macchiato, which now has the perfect amount of cum in it, I mean cream. I nod, "Uh huh."

"I say, uh…" Drakken looks out the window and sees a random guy walking a black labrador along the sidewalk, "I say to man, 'Come here, man.' Or man say to dog, 'Come here, dog.' Yes? Is that how you make man come?"

I snicker to myself, thinking of the various ways to make a man come, none of which involve black labs or leashes. What can I say? I'm plain vanilla in the bedroom *and* the elevator.

Drakken grins. "What is funny?"

"Nothing," I snicker.

"Okay. So tell me, how do I make come?"

I snicker again. "Ahhh…" Do I really want to have a grammatical discussion about the difference between 'come' and 'cum' in the middle of a crowded coffee shop? YOLO. I lean over the table and whisper, "Come also means *orgasm*."

"Orgasm?" Drakken says a bit too loudly. "Maybe I know this word. Is, how you say, man and woman make, uh, make sex. At end of sex is orgasm, yes?"

I nod, blushing, thinking a million different dirty thoughts.

The hipster guy scrolling through his smart phone at the table next to ours glances over, clearly eavesdropping.

Drakken's brows knit thoughtfully, "So, come is also orgasm?"

I nod again, on the verge of folding my arms on top of the little round table and burying my face out of embarrassment.

He asks, "At end of sex is come, yes?"

I snicker, "Lots of cum."

Drakken nods knowingly, "All woman like much comes for sex, yes?"

Hipster guy snickers, totally listening but pretending not to.

I can't believe Drakken and I are having this discussion. I'm glowing red. Whatever. I'm sure hipster guy and everyone else inside Bean There Done That knows about the birds and the bees. I whisper, "Yes, women like to come."

Drakken grins, "You like come, yes?"

This is so embarrassing but it's also hilarious. I laugh out loud.

Hipster guy chuckles and shakes his head, trying hard to concentrate on his smart phone but failing.

"Is okay to like come, yes? Man like come too, yes? Man like come very much."

Hipster laughs noticeably.

This conversation is ridiculous. Is Drakken doing this on purpose? He has to be. He isn't *this* dense.

Drakken frowns, "I say wrong?"

My forehead bonks against the table top and I roll it from side to side, giggling hysterically.

Drakken chuckles, "You are crazy girl."

I sit up and try to get a hold of myself. My eyes are watering.

Drakken's blue eyes twinkle with amusement while he sips his cup of coffee, which he filled with cum earlier. I mean cream.

I start to giggle and fall face forward again.

Drakken's phone rings. He pulls it out of the pocket of his jeans and looks at the incoming number. "Is business. Important call. I talk now, okay?"

I lift my head off the table, still grinning from ear to ear and say, "Sure."

Drakken stands up and walks outside.

Chapter 7

RIVER

While I wait for Drakken to finish his call outside, I glance around at all the funky original art hanging on the walls of Bean There Done That. This month, all the paintings depict cats wearing Victorian era ball gowns with huge hoop skirts. It makes me think of book titles like *Sense and Sensibility and Cats*, or *Pride and Prejudice and Cats*. Both sound hilarious. If no one has written them, someone should.

"Hey, Riv. What are you doing here?"

I twist back around in my seat.

Cage stands there with a messenger bag slung over his shoulder.

Great. Just my luck.

"Hey, Cage," I scowl sourly. I have no desire to deal with him right now. My stomach flip-flops unpleasantly. I was having a great time until a second ago.

"Mind if I join you?" he asks, sitting down before I can say no.

Was the scowl on my face not clear enough?

Cage smiles and sets his bag on the cement floor. "I haven't seen you here in forever."

I stopped coming here after Cage and I broke up. "What do you want, Cage?" I sigh despondently. I wish he'd leave.

"I just came in for coffee. I saw you here alone, so I thought I'd join you."

"I'm kind of here with someone."

"I don't see anybody," he chuckles.

I glance out the window and notice that Drakken has wandered off. I assume he's engrossed in his phone call. I hope he comes back soon. I give Cage a sour face, hoping he'll take the hint and leave.

"You look beautiful, Riv."

Cage was never good at figuring out what I wanted.

"Riv, you have no idea how much I've missed seeing you every day. It's like part of *me* is missing without you in my life."

I roll my eyes. "And you're just figuring this out now?"

I thought he'd finally given up on winning me back when he stopped coming into the spa to give me presents a while back. I guess I was wrong.

Although I'd like to tell Cage to leave, I don't want to be completely rude. I decide my strategy will be to say nothing more until he takes the hint that I'm not interested and I'm never going to be.

He emotes, "I miss coming here with you on Saturday mornings to people watch. Remember that? I miss hearing your laugh. It's been so long since I've heard you laugh. I'm starting to forget what it sounds like. I don't want to forget, Riv." He's using his Mr. Charming Matthew McConaughey tone of voice. His romantic artist voice.

I hate that voice.

"More than anything, Riv, I miss seeing your smile."

He can keep on missing my smile because I'm nowhere close to smiling right now. Without thinking, I say sarcastically, "Is that why you stopped coming by the spa to give me presents at work? Because you missed me so much?"

"Ouch," Cage chuckles. "I deserved that. But you have to see it from my perspective."

"No I don't," I sneer.

"You made it clear you didn't want me coming to your work. So I totally respected that. Stone made it clear he didn't want me coming around your apartment. I respected that too."

"Have you heard of the phone?" I say snidely. "It's this wonderful modern invention that has been around since long before the day you left me without any explanation. And there's also this thing called email. You know what email is, don't you? Or texting? You never even texted me, Cage."

He shrugs sheepishly. "Sorry."

"Sorry?" I blurt. I'm about to lay into him when I stop myself.

Why am I letting myself get sucked into a relationship discussion with Cage? This feels way too familiar, and familiar is the last thing I want to feel for Cage. He lost his privileges when he left.

I glance around, looking for Drakken. If he doesn't come back soon, I'm going to excuse myself from this awkwardness and go find him.

"Yes, Riv. I'm sorry." Cage sighs. "I wasn't always the perfect boyfriend to you, but I promise that I always loved you with all my heart. Even when I left, I loved you, Riv."

"Then why did you leave?" I demand with obvious sorrow. I'm on the verge of tears. My heart hammers in my chest like it's trying to jump out of my body and right into Cage's hands. This is so unfair that he's doing this now. "Wait, don't tell me. I don't want to know." I won't allow myself to open up to Cage. He doesn't deserve it. "You need to leave, Cage. Now is not the time for this discussion. I think a more appropriate time would be never."

He winces noticeably. His face collapses into desperate sadness. "But I still love you, Riv." He barely chokes out the words.

Oh, no, no, no.

He can NOT be doing this now.

Despite my anger, his words pierce my heart. I don't want them to, but they do.

I still have unresolved feelings for Cage. That's what happens when someone disappears on you and you don't get closure.

I take a deep breath, trying to calm myself before I blurt out something I regret. I may not be completely over him, but that doesn't mean there's anything left between us worth salvaging.

I sigh, "Why can't you leave me alone? You had plenty of chances to fix things between us a long time ago. If you'd have come back to me a day after you left, or a week, or even a month, we could've worked it out. But it's been nearly a year. I'm done with us. Let me rephrase that. I'm done with *you*, Cage. For good. I'm dating now." That's a bit of an exaggeration. I don't know what exactly Drakken and I have going, but Cage doesn't need to know one way or the other.

Concern withers his face. "Who are you dating?"

"Nobody you know," I say dismissively.

He takes a deep breath and waves his hand weakly. He looks nearly broken. "Look, Riv. I don't care about who you're dating. If you would just let me explain what happened when I—"

"I told you, Cage. It's too late for explanations. You had your chance."

Chapter 8

DRAKKEN

I press END CALL on my phone and sigh with frustration. Running a large business is a monumental task. There are fires to put out seven days a week. But without daily attention, there is no way to make my venture successful.

I wish I could turn off my phone while I spend time with Rivka, but it's simply not an option.

With a sigh I slide my phone into the pocket of my new blue jeans.

It rings the second I do.

I swear, if this call is not from someone important, I'm not going to answer. I want to rejoin Rivka inside so we can discuss English. I was having so much fun with her.

I pull out my phone to examine the number.

313 999 561-666

Every muscle in my body tenses.

Anger boils my blood.

I restrain the urge to hurl my phone over a building. I press IGNORE CALL.

HE is why I can't ignore my business for a single minute.

HE is why my business MUST succeed.

No matter what I do, HE always finds me.

If I don't get my business off the ground, I won't have the resources I need to craft a livable future for myself. HE has so much money, he will follow me to the ends of the earth until he gets what he wants.

Because HE never forgets a promise.

Ever.

The phone rings again.

313 999 561-666

The fire inside me ignites and I growl under my breath, "Stop calling me!"

I grimace and twist the phone in both my hands until the edge of the screen pops off the case. Yet still it rings.

"Stop!" I hiss and twist again. The screen finally crackles into shards and the ringing stops. I keep twisting until the case crumples and breaks. I drop the broken pieces into a garbage can near the front door of the cafe.

A young Asian woman with a bright red streak in her black hair sitting at a table outside the cafe looks up from her laptop and stares at me as if I'm insane.

At the moment, I'm close to it. I seethe with rage, on the verge of exploding. I heave heavy breaths like a steam engine chugging up to speed. I'm going to blast through anything and everything in my path.

All because of HIM.

HE won't stop until he has ruined me completely.

HE will never give me a moment's rest. Ever.

HE will persist until he takes everything I have.

HE took HER from me already.

If HE finds out about Rivka, I fear he will attempt to take her too.

I can't let that happen.

The young Asian woman with the laptop folds her computer shut, picks up her cup of coffee, then scurries inside the cafe.

I can only assume that to her, I look like a fuming monster.

I exhale heavily, trying to regain control. Slowly, I calm and more rational thoughts return.

Perhaps I'm foolish for spending time with Rivka. I'm putting her in tremendous danger, yet she has no idea.

How is that fair to her?

Perhaps I need to let her go before she gets hurt.

Perhaps I need to walk into this cafe right now and tell her I can't see her anymore. Not for English lessons, nor for any other reason.

It's the only way I can truly protect her from HIM.

It will break my heart, but perhaps it's the safest and most loving thing I can possibly do.

Perhaps some time in the future, after my business succeeds, I can reconnect with her. Until that time, it's not fair to put her at risk so that I may indulge my own whims. I clench my fists and resolve myself to the hard thing I must do.

The difference between a boy and a man is that the boy does what he wants, while the man does what he must.

No matter how much it hurts.

With my stone face in place, I march into the cafe.

Chapter 9

RIVER

"Come on, Riv," Cage pleads desperately. "I'm pouring my heart out here. Can't you see that?" He reaches over the table and squeezes my hand. "How can I get through to you?"

"Please don't." I tug my hand away. "You should go, Cage. I don't want to have this conversation with you. Not now, and not ever." Despite my resolve, it hurts me to my heart to push him out of my life when he's pouring out his emotions like this.

"Please, Riv. I need to explain to you what happened. Why I left. Please. Just give me that much, Riv. Please?"

I've never heard Cage beg with such utter desperation. Not once in our entire relationship. He was always the cool guy. Always laid back like nothing was ever a big deal. I don't know if he's doing this on purpose to manipulate me, but it's affecting me. I don't want it to, but it is.

I fold my arms across my chest. "What, Cage? What could be so important that you left me nearly a year ago without any explanation whatsoever?"

He reaches reluctantly across the table for my hand again. "Riv, my dad is—"

A heavy hand falls on Cage's shoulder.

Drakken.

Cage twists around and growls, "Who the fuck are you?"

Drakken hauls Cage to his feet by the shirt.

"What are you doing?!" Cage protests angrily, his arms flailing helplessly.

"You go!" Drakken barks and points his fisted finger toward the door.

"Stop, Drakken!" I blurt, but nobody hears me.

"What the fuck, man!" Cage yells as he twists suddenly and shoves Drakken as hard as he can, tearing free from Drakken's grip but also tearing his shirt in the process and knocking his chair to the cement floor.

The chair clatters loudly, startling everyone in the room.

Cage is by no means a small man. He's tall and muscular and he knows how to fight. I saw him punch a guy out at a bar once like he'd done it before. Right now he looks uncertain. But the anger on his face is plain as day.

In a calm voice, Drakken says to Cage, "You go now or I go very mad."

"Fuck you, buddy!" Cage appears to be sizing up Drakken, considering whether or not to throw a punch.

The electric tension bristling between the two men is palpable. They're two thunderheads about to crash together and shoot lighting out in bright forks. The room is dead silent. Everyone in the coffee shop is watching in anticipation of a fight. Even the baristas behind the counter.

Nobody moves with the exception of a random Asian girl with a red streak in her hair who sat down a second ago. She hisses to herself, "Is everybody in this place crazy?" She folds her laptop closed and trots out the front door, hunched over like she's ducking machine gun fire.

"You go," Drakken repeats to Cage.

"Drakken, stop!" I plead.

Cage's eyes flash at me, "You know this lunatic?"

"Yes." I stand up and step between Cage and Drakken.

Cage's face softens somewhat and he says, "We need to talk, Riv. It's important. I swear. It's my dah—"

"You go," Drakken growls loudly, looming up behind me.

Cage never breaks eye contact with me. He glares for a long time while his face clenches with anger.

This is way too much drama for me to deal with. I say softly, "Please go, Cage."

After a long painful moment of indecision, Cage breaks eye contact before yanking his messenger bag off the floor. He kicks the overturned chair on the floor on his way out. The chair slides across the cement and clatters against the empty chair abandoned by the Asian girl.

Relief slowly settles over everyone in the room.

Chapter 10

RIVER

"I so sorry, Rivka," Drakken says quietly, picking up the fallen chair. He sits down on it and scoots it up to our table.

"What the eff was that?" I hiss, sliding into my own chair.

The people inside Bean There Done That slowly start to bustle and conversation resumes.

I hear random people speculating about what just happened.

Some guy mutters, "What an asshole."

I feel like a total idiot.

Drakken nods his head deferentially, "I so sorry, Rivka. Is bad for me to do bad to man."

A random woman mumbles, "Somebody should tell him to leave."

Now that the immediate danger of a fist fight is over, I'm suddenly furious with Drakken. "Do you always act like this?"

Drakken frowns, "Sorry. I no understand."

A girl says, "That guy is cray-cray."

I roll my eyes and huff, "Drakken, you just walked in here and tried to start a fight for no reason. What is wrong with you?! You don't even know Cage!"

Drakken grinds his jaw. His eyes flick back and forth. "I know him."

"What?! How?"

The same girl says, "What a drama queen. She's as bad as he is."

I can't take this. I grab my handbag off the floor and stand up.

"You go?" Drakken asks uncertainly.

I'm guessing he's not picking up on all the random conversations like I am. I offer him my hand, "Come on, let's go."

I take Drakken's hand and we walk outside. Traffic whizzes past the sidewalk as we walk by clothing stores, furniture stores, restaurants, and plenty of parked cars. A Parking Enforcement car cruises by hungrily, looking for violations.

"How do you know Cage?" I ask.

Drakken smears his hand across his mouth. "I see him at hotel with flowers for you."

"What?" I have to think back. Cage hasn't brought me flowers since the day Drakken bought me a million roses. I suddenly piece it together. "Did you buy me all those rose bouquets because you saw Cage bring me a bouquet?"

Drakken nods sheepishly.

I laugh, "I didn't realize you were such a stalker, Drakken!"

"Stalker? What is stalker?"

I shake my head, grinning. "Never mind. Anyway, is that why you came inside the coffee shop and manhandled Cage like that?"

Drakken concentrates on my words, "Uhh... yes?"

I roll my eyes. I can't believe Drakken is jealous. I thought he was too disinterested to be jealous. I'm just glad he didn't fight Cage. He probably would've kicked his butt.

Drakken asks uncertainly, "You teach English now?"

"Sure," I smile. "But let's go someplace else, okay?"

"Okay," Drakken grins.

We end up driving all the way to Venice Beach. We sit at an outside table in a cafe beside the boardwalk. There's so much commotion from the thousands of tourists and locals, there's no way we'll bump into Cage here.

I reach into my handbag and pull out a copy of Green Eggs And Ham by Dr. Seuss and lay it on the shiny stainless steel table. I have no idea if you're supposed to use children's books to teach someone a language, but it seemed like a good idea when I checked it out from the library this morning.

Drakken laughs, "Is for me?"

I smile, "Yeah. I thought it might be fun." I slide my chair around so I'm sitting next to Drakken. So it's easier to point out things in the book. Not so that our knees are touching like they are right now. I'm just teaching, that's all.

Drakken is so busy flipping through the book, he doesn't notice the knees. He blurts, "Is kid book! Is for baby!"

"Is that okay?" I ask uncertainly.

He sips his coffee and shrugs, amused. "Okay. We read baby book. What is green eggs? Is bad eggs, yes? For garbage?"

I laugh, "No, silly! You have to read it."

"Okay, I read." He opens up the book and examines the first picture. "Sam is funny dog man with red hat!" He chuckles. "He drive his funny dog!"

We read through the entire book together, laughing at every page, totally unaware of the existence of the menagerie of people surrounding us.

Later, when Drakken closes the book, he smiles, "Is very fun book." His blue eyes beam into me.

Drakken is so damn handsome it's ridiculous. I can't help but notice several women at the nearby tables stealing glances at him. Even in Los Angeles, home of the most beautiful people on the planet, Drakken stands out.

I smile back at him.

I wasn't sure what I was getting into when I agreed to teach him English, but I never imagined I'd have this much fun. I don't want our day to be over.

"So," I grin, "what do we do now?"

"No more English. My head is crazy with crazy words!" he chuckles. "But is so much fun. Dr. Seuss is very good doctor!"

"Maybe we should go do something else," I suggest tentatively. "Like take a study break?"

Drakken arches an eyebrow thoughtfully.

The warm weather has my entire body buzzing in anticipation. Is it possible that Drakken and I will spend the entire sunny afternoon together? It would be the first time ever that we've done anything remotely resembling a regular date, and outside The Beverly Hills Resort no less.

Not that I'm getting my hopes up. Because my hopes are already as high as hopes can go. There is no up left for them to travel.

"We go walk, okay?" he smiles.

"Okay!" I literally hop up from my seat and throw the book in my handbag.

A minute later, we fade into the crowd of people strolling up and down the Venice Beach boardwalk. Between the shops, the people, the street vendors, the street performers, and everything else, there's a million things to look at and focus my attention on.

But all of it disappears the second I feel Drakken slide his fingers around mine. My entire universe shrinks down to our hands.

After all the amazing orgasms he's given me at work, nothing compares to this.

Suddenly, all my doubts about Drakken are gone with this one simple gesture.

Who knew hand holding could be so powerful?

Chapter 11

RIVER

So much for hopes.

After our initial English lesson, the only time I ever see Drakken is for our two hour lesson on Saturdays.

That's it.

We don't even fool around at work anymore.

That definitely has me worried.

I know sex cools off in any relationship, but I think it's safe to say that Drakken and I never *had* a relationship. At best, we were friends with a few benefits. Now I don't even have that.

That's why I call an Emergency Meeting of the High Council. I need some solid advice. So I ask both Julietta and Finch to meet me at ReaXion for lunch on a Sunday.

ReaXion is a buzzing new restaurant on Melrose. Our table is on the crowded garden terrace. Sun filters through the glowing green vines that coil around the overhead trellis. A fountain burbles next to our table while we all nibble on our salads and share a bottle of white wine.

I set my fork down on the edge of my plate and say, "Ladies, I need your advice. You know everything I've gone through with Drakken, right?"

They both nod.

I continue, "It seems like any forward progress in my relationship with him has stopped and now we're going in reverse. The question is, do you guys think I'm wasting my time with him?"

Julietta sips her wine and grins seductively, "I've seen him. Believe me, you're not wasting your time."

Finch blots her lips with a linen napkin, "I second that. If you get tired of him, send him my way."

I chuckle and roll my eyes. "I'm trying to figure out how to get him to spend more time with *me*, not you guys. Duh."

They both giggle.

Finch asks, "Did you ever figure out what the deal is with that Svetlana chick? Are those two hooking up? Maybe she's the problem."

I say, "I took Drakken at his word. He told me she was just his assistant."

Julietta smirks, "You know what that means."

"What?"

Julietta makes a circle with her index finger and thumb, and pushes her other index finger slowly in and out of the circle.

Finch winks and sips her wine and nods, "That's what I'm thinking."

I roll my eyes, "I don't think they're having sex."

"Seriously?" Julietta demands doubtfully. "The boss banging the secretary is the oldest cliche in the book. It would explain why he isn't pushing you for hook ups any more."

I sigh, "You might be right, but I don't have any proof."

Finch says, "I've seen the two of them walking through the lobby and chatting plenty of times. She is way more than his assistant. Trust me. She knows him well. I can tell."

I suggest, "Maybe they *used* to have sex."

Julietta says, "You should just ask Drakken straight up what his deal is with her."

"Maybe," I sigh uncertainly. "But I don't want to pressure him. What if they *aren't* sleeping together? Then he'll think I'm psycho jealous. I know it sounds stupid after everything he and I have been through, but I don't want to scare him off."

Julietta waves her hand, "If he runs off that easy, forget him. You deserve someone honest who shows up. Not a player who only comes around when it's convenient. I mean, it doesn't matter how much money he has or how hot he is. If he won't respect you, what's the point?"

"True," I nod.

"By the way," Julietta says, "I hope you're charging him good for all those English lessons. A rich guy like him can afford it."

"I don't charge him anything."

"What?" she goggles. "You can't be doing that shit for free, girl! I don't care how fine the man is!"

I shake my head, "No, not like that. He pays me without me asking. After the first lesson, he handed me five hundred bucks. I said it was too much, but he insisted. Now he pays me that much every time."

"No way!" Finch blurts. "I need a sugar daddy like Drakken! The rich bitch is buying lunch today!" She points at me like she's announcing it to the entire terrace.

"Shut up, Finch!" I hiss and roll my eyes dismissively, "He's not my sugar daddy and I'm not even close to rich. All the extra money goes to paying down my credit cards and tuition fees." I take a bite of my toasted beet salad which has sherry vinegar and candied Marcona almonds. Yum.

Julietta winks, "If you ever get tired of giving him English lessons, let me know and I'll give him some Julietta lessons."

"I'll *totally* do that," I lilt sarcastically while covering my mouth and trying not to spit out my food.

Finch asks, "Did you ever find out where he gets all his money?"

I wrinkle my nose, "I think he might be a pimp."

"WHAT?!" Finch and Julietta echo.

I nod uncertainly.

Irritated, Julietta asks, "When did you find this out? And why didn't you tell us sooner? Him being a pimp changes everything, girl."

"I don't know, a while back?"

Finch hammers the table and frowns, "No more holding out on us, River Freeman! Spill your shit now, bitch!"

Julietta frowns, folds her arms across her chest, and purses her lips. She cocks her head toward Finch, "What she said."

I wince, "Well, I don't know if he's a *pimp* pimp."

Julietta rolls her eyes, "Oh, okay."

I add quickly, "But he did hire some hookers for one of his business partners."

"He *what*?!" Finch blurts.

Julietta's eyes light, "I *knew* he was a drug lord!"

"Drug lord?" I ask quizzically. "How did we make the leap to drug lord?"

Excited, Julietta says, "Drug lords hire pros all the time, girl! Don't you know that?"

I roll my eyes and sip my wine, "That seems like a stretch."

"Haven't you seen Breaking Bad?" Julietta asks with great authority. "Drug lords come in all shapes and sizes these days, Riv. Who would've thought mild-mannered Gus Fring had his own meth empire?"

I chuckle, "That's a TV show, Jay."

She shakes her head, irritated, "Didn't you say Drakken makes trips down to Long Beach and San Diego?"

"Yeah, so?"

Julietta shakes her head, "I'm telling you, he's a drug lord. Drugs cross the border in S.D. all the time. And Long Beach is a huge port. Tons of ships bringing stuff in every single day. I'm envisioning cargo holds full of crates, and the crates are packed with straw and thousands upon thousands of hollowed out ceramic donkeys full of cocaine. Oh, and the donkeys have little ceramic sombrero hats." Julietta smiles proudly.

I pause with my fork full of salad halfway to my mouth and smirk, "That's insane, Jay. Drakken doesn't run his own Mexican drug cartel. Even if he did, he's not Mexican. I'm pretty sure he's from somewhere in Eastern Europe. Wouldn't his drugs come into the U.S. from the East Coast?"

"Just sayin'," Julietta nods knowingly. "It *could* be drugs. Maybe not Mexican. Maybe Russian mafia, or one of the other mafias." She sounds totally serious.

I smirk doubtfully, "*Other* mafias?"

"I agree," Finch says.

"You too?" I scowl. "This is so stupid. Remember I told you he had that business banquet thing at the resort?

"So what?" Julietta says doubtfully.

I sigh, "Everyone was wearing tuxes and stuff. They even had a Power Point presentation. I think he runs a company that makes breast implants or something."

Julietta shakes her head with great authority, "That's just a front. I bet they fill the breast implants with liquid heroin."

"Liquid heroin?" I say skeptically. "You have been watching *way* too much Breaking Bad."

"Serious, girl," Julietta says emphatically. "Organized criminals are smart. Who would think to check breast implants for liquid heroin?" She looks at Finch for support.

"Right?" Finch nods like everything Julietta is saying makes perfect sense.

I can't tell if Finch is serious or if she's just playing along with Julietta for fun.

"Whatever you do," Julietta says ominously, "Don't let him give you breast implants. The dogs at the airport can smell that shit. You don't want one of those trained German Shepherds biting you in the tit."

"Ew," Finch mutters.

I grimace at the image and hold my hand to my chest protectively.

"Or worse," Julietta continues, "you don't wanna get locked up abroad and have your implants removed by some crap-ass toothless surgeon who has dirty hands and operates with rusty scalpels." Julietta shivers at the thought.

Finch nods, "Totally."

An air of epic drama hangs over our table.

I shake my head and laugh, "That is the stupidest thing I've ever heard, Jay! You need to get out more. Have a fried cockroach." I toss one of my candied almonds at her salad.

"Get that off my plate!" Julietta squeals. "What is it?!" She jumps up onto her chair, squatting with both feet on the seat like she's expecting an entire army of flesh eating cockroaches to carpet the tiled floor of the garden terrace and begin devouring every human in sight from the toes up.

"Re-LAX, Jay," I say. "It's just a candied nut. Like you."

Slightly embarrassed, Julietta slides into her seat. "In that case..." She plucks the nut off her plate and pops it in her mouth. "Mmmm. I shoulda ordered what you had," she grins.

"Here," I giggle, "have another nut, you nut." I fling one onto her plate but it hits the edge and bounces right into her cleavage. I cackle gleefully, "Whoops!"

"Hey!" Julietta barks. She picks up her water glass like she's going to dowse me with it and start a full on food fight.

Finch giggles, "Calm down, you clowns! We're supposed to be giving Riv useful advice about her dating sitch."

"Exactly," I say and fire some rubber eye daggers in Julietta's direction.

"What?" she says innocently.

I shake my head and chuckle doubtfully, "Liquid heroin? Inside *breast* implants?"

While digging brazenly around in her bra for the candied nut, Julietta barks, "Look it up on the internet, bitch!"

"Peace, you two," Finch says. "Look, Riv. All you have to do is ask Drakken to take you out on a real date. What's the worst that can happen?"

Julietta pries the nut out of her cleavage and thunks it down on the table cloth. With an authoritative pout, she blurts, "Heroin breast implants."

After a moment of absurd silence, the three of us break into snickery laughter.

Chapter 12

RIVER

The waters of the Pacific Ocean are so close they nearly lap the white sand at the foot of Nobu, an upscale sushi restaurant on the Malibu beach.

Drakken and I sit on the outdoor deck, enjoying the view as the sun sets on the Pacific. I never get tired of seeing it.

Coming here was his suggestion. He said he was tired of coffee shops, and he wanted to start having English lessons twice a week. So we're here on a Wednesday night.

It's sort of a date, sort of not. But now I'm seeing Drakken twice a week. Maybe I don't need to bite the bullet and ask for a real date like Finch suggested. Maybe everything will work out without me having to do anything.

At the moment, the future state of my relationship with Drakken is the last thing on my mind because his eyes are mesmerizing me.

I never get tired of gazing into them.

Although they're ice blue, they always warm me to my core. A contradiction, like the man himself. When the heat gets to be too much, I gaze out at the view to the west.

The sun has gone down, but the sky above glows a brilliant pink. The scattered clouds above the horizon glow gold, casting a soft warm light over everything.

"Isn't the sunset gorgeous?" I say.

"Yes. I like it very much," he says. "It is *gorgeous*." He arches a brow and asks, "Do you know what also is gorgeous?"

I grin bashfully, "No, what?"

"Your Eyes. Your hair. Your face. Your heart." He smirks, "Your ass... Your rack..."

"Drakkozsha! Where did you learn those words?!" I demand jokingly. "Not from me, I hope!"

"I learned from friend," he winks.

"Some friend," I quip.

"He is guy friend. With guy talk."

I roll my eyes, "Of course. By the way, don't use the word 'rack' if you want to compliment a woman. It's crass."

"Crass? What is—what *does* crass mean?"

"Crass means rude or insulting, which means it hurts peoples' feelings."

He nods, "Yes, I understand. What word do you like? One is not *crass*? For your, uh…" he flicks his eyes at my chest.

I blush, "Oh, uh, I never thought about that."

He brazenly stares at my chest.

"Stop staring at them!" I giggle.

"Why?" He chuckles, "You like it. You like for me to look at you. To hunger for you. To hold you in my hands. I keep staring until you tell me a good word." He flashes a devilishly cocky grin.

I swear I can almost feel his eyes caressing my breasts. At least it seems that way because my bra is suddenly tight and compressing my nipples deliciously.

"Call them breasts," I gasp.

"I know that word. Is nice word. Beautiful word," he winks. "*Your* breasts are beautiful. But word is not good enough for your breasts." He shakes his head. "No, your breasts are more than a word," he grins, "*better* than a word. A word is not strong enough for power of your breasts. I *need* to hold them in my hands. I think of your breasts often. During meeting with business partners. Driving my car. In shower."

"Drakka! Stop!" I hiss. "Everyone can hear you."

The deck of the restaurant is full. The sound of animated conversation, beer bottles clinking together, waiters pouring ice water, and people laughing fills the air.

"There are no people, Rivka. There is only you, there is me, and nothing else. Nothing. I see only *you*. I hear only *you*. I smell only *you*." He inhales a long breath.

"You can't smell me from across the table," I scoff.

He inhales deeply and moans, "Ahhh. Is good." He flashes a cocky grin.

I'm not really sure how you prove you can smell something or not, but at the moment, I don't care. I'm too busy basking in his intense affection.

His eyes are locked on mine. They have been locked on mine since we sat down.

I am mesmerized.

The icy flame in his gaze travels from his eyes directly into mine, dribbling down my chest, pooling like liquid fire in my lap. I start to squirm in my seat. What were we talking about again?

This is why I always forget to ask Drakken what he does for a living, or press him to take me on a real date, or discuss the state of our relationship.

He enchants me every time we're together. Whenever I'm with him, I forget about everything. I'm so in the moment, I don't think about our pasts or our futures or anything else. I only think about the now. And right now, I feel like the most precious woman on the planet.

Drakken is going to melt me with his sultry gaze.

I grab my ice water and gulp two cool swallows.

ASK HIM ALREADY!! Julietta's voice echoes in my head. I jump in my seat.

"Are you okay, Rivka?" Drakken asks.

"Yeah, I'm fine," I shake my head dismissively.

Last night when Julietta and I were chatting outside our bungalows, she pressed me over and over to make Drakken tell me what he does. She said if he won't tell me, then it's proof he does something illegal.

DRUG LORD!!

One thing is for sure. Drakken *never* talks about himself. He must be hiding something, right?

It could be awful.

HEROIN BREAST IMPLANTS!

It could be terrible.

RUSTY SCALPELS!!

It could be the biggest deal breaker of all time.

TIT BITING GERMAN SHEPHERDS!!!

Maybe I don't want to know about it.

Julietta also said if I never ask Drakken the hard questions, our relationship won't ever move forward.

She's totally right about the last part. And seriously, if you're gonna date a guy, shouldn't you know what he does for a living? Especially when he's hiding it?

Time to let this cat out of the bag.

"Drakkozsha, can I ask you a question?"

"Yes. Any question."

"Um, what exactly is it that your business does?"

The cat is out of the bag.

"It is... how do I say... uhh... I am not sure of words... " he says evasively. He sips his sake.

"Do you mean you don't know the words?"

"No, is..." he trails off. His cat is still in its bag.

"Is what?"

"Is secret business."

That's not the cat I was expecting.

DRUG LORD!!

Julietta better not have been right. I take a big swallow of my own sake.

I need liquid courage if I'm going to press Drakken until I get to the bottom of this.

The waiter brings our sushi and sets the various plates on the table with a smile. His sudden appearance causes both my cat and Drakken's to jump back into their bags.

How do waiters always manage to interrupt so perfectly? Screw it. I'm not giving up yet. But I will bide my time until no waiters are in sight. Cats can be skittish, and usually wait till the coast is clear before they come out of the bag.

After Drakken and I have eaten our fill, I untie the cat bag again. "Anyway... I was asking earlier about what you do?"

He nods. "I remember. It is better I show you."

HEROIN BREAST IMPLANTS!!

"What do you mean?" I ask, hiding my anxiety.

"It is secret business. You must sign non-disclosure agreement that you will keep secret."

"I can do that." I'm not sure what I'm getting myself into, but I've heard of non-disclosure agreements. Julietta has to sign them whenever she works on movie projects. If it's just keeping a secret, I'm good to go. I've never been a gossip.

"I have good idea," Drakken smiles. "I get paperwork ready tonight. On Saturday, I show you business. Will be like date."

That was easy. All I had to do was let the cat out of the bag, and I killed two birds with one cat. Sorry, birds. Cats are natural predators and they have to eat meat to survive.

"I hope you like excitement," Drakken says suggestively.

"I do," I purr. "I can't wait to find out more about what you do for a living."

DON'T LET HIM GIVE YOU A HEROIN BREAST IMPLANT!!!

I roll my eyes to myself. Drakken probably just runs a computer business or some internet start up. Julietta is probably making a big deal out of nothing.

Everybody knows that cats and curiosity always turn out for the best.

RUSTY SCALPELS!!!

Chapter 13

RIVER

An orange and gray L.A. Metro bus pulls away from the distant bus stop on the street. Cars circle the crowded parking lot, looking for spaces. Saturday morning sunlight glints off the car windows.

I stand in the shade beneath the awning of a Vons grocery store, holding my purse and a sweater in case it gets cold later.

I'm waiting for Drakken.

I told him to pick me up here because it's way easier to find Vons than my bungalow. But it was really an excuse to spare him from being interrogated by Stone over a water board.

While I wait, I check my phone.

A new text from Julietta reads:

Don't let him kidnap you! If you end up a sex slave with heroin breast implants, I'm not coming to rescue you!

I smile to myself and slide my phone in my purse. My heart accelerates when Drakken's red Lamborghini turns into the parking lot.

I wave excitedly.

The gleaming red car rolls to a stop in front of me.

The people walking in and out of Vons all stare at it. The priceless super car sticks out like a sore thumb. Nobody in my neighborhood drives a car this nice.

The driver side door opens upward and Drakken steps out wearing a faded T-shirt and torn jeans. I can't tell whether or not they're designer clothes made to look old, but it doesn't matter. He looks completely dressed down, which matches my fitted T-shirt and skinny jeans. Drakken told me to wear comfortable clothes for our adventure today.

His bright smile beams beneath aviator shades. His slight beard stubble and strong jaw give him a rugged look that fits with the aggressive side of his personality. The side he normally keeps restrained beneath his tailored suits.

The dragon fire.

Phew! I'm going to swoon thinking about it.

Drakken walks around the car and opens my door for me. "You look beautiful," he smiles casually.

"You think?"

"You are always beautiful, Rivka. No matter what you wear. Your face is like sunshine to me. Your eyes like, uhh… bed pillows."

"Bed pillows?" I smile uncertainly.

He chuckles, "I can't think of good word. But I like bed pillow. Is soft place to lay my head and feel safe, yes?"

"Awww," I coo. "Bed pillows it is."

He brushes his thumb across my upper arm.

Goosebumps ensue.

He motions toward the Lamborghini. "Your chariot awaits."

"Hey! That's a new word for you!"

He smiles, "Is same word in my language. Is easy to remember. And I heard line in American movie as kid."

I wink, "That explains why you pick up English so fast."

He shakes his head, "Is not movies. Is you. Your help is make all the difference. And your bed pillow eyes," he grins.

I grin at him as I step into the leather seat. It's luxurious. I could get used to this.

Drakken closes my door and we drive toward the freeway.

I ask, "Did you finally figure out how to drive this thing?"

He chuckles and smiles, "Yes."

"No more problems with the computer thingy?"

"No. I know car very good now."

When he pulls onto the 10 freeway, he floors it and I'm pushed back into my seat like we're riding a roller coaster.

"Holy crap! This car is fast!" My heart races and my fingernails dig into the leather armrest.

"Is not that fast," he smiles.

"Maybe for you. Wow! My heart is pounding in my chest."

He chuckles, "Relax. You are safe with me, Rivka."

We cruise lazily through traffic until we get off of the 405 freeway at the offramp for LAX, L.A.'s main airport.

"Are we flying somewhere?"

He grins, "Yes."

"No way! I've never been on a plane before!"

"Is first time?"

"Yeah."

"Is very fun."

"I can't wait!"

We drive on an access road that runs alongside the main runway. A huge 747 passes over us. Its engines roar loudly as it comes in for a landing.

"Where are we going to fly? New York? Paris? The moon?" I'm so excited.

"Moon?" he chuckles.

"Yeah," I grin.

"Not today," he winks. "Maybe next time."

There are tons of small planes parked on the other side of the chain link fence that runs along the access road. I wonder if one of them is his.

Our car slows and turns into a driveway with a security gate. There's a little guard booth next to the gate.

Drakken rolls his window down.

The sleepy looking security guard steps up to the car and says, "Name?"

"Drakken Skalakova." He hands the guard his passport.

I whisper to Drakken, "Oh, um, I don't have a passport." We better not be flying out of the country.

DON'T GET LOCKED UP ABROAD!!!!

Drakken mutters, "Is okay. You don't need one for today. Maybe next time," he winks.

I smile at him, relieved.

The guard thumbs through Drakken's passport for at least a minute. He leans into the car window and says, "Sorry sir, but I have to call this in. Hold on a second." He retreats into the booth and picks up a phone.

I ask, "Is something wrong?"

"No," Drakken smiles. "Is normal."

The guard leans out of the booth a minute later, "I'm so sorry to keep you waiting. TSA will be here shortly."

Drakken nods at the guard before rolling up the narrow window of the Lamborghini.

"TSA?" I hiss. "Isn't that the airport police? For terrorists and stuff?"

"Yes," Drakken says casually.

"You're not a terrorist, are you?" I ask nervously.

Drakken chuckles, "No. Is okay. TSA always check."

A minute later, a police car with flashing reds and blues pulls up and parks behind the Lamborghini.

Are they blocking us in in case we try to make a run for it?

My nerves start to jangle. I have no idea what's going on. But police cars usually mean bad things involving criminals.

DRUG LORD!!

RUSSIAN MAFIA!!

HUMAN TRAFFICKING!!

SEX SLAVERY!!

HEROIN BOOB IMPLANTS!!

For all I know, Drakken could already be in trouble with the U.S. Government and he's going to fly me out of the country and we're never coming back.

Ever.

The two TSA cops chat with the sleepy security guard, who is now wide awake. The three of them nod a lot and keep looking at our car. Finally, the taller TSA cop leans over Drakken's window.

Drakken rolls it down and says, "Yes?"

The tall TSA cop holds up the passport in front of him then glances at

Drakken's face. "Good morning, Mr. Skalakova."

"Hello," Drakken says calmly.

"What is your business at the airport today, sir?" The TSA cop sure sounds official. And suspicious. Are they always like this? I have no idea. I hope Drakken isn't in trouble.

"I fly my plane," Drakken says. "Control tower has flight plan. Is all clear."

The TSA cop says, "Just a moment while I call the tower to confirm." He steps into the security booth and makes a call on the phone.

Is he calling in reinforcements? Are twenty cop cars gonna show up with machine guns and laser beams or whatever, and I have to watch while they pin Drakken to the ground and point guns at his head and cuff him?

I swallow the lump in my throat and hope Drakken doesn't notice.

Drakken squeezes my knee, "Is okay, Rivka. No trouble, I promise."

The TSA cop finishes on the phone and approaches the car again. "I'm so sorry for the delay, Mr. Skalakova. You're all clear. Have a nice flight," he smiles.

The security gate opens.

"Thank you," Drakken says to the cop before driving slowly onto the tarmac.

I breathe a sigh of relief.

"Don't be scared," Drakken encourages. "I promise, I take care of you. Only good things for you, my Rivka. Okay?"

His Rivka? I like the sound of that. I smile at him.

Up ahead, a fancy silver helicopter sits on the runway. A Range Rover and a Mercedes are parked next to it. A bunch of people mill around like they're getting it ready to fly.

I ask, "Drakken, is that your helicopter?"

As we get closer and closer, he arches an eyebrow and smirks, but doesn't answer.

"Are you going to take me on a helicopter ride, Drakken? That sounds like fun!"

As we pass the helicopter, Drakken scoffs, "No. Is not my helicopter."

"Oh, um, which one is yours?"

"Is over this way." He turns the car to the left.

All I see are rows of those little planes with one propeller. The kind I see flying over my neighborhood now and then. The ones that hold like two people. I imagine a helicopter is way cooler. Since I'm feeling a bit saucy, I say, "What, don't you know how to fly a helicopter?"

"No," he shakes his head, one arm draped over the wheel of the Lamborghini as we cruise slowly past all the little planes.

I quip, "I thought all the cool billionaires knew how to fly helicopters."

"My plane is much better than helicopter."

From what I can see parked on the runway, I doubt it. But I'm not complaining. Any plane ride will be the best I've ever had. Especially if it's with Drakken.

We drive all the way past the little planes and park beside a big nondescript brown building.

"Where's your plane?" I ask.

"Inside hangar." He climbs out of the Lamborghini and strolls around to get my door.

The door lifts silently and he offers his hand. I take it and climb out of the car. "You're always such a gentleman, Drakken."

"And you are always such a lady, Rivka."

The hangar has a small door with a key code. Drakken swipes an electronic card past it then punches a bunch of numbers into the keypad. It's seriously like fourteen numbers. How does he remember all that?

The door opens and he motions inside, "After you."

I grin at him nervously. Moment of truth.

He arches an eyebrow expectantly.

I can't stand here forever. But who knows what's inside? Don't drug lords use small planes to fly drugs across the Mexican border all the time? That's what I've heard, and I didn't hear it from Julietta.

Was she right all along with her crazy ideas?

She better not be.

But if I see crates full of ceramic donkeys wearing sombreros, or boxes of boob implants, I'm the eff outta here.

I step inside the door, prepared for anything.

Chapter 14

RIVER

A small office with a filing cabinet and a cupboard with a coffee machine on top greets me. A few cheap airplane posters hang on the walls. Not at all what I was expecting from Drakken the Drug Czar.

It's actually kind of boring.

Maybe it's just a front for something illegal. Fronts are supposed to be boring.

Naw, it's just an office.

Right?

A big man sits behind a desk reading a book called *The Right Stuff*. Whatever that is. Sounds sort of like porn to me. The man sets the book down and looks up. Drakken pulls the outside door tightly closed. The big man stands and I notice he wears a bulky police style belt with pouches and a pistol in a holster.

Guns?

Gulp.

Why do they need guns?

DRUG LORDS!!!

RUN FOR IT, RIV!!!

Good thing Julietta isn't here. I do my best to dismiss her crime movie logic and tell myself that this guy is just a security guard. But if I see those ceramic donkeys or boxes of breast implants, I'll grab that guy's gun, take Drakken hostage at gun point, and demand they release me.

"Good morning, sir," the big man says to Drakken.

"Ahoj, Lubomir," Drakken smiles. "Please to meet my good friend Rivka."

Lubomir steps out from behind the table and shakes my hand. "Good to meet you. Mr. Skalakova say many nice thing about you." His accent sounds a lot like Drakken's. He also has the same dark hair.

"Nice to meet you too," I shake his hand and notice his is gigantic. Even larger than Drakken's. Lubomir is a walking Rocky Mountain.

"Do you want to see plane?" Drakken asks.

"Yeah," I smile.

We walk through an interior door into a huge airplane hangar. Overhead fluorescent lights cut the gloom. The room is filled with planes of every size and shape.

"This place looks like an airplane museum!" I blurt. "Are all of them yours?"

"Yes," he grins.

Yeah, Drakken is stinking rich.

The first one we pass is like all the little ones outside with one propeller and room for maybe two people.

I scoff, "This looks like a putt-putt plane from a Pixar movie! I bet it can't get out of it's own way!"

He grins but doesn't respond.

We continue walking past another larger plane. It has two propellers and could probably hold ten people. A plane like this probably goes faster than a helicopter. It might be fun.

AND IT WILL HOLD WAY MORE DRUGS!! RUN FOR IT WHILE YOU STILL HAVE A CHANCE!!!

"This one?" I ask nervously.

"Nope."

The next plane we pass is an old one painted bright yellow. It has two wings, one on the top and one on the bottom, and one engine. There's no roof over the two little seating compartments. "What do you call this one?"

"Open cockpit biplane."

"So we'll get the wind in our hair? Like a convertible car? But a convertible plane?"

"Yes," he grins.

"That sounds fun!" I smile.

"It is fun. But car not go upside down like plane, or loop the loop."

"Wow, that sounds like a roller coaster! I can't wait!"

"We not fly this plane. We fly plane in back."

"Oh," I try not to sound disappointed. I wanted to fly in the convertible plane.

Our footsteps echo in the huge hangar as we walk up to the next plane, which is a small jet. It looks super expensive, like the private planes rich people fly in all the time. "Wow, what's this?"

"Gulfstream G650. Luxury passenger jet."

"Are we going on the Gulfstream?"

"No."

"So which plane *do* we get to fly?"

"This one," he smiles proudly.

We stop in front of a huge sleek black plane. A couple guys in jump suits are climbing around it doing mechanical stuff.

I goggle, "Wow! This looks like a space ship or something from a movie!"

"Is not a space ship," he grins. "Is fighter jet. F/A-18F."

"This is so stupid!" I stamp my foot and laugh, "You own a *fighter* jet?"

"Several," he grins.

Holy shizz!

I stop myself short of asking how rich he actually is. I can't imagine how much one of these planes costs. But I bet it's way more than his Lamborghini. Or a hundred Lamborghinis.

"You know American Blue Angels?" Drakken asks.

"Yeah. They're the Navy guys who do all those crazy stunts at air shows. My brother made me drive with him down to San Diego once to watch them fly at the Miramar Air Show."

"Then you know F-18," he grins and glances at the black fighter jet. "Is same plane Blue Angels use."

"No way!" I grin.

"Yes. My country has acrobatic team too. Is called *Nochnee Yestrabay*."

"What?"

He shakes his head. "Sorry. In English, is Night Hawks. We use black planes. This is mine." He pats the nose of the jet affectionately.

"Oh," I nod thoughtfully. "Wait, are you one of the pilots? Of the Night Hawks?"

He nods.

"Holy crap! The way those guys fly is super dangerous! You do that kind of stuff?"

"Yes."

Nervously, I say, "You're not going to make me go up in the air and do all that super dangerous stuff, are you?"

He arches his eyebrow, "Only if you want. We can go slow or fast. Is up to you."

"Ahhhh…"

"You no worry, Rivka. I keep you safe. She is good plane," he pats the nose again. "Like your Sheena. She never let me down."

"You remember Sheena!" I grin.

"Yes."

My heart thumps noticeably as I say, "Okay! Let's go flying!"

I have no idea what I'm getting myself in to.

Chapter 15

RIVER

The first thing we do is go to Lubomir's office to sign the paperwork. It turns out that not only do I have to sign the non-disclosure thing, but I also have to sign an insurance waiver and an accidental death waiver.

"Am I going to die if I sign this?" I ask nervously, holding the pen over the paperwork on Lubomir's desk.

Lubomir chuckles, "Drakken is best pilot you will ever fly with. You are safe with him."

Drakken smiles at the man.

"That's a relief," I say. But there's still that chance something will go wrong. You never know. I wince and ask Drakken, "I'll be okay, right?"

"Rivka, I never do anything to hurt you, okay? I have flown this plane many, many time, I can't count how many. Is like riding bike for me."

If I gotta die some day, it may as well be in the cockpit of a high performance fighter jet with the most handsome man ever at the controls. After my YOLO moment, I sign all the papers.

Lubomir collects the stack and shuffles them together before sticking them in the filing cabinet. He smiles at me, "You will be okay."

Neither of them seem worried.

I hope I don't sound like a wimp.

And I really hope nothing goes wrong.

Stone would kill me if I was killed in a plane crash. Come to think of it, he'll kill me if I tell him I got to fly in an F-18 and he didn't. I'll worry about that part after I survive.

Two hours later, we're standing outside the hangar in the sunshine next to the magnificent F-18. We both wear bulky flight suits and have helmets that come with gas masks.

Drakken walks me around the plane, explaining how the various parts work.

"How fast does this thing go?" I marvel.

"Faster than sound."

I furrow my brow, "What does that even mean?"

"It mean, if I shout at you from far away, plane gets to you before my voice, yes?"

"Wow! That's freaking fast!"

He grins, "Very fast. F-18 is almost twice as fast as sound."

"What! No way!"

"Yes way," he chuckles.

"So, if I'm ever mad at you, and I start yelling at you, you can jump in this plane and fly away so fast you won't be able to hear me yelling?"

He frowns and thinks about it for awhile, processing my words. "Yes," he chuckles. "But I never run away from you. You yell, and I still listen, okay?"

"Because of my bed pillow eyes?" I bat my eyelashes comically.

He laughs, "Yes. Because bed pillow eyes."

I shake my head and smile. I love this guy. I mean, I *like* this guy.

Drakken hollers at one of the men in a jump suit, "Radek! Is plane ready?"

Radek nods, "Cross checked, fueled, and ready to fly, sir."

"Thank you, Radek."

I lean into Drakken and whisper, "Do all these guys work for you?"

"Yes. All of them. Why?"

"Just curious," I shrug. Drakken sure is polite to all his employees. He's awesome. Even if he is a drug lord like Julietta said, he's probably the nicest drug lord there is.

Drakken helps me climb up a narrow ladder that hangs from under the plane's wing. He slaps my butt when I'm halfway up.

"Hey!" I blurt.

He chuckles, "Is to help you into plane."

"I think you need a firmer grip if you're going to actually help," I say sarcastically.

He reaches up and squeezes my ass.

Radek and the other crew guys in jumpsuits cheer and whistle.

"Stop!" I say to Drakken bashfully.

"I get good grip, no?"

"No!" I swat down at him.

He releases me but climbs up the ladder until his chest bumps against my ass.

I wiggle my butt in his face.

He snickers, "We fly plane or not?"

"You started it," I whine.

He laughs, "Get in plane."

I climb the rest of the way. "Do I sit in the front seat or the back?"

"Do you want to fly plane?"

"Yeah!"

"Then we both die," he chuckles.

"Hey!" I bark.

"Is up to you."

"Okay," I grouse. "I'll sit in the back." I lower myself into the narrow cockpit.

Drakken leans inside and fastens my seatbelt. It has a bunch of straps and a thousand buckles. He pulls everything really tight.

"Does it have to be that tight?" I ask.

"Yes. We go upside down."

"Upside down?" Now I'm getting nervous.

He nods.

"Do I get an airsick bag?"

Drakken chuckles and asks Radek for one. Radek trots off to get it. To me, he says, "Don't touch yellow and black handle between legs, okay?"

"Why? What's it do?"

"It eject you out of plane."

"What?" I ask in total disbelief. "Why would you want to do that?"

"If plane has problem." A grin widens across his mouth. "Or if you yell too much, I eject you, okay?" he winks.

"Drakken!"

He chuckles. "I not make you eject. Is joke. I make you safe. Okay?"

Now that I'm buckled into this gigantic fighter jet, I don't want to let on that I'm nervous about flying. I imagine it's scary enough to fly on a regular plane like everybody else. But a frickin' fighter jet? The bird-sized butterflies in my stomach suddenly flap their wings. I think they want to get out of this plane as badly as I do.

"Put helmet on," Drakken instructs. I do, and he checks that it's fastened properly. When he finishes, he climbs into the front seat of the jet and straps himself in.

A minute later, he says, "Ready for fly?"

"Yeah!" I don't know why I sound so excited. I'm ready to poop my pants. The poop urge worsens when Drakken starts the huge engines. They whistle and whine up to speed behind me. The entire plane rumbles. I'm sure Drakken's Lamborghini has nothing on this plane.

Drakken eases the plane forward and we creep out toward the main runway.

A Southwest Airlines plane comes in for a landing, speeding past us. Its big engines thunder as it flies by and touches down.

Being so close to these big planes is kind of intimidating.

Drakken chatters back and forth with the air traffic control guys. They speak in some kind of code, talking about information hotels and whiskey foxtrots. I have no idea what they're saying.

The Delta jet in front of us turns onto the main runway. Its engines roar louder and louder as it accelerates into the distance and lifts up into the air.

We're next.

This is it.

We roll forward and turn onto the main runway.

I have no idea what to expect.

The engines rev up even more and get really loud.

Drakken says, "Tower clear us for takeoff. Are you ready, Rivka?"

"Yeah," I say on my headset mic.

"Here we go!"

The jet accelerates and I'm pushed back into my seat.

"I turn on afterburner," Drakken says.

The plane suddenly rumbles and I'm pushed even harder into my seat. The nose of the plane comes up and we lift off the ground.

I feel myself sink into my seat. "Oh my god!" I squeal. "I'm flying! This is so cool!"

Drakken chuckles, "Gear up."

I feel the bottom of the plane vibrate and thunk as the wheels come up.

"Remember I teach you how to breathe?"

"Yeah?" Earlier, Drakken spent a half hour explaining to me this weird breathing technique that fighter pilots use so they don't pass out when all the blood rushes to your feet during hard turns.

"We breathe now, okay?"

"Yeah! I'm ready."

"Squeeze legs, take deep breath."

I do. I also clench every muscle from my waist down while I breathe shallowly. It makes all the blood rush to my head. I can feel my face getting red. It seems totally unnecessary, but I do it anyway.

"Ready and NOW!!!"

The plane suddenly points straight up and rumbles like a rocket ship. I'm hammered into the back of my seat and my body literally weighs a ton. My arms feel heavy. My face feels heavy. Even my eyeballs feel heavy. I can barely move.

Holy crap.

My blood drains from my head and my vision narrows into a tiny opening in a field of black.

"Breathe, Rivka."

I do my best to copy Drakken's breathing, which I hear over the headset, but my body is telling me that something is horribly wrong.

Before I have a chance to panic, I feel my body lighten as all the extra weight falls away. But I'm breathing really hard, like I just ran a mile.

"You okay?" Drakken asks from the front seat.

"What!" *gasp* "The!" *gasp* "Fuck!" *gasp* "Was!" *gasp* "That?!" I laugh.

"Was very fast takeoff," he chuckles.

"Wow, Drakken. I've been on some crazy roller coasters before, but none of them could've prepared me for this!"

He chuckles again, "You like?"

"Uhh... I'm not sure yet," I laugh. "That was seriously—" *gasp* "—insane." *gasp* "What now?"

"Now we fly north of city. Then very much insane, okay?"

"Um, okay? Just don't kill me," I giggle nervously.

"Don't worry, Rivka. I never let anything bad happen to you. Now we fly to Santa Barbara forest for open air space."

"Okay."

The plane accelerates gently and the ground whizzes by below.

"How fast are we going?"

"Five hundred sixty knots."

"How fast is that?"

"Almost speed of sound."

"Wow! Does that mean if I start yelling at you, you won't hear me?"

"No," he chuckles. "We go same speed. So no yell, please." He sounds amused.

For a few minutes, we fly in silence.

While enjoying the view, I say, "It's so peaceful up here. So quiet, so beautiful. What do you feel when you fly, Drakkozsha?"

He doesn't answer right away. When he speaks, his voice is choked up, "I feel free in sky. Nothing hold me down. Not man, not gravity. Nothing. Flying is freedom. Freedom." He almost sounds angry now, like he's holding something back. The pain in his voice is obvious.

I want to ask him about it. I want to ask him about the scars on his back. We've never talked about them. Though he carries a burden of terrible pain, I'm pretty sure he doesn't want to talk about it. He's had a million chances. If he did, he would've brought it up by now. But some pain gets buried so deep, you never want to talk about it.

I feel a burning desire to ask him to open up to me. That's how the healing happens. By sharing it. Letting it out. Add to that the fact we're in the most isolated and romantic place I could ever imagine. Me, Drakken, high above the entire world where no one can touch us. What better time to open up to each other?

"Drakken?" I ask tentatively over the mic.

"Yes, Rivka?" The tenderness in his voice makes my heart swell with, um, what's the word? It starts with an L. But I barely know this man. He is still a closed book, a guarded secret.

One way to change that. "Can I ask you something?"

"Anything, Rivka."

Suddenly, I stop myself. Something tells me this is the wrong place to do this. I remind myself where we are. We're flying in an F-18. It's not like we're at a restaurant and he or I can walk out if someone's feelings get hurt. We're stuck up here, thousands of feet in the air, and he's the one flying the plane. Now is probably not the time to get into Drakken's personal issues. It can wait.

"What is it, Rivka?" Drakken asks with concern.

"Uh…" I try to think of something to talk about that isn't a potential trigger topic for Drakken. I immediately blurt out the next words that come to mind. Unfortunately, triggers can come in all shapes and sizes, and sometimes you don't realize you're pulling one until the bullet is already shooting out the end of the barrel.

Chapter 16

RIVER

"So," I say casually, "do you take all your dates up in your jet fighter to impress them?"

Drakken chuckles over the headset mic, "I thought you have other question. What do you mean dates?" he asks, amused. "Dates is fruit from tree, yes? Do I press them in plane? To make wine? From dates?"

"No—" I giggle, still completely unaware that I've pulled Drakken's trigger.

"Is make no sense, Rivka," he chuckles. "I very I confused."

"No, silly!" I laugh innocently. "I mean like your *girlfriends*. Do you take them up in your plane to show off, to impress them with how cool you are?" It vaguely occurs to me that this is the sort of thing a teenager worries about, but I'm so busy trying to translate things for Drakken, I don't really think about the underlying content of what I'm saying.

After a tense and confused silence, Drakken grunts, "I have no girlfriend, Rivka. I tell you before. I have no girlfriend for..." He chokes up, unable to continue.

Whoops.

Now I'm thinking about the content what I'm saying.

I suddenly remember that day in the Sunset Suite when everything went wrong. Before Drakken's blow up, I insinuated that Svetlana was his girlfriend, I acted like an insecure teenaged drama queen. Rather than asking him for clarification, I went on the attack with the accusations. I'm surprised he didn't blow up at me right then.

I'm sort of surprised he's not blowing up at me now.

Once again, I'm assuming the worst about Drakken. I'm assuming he brings bimbo after bimbo up here to show off what a studly pilot he is. I mean, if I *hadn't* been assuming the worst, why would I have asked him the question in the first place? I can be totally immature when the opportunity presents itself.

I back pedal anxiously, "Sorry, I meant dates, not girlfriends. A *date* is what you call it when you take a girl out to dinner or a movie *before* she becomes your girlfriend. You know, because you like her and *maybe* want her to be your girlfriend, but she isn't yet *officially* your girlfriend. You're just getting to know her. Know what I mean?" All my overly dramatic back pedaling is making it worse. Considering the embarrassment brake is still on, this shame train is going nowhere fast.

Time to shut my mouth.

After lengthy silence, Drakken mutters angrily, "I have no girlfriend for very long time, Rivka."

"What?" I blurt.

BLAM!

The trigger has been pulled, and I was the one who pulled it. But somehow I still haven't figured out what I've done.

"No girlfriend," he growls. "No girlfriend since—" He stops himself short.

No girlfriends?

Why can't I help but imagine that a guy like Drakken has already been through more girlfriends in his life than George Clooney, Johnny Depp, Ian Somerhalder, and every boy in every boy band ever, *combined*? I mean, Drakken is *that* hot. And he's a billionaire fighter pilot. Him being a player is the *obvious* conclusion.

What can I say?

I suddenly stop myself.

I can say that I jump to way too many conclusions and I'm way too slow on the uptake today. I roll my eyes at myself. When am I ever going to grow up?

Finally, *finally*, I realize how badly I've pulled Drakken's trigger. I sigh apologetically, "Drakken, I—"

"I no want girlfriend," he blurts. "Okay?"

BOOM!

That's the moment when the bullet hits my heart. My entire body tenses with sudden fear. Nausea sweeps through me.

What have I done?

I just ruined everything. But it's my fault. I pulled the trigger.

My eyes water instantly. Why couldn't I have kept my mouth shut? Why did I have to assume the worst about Drakken? Every step of the way, he's proven to be the best. His intentions, his motivations, everything. He's a good guy. I'm the one making a mess out of things. Me and my insecurities.

"I no want girlfriend for long, long time..." he sighs.

Oh, wait. I thought he meant he didn't want *me*. Where is he going with this?

"Rivka, I want you. Up here. Is why I take you here."

Wait, what the fuzz?

Now I'm totally confused.

Did he just say he wants *me*, or wants me *up here*? Like, flying with him? But not *wanting* me wanting me?

Considering all I can see is the top of his helmet, I can't tell. Girls, never have a heart to heart in an F-18. It's way too complicated.

He continues, "Up here is fun. Up here is my happy. I want to show you my happy, Rivka. Only for you. Okay?" His voice is thick with emotion. "You are only person I bring up here to show my happy, okay?"

"Really?" I sniff.

"Is true. Only you, Rivka. Only you."

I nod silently and smear a tear from my cheek. How could I ever doubt a voice like that? "Thanks, Drakka."

Okay, that's it. I'm officially not going to read anything negative into anything else he says or does from here on out. I'll just take Drakken at face value, and I'll assume the best until proven otherwise. I'll assume that he is a good guy. It's the least I can do after all I've done.

I sigh with relief, "You're so sweet, Drakken."

"You're sweet too, Rivka." The smile in his voice is obvious. "I am very happy for you being here with me."

I feel a thousand times lighter.

Now I really need to change the subject to something less intense. "So, um, where are we going again?"

"We fly to mountain east of Santa Barbara.

"Oh. How long until we get there?"

"We here now."

"What?" I gasp. "That took like ten minutes! It takes an hour and a half by car!"

"Is fast plane. You ready for upside down now?"

"Do I need to do the breathing thing like when we took off?"

"No. Is no G's."

"Okay, whenever you want."

"Okay. Three. Two. One."

SPIN!

I'm instantly hanging from my seatbelt harness thing. No wonder Drakken made it so tight. I look up and see the ground. "Wow! This is awesome! We're flying upside down!"

SPIN!

Back to normal.

"You like?"

"Yeah I do! Do it again!"

"Three. Two. One."

The entire world spins around the plane, the ground and the sky switching places so fast I can't keep track. We stop after the third revolution, right side up.

I'm super dizzy. "Holy crap! That was incredible! I bet you can't do that in a helicopter."

"No," he chuckles. "Only in fighter jet. Now we fly low altitude, okay?"

"All right."

Drakken takes the plane down toward the forest. The trees whip by really fast. I glance at the gauge that tells the altitude, and it says three hundred feet. That's super high, but it sure seems really low all of a sudden.

We whip around tree covered hills, rolling randomly, going up, down, over hills, around small mountains.

I feel like we're in a video game.

But it's real.

With Drakken flying, I feel safe the entire time. If it was me, I'd be dead already.

The plane descends even lower and rolls from side to side along a winding canyon with a river snaking along the bottom. Trees and hills wall us in on both sides. Everything flashes by in green and brown blurs. Stone would have a blast if he were here right now. He'll be super jealous when I tell him about it later. I know he loves going fast on his motorcycle. But his bike isn't this fast. No way.

Frankly, I'm sort of freaking out.

Drakken weaves the fighter jet expertly along the course of the river. But we come *really* close to tree tops and hillsides at about three different points. Each time, I'm convinced we're gonna crash, but the plane turns hard, and everything is fine until the next turn.

It's super scary but exhilarating at the same time.

I'm sure this is normal for Drakken. The entire time, he reminds me when to breathe.

At one point, he levels off. "You okay, Rivka?"

"Yeah, but I think I need a break." My head is spinning and so is my stomach. "Where's that airsick bag? Oh, I found it." I don't use it, but I will if this continues. I don't want to sound like a wimp, so I don't say anything.

"Sorry. Is normal for me," he says over the mic. "I forget is very hard for new person. We fly easy now. You rest. Then we make loop the loop."

"Oh yeah! We can't forget that!"

He chuckles, "You are strong girl, Rivka. Very strong."

I smile, "Thanks." It's kind of weird not being able to see his face. All I can do is look at the top of his helmet over the seat back. But hearing his voice over the headset totally sets me at ease. "It's so beautiful out here. All there is is the beautiful blue sky, the beautiful mountains, the beautiful trees, and the beautiful clouds." I sigh romantically.

"And you."

"What?"

"You are beautiful like mountain and tree and sky."

"Awww," I coo.

"Do you want to see cloud up close?"

"Can we?" I ask enthusiastically.

"Anything for you, my Rivka."

The next thing I know, we're up high again, and flying through the clouds. Big fat puffy cumulus clouds, piled one on top of the other like columns of white cotton candy that billow upward. The plane swings from side to side as we fly around the cloud columns, weaving in and out. It's unbelievable.

"This is incredible, Drakken! It's like flying in a dream world!"

"You are dream world for me, Rivka."

Awww. He always knows what to say.

"Ready for loop the loop?" he asks.

"Yeah!"

Nope.

I spoke to soon.

The plane shoots straight up in the sky. This time, I weigh more than a thousand pounds. The blood in my brain is saying bye-bye. The blackness narrows my vision down to the size of a quarter.

I do my best to match Drakken's trick breathing as the plane loops upside down, and continues around until we're pointing straight at the ground.

I am scared out of my mind.

We're going to crash straight into the ground and die a horrible death. I barely have time to think about it because the blackness expands and my vision shrinks to the size of a colorful dime.

Then all the color fades away to gray...

Chapter 17

RIVER

"Drakka! The ground is made of clouds!" I jump up and down on a cottony white world of puffy clouds in every direction. The cushiony clouds are like a spongy trampoline. Each time I jump, I float up ten feet in the air like there's almost no gravity, then I float gently back down.

Drakken jumps too, and he's having as much fun as I am.

I can't remember when we left the F-18 and came out here, but it seems like hours ago. When I'm out of breath and giggling, I fall backward onto the blanket of clouds. The landing is softer than snow and pillows. "It's so comfy, Drakka! I think I'll take a nap. Hey look!" I blurt and point up at the sky. "It's a dragon!"

A huge blue dragon with a long tail beats its wings far above us. It circles slowly, like eagles do when they're looking for lunch.

Drakken floats down and stands over me. His head blocks out the dragon overhead. He smiles and coos, "Wake up, Rivka."

"No!" I laugh sleepily.

"Wake up, Rivka… *wake up…*"

The world suddenly becomes hyper-colored, the sky bluer than blue, the clouds whiter than white, but with red outlines. Something is happening. No! I'm not done with my cloud nap!!!

…Wake up, Rivka…

"Rivka? Are you okay back there? Rivka?"

A distant whine comes closer and closer as the blackness subsides and the world fades into view. My stomach is bunched up in nauseous knots. My entire body jingles with tingles, like when you sit on your leg wrong and it falls asleep, but it's not just my leg. Every muscle in my body has fallen asleep.

"What happened," I groan groggily.

"You fall asleep, Rivka. Too many G's. I do loop too hard. Sorry. Are you awake now?"

I smear my fingers against my face and choke down bile. "Where's the vomit bag?"

"In your hand?" he suggests.

"Oh. Yeah." I glance at my arm absently. I try to lift it, but it weighs a ton. I don't quite need the airsick bag, but I might. "Where are we?"

"Still in F-18."

"I think I blacked out."

"Yes."

"How long was I passed out?"

"Only five or ten seconds, I think."

"That's it?" I blurt.

"Yes," he chuckles.

"I was dreaming you and I were running around on top of the clouds for hours!"

"What?" he says with amusement.

"Yeah," I swallow acid. "The ground was made out of clouds, and I was jumping up and down on them and I saw a blue dragon."

He laughs, "Is good dream, yes?"

"Totally," I smile sleepily. I almost miss the moment when my stomach climbs up my throat. I jam my face in the vomit bag. Good thing I had a light breakfast. Nothing comes up, but I wretch anyway. A cold wave washes over me and my head falls back against the seat. Then a hot flash passes through me. I groan, "Ohhhh, I'm so exhausted." I swallow thickly. "I feel like I ran a marathon."

He chuckles kindly, "Is okay. Flight is almost over. I give you smooth airliner landing, okay?"

I don't know what that is, but hopefully it won't make me hurl.

As promised, we land gently at LAX twenty minutes later. I barely notice when the wheels touch the runway.

A sense of relief washes over me as the plane slows to a crawl.

I never thought I'd be so happy to be back on the ground. Then again, I never thought I'd be bouncing around on top of the clouds with a handsome fighter pilot and a blue dragon.

We taxi back to Drakken's big brown hangar. When the plane comes to a full stop, I'm even more relieved. But I'm so tired I can't move. The glass canopy raises up. A cool breeze blows across my face.

The breeze has never felt so good.

Drakken unbuckles himself and hops out of the front seat in two seconds. I'm stuck in my harness. I can't figure out the buckles and I'm not even going to try.

Drakken stands outside the cockpit, leaning over me. "Need help?" he grins.

I nod and sigh, "Please."

He chuckles as he unbuckles me, "Tired?"

I roll my eyes and smile, "Yeah."

"Happy to be on ground?"

"Looking forward to it," I grin weakly. "As soon as I get there."

Drakken finishes unbuckling me like a baby in a car seat. "Okay?"

I reach both arms up to him, "Help!"

He grins, wraps my arm around his neck, and pulls me to standing.

I almost collapse. "Whoa! I can't stand right now."

Drakken supports my weight and smiles as he helps me stumble out of the cockpit. When my feet are on the wing, he slings me over his shoulder like I weigh an ounce, then backs down the ladder like I'm his prize.

Drakken sets me on the ground.

I try to stand up on the cement, but my knees are wobbly, and I feel cold and clammy all over. I slide down Drakken's chest and sit on the ground cross-legged, leaning against his leg.

Radek, Lubomir, and the other ground crew are all milling around. They all chuckle at my inexperience.

I quip, "I've never been happier to have my ass on the ground than I am right now." I lean over sideways and literally kiss the cement.

More laughs from the crew.

"Is good," Drakken chuckles.

Chapter 18

RIVER

"I can't believe how tired I feel. I can't even move." I sit on a bench in my flight suit, slumped over and exhausted.

We're back in the locker room.

"Is okay," he grins. "I change you."

"You don't have to do that, Drakkozsha. I can do it." Despite my refusal, I end up sitting in a lump on the bench while Drakken climbs out of his flight suit and hangs it in the locker labeled SKALAKOVA.

He stands in front of me wearing only his boxer briefs. He is incredibly handsome. That body of his is perfect.

I wish I wasn't too tired to do something about it. Later. Definitely later.

Drakken smiles at me, "I help, okay?"

He leans down and kisses me gently before unzipping my flight suit. He slides my arms out, then removes my shoes and slides the legs off. I'm a rubbery doll the whole time. He hangs the flight suit in one of the other lockers.

I sit in my panties and T-shirt, which I wore under the flight suit, still slumped on the bench. "Are you gonna have your way with me? I'm helplessly exhausted and nearly naked. I'm totally defenseless right now... "

He smirks, "You are too sleepy. I wait until after dinner, when you are not defenseless. Then I have way with you, okay?"

"Promise?" I grin.

"Promise." Drakken pulls my clothes out of my locker and helps me into them.

"Thanks," I smile sleepily. "I couldn't have done it without you."

"Now I dress." He slides on his jeans and stretches his T-shirt over his head.

I hold my arms out to him like a little kid.

He takes my hands and pulls me to my feet.

I fall into his chest and snuggle against him. He smells so good. "I'm so sleepy, I could take a nap right here."

He chuckles, "Okay. I stand still. You sleep." He wraps his arms around my waist and pulls me against him.

"Mmmmm, I like it right here." My eyes close and I breathe evenly.

"Stand for sleep is no good," he mutters.

The next thing I know, he picks me up and cradles me like a baby.

"Can I stay here all day?" I sigh.

"Until arms get tired," he says.

"How long will that take?"

"Maybe one hour?"

"Okay," I sigh like I'm accepting the offer. Then I fake snore, "*Hoch-shh, hoch-shh, hoch-shh...*" I start giggling.

"Is okay," he chuckles. "You sleep. I carry you outside."

True to his word, Drakken walks me out of the locker room and into the hangar with all the planes. The men work on the fighter jet. They all turn to watch.

I wave at the men.

They smile and several laugh.

"You have sleeping baby," Radek jokes.

Drakken quips, "Shhh. Don't wake her up. She take nap."

The men laugh again.

Now I feel kind of stupid being carried. "You can put me down if you want," I whisper to Drakken.

"Is okay. You need rest. I carry you to Gulfstream. You take nap."

"The Gulfstream? Isn't that the big private jet?"

"Yes."

I look around the hangar, noticing it's gone. "Where did it go?"

"Is outside. Waiting for us."

"What?! Are we going someplace?"

"Yes."

"Where?"

"Is secret," he grins.

"Aw, come on, Drakken. Please tell me."

He smiles, "Is secret."

"Are we going to the heroin boob implant factory?"

"What?" he chuckles.

"Nothing," I grin.

I guess I'll find out when we get there.

Chapter 19

RIVER

The Gulfstream waits on the runway.

Drakken carries me up the stairs.

A beautiful young woman in a flight attendant uniform greets us inside the plane. "Good afternoon, Mr. Skalakova."

"Ahoj, Edita," he replies. "Sleeping baby is Rivka."

I snicker, "I'm not a baby! Put me down! I have legs."

Edita chuckles, "Is okay. Mr. Skalakova say many nice thing about you."

Drakken sets me down.

The interior of the Gulfstream is incredible and luxurious. It looks like the living room in a small mansion. White leather easy chairs, glimmering wood cabinets and table with a flower arrangement and computer monitors mounted on brackets. The back wall is also shiny dark wood, and has a regular interior door mounted in it.

"What's back there?" I ask.

"Main galley, second bathroom, and master suite," Drakken says.

"This plane has a bedroom?"

Drakken smiles, "Yes."

"Wow." I can't help but think of the Mile High Club, of which I'm not currently a member. Maybe Drakken can get me a membership card before the plane lands. Does it count if you use a bed? Or does it have to be in a cramped bathroom?

Edita asks, "Would you like drink while we taxi?"

"Oh, uh, water is good," I smile.

She walks to the front of the plane.

Drakken and I sit down in the white leather easy chairs, which have seat belts, and we buckle up.

Edita returns from the galley with a tray holding two glasses filled with ice water. Each glass has a cucumber slice, a small wedge of watermelon, and a mint leaf.

"Thank you," I smile and take a sip and enjoy the cool refreshing flavor. "Wow, that is some good water."

Drakken takes a huge swallow of his water, "Yes. Is very good."

Edita smiles, "Thank you. If you like more, I have pitcher in galley. I pour after takeoff."

"Great. Thanks, Edita," I smile.

She returns to the galley area at the front of the plane.

The plane starts moving and slowly taxis along the runway.

I ask Drakken, "Do I have to do the breathing thing again when we take off?"

Drakken chuckles, "No. Is not like F-18. Gulfstream is for smooth flight. No loop the loop or high G's."

"Okay, phew," I grin. "I don't know if I can take any more G's today."

He laughs and squeezes my knee, "You do very good in F-18. You are strong girl."

"Thanks." I only half believe him. I'm still wiped out after all of Drakken's fancy flying.

"Are you ready for more fun today?"

I grin, "I'm ready for anything…"

Chapter 20

RIVER

"Wake up, Rivka," Drakken mutters in my ear. "Is Golden Gate Bridge."

Drakken smiles at me. His blue eyes gaze into mine. His face sure is nice to wake up to.

"Huh?" I blink my eyes. "Was I asleep?" I yawn and cover my mouth.

He kisses my cheek, "You fall asleep as soon as plane take off."

Out the window, the red bridge spans the blue waters of the San Francisco Bay.

I smile, "How come they call the bridge golden when it's actually red?"

Drakken smirks, "I has no idea. Look over there at little island with building. Is Alcatraz. Famous prison."

"Is that where we're going?"

"No."

"No?" I sound disappointed.

"We go to California wine country. For dinner."

"What?!"

He grins, "I tell you already, is special place."

We land at the Sonoma County Airport a few minutes later. A limo waits for us on the runway. Drakken and I climb into the back.

During the drive, the limo climbs a curving road into the mountains. Jagged rock formations and trees grow along the roadside. Eventually we descend into a huge green valley. I can see vineyards along the hillsides.

"Where are we?" I ask.

"Calistoga," Drakken says.

We turn down several roads and end up on a private driveway. A fancy sign reads "Chateaux de l'Amour" in script letters.

The limo stops at the end of an empty parking lot and the driver opens our door.

Drakken steps out and offers his hand.

I take it and climb out of the limo.

A giant castle towers over us. It has stone walls, a bunch of big turrets like giant chess pieces, you know, the castle kind, and the really narrow windows.

"What the eff?!" I blurt. "Is this your castle or something?"

"No," Drakken chuckles. "Is Chateaux de l'Amour. Is winery. My castle is much bigger," he winks.

Is he joking? I can't tell. "This place is beautiful, Drakken!"

"We have dinner here, okay?"

"Okay? This is perfect! I've never had dinner in a castle before!" I jump up and throw my arms around his neck and kiss him passionately.

A guy in a tuxedo walks up beside us. He wears white gloves and holds a silver tray with two glasses of champagne. He smiles politely, "Sir. Madam."

"Hi," I say to him shyly.

Drakken takes both glasses off the tray, "Thank you."

The waiter bows his head slightly before turning and walking methodically back up the curving staircase that leads to a pair of huge arched wooden doors.

At least a dozen male and female waiters in formal attire, all wearing white gloves, line both sides of the staircase.

I lean toward Drakken and whisper, "Are all these waiters here for us?"

"Yes," he smiles.

"Did you like, rent this whole place out? Just for us?"

He smiles, "I want quiet dinner. Usually is very busy here."

"Really?"

He nods.

"*Really?*" I demand.

"Yes."

I think my panties just got wet. "Wow, Drakka, you didn't have to do that. We could've just gone to T.G.I. Friday's and I would've been happy."

"What is Teejee Eye Friday's?"

"Nothing compared to this," I quip.

We walk up the stairs holding hands.

All the waiters smile and say, "Good evening."

When we reach the stone landing in front of the tall arched doors, I whisper to Drakken, "Is it bad that the waiters are making me feel underdressed?"

We're both still in our T-shirts and jeans.

"Is okay. We change clothes after tour."

"Change clothes? I didn't bring any clothes!"

"I have clothes sent for you."

I plant my fist on my hip, "Do you even know my size?"

"Yes. I ask Finch at hotel. She tell me your uniform size. I use that."

My eyes pop, "Wow, pretty sneaky, Drakken."

"Sneaky? What is sneaky?"

"You," I giggle and wrap my arms around his waist and lean my cheek against his muscled chest as we enjoy the view from the landing. Endless rows of grape vines surround the castle. It's super quiet and totally peaceful out here. "What time is dinner?"

"We eat when sun go to sleep," he winks. "At sunset."

I grin at his joke.

"What do you wanna do until then?"

He arches an eyebrow and flashes his cocky grin. "Is up to you."

"Does this place have the king and queen's bedchambers or whatever?"

"Yes."

"What! That's awesome! Can we sneak in and mess up the bed?"

It takes a moment for Drakken to process my words, "Yes. We can mess up bed all night, if you want."

"All night? Did you rent a room or something?"

"Yes. We stay in King's Bed Chambers. If you want. Or we can fly home tonight. Is up to you."

"What?!" I screech. "Are you serious?"

"Yes. We have whole castle for all night and tomorrow morning."

I can't believe this. "How much did this all cost?" I slap my hand across my mouth, embarrassed. "Never mind, you don't have to answer. Thank you so much, Drakken. I can't believe you did all this for me." I think I'm going to cry, and we haven't even tasted the food or walked inside the castle yet.

He smiles. "For you, Rivka, is worth it. Smile on your face right now make me so happy, I have no words to tell you how I feel."

I hug him. It's the only way to express my gratitude at the moment.

"Good evening," a man says behind us.

We turn around and a handsome older guy with short dark hair smiles at us. He too wears a tuxedo.

"Welcome to Chateaux de l'Amour. My name is Terrence Sterling. I will be overseeing your stay here tonight. If you have any questions, I will be happy to answer them. If you like, you are free to tour the castle and the grounds. Throughout the Chateaux, you will find a hand bell resting in the corner of every room. Should you need assistance at any time, whether to ask directions, or refill your champagne," he nods toward our glasses, "request an appetizer, or merely to have one of our waitstaff give you the history of whatever room you happen to be in at the time, we will answer your summons and fulfill your request. Remember, just ring the bell." He bows his head deferentially. "May your stay here surpass your wildest expectations."

"Thank you," I say.

"Before I go," Terrence says, "Can I answer any specific requests?"

"Uh, I sort of need to go to the bathroom," I grimace. I hate to ruin the moment, but even kings and queens have to pee. Especially after a plane flight and long drive.

"Certainly, madam," Terrence says politely. To Drakken, he says, "Shall I take the lady to the royal bath?"

Drakken nods.

"Very good," Terrence smiles.

"Oh," I interrupt, "I don't need a bath. Just the toilet. I really have to go. Sorry."

"Completely understandable," Terrence nods indulgently. "If you'll follow me, madam, I'll show you the way."

The three of us walk through the arched doors. Inside, the castle is more impressive than the outside. Stone walls, high ceilings, giant tapestries, suits of armor, hanging chandeliers with real candles. And all the candles are lit. I feel like I've time travelled back to the Middle Ages.

We turn the first corner and Terrence points down a short hallway, "The ladies room is to the left."

I hustle down the hallway and take care of business. When I emerge, Drakken is leaning against the stone wall.

"Is good?" he asks.

"Yes," I sigh dramatically. "I was about to spring a leak."

"Spring a leak?" he says, confused.

"Do I have to be English teacher today?"

He smiles, "No. Is okay. No English lesson today. But you use simple words, okay?"

"Deal. Shall we look around?"

"Yes." He presents his elbow and I take it.

We walk from room to room, looking at everything. There's a huge dining room with a really long wooden table and about fifty chairs around it.

I quip, "Are we gonna eat here? With you at one end and me at the other?"

"If you want."

"Here, sit down," I pull out the chair at one end of the table for

Drakken.

"You get chair for me?"

"Yeah. Sit down"

"Okay." He sits in the chair, which has a really tall back.

I jog to the other end of the table and sit in the other tall chair. Then I holler, "Can you please pass the salt?!"

Drakken chuckles. "Okay. Is too big. We eat someplace else. We eat anywhere in castle. Okay?"

"*Any* place?"

"Yes," he smiles.

"Really? That's so cool! Can we eat on the roof? On one of the towers?"

"I don't know. Ring bell and ask."

"Huh?"

"Remember bell? For service?"

I look around at the four corners of the room and spot a hand bell on a little table. I jump out of my chair and jog over to it. I'm literally giddy with excitement. I pick it up and jingle it several times. It's a lot louder than I expected. "Whoops." I silence it with the palm of my hand.

A moment later, Terrence walks in. "You rang?"

I almost laugh. "Uhh… I was just wondering, can we eat on one of the towers?"

"Anywhere you like," Terrence smiles. "Just let us know which tower, and we'll set the table there."

"Okay. We'll look around first."

"Excellent. Anything else?"

"No. Thanks!" I smile.

Terrence disappears.

I whisper to Drakken, "I can't believe the bell thing works!"

He grins, "Is nice, yes?"

"I could get used to this."

A strange expression crosses his face, but it's gone as quick as it came. He stands up, "Would you like to see rest of castle?"

Did I annoy him? Am I being totally shallow right now? "I was just joking about getting used to this, Drakken. You didn't need to take me here to impress me. I meant what I said about T.G.I. Friday's. I'm a simple girl. I don't need all this flashy stuff to be happy. I just like hanging out with you. No matter what we do. Does that make sense?"

He listens closely and nods, "Yes, is make sense." He smiles warmly. "I take you here to make you happy, Rivka. Your happy make me happy."

After a moment, my enthusiasm elbows my uncertainty out of the room and a smile spreads across my face. "Let's go see the rest of this place!" I pull Drakken's arm and he follows, chuckling merrily.

Chapter 21

RIVER

My favorite part of the castle is the dungeon. Well, it's the wine cellar and barrel room, but you have to take stairs down to it and go through a long narrow stone hallway with torches along the walls. The torches aren't lit, there's recessed lighting overhead, but I can totally imagine how dark and dingy this place would be back in the day.

The barrel room has stacks and stacks of wine barrels piled to the ceiling. The room seems to go on forever.

We walk all the way to the end, where it's dark. Drakken pushes me behind a stack of wine barrels and we make out like crazy.

The whole time, I wonder if one of those tuxedoed waiters is going to pop out of the woodwork and ask if we need a bed rolled out.

Drakken squeezes my breast through my T-shirt and I giggle, "What if the waiters hear us?"

"I pay them to not listen except when bell, okay?" he chuckles while he nibbles my lips in the shadows.

I reach down and feel Drakken's hard cock straining against his jeans. Can't have that. I unbutton his fly and pull him out. I'm not usually this crazy, but I'm in a freakin' castle with a king of a man, and the dark wine cellar seems likes a good place for a royal B.J.

"Shall I kneel for the king?" I ask coquettishly as I squat down in front of his erect cock.

"Rivka!" he whispers, "You are crazy girl today..." He hisses pleasurably.

I grin up at him, "Just my way of saying thanks." I tease the underside of his manhood with my tongue. "Besides, I'm ready for an appetizer." I think all the champagne I drank went straight to my head. Which is why I go straight for his. I take his throbbing cock into my mouth and work it urgently. I pump the shaft and tickle his balls with both hands.

He moans and leans his head back against the stone wall. "So good, Rivka," he whispers. "You make me come soon..."

His cock strains in my mouth. I taste pre-cum on the tip.

"Stop!" he hisses. "I make you come first."

I love that he thinks about me. But sometimes it's better to give than receive. I work his shaft and lick and suck ravenously.

He places his palm on the side of my face. His thumb caresses my earlobe, and for whatever reason, that drives me crazy. I'm totally wet and the only thing I want is his cock inside me.

But I'm not going there. We've never crossed that bridge. Best not to tempt fate twice.

He can take care of me later.

Now it's his turn for pleasure.

I run my free hand under his T-shirt and caress his rock hard abs. His stomach is super tense because of what I'm doing with my tongue and lips.

"Is so good, Rivka. Is, is, oh… so… Ah! Yes! Ahh!!!"

My thighs quiver deliciously when he explodes in my mouth and gasps for breath. I almost come when I taste him and swallow his luscious seed. It's such a complete turn on. Something about having sex in a dark dungeon.

I milk every last drop of Drakken's cum as he sags against the stone wall.

Chapter 22

RIVER

"Are you hungry to eat?" Drakken asks when we're standing on one of the castle walls gazing out at the vineyards.

"Wait, what kind of eating are we talking about?" I quip. My panties are still wet after the wine cellar, and I can't stop thinking about cocks and orgasms.

Drakken grins, "Food kind. We can eat on tower. Or we can go to royal bedroom and I can eat you for dinner." He flashes me a sensual grin.

I laugh joyfully, "You just made a sexual innuendo joke in English, Drakken! That's your first one! That's a big deal!" I smile from ear to ear.

"Is so much harder in English."

"I know, but that's progress!" I clink his champagne glass with mine. "And that's not the only thing that's hard…" I reach down and squeeze his package through his jeans. "Oh shizz! I was joking, but you're hard again!" I hiss quietly because I don't know how close the nearest waiter is.

He nods. "Because I think about how wet you are after blowjob in wine cellar. Is make me very hard."

I blurt laughter but say in a quiet voice, "*You're* hard?! I'm soaking wet!!"

"You want me to eat you now? Or we wait until after dinner? Sun go down soon."

"You can *go down* as soon as the sun does," I snicker and wink.

"*Then* I eat you as dessert," he grins.

I clink his glass again, "You're on a roll with the sex puns, Drakken! Keep 'em coming."

"I keep *you* coming all night," he chuckles.

I fold at the waist and cackle loudly. Not only am I super buzzed, I'm also super horny and I couldn't be happier.

"Are you ready to try on dress?"

"You got me a dress?"

"Yes. Is in royal bedroom."

"Let's go!" I pull him along the castle wall and we descend a spiral staircase to the castle proper.

"This way." Drakken leads me down a long hallway. We turn a bunch of times until we arrive at a pair of old wooden doors, the kind with the huge iron hinges and iron rivets. The handle is a fat iron ring.

Drakken opens the door and I walk inside.

"Wow," I marvel. "This... this is *enchanting*."

Outside the bedchamber, the castle is Henry the V. Inside it's Louis the XIV. The room is filled with opulent gold leaf and canary blue baroque furniture. Royal velvet curtains, also in canary blue, drape over the exorbitant four poster bed, and are gathered back from the windows with gold ropes. Crystal chandeliers float like frozen snowflakes above the inlaid wood floor. I imagine there are some ladies in waiting around here somewhere...

I spot a pink princess gown on a dress mannequin in the corner.

My jaw drops.

I turn to Drakken, on the verge of drooling, "Is that my dress?"

He nods, "Yes."

"It looks like a fluffy pink birthday cake!" I rush over to it. A bejeweled pink corset rises out of a frilly hoop dress made from pink ruffles and fluffy taffeta layered over lace. Embroidered silver detailing is woven throughout.

I bite my lip and smile at Drakken. "It's beautiful," I mumble, barely able to get the words out. It looks good enough to go in the Smithsonian or some other world class museum.

"Is yours."

"Thank you, Drakken." I gasp, "Oh, no! Shoes!" I wince and hold one of my feet up behind me. "All I have are my running shoes. I can't wear them with this dress!"

"Is okay." He walks to the corner and lifts yet another handbell off the baroque table. He rings it.

"Oh, that's okay," I say. "Nobody is going to see my sneakers under the dress anyway."

Drakken opens the bedroom door and three of the waitresses carry in a dozen shoe boxes. I spot the embossed silver Jimmy Choo logo right away.

My eyes goggle and I blurt, "Don't tell me I get to pick my shoes!"

Drakken grins, "No, only shoe size. Shoe is match dress. What size are you?"

"I'm usually seven and a half."

Drakken looks through the boxes until he finds one and takes it from the woman. "Thank you."

She nods and smiles.

Drakken walks over to me. "Sit down. We try shoe first. Put on dress after."

"Okay."

I sit down in one of the plush hand-carved baroque chairs. Drakken kneels and slides off my running shoes. He opens the shoe box and pulls out bejeweled pink peep-toe platforms.

I gasp. "Wow, that is totally luxe!"

Drakken slides the shoes on my feet Prince Charming style.

I stand up and twist around, trying to get a better look. "Is there a mirror around here?"

One of the waitresses motions toward a door, "This way."

I follow her into a bathroom that looks like a ballroom, but it does in fact have a marble bathtub with gold faucets. There's a floor length mirror on a wooden easel in the corner.

Yeah, the shoes are awesome.

I can't wait until I see myself with the dress on!

Drakken leans his head through the doorway. "Have women help you dress. I change in other room. I wait for you downstairs."

"Okay," I say excitedly.

Chapter 23

RIVER

I descend the staircase to the main lobby of the castle where all the suits of armor are. My dress came with elbow length pink gloves.

I'm bedazzled pink confectionary from head to toe.

Drakken stands at the bottom of the stairs in a white tuxedo with a pale pink vest and matching bow tie, and white gloves. He looks damn handsome.

He takes my hand and purrs, "I am ready for dessert. You look like pink birthday cake."

"That's what I thought!" I grin. "Don't worry, you can have a slice later..."

I hook my arm around his elbow and we make our way to the tallest tower and up to the roof.

Terrence stands at the top of the spiral stairs. He says, "Your table, my lady."

Fine crystal glasses, silverware, and gold enameled dinnerware sparkle atop a pale pink linen tablecloth. A garland of pink roses is draped around the table. Pink and white rose petals are scattered across the stone floor.

"We match the decor," I smile.

Drakken grins and pulls out my chair for me.

"Thank you, sir," I quip and sit as he slides my chair forward.

He sits down across from me.

We're close enough to hold hands, which we do.

Terrence steps up to our table and asks, "Would the lady care for a drink?"

"Oh, um, you have wine, right?" I joke.

Terrence looks genuinely amused, "But of course. Shall I chose something for you to go with the appetizers?"

"That would be awesome."

Terrence bows and walks down the stairs.

I look out at the setting sun, which is a red globe balanced on the edge of the distant mountain range.

"Is nice, yes?" Drakken asks.

"Drakken, this is the nicest dinner I've ever had! And we haven't even eaten yet!" I'm so excited it's ridiculous.

He smiles and squeezes my hand.

A waiter walks up the spiral staircase carrying a tray of appetizers. He sets them down on the table and says, "Bacon wrapped dates stuffed with blue cheese."

I lean over to Drakken, "Should we take our gloves off before we eat?"

"Yes." Drakken tugs his gloves off one finger at a time with distinctive panache before setting them on the edge of the table in a neat stack. He seems very at ease dining in formal wear.

"You make it look so easy," I muse.

"Practice," he says confidently.

"All I can think about is whether or not I'm going to drop a greasy bacon wrapped date in my fluffy pink lap when I finally get my fork into one."

He chuckles, forks up a date and leans over the table, his hand cupped beneath. "I feed you, so no spill."

I lean forward and take a dainty bite. "Mmmm! Yum! That is so good!"

He eats the other half and chews thoroughly until he swallows. "Very good."

"It's delicious, right?"

"Almost as delicious as you, Rivka," he winks.

I quip, "Make sure you save room for dessert. We're having cake," I say suggestively. "I hope you like pink frosting."

"Is my favorite," he winks.

Chapter 24

RIVER

I stand alone in front of the full length mirror in the royal bathroom, still wearing my pink birthday cake princess gown, examining the dress. It really is exquisite.

"You can't even tell," I moan. "You, *oh god," moan* "you can't." *moan* "Even." *moan* "Tell…" My words echo off the marble floor and walls as my head tips back and I sigh heavily, "Ohhhhh…"

I don't know what Drakken is doing under my dress, but I'm pretty sure it involves his tongue, all his fingers, and both thumbs. And of course, my drenched wet orifice.

I asked him to climb under my dress because I thought it would be funny to see if he could do it without being noticeable, but he is taking the whole thing very seriously.

I would've collapsed by now, but his powerful hands grip the backs of my thighs and hold me up. My upper body is rubbery and wiggles loosely as pleasure fountains up from my core. A moment later, my eyes flutter and an orgasm washes down my spine as I rain all over his face.

A few minutes later, Drakken has finally stopped licking and fingering. He releases me and emerges from under the dress, still in his tux.

Still breathless, I joke, "How was the cake?"

"Sweet. And spicy," he smears his slick fingers across his tongue and sucks the tips, savoring my flavor. "You taste like cinnamon and honey."

"No I don't," I scoff.

He smiles and wraps his arms around my waist and kisses me forcefully. All I can taste is his raw masculine passion. He moans into my mouth and pushes his hips against me.

The fluffy princess gown has so much material, I can't feel him through the dress, so I reach down and make sure he's hard. Yup. Like steel.

I wink, "We need to unsheathe your sword, Sir Knight. Would you be so kind as to help me out of my dress?"

"Anything for you, my lady," he winks.

We remove my fluffy dress in stages. Drakken drapes each piece over a baroque chair in the corner.

He turns to face me across the expanse of the marble bathroom. A cocky grin spreads across his face. "Is nice," he murmurs.

I stand in a bejeweled pink corset, garters, thigh high pink stockings, and the pink peep toe platforms. No panties, of course.

"You are gorgeous, Rivka. All day, I think about this moment. I picture you in my mind in pink dress, but picture is no good compared to real thing."

I giggle bashfully. I'm not used to being ogled and complimented like this. Especially not by the most incredibly handsome blue-eyed beau I've ever laid eyes on.

He begins unknotting his bow tie as he steps slowly toward me. "I am hard all through dinner thinking about you. When I watch you eat, I want you. I want your mouth…" He slides his bow tie off his neck and drapes it around mine. He kisses my top lip softly. "I want your lips…" he kisses my bottom lip then bites it gently. "I want your tongue…" He slides his into my mouth for a brief hot tease, then withdraws. "I want your wetness…" His hand cups my wet folds.

I'm still soaking wet from the orgasm he already gave me. "I think it's your turn," I grab his cock through his slacks.

"No," he removes my hand. "I not done with you, Rivka. Come," he slaps me on the ass and walks to the door of the royal bathroom. "Come, Rivka. Now."

I walk across the bathroom, my heels clicking quietly on the marble.

"Sit," he points to the giant four poster bed with the canary blue velvet curtains tied around the posts.

I sit on the foot of the bed, knees together. He kneels and removes my shoes.

"Stand and turn around," he commands.

I comply and he unlaces my corset. I lift it off and his arms suddenly snake around me. Strong hands cup my breasts, pressing them against my chest and kneading them greedily. He pulls me into his chest and I tip my head back against his muscled shoulder.

His hands roam all over my body while he nibbles my ear. He caresses my breasts, my stomach, the inside of my thighs. A hard finger slides inside me. I close my eyes and moan, "Mmmmm. Yes. More of that."

He releases me and steps away.

"Where are you going?" I whine. "I was just getting into it."

He grins and opens one of the baroque cupboards and pulls out a white box with a pink bow. He hands it to me. "Open."

I unknot the bow and lift off the lid.

Inside the box, two pairs of golden handcuffs rest on top of a nest of pink velvet.

"Handcuffs?" I ask uncertainly. I've never done handcuffs before, or anything kinky. Sure, I've done a bunch of different positions, but nothing too weird.

He nods. "Put them on. One on each wrist."

"Um...do I have to?"

"No," he says casually.

"What happens if I put them on?" I ask uncertainly.

HEROIN BREAST IMPLANTS!!

SEX SLAVERY!!

DON'T DO IT, RIV!!!!

Drakken says seductively,

"I will make you come harder than you ever come before..."

"I like the sound of that," I grin. "What happens if I don't put them on?"

He smirks, "I make you come, but less hard."

I giggle, "You already made me come really hard in the bathroom. How hard can one person come?"

"You can never come too hard, Rivka."

"Okay..." I lift one pair of golden handcuffs out of the box.

DON'T DO IT!!!!

I set the handcuffs back in the box. "Can I ask you a question, Drakkozsha?"

He slides his hands into his pockets, "Anything."

My heart starts to pound in my chest.

It's high time I ask Drakken what he does for a living. If he's a drug czar or any other kind of criminal, I want to know before I put the cuffs on. If it turns out he *is* a criminal, it's going to ruin the moment and probably the rest of the weekend.

Maybe I should drop the subject. I can always ask him come Monday. Then I can spend the rest of the weekend coming.

I bite my lower lip uncertainly.

I can't keep *putting* it off just to keep *getting* off. I fist my hands and push them into the tops of my thighs. "Drakken, what does your business do?"

He narrows his eyes for a moment, then runs one hand through his short black hair.

"Is complicated," he sighs heavily.

Great.

There went my weekend.

No more coming and time to get going.

Chapter 25

RIVER

Drakken throws his head back and laughs for a long time. When his laughter fades, he chuckles, "You are thinking I am Russian mafia?"

I nod sheepishly.

We sit side by side on the foot of the bed.

"No, no, no. I am not Russian. And not criminal. I own airplane business."

"An airplane business?" I gawk. "Why didn't you tell me before?" I slap his leg.

"My company make research and development for other aeronautic companies. Much of our work is top secret. For government."

"Oh," I say dramatically. "Which government?"

"Different ones," he says casually.

"Is it for the U.S. government?"

"No."

"Then what are you doing in Los Angeles?"

"I have many business partner here for side project."

I narrow my eyes, "It's not illegal, is it?"

He shakes his head, "No, no, no. Side project is legal. But is very experimental, and worth billion of dollar if I get business off ground."

"I get it." I pat his leg.

What a relief. When I get home, I'm going to give Julietta a hard time for making me so paranoid. But that can wait. Now I'm ready for Drakken to give me a hard time. The hardest time ever. I hold up one of the golden handcuffs, "So, what're we gonna do with these?"

"Is depends. Have you been bad girl, Rivka? Or good girl?" His eyes twinkle with mirth and the promise of earth shattering orgasms.

"Haven't you heard?" I say seductively. "Bad is the new good..." I wink, "...and I've been really bad..."

"Then you must be punished," Drakken grins, "Put handcuff on."

"You or me?" I quip and bite my lower lip, crinkling my nose.

He chuckles, "You really are bad girl. You know what bad girl need?"

"Uh...orgasms?" I giggle. I haven't done the bondage thing before.

He grins, "No, bad girl need spanking!"

Before I can respond, he's tickling my ribs and I'm laughing like crazy and hunching over, trying to protect my sides. This makes it easy for Drakken to throw me over his lap and start the spanking.

Whack!

"Ouch!" I blurt, still giggling.

Whack!

He's not hitting me very hard. I don't know what I was expecting, but the only thing I really feel is a pleasurable sting on my ass.

Whack!

I go with it. I purr, "I've been really bad, Mr. Skalakova. I don't know what I was thinking when I spilled coffee all over your billion dollar presentation notes."

"What?" he pauses, clearly confused.

I wink up at him, "I'm pretending. This is a fantasy, right?"

He chuckles, "Okay, yes. We are in skyscraper office and presentation is in five minutes."

Whack!

I love that he can play along too.

He says, "I spank you for every page of note you ruin."

Whack!

The tingling on my ass slowly transforms into something rather delightful. Every time he spanks, puffs of pleasure explode throughout my pelvis. I kind of like this.

"You has been very bad, Rivka."

Whack!

After I lose count on spanks, his hand comes to rest on my butt cheek. Then it slides down my ass and delves between my legs. His fingers work their way down to my drenched folds. I'm totally turned on.

"You are so wet, Rivka," he hisses with obvious approval. "Only bad girls get wet."

"Mmmm-hmmm," I moan.

His fingertips massage my labia in slow strokes. "Very wet," he groans, his own arousal apparent. "You know what I do with bad girl who is very wet?"

I shake my head, unable to speak because the sensation of his fingers is driving me crazy.

"I punish wet girl."

A thick fingertip slowly pushes into my hole.

"I punish her by make her so wet she never forget how bad it is to be wet."

I don't think I've ever been so entirely focused on the sensation of something entering me as I am right now. His finger goes in to the hilt, then withdraws slowly, only to slide back in to the end of heaven. Wow, if this is what bad gets you, bad really is the new good. Oh my god, I have died and gone to sexual heaven.

"Bad girl..." he groans, clearly mesmerized by whatever he's experiencing on his end.

"Oh," I whimper with genuine delight, "I'm going to come, Drakka..."

His finger slowly withdraws.

All the way.

Wait! I was enjoying that!

He sits me up on the bed.

I notice he is rock hard in his slacks.

He stands and glares down at me, "Bad girl is not allowed to come until I say she can come."

I am on the verge of a really powerful orgasm, and I don't want to lose it. Without thinking, I slide my fingers between my legs and rub my clit. I hood my eyes and smirk at Drakken while I touch myself. Two can play at this punishment game. I slowly lick my lips...

"Stop!" he roars. "No come until I say come!"

His voice is so commanding, it shocks me and I stop what I'm doing, withdrawing my hand from between my legs.

He points forcefully, "Put one handcuff on each wrist."

I notice the cuffs are padded. I pop one open and ratchet it around my wrist, then do the other wrist with the other pair.

I plant my hands on the edge of the bed, not sure what comes next. I mean, besides coming...

"Now what?" I ask.

"Lie down on bed," he commands.

"Yes, sir." I scoot my ass up on the covers and lie my head on the fluffy satin pillows. I do the obvious and spread my arms out. They're too short to reach the wide-set posts. "I can't reach."

Drakken walks around to one side of the bed and snaps the cuffs around an iron ring bolted to the headboard.

Now that I'm actually attached to the bed, I'm pointedly aware of the fact that I'm not going anywhere. What if there's an earthquake? Northern

California is notorious for earthquakes. They strike when you least expect it. Usually when you're hand cuffed half-naked to a bed.

He walks around to the other side and fastens the other cuff to the other ring.

I wiggle the cuffs, "Now I'm stuck. All locked up with no place to go."

He slides off his tuxedo jacket.

"Are you gonna give me a show?"

"No show."

"Why not?"

"Bad girl must have punish. You think for long time about spill coffee on my billion dollar presentation note. And think about how bad you are to be so wet."

He folds the jacket over the back of one of the baroque chairs. He lays his pink vest on top then sits on the chair and removes his shoes and socks.

He stands and walks to the foot of the bed and unbuttons his shirt slowly, staring at me the whole time.

Chest.

Followed by abs.

Followed by him stretching out of the shirt with languorous slowness like a waking predator stretching before the hunt.

He bunches the shirt in one hand.

"Nice body," I quip.

Nice is an understatement. Perfect is more appropriate. Manly muscles doesn't do it justice. Dangerous is a better word. You could chip a tooth on those abs of his. I plan on trying as soon as his stomach gets within nibbling distance.

I mutter, "Come here, you animal…"

He tosses his white dress shirt in the air and it billows down onto my face.

"Hey!" I bark. "What was that for?"

"For you to smell," he chuckles. "While you think about how wet you are."

All I can see is white dress shirt.

I hear his bare feet pad across the wood floor. A door creaks open. I hope that's not the front door to the room. I don't want him deciding now is a good time to take a tour of the vineyards or have a long chat with Terrence and the waitstaff. Although I'm really enjoying all this fantasy role-playing, I don't think I like the idea of him abandoning me completely.

The door closes and I realize it's the bathroom door. Phew.

With him gone, I feel anxious, so I'm trying to ease my nerves with humor. I holler, "I hope you're going number one, because I don't think I'm comfortable waiting any longer than that!"

He doesn't respond.

Silence.

I squirm around on the bed. You really can't move much when both your arms are pinioned to a headboard.

After another minute, I holler, "You're not reading a magazine are you? Aviation Weekly or whatever?"

No answer.

They say anticipation heightens the reward. I don't know if that's true. But it heightens anxiety. I'm getting hot under his shirt from all my breathing. I blow hard, hoping to somehow blow his shirt off my face. Not a chance. Too heavy.

I inhale deeply afterward, and that's when I smell his scent.

It's all over his shirt.

He totally knew what he was doing.

I'm cocooned in Drakken scent.

It is most pleasant.

In fact, I might have to ask Drakken to let me keep this shirt for my own bed. It will remind me of our unforgettable time at Chateaux de l'Amour. As I reflect on it, I remember Drakken's words, and find myself thinking all about how wet I am.

It's all I can think about.

Well, my wetness, the spankings, and his finger going in and out like it was the best fucking I've ever had. In, out, slip, slide, pleasure, pleasure, pleasure...

Lying on this comfy bed, with his pheromone laden shirt permeating my senses and thoughts of his manly hand penetrating my feminine defenses, all I want to do is come like crazy.

I can take care of that. I reach down to slide my fingers through my wet folds and—

RATTLE!!

Stupid handcuffs.

Stupid Drakken!

I squeeze my thighs together and rub them back and forth because it's all I can do. I feel tingling inside my core, and working the muscles down there does heighten the pleasure slightly, but it isn't going to get me over the edge of the orgasm waterfall. At the moment, bound as I am, only one thing will do.

I need a man.

"Hurry up in there, Drakken!" I plead before fading into frustrated chuckles.

Sooner or later, I'm going to die from the overwhelming pent up desire that throbs between my legs.

About four hours later, or four minutes—it's hard to tell—the bathroom door opens.

I hear Drakken pad out and sit on the foot of the mattress.

"Finally," I grouse.

He unhooks my garters and slides off each stocking with agonizing slowness.

Something brushes across the inside of my upper arm, shocking me out of my Drakken drenched fantasy.

I shriek, "A spider just crawled across my arm! Get it off!"

Whatever it was is suddenly gone. And whatever it was, it took my arousal with it.

"Did you kill it?" I ask frantically. "I hate spiders!"

"Is not spider. Is feather."

"No fair! I'm totally ticklish!"

"I know. You show me earlier. That is why I bring feather. I must punish bad girl."

"I don't know about that," I say skeptically.

"Relax. I am right. You will see. I mean, feel."

I snicker under his dress shirt, "Are we having another English lesson?"

"No. Is sex lesson," he chuckles. "For bad girl who do not learn lesson first time..."

The feather brushes across my skin again.

Now that I know it's not a spider, it's easier to enjoy it.

Drakken works the feather along my arms, around my neck, down my chest, between my breasts and around each one. A breeze of pleasure trails behind wherever the tip of the feather touches. He tickles my nipples with it and a mist of pleasure billows inside each breast.

This feels amazing.

I still can't see anything, so I close my eyes and enjoy it. The burning coal in my core reignites when he caresses my navel. I fall back into the warm embrace of fiery arousal.

The feather trails downward, skipping over my entrance, then slides down my quivering thighs.

When the feather reaches the sole of my foot, I jiggle my leg involuntarily. "It tickles," I giggle.

"If you relax and let feeling flow, pleasure will be more."

"I'll try," I sigh.

Sure enough, the light brushing of the feather across my feet becomes a sizzling windstorm that climbs up my legs and feeds the blazing heat inside me.

The thing I'm not at all prepared for is what happens when that demon feather goes to work on my ribs. The pleasure overtakes me. My eyes turn up into the top of my head. My mouth opens wide in a silent moaning gasp. I can't inhale because the feather is making every muscle in my abdomen spasm. The electricity unleashed courses through my body. I'm hyperventilating and my erratic breathing heightens everything.

Drakken is going to tickle me to death with the feather. The tickling is short circuiting my brain. I am on stimulation overload. Rather than run from it, I fall into it.

Falling, falling, falling.

I'm ready to die.

Every muscle in my body squirms to escape the onslaught of ecstasy, but my wrists are trapped by the handcuffs. I pull against them, wanting desperately to touch myself, to bring the release that is dying to come out.

Come, come, come.

But I can't.

I'm right on that edge of bliss, but I can't cross over until someone presses my magic button.

I feel Drakken shift his weight around on the bed.

Something hot and hard presses between my closed thighs. I'm pretty sure it's his finger, but at the moment, it feels like a throbbing cock. At least that's what I'm telling myself. I desperately want it to be his cock. Drakken and I still have not had intercourse. Not that I'm complaining. What I'm experiencing at the moment is proof that you don't have to have a cock handy to come hard. I relax my legs, opening myself up to him.

Then he enters me.

I tell myself it is in fact his cock.

I tell myself that this incredible man is inside me the way I have longed for since that fateful evening in the Sunset Suite. If I can't have the reality, I will gladly indulge in the fantasy.

The fantasy is incredible.

I rise again on hot clouds of wet ecstasy as he penetrates me and fills me up.

But it's not quite enough to lift me to oblivion.

As if he's reading my thoughts, he finally, *finally*, presses my magic button. Something, probably his thumb, gives my clit the treatment it deserves in slow languid circles.

Orgasmic waves begin to build inside me. They increase in rippling peaks of mounting intensity.

Mounting...

A powerful orgasm unfurls inside my pelvis. My breath comes in great gasps as I moan and moan and moan.

"Ohhhhh, ohhhhh, ohhhhh... Oh, Drakken..."

Heat blooms and pours out from my core, drenching my body with golden syrupy waves of pleasure that flow to the tips of my fingers and my toes.

For what seems like several minutes, I float inside an orgasm. It is intense, all consuming, and feels oh so fucking good.

Slowly, the sensation fades.

But the afterglow remains.

I pant, eyes closed, my hot breath heating my face beneath the shirt.

Suddenly, the shirt is lifted away and a cool breeze settles on my face.

I open my eyes to a slit. I can't open them any farther because even my eyelids are basking in the afterglow of my white hot orgasm.

Drakken leans over me, smiling warmly. "Is punishment for bad girl good?"

"Mmmm," I sigh. "That was amazing, Drakka. You can punish me like that any time you want," I purr.

"Did you come hard?"

"I did. But I'm not sure that's the *hardest* I've ever come before."

He frowns. "*Not* hard?"

I nod listlessly, "It was different. Almost like melting. Not hard, but it may very well be the best orgasm I've ever had..." I grin and sigh sleepily. "Oh my god. I feel so damn good right now." I draw a slow breath of air. "Almost like I'm stoned or something."

He nods, pleased with himself, "Is good."

I giggle, "You're a bit cocky, aren't you?"

"Yes," he grins. "I am very much cocky."

I chuckle. "Well, I hate to break it to you. As good as that orgasm was... still is, wow. As good as it felt, it definitely wasn't the *hardest* I've ever come."

"Oh? Are you challenge?"

I nod. I'm about to say something, then I stop myself.

Do I tell him that there's something about coming when a guy has his cock inside you and you both come together that overshadows every kind of orgasm a woman can have? No, I can't say that. It would probably just hurt his feelings.

He nods, "Is okay. Now I make you come harder than you ever come before."

I smile, "You don't have to, Drakken. It's your turn. Let me make you come. Take these handcuffs off and I'll make you come so hard your dick will shoot off your body like a flesh rocket." I chuckle at my own joke.

"Flesh rocket?" he grins. and shakes his head. "You has crazy ideas,

Rivka."

"I'm joking. Just uncuff me and I'll give you a blowjob you'll never forget." I give him a sexy wink. "You've been pretty bad too, you know..."

He shakes his head. "No."

"No? You haven't been bad?"

He smirks, "I am all ways bad."

In a stern tone of voice, I admonish, "Then I have no choice but to give you a blowjob, young man."

"You give me blowjob in barrel room. I am more bad than that."

I'm not sure where he's going with this. "You don't want something with whips and paddles, do you?"

"No."

"Chains and ball gags?"

"No."

"Squirrels and gerbils?"

He smirks, "No."

"Okay. Um, how about a parade of sailors with their bouncing cocks out?"

"Sailors?" he chuckles.

"I'm sorry," I sigh, "I'm not sure what you want. Can you uncuff me now? So I can give you a blowjob?" Sometimes, the simple solution is the best one.

He unfastens his slacks and slides them down to his ankles. His mammoth cock is rock hard.

I would really like to lick it. But there's nothing I can do cuffed to the bed.

He steps out of his slacks and stands beside the bed. His thick erect cock is a foot away. It's also nearly a foot long, by my estimates. If only I could grab it, I would go to town.

He grins down at me. "You want my cock."

"Was that a question?"

"No. You want it. I can see it in your face."

"Yes, I want your cock. So what?"

"How bad do you want it?"

I smirk, "Are you trying to make me beg?"

"No." His gaze dances around uncertainly for a moment. His face struggles through a range of expressions. He's thinking about something. "I, uh, I want to know if, if you... do you want my cock inside you?"

Okay, that's weird. He went from sixty-nine shades of Drakken for the last hour to suddenly...nervous.

Now would be a good time for the sailors and their bouncing cocks to Riverdance into the room and break the tension that now strains the moment.

"I hate to ruin the mood," I say cautiously, "but I think I'm ready for the handcuffs to come off. My arms are sort of falling asleep."

He nods, his head hanging, hiding his face.

He picks up the box that held the handcuffs and pulls out the keys. Then he quietly unlocks the cuffs.

I sit up on the bed cross legged and rub my wrists. Even with the padding, it was somewhat uncomfortable. But well worth the experience.

Drakken's erection is gone.

He sits down on the edge of the bed beside me and I rest my hand on his back.

He hisses and flinches.

The scars.

All those jagged scars.

IS TOO MUCH!!!

I yank my hand away. "I'm sorry," I say softly. "Do you not want me touching your back?"

He turns his head and pins me with his wounded blue eyes. They are dark in the faint glow of the chandeliers. But the sadness in them is clear as day. In a choked voice he says, "Is okay. You can touch."

I rest my hand on his back and feel the puckered and melted flesh. At a moment like this, I would normally rub his back gently but the silent scars scream beneath my palm. I hold them gently, imagining my healing energy flowing into his body. I send him all the loving kindness I can.

I whisper, "Do you want to talk about it?"

"No. It will make me sad. I don't want to be sad now, okay?"

"Okay," I murmur.

Despite Drakken's remarkable progress with English, I know that what remains of our language barrier makes it difficult to talk about complex issues. Now is not the time to fumble through such a delicate conversation.

I lean against him, my breasts pressing against his muscled arm, and hug him. I kiss his cheek, his ear, the corner of his mouth. I squeeze my arms around him and hug him lovingly.

I can't escape the feeling that the handcuffs and the feather and the dominance were all an act for my benefit. Maybe he wanted to avoid the disaster we had the last time we were in a bedroom by putting on a big show. I don't know. I certainly enjoyed it.

But it lacked that flow, that special magical connection I felt on our fateful day in the Sunset Suite, before our love making collapsed into a waking nightmare.

It suddenly occurs to me that Drakken has *avoided* bedrooms entirely ever since. Every time we have fooled around, it has been in a public place like an elevator or kissing in his car or whatever.

But never in a bedroom.

Has he been avoiding bedrooms on purpose? Is he afraid that he'll freak out again? The idea frightens me too, but I'm not walking out of here, no matter what happens. I could never walk away from the man in my arms right now.

This man, the quiet one, the shy one, the sad one, is the real Drakken. This is the man I want to connect with soul to soul. The man I want to comfort and care for more than I've wanted anything in my entire life. The man I want to hold and heal and bring back to happiness.

I whisper, "What do you want me to do, Drakkozsha?"

"Make me forget. Okay?"

I don't know what it is he wants to forget, but I know exactly what he needs.

"Make me forget, Rivka," he repeats hoarsely.

I gaze into those ice blue eyes and shine all of my love into this man.

Flow.

I feel it.

He feels it.

That sacred connection we shared months and months ago is back as if it was never gone.

It's all about the flow.

Chapter 26

DRAKKEN

I gaze into Rivka's liquid blue eyes.

I feel love emanating from them like a beacon of hope.

The sensation is unmistakable. It is the same sensation that SHE gave me before SHE was taken away by HIM.

It takes everything I have to confront my past in this moment and not run away from Rivka.

I am drowning in painful memories.

I now regret insisting on the handcuffs this evening. I foolishly believed that focusing on sex games would distract me from my inner turmoil and allow me to enjoy myself. The games worked while I was giving Rivka pleasure, but once the focus shifted to my pleasure, the suffocating pain returned full force.

The only thing holding me together in this moment is the strength and power of Rivka's heart.

I feel it with certainty.

If not for her, I would explode and tear apart every piece of furniture in this room until I was surrounded by the same broken wreckage that fills my heart.

But I don't.

Because of Rivka.

Only she can soothe my pain and cool my burning fury…

Chapter 27

RIVER

"Lie down," I say softly.

He scoots all the way onto the bed and rests his head on the pillows.

I feather kisses across his face like warm and loving snowflakes.

He needs me to make him forget.

I *need* to be needed right now.

With my heart wide open, pouring every ounce of my love and healing energy into him, I am totally exposed. I need *him* to accept my love, to make me feel safe and confident that he still wants me when I am baring my very soul to him. It takes every last bit of courage I have to stay open.

I kiss the tip of his nose gently then gaze into his eyes.

The stone mask is gone. The dominance is gone. His face is soft, fragile, breakable.

Flow.

Our exchange of honest emotional energy is overwhelming.

His mouth finds mine and our lips tangle together with desperate need. Our tongues fight. The passionate loving man that hides beneath all his masks and facades and his profound anger begins to finally emerge.

I glide my hand across his chest, caress the skin with my fingertips, tickle his abs, then grab him by the root.

He is stout and strong. Hot and pulsating in my hands. His need for me could not be more clear.

I kiss my way down his chest, fully prepared to rock his rock hard world.

"No," he mutters.

The flow closes.

Shizz.

I freeze in place and rest my face against his abs.

So close.

His cock juts magnificently in the air, only inches from my mouth.

I don't know what to do.

He rolls to the side of the bed.

I sit up on my knees and cover my breasts, hugging myself. I don't know where this is going, but I'm worried and uncomfortable all over again.

What happened to our flow?

He opens a drawer beside the bed and pulls out a box of condoms. "We use these."

"What?" I frown nervously. "For a blowjob?"

"No."

I rest my palm on his arm. My face knots with worry, "Are you sure?"

"Very sure."

"I only want to do this if you want to do this, Drakkozsha." Oh boy, I *really* want to do this. But only if he does too. I don't want another disaster on my hands.

The jagged memories of that day slice painfully through my mind.

IS TOO MUCH!!!

GO!!! GOOOOO!!!

He sits up and rests his hand on the inside of my thigh. His cock still points straight up. A droplet of pre-cum glistens on the tip, declaring his desire. "I want this, Rivka. I want you. I want to have sex with you. Right now."

"But last time..." I trail off, afraid to say more.

"Last time, we has no condom. Now I has condom. I want you, Rivka. I never wanted a woman so bad as I want you right now. Never in my..." he droops his head. His voice chokes up, "never in my life has I wanted a woman so bad it make so much hurt."

Tears fall onto his chest, reflecting the soft glow of the chandeliers like glittering diamonds. He lifts his head and tears stream down his cheeks. "Make me forget, Rivka. Make me forget."

FLOW.

Powerful, open, soul-shattering flow.

As long as I feel the flow, everything will be as it should.

I glance down at his manhood. Still rock hard. It twitches in time with his heartbeat.

Twitch, twitch, twitch...

Pre-cum has dribbled down the head of his cock. He wants me. There's no doubt about it.

IS TOO MUCH!!

FLOW.

All that matters is our flow.

I am not afraid...

I reach down and hold him in my hands. I rub the pre-cum around beneath my thumb and massage the tip with one hand. With the other, I caress his shaft languorously.

He leans on one arm and his head falls slowly backward. He moans with desperation and distinct satisfaction, "Aaaahhhh..."

With that moan, I know everything is going to be okay. He's finally letting go. Finally giving in to our connection.

The pure thrill of *his* enjoyment brings a smile to my face and fills me with happiness and unabashed desire.

I need him inside me as badly as he does.

"Remember," I murmur. "I am on the pill still."

He tilts his head forward. A seductive smile relaxes onto his face. "Yes. But we use condom, okay?"

"Sure." It doesn't matter why.

He peels the box open and pulls out the roll.

I take it from him. "Let me do that." I tear a packet off the strip and open it. I roll the slippery condom onto his length.

"Lie down," I say confidently and press my hand against his chest.

He sinks into the plush comforter.

I swing my knee over his waist and hover above him. I reach between my legs and position his cock at my entrance. Between my wetness and the lubrication on the condom, there is no resistance.

Slowly, I sit down.

"Ahhhhhh..." he groans.

Slowly, he fills me.

I bite my lower lip and suck in air across my teeth. "Ohmygod." I close my eyes and everything ceases to exist, save this man and our intimate physical and emotional connection.

Our flow.

I relax my legs completely, sinking down until I'm sitting on his lap, savoring the feeling of being exquisitely and perfectly full.

Flow.

Drakken sighs, "Is so good, Rivka. So warm."

I lift myself up, squeezing my kegels as hard as I can, milking the pleasure out of him.

"So tight," he gasps.

I sit back down, sliding down his hardness. My clit tickles along his length and it feels fantastic. Drakken's cock was made for me. It's that simple. I don't know if it's Drakken's girth, his shape, or what, but his throbbing cock is rubbing right up against my clit every time I move.

Again, I lift myself up and lower myself down. Each time I do, my clit sings with pleasure.

Drakken grabs my waist and thumbs my hip bones tenderly, "So womanly," he says with obvious admiration. "So beautiful…"

I'm surprised that he likes them.

I lean forward and plant my hands on his broad chest and start a slow steady rhythm. Up and down, up and down, grinding my pelvis when I reach the bottom, shocking my clit each time.

"Ahhh, so good," Drakken moans, thrusting up with his cock.

Every cell in my pelvis is sizzling with pleasure and flow.

Drakken pushes his palms against my breasts, massaging them lightly against my chest.

I hang my head and sigh, "This feels so good, Drakka." I rock and rock and rock. "I'm going to come. Oh god, I'm going to come. Drakka…" I'm breathless. "Drakka…"

He responds by grabbing my ass, digging his fingers into the muscles as I grind and grind and grind.

I scream, "I'm coming, Drakken! I'm coming!"

"Yes, come for me, Rivka. Come," he growls.

I lose the ability to coordinate my muscles and fall forward onto his chest as the orgasm sweeps through me. He frantically pounds his hips upward, drilling into me repeatedly as my entire body spasms.

As my orgasm fades and he slows to a stop, I'm draped over him, heaving heavy breath after heavy breath.

Several minutes pass before I can speak. Finally I sigh, "That was incredible, Drakkozsha."

A fountain of energy flows out from his manhood into my womanhood, a river of potent energy that fills me up, traveling up my spine and shooting out my scalp like a geyser. I've never felt anything like it. It's as if Drakken is shooting a column of sexual fire up into me and it's exploding out of me.

Curious, I ask, "Did you just come or something?" It's the only explanation I can think of.

"No."

"What? No way," I laugh softly.

"No. I save my come to give you hardest orgasm ever," he smirks.

I love that he is now relaxed enough to make a joke. "I think you already did," I giggle.

"No. Not yet."

"Are you serious?" I ask skeptically.

He smiles and nods.

I totally don't believe him.

He grins, "Now is your turn. Lie down."

"Is that an order?" I balk.

"Yes," he grins.

"Okay then," I smile, ready for anything.

Chapter 28

RIVER

I twist onto my back and position my entrance right below his straining cock.

He reaches under my ass and lifts my hips off the bed with powerful arms. Rather than thrusting up and down with his pelvis like a normal person, he lifts my hips up and down so that my wet folds slide against the underside of his cock. Leave it to a man with a hard-on to do things the hard way. In this case, it's the best way. He's not even inside me, but it feels amazing to be manhandled so expertly.

After several sensual strokes, he repositions his hands so that my hips are now held aloft by one strong arm. With his free hand, he grabs himself by his thick root and jams himself against my wet entrance until his hot manhood forces its way inside me.

Then he holds me up with both hands and slowly fucks me, pulling my hips toward him while arching his back, then pulling my body slightly away as he withdraws. He's doing all the work, which is awesome, but I can't resist the urge to wrap my legs around his waist and make this a two person maneuver. I arch my own back in time with his movements.

Drakken thrusts with increasing urgency. The ecstasy of aggression etched onto his face is all it takes to give me another mind blowing orgasm. I buck against him with my own angry need. Eventually, he slows as I breathe it out with hitching breaths.

"That was incredible," I gasp.

Still inside me, he lowers me to the bed and leans forward, kissing me. "Now I fuck you. Hard." He's all hot fiery passion now. He's a hungry beast ready to feed.

I snicker wistfully, "I thought you just did."

He shakes his head. "You will now come harder than you ever come before. Okay?"

"Drakkozsha, if you say it like that, you'll jinx it."

"Jinx?"

"Uh, it won't happen because you *want* it to happen."

He arches an eyebrow and flashes his cocky grin. "It *will* happen because I want it to happen."

"Okay," I warn, "but don't wait for me to come. Just come whenever you're ready." What I don't tell him is that I think I may have run out of orgasms for the evening. You can only have so many in a day from what I understand. I think we passed my personal best about two orgasms ago.

"I come only when you come," he warns.

"Okay," I lilt. I'm gonna have to take one for the team, not that that's a bad thing under the circumstances.

Drakken begins a slow steady rhythm.

It feels fantastic, but I don't know if I'm actually going to come.

Drakken doesn't seem worried. He starts kissing me hungrily, and I become totally engrossed in his tongue. Despite all the sex we've had tonight, I can't get over how much I love kissing this man. Yes, love. He's an incredible kisser. Like fine wine. So many layers, so many different tastes and notes and all that wine stuff. It's mesmerizing. Almost like getting a good massage. You just want more and more and more...

I don't know how long he has been steadily thrusting, maybe ten or fifteen minutes, but his pace has accelerated.

The next thing I know, I'm coming. Or I should say, an orgasm is coming. It's on the way and I know it's going to be huge. I didn't think I had it in me, but I do. I feel it coming like a freight train miles down the rails. It's a dot in the distance, but I know when it gets here, it's going to be a million tons of thundering steel, just like the silken steel thundering and pistoning inside me.

Drakken is truly fucking me with methodical force.

My orgasm builds...

"Rivka, is... so... good... I feel you squeeze me. Is... so... good..." He winces, "Ahh, so good. Now you come for me. You come hard, Rivka."

I'm down with that.

His strokes grow harder and longer.

I'm tightening up like a vise around his cock.

"Fuck!" he grunts. "Ahhh! You're going to make me come!!!"

I was right. Here comes my train.

It doesn't pull into the station.

It blasts right through it.

An orgasmic shockwave slams into me and I am coming *hard*. My whole body locks up. Every muscle pulls tight. My core fists around Drakken as he explodes inside me, ramming his cock again and again and again up to the end of my tunnel.

"Rivka!" he shouts. "Rivka!!! I'm coming! Rivkaaaa!!!"

My legs constrict around his waist and I scream and frantically claw his back with my fingers. Good thing I have short fingernails because of my massage work, otherwise I'd be tearing his back open.

IS TOO MUCH!!

Damn right it is.

I literally stop breathing because the orgasm is so incredibly powerful and earth shaking, I *can't* breathe.

Remember what I said about those Northern California earthquakes?

They can strike at any time.

And when they do, they do in fact shake the earth.

I nearly black out from the lack of oxygen. And because this is the hardest orgasm I've ever had in my entire life.

Drakken wasn't exaggerating.

Chapter 29

RIVER

A sea serpent rises from the murky water and watches me closely, it's eyes floating just above the glassy surface.

That's how it appears as I watch Drakken's head rise out of the warm water in the royal bathroom's giant marble bathtub.

The tub is huge, and we sit facing each other, our legs fully stretched out. Who doesn't love a big bathtub?

After our incredible sex, a soak seemed mandatory. We've been in the tub for over an hour, and have refreshed the hot water numerous times.

We gaze dreamily into each other's eyes, communicating without speech. Our connection is complete and beyond words.

We're both submerged up to our noses in the liquid warmth.

I am at peace.

The bathroom is completely serene. It's super late and the castle, which is surrounded by tranquil vineyards and mountains for miles, is totally silent. It's a wonderful change from my bungalow in Los Angeles, where silence doesn't exist.

I never knew how much I missed the silence. It makes the world feel much larger and more welcoming.

I love that feeling.

I also love the feeling of Drakken massaging the soles of my feet under the warm water.

All in silence.

I feel completely connected to this man. I never want the feeling to go away. The idea of losing what we have right now sort of freaks me out.

And the person I most blame for that fear is not Drakken.

It's the man who gave me my very first set of adult baggage.

Cage Hancock.

I'll probably never get entirely over the fact that Cage left me without an explanation. The same questions still gnaw at me.

Why did he leave so suddenly?

What didn't he tell me?

I don't know. I'll probably never know. Sadly, the not knowing makes it easy to imagine countless horrid scenarios. That's why the sense of betrayal was so intense.

And that's why the same questions gnaw at me when it comes to Drakken. I know almost nothing about him.

What is Drakken still hiding?

Will he suddenly leave me some day for no reason?

I shiver noticeably in the hot tub, despite the enveloping warmth.

Drakken slowly lifts his mouth above the water and says softly, "Are you okay, Rivka?"

The care and concern in his voice is clear, and it soothes me.

"I'm fine," I whisper. I refuse to let my doubt, or any permanent scars Cage gave me, ruin this moment.

Right now, I am here with Drakken.

This is *our* moment.

And that is enough.

Chapter 30

RIVER

I'm falling.

Falling, falling, falling.

The ground is rushing toward me.

I'm thousands of feet in the air.

A second ago, I was on the back of a great dragon, swooshing through the sky like I belonged up here and nowhere else in the world.

Then the dragon rolled suddenly without warning, flinging me off its back to plummet helplessly toward the earth.

I flail in the air, trying to slow my fall.

I'm going to die.

The dragon is now a shrinking speck soaring high above. It flaps its powerful wings, sailing into the clouds without me.

Every muscle in my body freezes in fear as I smash into the—

"Hnnh!!" I gasp awake in the four poster bed of the royal bedchamber.

Drakken is gone.

After our bath, we had curled up and fallen asleep, twined together in a warm embrace.

Now he's gone.

The sheets where he'd lain are cool.

When did he leave? Is he still at the castle? Or far away and who knows where?

I sit up in bed and slide my feet onto the cold floor.

The empty room is almost totally dark, but a faint silver glow sifts through the windows.

The moon is out.

I tiptoe across the room and notice Drakken leaning against one of the open windows.

I sigh with relief.

My heart relaxes.

I approach him cautiously and whisper, "Drakken?"

He leans with both hands against the wide open window frame, gazing out at the glowing moon. With his arms out, the wings of his dragon tattoo are spread, ready for flight. He turns and whispers, "Hello, Rivka."

I step closer until I'm an inch away and feel his body heat.

He wraps one arm around me and I fold into his side, fitting perfectly, skin to skin.

With his arm around me, all my tension and fear disappears.

"Couldn't sleep?" I murmur.

"No."

"What's on your mind?"

"Business," he sighs.

"I imagine a billion dollar deal is stressful."

He chuckles softly, "That is understatement. So much is on line for me, is not very funny. That is how you say it, right? Not very funny?"

"Not *even* funny," I grin.

He nods thoughtfully, "Not *even* funny."

I wrap my arms around his waist and lean my cheek against his muscular chest. "Come to bed, Drakkozsha. Forget about it until tomorrow."

"Is not so easy." He heaves a sigh and gazes back at the moon. "When I was boy, I think about going to moon every day. I read all about astronauts as little kid, every book I find. I dream to be astronaut and walk on moon like Neil Armstrong and Buzz Aldrin." He smiles down at me. The look of joy on his face is unmistakeable.

I smile up at him.

He asks, "Do you know only twelve men have walked on moon? And they were all American?"

"No, I didn't know that."

"Is true. Some people say it is conspiracy, that moon walk never happen. I don't believe that. But I know those twelve men are very lucky to walk on moon."

"How come no one goes to the moon anymore?"

"Is too expensive. And no reason to go."

"Oh. Makes sense. No oil deposits or bars of gold, right?" I quip.

He grins, "Yes, no bars of gold. Or Transformers robots," he winks. "I am young man still. I hope maybe some day, man go to moon again. Or maybe planet Mars. Maybe *I* go to Mars." He says it with great passion and stares out at the stars in the night sky like he could reach out and grab them.

"If you go to the moon or Mars or wherever, will you take me with you?" I grin.

He squeezes me against his side and kisses my forehead. "Yes, Rivka. I take you to stars with me."

"Awww," I grin.

"You climb on my back, and I fly you there now, okay?" he grins.

"Now?"

"Yes. I flap my arms and I fly us to stars like I am dragon."

Whoa, that is really weird he just said that.

He squats down, "Jump on my back. I fly us there."

After my dream, I don't know if that's a good idea. "Uh, you're not gonna jump out the window or anything crazy, are you?" I ask nervously.

"No," he chuckles and smirks back at me. "Just climb on my back."

Reluctantly, I wrap my arms around his neck and my legs around his waist.

My naked breasts press against his scars. They are ragged reminders of his painful past.

What happened to this poor man?

Drakken doesn't seem to notice I'm touching his scars. He jumps up abruptly and shouts, "Whoosh!"

I shriek.

We don't go out the window.

Drakken jogs around the big room with me on his back.

"We fly to moon, Rivka!" he whispers jubilantly.

I giggle gleefully as he swoops up and down like a flying dragon.

I pray to the gods of the moon and the stars that Drakken never drops me.

Because I'm pretty sure that when it comes to Drakken, my heart is already thousands of feet in the air.

Chapter 31

RIVER

The next morning, Drakken and I eat breakfast on top of the castle tower. Cool fog blankets the lush green valley of vineyards below.

I have the comforter from the royal bed wrapped around me to keep warm. Terrence was kind enough to bring up a space heater, which points at me. Drakken wears only his T-shirt and jeans. The cold doesn't bother him one bit. He's not even wearing shoes or socks.

I mop up the pool of real maple syrup on my plate with a wedge of waffle and ask, "How do you stay so warm when it's so cold?"

"Cold?" He chuckles, "Is almost sixty degrees! This is summer weather in my country."

I'm about to say something when Drakken's phone rings.

He pulls it from his pocket and examines the number. "Sorry. Is Svetlana. I must answer." There is a questioning look on his face, like he's waiting for me to approve.

Hearing her name makes me cringe. Every time I've bumped into Svetlana, she's always weird and blames me for every bad thing that happens to Drakken.

"Okay," I sigh and nod.

He answers the call and holds the phone to his ear, "Yes?" He nods. "Charles wants to meet today? ... When? ... Now? On Sunday? ... I am in Northern California. ... Is not so urgent he cannot wait until Monday?" Drakken nods, "Mmm-hmm. Mmm-hmm." He rolls his eyes and sighs, "Okay. Tell Charles I will be there in three hours. ... Yes, three hours. If we drive to airport now, it will take three hours to get to airport, fly to LAX, land, and meet him at office. Is no sooner I can make it ... Thank you. Good bye."

Drakken ends the call and turns to me, "I am sorry. Crazy business partner wants to meet today. I am hope you and I stay here at castle until afternoon, but I can't. I'm sorry."

"Oh, that's okay, Drakken, I totally understand. I've had a wonderful weekend with you already."

Thirty minutes later, the limo drops us off at the Sonoma County Airport and we board Drakken's Gulfstream G650 jet.

Edita greets us, "Hello, Mr. Skalakova. How was weekend?"

"Perfect," he smiles.

"And you, River? Did you have fun at castle?"

I grin, "You know about it?"

"Yes, I read about it on internet. Is very romantic, yes?"

I beam with happiness, "For sure."

She winks and says, "Would you like beverage? Today I make water with fresh strawberry, lemon, and basil."

"Oh, that sounds great," I grin.

"And you Mr. Skalakova?"

"Please," he nods absently while checking his smart phone. To himself, he mumbles, "Acch, Charles is demanding baby today. Why he cannot wait until Monday?"

The pilot steps out of the cockpit in his captain's uniform. He smiles at me then turns to Drakken. "Sir, I sorry to interrupt."

Drakken looks up from his phone. "Yes, Vladan?"

"We just receive request from ODTN. They ask if we can make a Class-1 delivery flight." Vladan also has an accent nearly identical to Drakken's.

"Of course," Drakken says. "When?"

"Now, sir."

Drakken rolls his eyes, "I have meeting with Charles in two hours. Where is drop off?"

"New Mexico, sir. Grant County Airport. Is small airport, has no major carriers."

Drakken nods. "Where is pickup?"

"Oregon, sir."

Drakken nods, "How long is flight time?"

"About four hours, sir. Recipient is small boy. Six years old, I think."

Drakken shakes his head, his face sour, "Charles can wait. Tell ODTN we make transfer right away."

Vladan smiles appreciatively. "Yes, sir. Gladly, sir." He turns and walks back to the cockpit.

Drakken plops into one of the luxurious lounge seats in the cabin and buckles in.

I sit down next to him, "What was that all about? What's the ODTN?"

Drakken smiles at me, "Organ Donor Transfer Network."

I frown, "Are you delivering an organ to someone?"

"Yes. We pick up organ from donor hospital, then fly to recipient hospital."

"Oh." I say thoughtfully. "And what's Class 1? The pilot mentioned that."

"Class 1 is mean short organ lifespan. Either heart or lung. Heart or lung have shortest survival time once removed from donor. Transfer to recipient must be fast. Less than six hours. Better if shorter."

"Don't the big airlines like American or Delta or whoever usually do that kind of thing?"

"Yes. But Vladan say Grant County has no major carriers, which mean that big airline no go there. Two airports are far apart. They need fast plane to deliver heart in time, before heart go bad. I have fast plane."

"Oh," I nod.

"Is okay with you we make flight?"

"Of course it is," I smile. "Why do you ask?"

"If we make transfer, will mean we don't go to Los Angeles until late. Maybe four or five hours extra in plane with me," he smiles hopefully.

"Wait, you want me to come with you? To pick up the heart or lung in Oregon and fly it to New Mexico for a six year old boy who needs a heart transplant or whatever?"

"Yes. But only if you want. I can book you flight here at Sonoma Airport direct to LAX. Then you go home early."

"No way," I say confidently. "Let's go help that kid!"

Drakken grins, "I hope you say that."

When we're in the air, I ask, "How much does all the gas cost for all this extra flying around?"

"For this trip?"

"Yeah."

"Maybe, $15,000. With cost of flight crew, ground crew, airport fees, airplane maintenance, maybe $30,000."

"Whoa," I blurt. "You spend that much money just to help a complete stranger?"

He frowns, "Of course. With luck, we save a life today."

I smile warmly and grasp his hand.

He gives my fingers a gentle squeeze.

Little more than an hour later, we land at Portland International Airport. Edita opens the door and a guy hands her a red cooler with the letters OHSU stamped on the side. Vladan signs some paperwork. Ten minutes later we're back in the air because air traffic control gave our plane priority takeoff.

We circle the Grant County airport two and half hours later. It's a tiny isolated airport in the middle of nowhere, surrounded by miles and miles of empty brown desert.

Drakken looks out the window, "Ahh, I see. Look at runways."

I stare out the window, "What about them?"

"Three are dirt. Only one is asphalt. Big plane never fly here. Is why they ask us to help."

I look at the airport terminal, which consists of three tiny buildings with tin roofs. There's all of three putt-putt planes parked on the runway.

When we land, an ambulance is waiting on the tarmac for us. Edita opens the door and hands the red cooler to an EMT. More paperwork is signed by Vladan, then the EMT trots out to the ambulance and hops in. The red flashing lights come on and the ambulance speeds off.

I say to Drakken, "So now some six year old boy you've never met is going to get a heart transplant and live to be an old man?"

Drakken smiles, but not happily. "Survival rate past fifteen years is best outcome. Sometimes, is much shorter. But with luck, child will live long time."

"That's sad," I say quietly.

He nods, "But every year, is get better as immune drugs improve. I donate money to drug research. One day, lifespan will be more longer."

"Wow, Drakken. You sure spend a ton of money on this whole organ donor thing. That's very generous of you."

He nods and his brow furrows darkly. "Is for my, uh… *sister*. She has donor kidney."

"Oh, I'm sorry." I didn't realize he had a sister.

"Is okay. She take immune suppression drug every day for rest of life. Many kidney recipient live very long time. With luck, my sister live to be old woman."

This is news. Wow. I really know almost nothing about Drakken beyond the most basic facts.

But I do know one thing.

Drakken raises the bar on chivalry to a whole new level.

Chapter 32

DRAKKEN

After the Gulfstream touches down at LAX in the late afternoon, I walk Rivka across the cooling tarmac toward my Lamborghini. As always, I get the door for her.

She climbs into the car, "Thank you, Drakka."

"Anything for you, Rivka," I smile at her and lower the door gently.

This weekend has been incredible. I never imagined it would've turned out so well.

I never want it to end.

Perhaps we'll have dinner some place romantic. Or maybe she'll finally allow me to meet her hot headed brother.

Whatever Rivka and I do this evening, it will be wonderful.

Of that, I am sure.

As I walk around the back of the Lamborghini, my phone rings. Charles already knows I can't make it tonight. I called him on the satellite phone while we were in the air. I explained our ODTN drop off and my weekend holiday with Rivka. He was very understanding.

Whoever this is calling now, it's probably nothing.

I check the number, just in case.

313 999 561-666

I was wrong. It's everything.

Rage overtakes me.

I clench my fists.

No.

I breathe deeply and do my best to let go of my anger.

I won't let HIM ruin my time with Rivka today. In the end, HE may ruin my life, but today, he can't touch me.

Until he finds me, I am safe.

And, as long as he never knows of Rivka's existence, I am at peace.

For now, wherever he is, he can rot.

Chapter 33

RIVER

We sit in comfortable silence in Drakken's Lamborghini, holding hands across the console between the seats as we drive away from LAX.

This weekend has been a once in a lifetime experience every step of the way. But it's nearly over and I have this sinking feeling that once Drakken drops me off at my crappy bungalow, the carriage is going to turn into a pumpkin and I'm going back to scrubbing floors like Cinderella. Of course, that's silly. I didn't have to trick Drakken into thinking I was some rich princess for him to like me. He likes me just the way I am.

That's why he's so amazing.

As we drive north on the 405 freeway, I say, "I don't know about you, but after all the excitement this weekend, I'm kind of in the mood to relax."

"Where do you want to go?"

The obvious choices are his place or mine. Since Stone is probably home, that leaves Drakken's room at The Beverly Hills Resort. Since it's the weekend, Luciana won't be there. But Svetlana might. Maybe she'll be out shopping and I won't have to see her. "We can just go back to your room, if you want."

He smiles, "Is good."

When we drive up the hill at the resort and pass the roundabout in front of the main building, there's a veritable motorcade of black Town Cars parked under the awning. In the middle of all of the cars is a black Mercedes stretch limousine parked near the main doors of the resort.

"Why is all cars?" Drakken asks curiously.

"I don't know. Looks like someone important has arrived. Maybe it's the Queen of England," I smirk.

Drakken chuckles, "You think Queen come here?"

"Why not? The Beverly Hills Resort gets high profile guests all the time. I'm sure royalty from all over the world have stayed here plenty of times. I mean, doesn't everyone in the world know about Beverly Hills and Hollywood?"

Drakken nods as we drive into the underground garage and park. We walk into the elevator and I press 20. While the elevator rises, I wrap my arms around Drakken's elbow. I am in such a good mood right now.

Ding!

The elevator suddenly stops at the lobby. Someone else must have called the elevator.

For a second, I'm afraid Luciana is going to be standing there when the doors open with her fists jammed into her hips. She's going to give me a horrid look, and she's going to say, "I knew you were sleeping with Drakken all along! I have the sex tape footage to prove it! You're fired!"

Of course, that sort of thing is too ridiculous to ever happen in real life.

As the doors slowly open, they reveal not Luciana, but a tall severe man with short salt-and-pepper gray hair wearing a black suit. He is surrounded by a dozen tall burly men in similar black suits. All of them have short cropped black hair.

I wonder if these are the people who arrived in the black motorcade parked outside?

The eyes of the severe man narrow suddenly and his mouth shrivels into a tight white knot. He hisses under his breath, his face rippling with rage as he says a single word, "Drakken."

Wait, what?

Does Drakken know this man?

I glance up and Drakken's face is murder red. His entire body shakes with cataclysmic rage. He is a volcano ready to blow.

The tall severe man steps boldly into the elevator and—

CRACK!!

—slaps Drakken harshly across the mouth.

The sound of strained silence rings out loud and clear. The tension of the moment heightens to the breaking point. The twelve burly men are on their toes, ready to spring into action.

Drakken vibrates from head to toe. His hands shake visibly at his sides. A white hand print glows on his red cheek. The muscles in his jaw sizzle with restrained anger.

The tall severe man utters a string of harsh words in Drakken's native language. His tone is commanding and brutal. When he finishes, he stares Drakken down.

The two men are the same height and stand eye to eye.

The vibration shaking Drakken's body increases until he explodes with a feral roar of terrible power. He screams in the severe man's face.

The severe man remains absolutely motionless while the twelve burly men launch instantly into action, a chaos of muscle and force. Four of them intercept Drakken and ram him into the back wall of the elevator.

BOOM!!!!

I'm nearly crushed by the mass of men, but manage to squeeze to the side just in time to avoid getting pulverized.

Through it all, the severe man stands motionless, like the blackened eye of a hurricane amidst the flurry of spinning black suits, his face a grim stone mask that looks entirely too familiar.

"NOOOO!!!!!" Drakken roars as the four men pin him to the wall. Impossibly, Drakken launches all four men forward, hurling them out of the elevator in a mass of flailing limbs.

To everyone's surprise, Drakken vaults forward toward the button panel and slams his finger into the DOOR CLOSE button like he's launching every nuclear missile in every missile silo on the entire planet all at once.

The twelve burly men bob and weave uncertainly on the elevator landing, watching Drakken warily.

The severe man remains motionless, but his face is a dark turmoil of pure hatred.

Drakken stands hunched over like a lone gladiator facing a horde of barbarians, ready to take them all down in a bloody battle.

After what seems like an eternity, the elevator doors finally close. Drakken pounds one of the steel doors with his fist.

BOOM!!!!

The sound reverberates up and down the elevator shaft like a bomb going off and the entire elevator earthquakes around us.

A massive dent has appeared where Drakken's fist impacted on the surface of the steel. He shouts a string of words in his native language at the top of his lungs, his face pointed skyward while clenching his fists. The muscles and veins of his neck pop and bulge, red hot.

He winds up and punches the steel doors a second time.

BOOM!!!!

He roars.

"IS HIIIMMM!!!!"

Chapter 34

RIVER

"Drakken?" I ask uncertainly,

Drakken is non-responsive during the entire ride up to the 20th floor. He stands slumped, his chin in his chest, his eyes downcast and vacant.

When the doors open, he steps slowly onto the landing, having completely forgotten I'm here. He moves as if his body is made of lead.

I follow. "Drakkozsha? Are you okay?"

He doesn't look at me. He stares at the carpet and walks down the hallway like a mindless robot.

Now I'm scared. "Drakka? Who was that guy?" I ask anxiously. "And why did he slap you?"

Drakken doesn't answer. He just continues to trudge slowly forward.

"Drakkozsha, what's wrong, babe? Please tell me."

He doesn't answer.

We turn a corner in the hallway.

In a calm but firm voice, I ask, "Drakken, who was that man?"

He slowly stops and turns to look at me. His face is that same gray and hardened stone mask I saw the day we first met. Only this time, his eyes are filled with sorrow. He mutters faintly, "My father."

"Your father?" I blurt, totally confused. "Why did your father hit you?"

"He is terrible man."

I don't know what to say to that.

Drakken slogs the rest of the way to the Sunset Suite. He pulls out his keycard and slides it in the lock. He fumbles with the knob as if he's forgotten how the door works.

"Here," I say, "let me help."

Drakken's hands fall to his sides like a helpless child.

I pull the keycard out of the slot and slide it in again. Before I can turn the knob, someone on the other side opens the door.

A gorgeous woman with long golden hair and blue eyes stands inside the room. She wears a white pant suit and strappy gold pumps. When she lays eyes on Drakken, her lush red mouth curls into a greedy smile.

I don't like the look on her face at all.

Stunned, Drakken gasps, "Karina... I thought you were..."

I can't decide if he looks more stunned than he already did or not.

Drakken mutters, "Karina, how did you...?"

Karina smiles at him, "Your sister let me in."

Sister? The one with the kidney? Is she here too? Did she arrive with Drakken's father?

Svetlana walks up beside Karina.

"There she is," Karina smiles at her.

Svetlana looks as beautiful as ever. Her long dark hair cascades over a white button down shirt and tan suede jacket. Her blue jeans are belted low on her flat stomach. Although the outfit is casual, it looks like she bought it on Melrose for no less than $1,000.

As always, I'm the most underdressed person in the group in my T-shirt and jeans and sneakers.

"Hello, Drakkozsha," Svetlana smiles at him and kisses his cheek. Then she glares daggers at me. Beyond that, she doesn't acknowledge my existence.

Wait, what? Is bitchy *Svetlana* the one with the kidney? And now I can't hate her? This is way too crazy. My head spins like a whirligig as I try to piece everything together.

Svetlana kisses Drakken on the cheek. "Why didn't you tell me Karina was coming? I have not seen her in a very long time."

Karina smiles, "It has been years."

Drakken barely whispers, "I didn't know..."

Svetlana says, "I told Karina she can have my room now that she's here. I'll arrange for another room so you two can have your privacy."

Privacy? What the eff?

Karina grins happily at Drakken, "How I've missed you, Drakkozsha, my dearest." Karina drapes her arms around Drakken's neck and kisses him on the mouth.

This time, I watch with nauseous horror as Karina kisses Drakken full on the mouth, long and hard.

There's no mistaking it.

This is *not* an L.A. Hello Kiss.

This is the real deal.

Karina breaks the kiss and purrs, "I've just bought the perfect island in the Caribbean to use for our honeymoon, Drakkozsha. I can't wait to show you! We can take the Gulfstream tonight, yes?"

Honeymoon?

No effing way.

I. Am. In. Shock.

I hear Drakken's throat click as he swallows a rock.

When Drakken doesn't respond to Karina, her brow furrows. She finally notices me and sneers, "Are you the maid? The bathroom is filthy and I need fresh towels."

She seriously did not just say that to me.

The sneer on her face says she did.

There went my fairy tale ending.

No wonder Drakken is so guarded about his personal life.

He's a fucking liar.

I can't believe I let myself get sucked into the middle of all this drama.

I should've known.

I turn to Drakken and say with ample sarcasm, "Apparently, I'm nothing more than an ignorant maid who is too stupid to know any better." I turn to Karina and leer, "I'll go get your towels right now." Then I sneer at her, "Ma'am."

I curtsy disrespectfully before turning around and storming down the hallway toward the elevators.

That bitch is going to have to wait a long time for her fucking towels.

I'm going home.

Book 4

Chapter 1

RIVER

"Drakken is *engaged*?!" Julietta demands.

I nod forlornly and gulp my Seven and Seven. I've been putting them back like water since we arrived at Bar 454.

I also filled Julietta in on everything that happened over the weekend, from flying in the fighter jet, to the castle in Calistoga, the pink princess gown, all the crazy stuff in the bedroom, and his surprise fiancée Karina waiting for us at The Beverly Hills Resort a few hours ago.

Now that I've had some time to process Drakken's bimbo bombshell, I'm over the anger. The hurt replaced it halfway back to my bungalow, followed by tears. Good thing Julietta was free this evening. I don't want to be alone right now. I'm apt to do something stupid.

Julietta's face twists into a disgusted scowl. "Drakken is a royal douchebag."

"Nah," I grimace, "he's just a regular douchebag. There's nothing royal about him." I gulp more Seven and Seven.

"True that. Now you can stop wasting your time on him."

"What do you mean?"

Julietta gestures with her Cosmo, "I don't know. I always thought he was weird. Too aloof. Too mysterious. Guys who hide shit always have hidden problems they don't want you to know about, you know?"

I scoff, "Oh, I know."

"It's better you found out now. Before things got too serious."

"I'll drink to that," I raise my empty glass and shake it in frustration. "Hey, bartender! I need another drink!"

All the bartenders are busy tending to the other customers.

"Do I have to flash my tits to get service around here?" I mutter. I'm not going to wait. I grab Julietta's Cosmo off the bar, intent on guzzling it. Liquor splashes over the rim and splats on the bar.

"Slow down, girl!" she chuckles. "I don't want you puking in my car."

I smirk at her, "I can hold my liquor."

Julietta shakes her head, "Since when?"

"Since now." I throw back the glass and swallow her drink down. I nearly choke myself and cough several times.

She giggles and rubs my forearm, "You're only supposed to drown your sorrows, not yourself."

I grumble apathetically, "And what was up with his freakin' golden handcuffs? That's when I should've bolted. Any guy into games in the bedroom is probably into games in general. It makes me sad that Drakken's vulnerability was a big fat lie."

"I know, right?"

"Totally," I groan. "It ceases to mean anything when he's *engaged*."

"More proof he wasn't worth it."

I feel tears brimming against my will. I guess I'm not done with the sadness. "I thought he was opening up to me. I thought we had a connection. I thought it was more than sex." I shake my head morosely. "Why did I even get involved? I should've known from the get go it wasn't going to last. Things never last with guys like Drakken."

Julietta shakes her head resolutely, "Stop beating yourself up, Riv. Sometimes things don't work out. You should forget about him and move on. That's what I always do."

"I'm trying." I sigh. I pick up my empty glass and shake it. "Hey, bartender!" I holler. "Help a poor girl out! My sorrows are still breathing!" I force a grin, trying to push away my despair.

"That's the spirit," Julietta smiles. "You know, our bartender is pretty damn cute. He's been looking at you all night."

"No he hasn't," I scoff.

"Has too. You're just too busy wallowing to notice," she winks.

"I'm not wallowing," I whine. Secretly, I perk up at the thought. All the whisky in my Seven and Sevens has scattered my fragile emotions in every direction. Now is not the time for me to hook up with a random guy. There's no way I'm doing a hungover walk of shame tomorrow morning. "I've told you a thousand times, Jay. I can't do short term flings."

"Maybe you need to step out of your comfort zone. Orgasms always make me feel better," she grins.

I roll my eyes, "I just had a bunch last night. Look where it got me?"

"Another Seven and Seven?" the cute bartender asks.

"Please." I smile at him and wink against my better judgement.

His thick dark hair is unruly on top and shaved on the sides. It looks good on him. He sort of reminds me of cute Tom from Vanderpump Rules, but with a raspy voice. Did we come to Sur and I didn't realize it? No, we're at Bar 454. This isn't him. But he's just as cute as Cute Tom. If not cuter.

While he makes my drink, Julietta leans over and whispers in my ear, "He's totally into you."

"Is not." I pull money out of my purse to pay.

He sets my drink on a cocktail napkin and pushes it toward me with a sly grin.

I slide my twenty across the bar.

"It's on the house," he winks. "You look like you need it."

"Is it that obvious?" I sigh and giggle.

"Pretty much," he chuckles, leaning his muscled forearms on the bar. Tendrils of ink creep out from beneath his rolled up cuffs.

Julietta nudges me with her elbow.

"What's your name?" he asks me, his eyes flickering invitingly in the dim light.

"Hey, Riv," someone says behind me.

I twist around on my barstool.

Cage.

"Oh no," I groan.

Julietta smirks, "Look what the ass dragged in."

I sigh, "What are you doing here, Cage?"

"Getting a drink. Hey, Shaun," Cage nods at the bartender. Shaun leans over the bar and they bump fists.

"This your woman?" Shaun asks Cage.

"She was," Cage grins at me, his mahogany brown eyes twinkling, "until I fucked everything up."

I shake my head. Why did Cage have to pick now to drop back into my life? "Cage, you have the *worst* timing."

Julietta cackles agreement.

Shaun glances at Cage, "The usual?"

"Yeah," Cage nods, "Extra dirty. Thanks, bro."

"You got it." Shaun turns around and grabs a bottle of Tanqueray gin from one of the mirrored shelves loaded with liquor bottles.

Cage squeezes behind Julietta and leans his hip against the bar.

"Do you have to stand back there?" Julietta asks, twisting around. "You're making me nervous."

Cage chuckles confidently, "I always made you nervous, Jay."

"You and earwigs," Julietta quips.

"What?" Cage laughs. "How am I like an earwig?"

"You crawl into people's ears and eat their brains, that's how."

I smirk. I'm not even sure what to make of that comment.

"What?" Julietta demands, drilling me with her gaze. "Cage is totally an earwig. He tried to eat your brain, didn't he?"

I nod, "Yeah, pretty much."

Julietta glares at Cage. "See? Now go find yourself a roach motel and don't check out."

Cage says thoughtfully, "Why would I want to go to a roach motel if I'm an earwig? Last I checked, roaches and earwigs don't get along." He winks at Julietta.

"Are you calling me a cockroach?" Julietta growls.

"Relax, Julietta," Cage drawls.

She frowns at me, "He just called me a cockroach!"

Cage picks up one of the paper cocktail napkins off the bar and waves it in the air, "Peace, Jay. I'm not here to fight."

I sigh. "Why *are* you here, Cage? Julietta and I were talking."

Shaun sets a cloudy martini in front of Cage. Three olives are submerged in the briny booze. "Want it on your tab, man?"

"Yeah, thanks," Cage smiles. He picks up the glass and salutes Shaun with it.

Shaun tips his head back in reply and grins before turning away to help another customer.

Shaun sure is cute. Maybe Julietta is right and he's into me *and* single. What am I thinking? It's way too soon. And I've had way too much to drink tonight.

Cage sips his martini and smiles. "Mmmm. Shaun makes the best dirty martini in L.A."

Julietta barks, "Cage, you make the best dirty asshole in L.A."

I cackle helplessly, fold my arms on the bar, and bury my face in them. Ahhh, Julietta. I'm so glad we're besties.

Even Julietta snorts at her own comment.

"To assholes," Cage grins confidently, holding up his glass, "The dirtier the better."

To my surprise, Julietta laughs and clinks her glass against Cage's.

"Where's your drink?" Cage asks me.

"Oh, uh…" I stammer and pick up my fresh Seven and Seven. "To assholes!"

The three of us clink glasses.

I have to admit, I'm tired of being miserable tonight. Cage seems to be in a good mood, and I'll take all the good mood I can get right now. But is it a good idea to have drinks with Cage? Considering everything that went down with Drakken and I in the last 48 hours? And considering I'm way past buzzed?

No.

Did I say I was going to do something stupid tonight?

Yes.

Chapter 2

DRAKKEN

I have to find Rivka.

She doesn't understand. I have no doubt at this moment she believes I'm a terrible person. I can only imagine what she thinks of Karina.

I need to explain.

If I can find her, I will beg her forgiveness. If she will hear me out, she will understand.

"Drakkozsha, where are you going?" Karina asks in my native tongue.

I ignore her and stride down the hallway on the twentieth floor of The Beverly Hills Resort toward the elevators.

I will find Rivka.

I will pour my heart out to her and hope for the best.

It's all I can do.

"Drakken!" Karina calls.

I ignore her.

I turn a corner in the hallway and stop short.

My father marches toward me, flanked by his battalion of security officers. The black suited men fill the hallway. There is no way around them.

I can only go through them.

"Drakken," my father hisses as he comes to a halt.

His men stand poised behind him, ready for action.

If I attack my father, they will pounce. I can't subdue all of them. If I attempt to penetrate their line and drive through them, they will likely bring me down. There are simply too many men.

This situation demands a hasty exit.

Unfortunately, on the twentieth floor of this high rise, my options are limited to the stairs and the elevators. If I had a parachute on a static line, I would dive through a window and float to safety. But my parachutes are all at the hangar.

My only option in this case is diplomacy. I slide my stone face into place.

"Father," I growl, staring him down. If there is one valuable lesson I learned from my father, it is to never back down. I clench my fists at my sides. My desire to tear his head from his neck in this moment is immeasurable.

I hate this man more than any other being on the planet earth.

My father stands stone still. He too is a statue. Not a hair on his head is out of place. Not a muscle moves unless he permits it. He betrays no emotion. "You have refused my calls." It is a cold statement of fact. "Why?"

"I have been...engaged in other affairs."

"What is so important that you cannot speak to your father about it?"

From another man, those words might convey love. From my father, they convey danger. Only danger.

"Business," I hiss.

"What business?"

I don't answer. I remain motionless. I cannot afford to show the slightest hint of weakness nor offer the slightest clue as to my activities here in America. My father is a shrewd and determined man. He will bore and probe at my defenses until he gets the information he seeks. I cannot allow that to happen.

"Drakka, my son."

Against my will, I wince noticeably. His endearment is a revolting lie that fills me with disgust.

"Tell me what you have been doing."

I say nothing. I will not bend.

A horrid smile eases onto his face, "If you do not tell me, I will find out for myself."

The gravity of his threat is clear.

My father has the resources to uncover every last detail about my secret work here in America. Although it will take him time to piece everything together, he will eventually get the answers he seeks. Then he will take action to shut me down. Everything I have worked so hard to achieve will crumble.

This is a disaster.

To make matters worse, when my father starts to dig, he will inevitably unearth information about Rivka. If that happens, she is in mortal danger. I need to warn her immediately.

"Does your sister know you're here?" my father asks.

I freeze.

Svetlana.

How could I forget my poor sister? I am a terrible person. Our father doesn't know she's here. Months ago, when I told her I was in Los Angeles, she insisted on joining me in secret. The only place she feels safe from our father is by my side. At the moment, the only thing protecting her from him is me.

I'm suddenly torn, my heart stretched to breaking. Ahead lies Rivka. I need to get to her. I need to explain my dire situation and hope that she can forgive me. Most of all, I need to keep her safe from my father. Behind lies my sister. My father must not know she's here. I need to get her out of this hotel unseen and to a place of safety. It's the only way I can protect her.

Curse my father. He is the source of all my troubles in this world. He is forcing me to chose between my beloved sister and...

...my beloved Rivka.

Chapter 3

RIVER

"I don't believe it," I gasp.

"I know," Cage says from across the table. "It sounds ridiculous, right?"

Julietta huffs beside me. I can't tell if she believes Cage or not.

I'm not sure if I do either. The only reason I'm listening to his story is because Cage is basically a decent guy. Yes, he left me without an explanation. But when we were together, he was never a bad guy. And maybe because I'm super buzzed and can't stop gazing at his sad mahogany eyes.

Cage really looks like he needs a hug right now.

The three of us sit in a red vinyl booth in the 1950s Diner-themed section of Bar 454. Our Formica table has one of those little chrome jukeboxes attached to the wall, but it doesn't actually work. If this place served milkshakes, I would've ordered one to absorb all the Seven and Sevens I've gulped down. I'm pretty sure the room is going to spin the second I stand up.

But that won't be for awhile.

Right now, I'm still processing Cage's crazy story. I ask, "Why didn't you tell me, Cage?"

He shrugs. "I was too embarrassed."

Julietta folds her arms across her chest. "I'm sorry, Riv. I don't believe any of this. It sounds too good to be true."

"Good?" Cage blurts. "Because of my mom, my dad almost died. How is that good?" He sounds hurt.

Julietta rolls her eyes, "Normal people call their girlfriends when something goes wrong, Cage."

Cage sighs, "I don't care if you believe me Julietta. It happened. My dad almost died because my mom is a fucking loser and a low life. And you're right, it's not normal. My family is not normal. *I'm* not normal. But I should've called you, Riv. I should've told you what was going on." He reaches across the table and grasps my hand.

I let him hold it. I know Cage well enough to know when he's being honest. His sad brown eyes are telling the truth.

He says, "You gotta believe me, Riv. When my old high school buddy Travis called and told me my dad was in the hospital, I lost my shit. I drove straight down to Riverside. When I got there, my dad was unconscious. There were sheriff's deputies swarming everywhere. They wouldn't tell me shit. And none of the doctors or nurses could tell me shit either. They just said my dad was in critical condition. It was a nightmare. It took all night to piece the story together."

"But you couldn't call Riv and tell her what happened?" Julietta ask skeptically. "Not once in six months?"

Cage gives Julietta a hurt look. "My dad was in critical condition. I thought he was going to die. I was by his side every single minute. When I wasn't, I was pestering the doctors and the deputies so I could figure out what the hell happened. It was nonstop. And the whole time, I was trying to wrap my head around the idea that my fuck-up mom was to blame."

Julietta shakes her head dismissively, "My mom would never do something like that to my dad."

"Is your mom hooked on crystal meth? Is she a crank whore who fucks guys for a fix?"

"No, but—"

"Then you don't know what you're talking about, Jay. My mom is a fucking loser and an embarrassment, and has been since I was a kid. I totally blame her for my dad getting stabbed. He was trying to help her out by letting her stay at his apartment until she got clean. Rehab never worked for her. Dad thought he could get her clean. I don't know what he was thinking. I guess he still loved her. I don't know." He sighs.

"That's so sad," I mutter.

Cage scowls, "Too bad her psycho pimp boyfriend didn't want her getting clean. He wanted her to keep fucking guys in exchange for more meth. Can you believe that? He treated my mom like his own personal drug slave." Cage shakes his head and chuckles grimly. "I guess she made a lot of money for him and he wasn't going to let my dad slow his cash flow by cleaning up my mom. So the guy snuck into my dad's apartment one night while my mom was there, and the guy tried to stab my dad to death in his sleep. In his own fucking bed. Can you believe that? Lucky my mom woke up when she heard them fighting and started screaming. Apparently the gun nut who lives next door heard them struggling, so he kicked down Dad's front door with a shotgun in hand. Too bad my mom's murderer boyfriend managed to climb out a window and take off."

Julietta winces noticeably, "Oh my god."

I squeeze Cage's hand. I feel terrible for him. "Oh, Cage. I'm so sorry."

"You guys good?" our waitress interrupts. She wears a black Bar 454 T-shirt and has an empty tray cradled in her arm.

"Yeah, thanks. We're good." I smile meekly.

"Let me know if you guys need anything else." She wanders away.

Cage continues, "When my dad finally woke up in the hospital, the first thing he saw was me. He cried for over an hour. He kept asking where Mom was. If she was okay. I couldn't believe he cared. She was the reason he was in the hospital in the first place. I kept telling him she was fine. I didn't tell him nobody knew where she was. For all I know, she's back with her pimp boyfriend. Or dead. I don't care. As long as she never comes back. When my dad got out of the hospital, he had a lot of trouble using his hands. He had a lot of nerve damage because of the knife wounds. So he had a hard time doing basic things. I had to buy all his groceries and cook for him. I shaved him and bathed him and wiped his ass."

I glance at Julietta.

She meets my eyes, but looks away quickly. In a whispery voice, she says, "I'm so sorry, Cage."

Cage nods, "Thanks. One night, right after I took my dad out for pizza and beer, just so we could feel normal and forget about everything for a few hours, we came home and found his apartment trashed. Nothing was stolen, but the place was wrecked. I think my mom's *boyfriend* was trying to send a message. The sheriff never did figure out who he was. My mom wouldn't tell them anything. Fucking bitch." He trails off bitterly. His eyes drop to our hands.

I still hold his in both of mine.

With his free hand, he caresses my fingers and the back of my hand with his thumb like I'm sacred treasure.

Chills run up my arms.

Cage used to love rubbing my hands just like this. He would do it whenever I was sad. I should be the one comforting him right now.

"I didn't want you to have to see any of it, Riv," he says earnestly. "I didn't want you to find out about my loser mom."

I nod, "You always kept her a carefully guarded secret."

He sighs heavily. "I'm tired of making excuses for her. I've done it most of my life and I'm fucking sick of it. All I wanted to do was get my dad back to health as quick as I could so I could pretend it never happened. My plan was to come back to L.A. and be the same good old Cage you remembered. It was stupid of me to think that way, but I did. And I'm sorry. Anyway, when Dad was finally able to take care of himself, I came looking for you."

"Oh, Cage," I sigh. "You should've told me when it happened." I lock eyes with him. "Cage, you aren't your mom. You shouldn't feel ashamed because of what *she* did. It's not your fault."

"Yeah," he mutters.

I squeeze his hand, "And you were being a good son to your dad. You were trying to take care of your family. How can I hold that against you?"

Cage arches an eyebrow, "You don't think I'm a loser because my mom is a drug whore?"

I shake my head, "You're a good person, Cage. You're good to your family, and you were always good to me. How could I ever find fault in that?"

All of a sudden, I feel like the dumbest thing I've ever done in my life was to shut Cage out when he came back. I should've given him a second chance, not given up on him. I am *so* lame.

What was I thinking letting a lying douche like Drakken into my life? I had a good man in front of me all along. And I threw him away for the biggest ass pole on the planet.

Correction. Second biggest ass pole.

I'm the biggest ass pole for not giving Cage a second chance.

Chapter 4

DRAKKEN

My father drills me with his steely eyes, awaiting my response.

To disobey him is an act of treason.

Must I wage war with my father to accomplish the simplest thing?

If I wait much longer, he will sense I am hiding something. I can't let that happen. But I can't act without a plan.

My mind races through the facts at hand. The only thing I know for certain is that my father is unaware of my sister's presence in the hotel suite behind me. Had Svetlana known our father was here in Los Angeles, she would've insisted we both leave the country immediately. The only thing protecting her in this moment is my father's ignorance.

Therein lies my advantage.

I need to lead my father and his men out of this hallway. If I can manage that, Svetlana might escape the building unnoticed. Then I can take her to safety.

Then I remember Karina.

Will she inform my father that Svetlana is here? I don't know. But it won't matter what she does if Svetlana and I are both gone.

Running is never my first choice, but in this situation, it's my only option. First, I need to create a distraction.

I like distractions.

I step up to my father and stand toe to toe. Eye to eye. The element of surprise cuts two ways.

I've imagined doing this for my entire life. It won't begin to make up for all the times he has done it to me, but it's a start.

I slap him boldly across the cheek.

CRACK!

His head whips to the side while his broad shoulders remain motionless.

My palm stings. It feels wonderful.

The twelve men in black suits behind him loom toward me like dark thunderheads.

I grin at them openly. I'm tempted to laugh maniacally, but I need to stay focused.

My father's face is a red stone mask. He reveals no emotion. His eyes on mine, he growls under his breath, "Take him down." His voice glints with a knife-thin edge of rage.

The dark suited men descend like rocks falling from the sky. My father turns on his heel and strides away as the fists fly.

I throw three blows for every one of theirs. Knuckles, knees, claws, teeth. I bite someone on the forearm. I tear another man's cheek open after I break another's nose.

My father departs, followed by two of his men, leaving the remaining ten to handle me. I will handle them. All that matters is that my father is out of the way and still unaware of Svetlana's presence.

The men pummel me from every angle. They're pulling their punches, but only enough to avoid killing me. I am his son, after all.

The melee continues for several minutes. I drag the men in the direction my father went, away from Svetlana.

Lightning lashes out from my kidney as a heavy blow lands against my lower back. I stumble forward, going down on a knee. I vault up and forward, away from the men, away from the Sunset Suite.

I can't do this much longer, but I'm not giving up yet.

After what seems hours, but is likely mere minutes, I have maneuvered the crowd of men within sight of the main elevators. My father is nowhere to be seen.

I break from the hailstorm of fists and crash through the door to the stairwell. I fly down flight after flight. Behind me, footsteps machine-gun down the steel stairs and echo off the concrete walls.

Down and around we go until I burst through the door on the first floor. I have a substantial lead, and know the layout of the resort quite well. I don't want to lose the men. I want them to follow. I turn down several hallways and slip out a side door into the darkening night.

Despite the twilight and the electric lights scattered around the grounds of the resort, the illuminated pathways leading to the tennis courts and the golf course are but silver streams running through a gloomy landscape of deep shadows.

When I have a significant lead, I turn a corner and dive into the nearest bushes. A moment later, black trousered legs flicker past. When I'm confident they're gone, I slide my phone out of my blue jeans and dial Svetlana frantically.

After two rings, she answers with laughter. "Drakkozsha, you are terrible! Where did you run off to? Karina is here waiting for you."

I hear Karina whine in the background, "Where are you, Drakkozsha? We barely said hello, my love!"

Svetlana giggles, "That was very rude of you. Karina has only just arrived. Don't you think you should spend some time with your fiancée?" She chuckles with careful good humor.

"Sveta," I say breathlessly. "Listen to me. Father is here."

"What?" she gasps. "Where? In Los Angeles?"

"No. In the hotel."

"Oh my god," her voice quavers. "Excuse me, Karina. I have a business matter to attend to with Drakken."

"Certainly," Karina says agreeably. Her voice is faint over the cell phone. "Take your time. I think I'll take a bath. Tell Drakken he can join me. But tell him not to make me wait too long," she singsongs. "I won't keep the water warm forever."

"Yes, of course," Svetlana says nervously.

I hear a door latch. Footsteps. A moment later, another door latches and then a bathroom fan.

"We are alone," my sister whispers.

"You have to leave now. Get to LAX. Vladan will fly you somewhere safe."

"Vladan? Won't father find out?"

"No. All of my men are loyal to me. They won't betray you, Sveta."

"Are you sure?"

The desperation in her voice breaks my heart. A daughter should never have to run in fear from her father. "Yes, Sveta. You must trust me. Go to LAX. I will tell Lubomir you are on the way. He will contact you en route and tell you where to meet him."

"What about Karina?" she asks nervously.

I consider for a moment. "Does she know father is here?"

"I—I don't think so. She would have mentioned it, don't you think?"

"Yes. She likely doesn't know."

"Is she going to be safe? With father here?"

"She will be fine. Don't tell her where you are going. Okay?"

"Are you sure?" Her concern is obvious.

"Yes. It is very important father not know you are going to LAX. I can't have him or his men following you there. Take only what you need. You must move quickly. Do you understand?"

"Yes." She sounds uncertain.

"You can do this, Sveta. You MUST do this."

After a moment she mutters, "Yes."

"Good. I will keep father's men occupied. But I can only do it for so long."

"I understand. I love you, brother."

"I love you too, sister. Now go quickly. Before it's too late."

I end the call and slide my phone into the pocket of my blue jeans. My body boils with stress. My armpits are soaked. I smear my hand across my mouth, trying to think.

I need to strategize. I have to relocate all of my assets. Luckily, I have enough pilots on my staff to fly all of my important aircraft out of LAX. The smaller planes can be left behind. I just hope I can scramble the men quickly enough to get everything into the air. Runway delays at LAX might very well be my undoing.

This is ridiculous.

I am literally fighting a war.

Against my father.

Once again, he is ruining everything.

I only hope that somehow I can find Rivka before I leave Los Angeles forever. At the very least, I need to apologize and say goodbye.

Chapter 5

RIVER

"You guys mind if I use the men's room?" Cage asks.

"Oh," I smile, "go ahead."

Cage slides out of the booth and squeezes through the crowd toward the back of the bar.

I catch Julietta smiling while she stares at Cage's ass. I blurt, "I thought you hated him."

She smirks, "I thought *you* hated him."

"I don't know. After that story, I feel like an idiot for not hearing him out sooner."

Julietta nods, "Me too. Assuming it's true."

"What, you don't believe him?"

"I don't know, Riv. I mean, he could've called you. If you were important to him, he *would* have called. Even if just to say he had family stuff to deal with."

"You heard him, he didn't want to be judged. How would you feel if someone in your family was a total freak?"

She scoffs, "Have you met my brother Romeo?"

"Yeah, yeah. But Romeo isn't that bad."

"*What?!* Romeo is insane, girl. *And* he's gay. But you don't see me hiding him from my closest friends. I'm proud of that wacky mother fucker. I mean, he's my *brother*, Riv."

"Yeah, but is he a drug whore?"

"No," she grins, "Just a cock whore."

I roll my eyes, "That's true. Anyway, that's different from Cage's situation."

"I guess," she sighs. "Just be careful. I don't want you getting your heart broken a second time. So don't go jumping into bed with him."

"First of all, my heart is already broken because of Drakken. And second—"

"Not like when Cage disappeared."

I dismiss her. "And second, are you the same Julietta I've lived next to forever? The one who said an hour ago that an orgasm from a stranger is the perfect cure for a broken heart? Miss One Night Stand? Miss... uh, Miss *Sleeve* and Leave?"

"*Sleeve* and Leave?" she chuckles. "What the hell does that mean?"

"You know, like, you *sleeve* them with your vag then you leave them?"

Julietta shakes her head and laughs, "*Leave* the comedy to the professionals, Riv. That is awful."

"What? A vagina is totally like a sleeve! A flesh sleeve!"

Julietta shakes her head, "That is terrible, girl!"

"What's terrible?" Cage asks, sliding back into the booth.

"Nothing," I blurt and flash my eyes at Julietta.

She rolls hers. "I warned you."

"Warned her?" Cage asks.

"Ahhh," I stammer, "yeah, she warned me not to have any more Seven and Sevens."

"Good call," Cage drawls. "Are you two gonna be safe to drive home tonight?"

"We'll take a cab," Julietta offers.

"Naw, you guys don't need to waste your money on a cab. I'll drive you. I've only had one martini."

"Are we going home now?" I ask. Why am I looking right at Cage when I say it? I blame the alcohol.

Cage shrugs, "Whatever you guys wanna do. It's up to you."

I gaze at Cage.

Did he fix his hair in the men's room, or was it always this rakishly perfect? Maybe I didn't notice earlier when he came in because I was mad at him. But right now, he's as handsome as ever. And it's not because I have Seven and Seven Spectacles. Cage has always been hot. And plenty capable of offering orgasm distraction.

Yeah, I'm definitely in the mood for something stupid tonight.

A stupid good orgasm, that is.

Chapter 6

DRAKKEN

My Lamborghini revs into the red as I dart through Hollywood traffic. I have already called Lubomir and given him instructions. The Gulfstream will be ready and waiting when Svetlana arrives at LAX.

I can only hope she makes it.

I did my best to lead my father's men on a wild goose chase to give her a window of opportunity to escape.

The only consequence is, I now have a tail.

A black Mercedes sedan follows me on Santa Monica Boulevard. It is several car lengths behind, but I have no doubt the car is tailing me. I can't risk being followed to Rivka's.

At the first opportunity, I turn on my right blinker and move into the right lane. The Mercedes follows suit two cars behind, fading into the right lane without signaling.

We travel with traffic for several blocks. When there is a sufficient gap ahead of me, I slow for a yellow light. The car ahead pulls through the intersection. The light turns red and I stop at the crosswalk. I signal right and turn my car slightly, as if I'm waiting for a gap.

Four lanes of north and southbound traffic pass me by in an incessant stream of metal and headlights. I scan the flow to the left and right, seeking an opening.

There it is.

A gap.

Coming from the north.

And another narrower gap from the south.

It will be close.

I clutch the Lamborghini and give it just enough gas to pull the tach out of idle.

Wait.

Wait...

NOW!!

I floor the gas pedal and smoothly engage the clutch. The powerful engine screams and the car lunges between oncoming cars.

Horns blare and tires screech.

The Lamborghini power slides into a left turn, the rear tires drifting silently across the asphalt as the rear end floats to the right. I steer into the skid and feather the gas.

A north bound delivery truck is about to slam into my rear end. Its horn bellows angrily.

The Lamborghini roars and I shoot forward out of harm's way.

I have no doubt several drivers are shaking their fists and cursing me. Southbound traffic slows in response to my interruption. Hopefully, they will delay traffic further.

With the Mercedes still trapped behind two cars at the red light and the impending southbound gridlock, there's no way my tail can catch me.

I head northward into the maze of the Hollywood Hills. They'll never find me up here.

Some time later, after I'm confident I've lost the Mercedes, I resume my journey to Rivka's home. When I reach her neighborhood, I park in a red zone beside a fire hydrant because there are no free spaces. I don't know where she lives, but I can deduce the location.

I remember the general area. With any luck, Rivka's blue Audi will be parked somewhere in view.

I walk down the sidewalk, scanning for her car. It only takes a few minutes to locate it parked behind a row of bungalows. Wrought iron bars fence off the property. There is no intercom button on the gate. I pull out my phone and dial her number. It goes to voicemail. I try again. No luck. Her phone must be off. She probably wants to avoid me. I don't blame her.

I scale the iron fence and drop onto the cement pathway.

I pause for a moment in the shadows. From the surrounding buildings, I hear Spanish voices cascading from various open windows. The sound of sizzling signals the cooking of dinner. I smell chili peppers and tomatillos. Ahead, a skunk waddles proudly past a garbage dumpster.

I can't help but smile. No one bothers a skunk.

After he departs, I creep forward in the shadows, listening.

Then I hear it.

The voice of Rivka's brother. I remember it clearly. Filled with anger. He wears his heart on his sleeve.

Is he talking to her in that tone? My blood boils at the thought. He best not be, if he wants to see tomorrow.

I listen carefully.

"Fuck him, Colin. Tell your boss he can suck your dick if he doesn't like it. You don't need that shit, bro."

It doesn't sound like it.

I rap the front door of the bungalow forcefully with my knuckles and wait patiently.

The door whips open.

"Who the fuck are you?" *her brother demands. He holds a cellular phone to his ear.*

"Where is Rivka?"

"Who?"

"River. Where is River? You—*your*—sister."

He smiles with tortured amusement, "I don't know who the fuck you are pal, but I'm not telling you where my sister is. Yo, Colin, I gotta call you back. ... Yeah, okay. Bye." *He tosses the phone to the side and shakes his arms. A display of aggression.* "Who the fuck are you, bro? You from the hotel?"

"Yes. No. Ahhh...I am guest there."

Her brother knits his brows, "'Guest there?'" *he mimics.* "Dude, are you from Russia or some shit?"

"No, I—"

"Never mind." *He shakes his head.* "I have no idea who the fuck you are. So get the fuck outta here."

He slams the door in my face.

If he won't tell me her location, perhaps I can find someone who will.

I won't give up until I find her.

Chapter 7

RIVER

"I've missed you so much," Cage moans into my ear. "I've dreamt about this for months. I need you like I need to breathe. I can't live without you, Riv."

I nuzzle my nose into his neck.

His powerful hands squeeze my ass as he picks me up. I forgot how strong he was from chiseling and hammering away at his marble statues all day long.

I wrap my legs around his waist.

Cage has a marble statue in his pants right now. He carries me into his dark studio.

Street lights shine in through a wall of windows with no drapes. We're surrounded by life-size marble statues of various rich Hollywood socialites and celebrities in various states of completion. Work benches and tools line the perimeter of the room.

It almost feels like we're being watched by all the statues, but I know it's just lifeless marble. I've been here plenty of times. I'm used to it.

So why do I feel so guilty?

Who knows, says the alcohol in my system. And who cares? There's a hot dick lodged between your legs.

Orgasms are a cure-all, drunk Julietta says in my head.

I think drunk Julietta has the right idea. Drunk River agrees.

"Oh, Cage," I moan.

He bites my neck then licks his way to my lips. His hot tongue forces its way into my mouth.

I yield.

He enters me.

Chapter 8

DRAKKEN

I knock politely on the door.

It whips open.

Light pours out.

River's brother bounds across the threshold and bumps his chest into mine. "Dude, get the fuck outta here!"

He's attempting to intimidate me.

I don't budge. In a calm voice, I say, "Please you tell me, where is your sister?"

"Do you not understand English? I'm not telling you where my sister is! Now hit the fucking bricks before I throw your ass to the curb!"

I remain calm. As with all storms, this one will eventually blow over. "You tell me where she is, I go. Okay?"

His face dances with uncertainty. I suspect he's not accustomed to a man who won't back down. "What the fuck happened to your face?"

"I have fight."

"What?"

"Is long story."

"You look like you got your ass beat, buddy."

"They was ten men. Many are in very much pain right now."

"Bullshit."

I have nothing to prove to him. "I have no time for, how you say, chit chat?"

"Huh?"

"Is very important for me to speak to Riv—*River.* Tonight. Very important. You help me, okay?"

He runs his hand through his hair.

The storm breaks, as does the man.

"Look, buddy. I don't know who you are. If you know my sister like you say, give her a call."

"I did. Is no answer."

"Then she probably doesn't want to talk to you."

"I know she no want to talk to me. But I have important thing to say. Very important."

"So tell me. And I'll tell her."

I shake my head. "Is very, uh, *complicated*, yes? Is how you say?"

"I don't know how you say shit, bro. If my sister doesn't want to talk to you, she doesn't want to talk to you. Got it?"

His stubbornness is forged in stone. I am wasting my time. "Thank you." *I turn and walk away.*

He chuckles, "For what?"

"For remembering me that any problem has two answer."

"What?"

"Good night." *I walk down the cement path, toward the street.*

"Yeah, okay. Whatever." *He slams the door behind me.*

When I reach the street, I dial my phone. "Greetings, Lubomir."

"Hello, sir."

"How is my sister?"

"She is safe, sir."

"Good. Has she left in the Gulfstream yet?"

"No, sir. We're waiting for clearance from the tower for takeoff. It should be less than thirty minutes until she is in the air."

"Excellent. I need you to track a cellular phone number right away."

"Yes, sir. What is the number?"

Chapter 9

RIVER

The pounding sound of running water wakes me. What the fuzz? Did I sleep next to Niagara Falls last night? Why is it so loud? What is making all that fuzzing noise?

I grab a random pillow and cover my face. Not so much because of the noise, which is louder than a bomb storm, but because sunlight is now made of daggers.

Ow, shizz.

I clamp my eyes shut. It's still not dark enough. I drank *waaaaay* too much last night.

What was I thinking?

How many Seven and Sevens did I go through? A thousand? Enough to keep Niagara Falls running for a year? More?

Two pile drivers pound rhythmically against the sides of my head.

I am never drinking again.

I finally realize that Niagara Falls is just the sound of someone showering under a billion gallon waterfall-style shower head. Is there a volume control on that thing? I want to shout, "Turn it down!!!" But I know my own voice would split my skull in half.

What the *hell* did I do last night?

Let's see, I came home from my disaster date with Drakken. I told Julietta I needed to go out for drinks so I could moan about it. We ended up at Bar 454 and...

Oh SHIZZ!!!

I went home with Cage!

I'm in Cage's bed!

How the EFF did I end up in Cage's bed?!?!

Shizz, shizz, shizz! What did I do??!!

"Oh Riv, I need you so bad..."

"Oh Cage..."

"I can't live without you, Riv..."

Lips. Licking. Tongues. Kissing.

Something about a hard cock. A *really* hard cock. And me liking it hard. Shizz!!!!

Why did I have to go home with Cage! I'm going to regret this. The fear crackling through every cell in my body says I made a huge mistake.

I jump out of bed.

The toxic waste in my stomach nearly jumps out of my mouth. The room spins and spins.

"Fuzz!!" I whimper softly. I'm still buzzed. But I need to get out of here before Cage finishes in the shower. If I don't, he'll never let me leave.

I stumble to the floor and gather up my wadded clothes. How am I going to put my pants on? I can't find the leg holes! Do I have the wrong end? It's a big ball of crumpled denim. Where's my bra? Where are my shoes?

There's a pile of clothes all over the floor. Cage never liked to pick stuff up. The first shirt I find is one of his T-shirts. Good enough. I just need something to cover my bra.

I finally unknot my pants and kick my feet into them. Shoes! There they are! I don't bother with socks. I pull my Nikes on while hopping toward the stairs. Purse! Where's my purse! I glance around frantically. Where is it? Maybe it's downstairs. I lean over the loft railing and scan the studio area below.

Which one of you statues took my purse?

Half of them stare at me blankly. The other half have their backs to me like I'm not worth the time of day.

You guys are no help.

I trundle noisily down the stairs and run into the kitchen.

My purse! It's on the marble topped island. I grab it and run for the front door.

"Riv?!" Cage hollers.

The water upstairs turns off.

"Riv, are you okay?!"

I rip the front door open and run outside.

I do the Sprint Of Shame to the nearby Metro tunnel and wait for a northbound train home. I stand impatiently amidst the crowd of Monday morning commuters. Nobody notices me in my T-shirt and jeans.

But they notice Cage when he jogs barefoot down the long subway stairs with a towel wrapped around his waist and no shirt on. "Riv!" he shouts. "Riv, wait!"

Oh no.

Thank god my Shame Train just pulled into the station. A flood of people exit the cars and I squeeze past them and drop into a seat by the window. It's the only one I can find.

"Riv!"

I duck my head below the window frame but I can't help peeking.

Cage is fighting his way through the crowd.

I forgot how good he looks with his shirt off. Not that I was looking. I duck lower in my seat.

"Riv! Wait!"

Just as he reaches the doors of the train, God—or somebody with a sense of sympathy—slides them shut.

As the Shame Train accelerates, I slowly pass by Cage.

He wiggles his hand in the air with his pinky and thumb out like he's holding a phone. His eyebrows lift hopefully. He mouths the words, "Call me!"

As the Metro train pulls into the dark tunnel, I clamp my eyes shut and groan. With my eyes closed, the swaying of the train makes me nauseous, so I open them and concentrate on not vomiting.

Alcohol is evil and nobody's friend.

Chapter 10

RIVER

I jog up the escalators out of the Metro tunnel. On the large street corner, people are crowded everywhere, waiting at crosswalks and bus stops, or walking here and there with purpose. Thousands of cars packed into the street do the same dance of waiting or driving. It is a cacophony of Monday morning activity and it is killing my head.

And wow, the sun is five times brighter than usual. I have to squint through slits so I don't go blind. The squinting makes my eyes itch. My skin feels like a wool sweater I want to peel off but can't.

After my jog out of the Metro station, I am temporarily exhausted. I stop where I stand. I need to regroup before I take another step. What am I doing again? People swim past me like an agitated school of fish, bumping me, nudging me, shoving me.

I'm too tired to care.

Wait a second. I'm late for work!

Luciana is going to kill me! Then she'll probably fire me. She'll interrupt the burial ceremony, say something nasty, then pay the undertaker or whoever to inscribe 'She was always late' on my tombstone.

I begin a fast paced walk, the best I can manage, toward my bungalow. Halfway there, I stop in front of a three-story apartment building and throw up all over some bushes. A cat yowls and runs out from under the leaves and my rain of vomit.

"Sorry," I groan and smear bile from my mouth. My skin feels cold and clammy. I'm so dehydrated I can't sweat. I drag myself toward home. Maybe I should call in sick. I'm in a bad way right now.

What a way to start my Monday.

At the end of yet another apartment-lined street, I turn the corner. My bungalow is just across this street. Movement in the corner of my eye catches my attention.

Drakken steps out of his Lamborghini.

Oh no.

I'm ready to puke again, and not because of the alcohol. I dry heave once, but the nausea subsides. I groan, "What do you want?"

"Rivka, are you okay?"

"Does it matter?"

"Yes, it matter. I call you many time. You no answer your phone. So I wait here for you all night. I is—*am*—very worry for you."

"You spent the night in your car? Waiting for me?" I feel a twinge of appreciation but the pounding in my head knocks it right out.

"Yes," he nods. "Is very important, Rivka. I need to explain."

"I'll say," I smirk, but continue walking toward my building, crossing the street.

"Rivka, wait. I must tell you."

I stop in the middle of the street. Another slimy cold flash slithers down my chest and churns in my stomach. "I can't do this right now."

"Riv! Where the hell have you been?" Stone demands, striding through the gate in front of our bungalows. He spots Drakken. "And who the fuck is this guy?"

"Uh…"

"Tell me what's going on, Riv. I've been worried sick. You were gone all weekend. I tried calling your phone. You never answered. What the hell?"

"You did?" I ask, confused. "Nobody called me." I reach into my purse to check my phone. "Oh, fuzz. My battery is dead."

Drakken nods, "Ach. I think so."

What does he mean by that?

Stone cocks a thumb at Drakken. "Do you know this fucking guy? He came by last night looking for you. Said he needed to tell you something important."

"Uh…"

"Rivka, please. I need talk with you. Please."

I glance between Stone and Drakken. "Uh…"

Stone barks at him, "She doesn't look like she wants to talk to you."

I can't do this right now, not with either of them. I wrinkle my nose, "Um, I'm sort of late for work."

"I take you," Drakken says instantly.

"No you won't," Stone chuckles. "She's not going anywhere with you."

Drakken's face hardens into a rigid mask. He stares at Stone for a long time. Then he looks at me and his face melts. It opens up, revealing that boyish vulnerable side of Drakken I've come to luh…I mean know. Come to *know*. He says, "Rivka, I tell you now. I tell you everything."

Another wave of nausea billows from my stomach outward. "I'm gonna hurl." I bend over at the waist and my insides do the taffy dance. If you've ever seen saltwater taffy being made, you know what my stomach is doing. If not, picture guts churning in ropey knots.

Drakken lays a hand on my back. "Rivka, are you okay? What happen to you?"

Stone barks, "Get your fucking hands off her, pal!"

"It's okay," I mumble. "He's not going to hurt me. Not with his hands, anyway." I smirk sourly.

"Want me to carry you inside?" Stone asks.

"No, I'm okay." I stumble toward the gate.

Stone jogs ahead and opens it.

I walk toward my bungalow and push through the front door. Stone follows me inside.

"You can't come in," Stone growls at Drakken.

Standing in the doorframe, Drakken looks at me hopefully. His face is soft.

I can't be rude to him. "He can come in," I mumble and stumble to the bathroom. I drop to the floor, about to hug the toilet bowl. Then I smell urine. "Damn it, Stone! How many times do I have to tell you to watch your aim!" I flop backward and slump against the side of the tub.

"Sorry," he says meekly.

I groan, "My head is *killing* me. I need water. Someone get me water."

Drakken and Stone both try and walk into the small bathroom at the same time. They bump shoulders.

"Watch it!" Stone growls.

"Excuse please," Drakken mutters.

Stone shoulders past, "I'll get it." He grabs my cup off the counter and fills it in the sink.

"Not tap," I sigh. "I need cold water. In the fridge."

Stone squeezes past Drakken.

Drakken lowers the lid on the toilet bowl and sits down. "Are you okay, Rivka? What happens to you?" His concern is obvious.

I clamp my eyes closed. "I drank too much last night. Now I'm paying for it. I'm still drunk."

Drakken chuckles, "Ah, yes. I understand."

"It's not funny," I frown without opening my eyes. I cradle my tender stomach with my forearms and rest my forehead against my knees.

"Sorry."

"Here ya go," Stone says.

I open my eyes and take the offered glass.

"Sip it. Or you're gonna puke again."

"Yeah." I gingerly sip. I close my eyes and savor the cold water. It feels wonderful on my tongue. I let out a semi-contented sigh. I just hope I can keep it down.

"Does he need to be here?" Stone asks.

I open my eyes.

Drakken's face shows concern. "Is very important I tell you, Rivka. I —"

Stone interrupts, "Why does he keep calling you that?"

"That's a good question," I smirk. "Why do you keep calling me that, Drakken? I thought it was a nickname for someone you cared about."

He nods knowingly and smiles. "You no understand."

"Damn right I don't understand. You're *engaged*."

Stone glances between me and Drakken. "Are you dating this guy?"

"Not anymore," I scowl.

"Rivka, engagement is not my choice. Is arrange marriage by my parent and her parent."

I frown, "What?"

"Is not right word?"

"Which word?"

"Arrange?"

"I don't know," I say. "It depends what you mean by arrange. Do you mean your parents and whatever-her-name-is's parents—"

"Karina."

I make a face, "and *Karina's* parents are *making* you and her get married?"

"Yes," he nods.

"Really?" I curl my lip doubtfully.

"Yes," he says.

Stone huffs, "Who does that old-fashioned shit anymore?"

"Old fashioned?" Drakken asks.

I shake my head, "Never mind." I shoot Stone a "shut up" glance.

"What?" he blurts.

"Let him talk," I warn. "Drakken, are your parents making you marry Karina?"

"Yes."

"Why?" I ask thoughtfully.

Drakken grinds his jaw. He inhales and sighs heavily. "Rivka, in my country, my father is king. And I am prince. I—"

"HA! HA! HA! HA! HA!" Stone guffaws. "You're not a fucking prince!" He looks at me. "Who the fuck is this guy?!"

"Um..." I don't know what to say.

Drakken shrugs and smiles. "I am prince. When my father die, I am to be king."

"Bull fucking shit!!" Stone chuckles. "This guy is pulling your leg, Riv! What other shit did he make up to impress you?"

Drakken doesn't respond.

I have to think about it.

"Buddy," Stone chortles, "You're a fucking idiot if you think my sister is dumb enough to fall for shit like that."

"Actually, Stone," I say thoughtfully, "Drakken never told me anything outrageous. In fact, he's never really told me much at all. I don't know the first thing about him." My brows knit. "Drakken, are you *really* a prince?"

"Yes."

I marvel at him, "How come you never told me?"

He smiles, "Would you believes me if I say I am prince?"

I snicker, "I guess not. So, you're an actual *prince*?" I wrinkle my nose.

"Yes."

"Is that why you have all those airplanes?"

"Yes."

"Airplanes?" Stone scoffs, "Yeah, I bet he told you all kinds of bullshit about having his own F-22."

Drakken shakes his head, "No. Is F/A-18."

"Yeah, right," Stone chuckles. "You don't have a fuckin' F-18."

"He does, Stone," I say.

"What? Bullshit."

I nod, "I flew in it."

Stone stares at me for a long time, examining my face.

"He does," I reiterate.

Stone's eyebrows float upward. "This guy has an F-18? An *actual* F-18?"

"Yeah."

"And you flew in it?"

"Uh huh."

"No way," Stone mutters.

"Yes way."

Stone looks over at Drakken and marvels like Drakken suddenly turned into a solid gold statue.

I smile. "Yeah, we flew to Santa Barbara on Saturday. In like, ten minutes. Isn't that right, Drakken?"

"Is true."

Stone gapes, "What the fuck! Are you serious, Riv?"

"Yeah. And he flew me to Calistoga in his fancy jet."

"Is Gulfstream G650," Drakken offers.

"What the fuck!" Stone gasps. "You have a fucking *Gulfstream*?"

"Yes. You want, I take you for ride."

"Fuck the Gulfstream, man! I wanna go up in your F-18!"

Drakken chuckles and I can't help but join him.

After a moment, Stone gives me a shrewd look, "I get it." He nods knowingly. "You two are *totally* bull shitting me."

"No, Stone, I swear—"

"Yeah, yeah. You didn't fly in no fuckin' F-18."

"I did!" I plead. "We did all those, what did you call them, hygiene maneuvers?"

Drakken chuckles, "Did you say hygiene? Is for teeth, like dental hygiene?"

"Oh," I smile and shake my head. "I meant high G."

Drakken grins, "Now I give *you* English lesson, Rivka."

"You did high G flying?" Stone asks.

"Yeah," I nod. "Loops and rolls. I even passed out on one."

Drakken nods, "On loop the loop. I sorry for too many G's."

Stone glances between the two of us. "What the fuck, Riv!" He laughs. "You got to fly in an F-18?!"

I hike my eyebrows and nod.

"Well, fuck me!" Stone says. "Maybe this guy is a prince!"

Chapter 11

RIVER

"So wait, let me get this straight," I say. "Karina wasn't some long lost love of yours?"

The three of us sit in the kitchen at the little breakfast table.

"Yes," Drakken nods. "I meet her first time five years ago. My father say me to marry her. I have no choice."

"Is she hot?" Stone asks.

Drakken winks, "Very hot."

I frown. "And I'm not?" I fold my arms across my chest.

Drakken pats my arm, "You are ten time more hot, Rivka."

Him calling me Rivka doesn't bother me as much now as it did five minutes ago. I blurt, "You haven't slept with her, have you?"

"No!" Drakken laughs. "Her father would kill me! My father would too! No sex before marriage. Is part of legal agreement."

"Really?" I frown.

"Yes. Is true."

"You got a picture of her?" Stone asks. "In your phone or something?"

"No," Drakken shakes his head.

That's a good sign. I'd be worried if he did.

"What's her name?" Stone asks and pulls out his smart phone. "I'll look her up on Google." He thumbs buttons on the phone.

"Karina Nakupovatska," Drakken says.

Stone shakes his head. "What? How do you spell that?"

"Give me phone, I type."

Stone hands it to him and Drakken thumbs in the name before handing the phone back.

"Holy shit! She's hot!"

I frown, "She's not that hot."

"Look at the picture!" Stone turns the phone so I can see it.

The photo of Karina looks like she's at some social function. She wears a bedazzled white gown and her hair is up in an elegant yet chaotic arrangement. Her makeup is flawless, and she looks like a movie star.

"That's her all right." I scowl.

Stone curls a smile. "Says here she's a princess. Damn, dude, why aren't you marrying a piece of ass like her?" His eyes search Drakken's.

Drakken stares at me intently with his ice blue eyes and says. "Because I no love her."

I shiver and feel the flow. *Our* flow. Now that I can feel it, I never want to break my connection with Drakken, whether Karina is his fiancée or not. She can suck it.

Stone mumbles, "It says here on the BBC News website that Karina Nakkapoopa—"

"Nakupovatska," Drakken corrects.

"—is supposed to marry Darkman Skaka-kaka—"

"Skalakova," I giggle.

"Yeah, whatever," Stone dismisses. "He's supposed to marry her later this year." He turns the phone so I can see it again.

"Let me see that." I take the phone from Stone.

Two pictures are side by side at the top of the article. One of Karina and one of Drakken. The caption below the photo reads, "Prince Drakken Skalakova will marry Princess Karina Nakupovatska later this year."

It's true. It's *all* true.

I skid the phone across the table like it's covered in poison.

Now I'm more confused. I was ready to believe that Drakken's engagement to this Karina woman was meaningless and true love would conquer all. Cut to happy ending, roll credits. But there's more to the story. Drakken is, in actual fact, a prince. And he's engaged to be married to an actual princess. Something makes me think his engagement is more than just a casual thing. Something called the BBC News. Despair strains my face.

Drakken reaches across the table and takes my hand. "I no want to marry her, Rivka."

"But you have to?" I ask.

"Yes…"

Defeat sinks into my bones. I *knew* it. I knew Drakken was too good to be true. Cut to tragic ending, roll credits, groan and throw popcorn at movie screen.

I sigh heavily. The truth is, Drakken and I *never* had a chance. If I had known about his engagement, I never would've gone out with him in the first place.

Drakken squeezes my hand. "Unless my project here in America succeed."

"What?" I ask hopefully. "What do you mean?"

Drakken releases my hand and folds his forearms on the table top, severing our connection, our flow.

It hurts.

Drakken hunches over and his face tightens. His entire body language has gone from open and relaxed to closed and tense.

"My father is powerful man," he says, staring at the table top. "He is king of my country. He has very much money and political power. More than you can count. He is to make me marry Karina."

"What?" Stone frowns. "How can he *make* you marry someone?"

"He put me in prison if I no marry her."

I gasp, "Are you serious?"

"Is truth," Drakken nods. "If I go home to my country, and I no marry Karina on wedding day, he put me in prison. But if I no go home, and he no find me, no prison."

I can't believe what I'm hearing. "Why would your dad put you in prison if you don't marry Karina?"

"Is political marriage. And for finance—*financial*—reason. Is hard to explain. For easy, think of marriage as business deal. Very big business deal between two country." He sighs heavily. "My father is king, and he think I am pawn."

Stone interjects, "I thought you said you were a prince?"

"Pawn, like chess. My father is king. He is try to make me do what he want, like pawn. He all ways make me do what he want. When I no do his want, he take from me. He take everything." Drakken's brow blackens and jitters with hidden rage.

WHAM!!

Drakken slams his fist on the table top.

My glass of ice water teeters and Stone grabs it. "Easy, buddy," he warns.

Drakken's head is still bowed. His jaw muscles shiver uncontrollably. "He take and take and take. Damn him!"

I reach over and squeeze Drakken's wrist.

He looks up at me. His eyes are wide and terrified.

"It's just me," I whisper.

Drakken stares at me like I'm a stranger.

I can only wonder what sort of craziness he has endured at the hands of his father. It's all so weird to me. Then I remember all the scars on Drakken's back. Did his father have something to do with them? I don't know what things are like in Drakken's country, but based on what I see in the news, anything is possible. People all over the planet are tortured or murdered for political reasons every single day.

In a quiet voice I say, "So you came to America to escape your father?"

"Yes," Drakken nods solemnly. "To build business for me. To make money for me. To make me free," he says bitterly, "from him."

"So," I say, "your airplane business needs to succeed just so you can stay out of jail?"

"Yes."

"What happens if it succeeds?"

"Then I never go home again."

I wince, "That sounds awful."

Drakken shakes his head, "Freedom is never awful."

Stone says thoughtfully, "You can say that again." Stone has spent his fair share of nights in jail for fighting.

Drakken gazes at me, "If I am free, I can marry woman for love, no for money. If am free, I can marry you, Rivka."

"Oh, Drakkozsha," I sigh.

Our warm flow resumes and melts my heart. It also scares me to death. I haven't been thinking about marriage. Not even close. I just spent the night with Cage. This is all too much. Too crazy. Too good to be true and too awful to be believed. I can't process all of this right now. I need some time to think about things.

Drakken's brows clench tightly and his eyes shut. "Now I have hard thing to say, Rivka."

I feel our flow freeze.

Wait! I needed time to think!

"Rivka, my father see you with me, yes?"

"Yeah. At the hotel yesterday. In the elevator. I had my arms around your elbow and I was leaning against you, thinking about how amazing our weekend was. Thinking about how much I luh—" Fear dribbles down my back in cold droplets. "How much I..." I can't say it because my mind has just pieced everything together. "Your father saw us. He saw me holding onto you. He must have known we were together. And if you're engaged to a *princess*, and you're seen hanging out with another woman— a lowly hotel masseuse no less—that would look very bad..."

Drakken nods slowly. "Yes."

"What would your father do if he knew what you, I mean, what *we* did?"

"What did you do, Riv?" Stone demands fearfully.

Drakken says, "If my father ever see you again, if he think you are with me like girlfriend, he will... he will..." Drakken's face shivers. "He will do *bad* thing to you."

"What?" Stone barks. "No fucking way."

"Shush, Stone," I hiss.

"No, Riv. If some guy out there thinks he's gonna hurt you for—" he scowls, "for *hooking up* with this guy, he's gonna have to come through me."

Drakken glances between me and my brother and sighs. "Can you defend against financial attack?"

"What?" Stone asks, confused.

"My father is very danger man. And very smart. He can take all money from your bank before you know is happening."

"I'm not worried about that," Stone chuckles dismissively. "We don't have any money in the bank, do we Riv."

"Um, no, but—"

Drakken shakes his head. "Money is only beginning. He can *sah*, uh, what is French word?"

I shake my head, "I don't know."

"He can, uh, *sabotage* your car. Or your home. Make gas leak. Start fire. Or he can take you."

"Take me?" I gasp. "Like, kidnap?"

"Yes."

Stone growls, "No one's kidnapping my sister."

Drakken looks at my brother thoughtfully and says, "Are you with Rivka ever day? Ever hour? Ever minute?"

"No, but—"

"If my father want to take Rivka, he will. If he take her, he..." Drakken trails off ominously.

My gurgly stomach threatens to heave up all of the ice water I drank in the past fifteen minutes. I swallow it back down. "Are you saying your father might try to kidnap me? Or... *kill* me?"

"Fuck no, he won't!" Stone barks.

"Shut up, Stone," I warn.

Drakken sighs. "If I never see you again, no." He nods, "If now is last time I ever see you, you will be safe. All ways safe. I promise. My father want me, not you. If he has me, he forget you."

I don't like the sound of this. "It sounds like you're his prisoner or something," I mutter.

"I am." Drakken swallows hard and his eyes water. "Rivka, I am sorry. My father is danger man. He will hurt you. I can no be with you ever hour,

ever minute. With me, you are never safe. With no me, then you are safe."
He swallows again. "So I go. I say goodbye."

"Drakken, no," I mutter.

"Yes, Rivka. Yes." A single tear slides down his cheek, leaving behind a
tiny River of wetness. The tear falls from his jaw and lands on the back of
my hand, which is resting on his wrist. Drakken pulls his arm out of my
grasp and lowers his hands beneath the table. "I will marry Karina and my
father will never know who you are or where you live. Then you will be
safe."

My stomach lurches. "I can't believe this, Drakken. This is crazy. You
shouldn't have to marry someone you don't want to."

"I has no choice. Is only way I know to make you safe, hundred
percent."

I shake my head. "No! This doesn't make any sense! Why would your
dad try to hurt you just because you *like* me?"

"Is no like, Rivka. Is love, Rivka. I *love* you, Rivka. With all of my heart,
I love you." He says it with complete conviction. His face is open and soft.
Tears stream down his face in Rivers.

The flow between us resumes with torrential force.

My body starts to shake. This is wonderful. This is terrible.

The kitchen is dead silent.

Drakken's ice blue eyes search mine. He looks completely helpless, like
a lost boy with no home who has never known love. Maybe he's never had
either.

"Oh, Drakken," I sigh sadly and sniffle back a tear. I'm torn between
thinking this is all a terrible nightmare and the stark realization that it's all
true. As crazy as Drakken's story sounds, I believe every word of it. But I
don't want to believe any of it. It makes me furious to think Drakken's
father is *this* awful. *This* horrible. What kind of father treats his son like
this? Anger boils up inside me. "This isn't fair, Drakken. It's not fair!" I
shout.

Drakken's face contorts with rage and he stands up suddenly. "No. No,
I will no let my father hurt you. No, no, no!" Drakken's face ratchets into
hard lines. He starts to pace the small kitchen. "No, no, NO!"

"Easy buddy," Stone warns.

"No!" Drakken shouts. "My father will no hurt you! NO!!" He slams a
fist into our refrigerator, denting the side.

Stone jumps up, "What the fuck!"

I grab Stone's arm. "Don't, Stone!"

"He just broke our fridge, Riv!"

"Sit down, Stone! Let me handle this."

"I can fucking handle this, sis."

"Shush. Let me do it." I step toward Drakken.

"NO! My father must die! He will no kill you! He will no KILL YOU!!"

"Drakka," I soothe. "Drakkozsha. Stop, babe. It's okay. Your father isn't going to hurt me. I promise."

Drakken looks at me. His face glows bright red. "You no know him, Rivka! He does terrible thing to many people! He is bad man! Very bad!!"

I don't know what to say to that. I do know that there are terrible men in this world who have done exactly what Drakken said to their own people. It happens all the time. I can't think about it. The horror of it would shut me down. Right now, the only thing that matters is comforting Drakken. His sadness and rage are breaking my heart.

"I can no see you, Rivka! Never another time! Is only way for you to be safe, okay?!" His chest heaves with effort. His lips peel back over clenched teeth. Agony consumes him. "I say goodbye to you. I marry Karina. For you to be safe. Okay?"

I feel his pain as if it were my own. I feel it because of the flow between us. Our connection is undeniable, and it is powerful. I won't let anyone hurt Drakken. Not his father, not anybody. I will protect him from every horrid thing on this planet.

"No, Drakken," I whisper.

"What?" he whines, sounding more like a frightened child than the powerful man I know him to be. "What can you do, Rivka? Is my father! He will kill you like he—" Drakken stops short, a look of horror shining from his eyes.

"What, Drakken? Tell me," I say with calm confidence.

Drakken shakes his head. "No. No, no, NO!" His face hardens. Then softens. Then hardens again. He clenches his fists as if trying to regain control of himself. "Rivka, I love you. I all ways love you. Until I die, I love you. But I go. I say goodbye. For you to have safe, I go. Goodbye, Rivka. Goodbye." He rushes past me and out of the kitchen, heading toward the front door. His footsteps are heavy but unrelenting.

I'm stunned.

I can't move.

What is happening?

None of this makes any sense.

I need to move.

I *have* to move.

I run after him.

When I catch up to him, Drakken is grabbing the front doorknob. He twists it. The door creaks open ominously.

This is it.

He's leaving. As weird and impossible and ridiculous and fantastical as the last thirty minutes of my life have been, it's all real. And it's all about to fall apart. The most amazing and mysterious and wonderful man I've ever met is going to leave my life as strangely as he came into it.

I can't help but think I'll look back on all of this in five years and wonder if any of it was real. Will I forget Drakken's ruggedly handsome face? The sound of his resonant voice? The touch of his strong and loving hands? The wonderful scent of his skin? Will every aspect of Drakken's existence fade from my mind and leave nothing behind?

No.

My heart says no.

My heart says I will never forget this man.

My heart says I love him.

My heart says I will fight for him.

After Cage, I never thought I would say those words ever again. After Cage, I didn't think I was capable of loving *anyone* else. My heart was smashed to bits when he left. But that was nearly a year ago. The heart is strong. It can heal. Mine did. Today, my heart shines bright and beats strong with my love for Drakken. It courses powerfully through my veins.

I whisper:

"I love you."

He stops in place, one foot hovering out the front door like a man about to jump from an airplane without a parachute. He slowly retracts his leg and turns to face me.

I pour my heart out to him. "Drakken, I love you. With all my heart, I love you."

His face is soft, alive, and filled with hope. His wet eyes twinkle and dance like blue stars. "I love you too, Rivka." His face collapses with sadness. "Is why I say goodbye." He spins and runs out the door.

"Drakken!" I scream. "No! Drakken!" I run after him and stumble onto the cement path that leads to the street.

Ahead, Drakken vaults over the front fence like he has wings on his back.

When I reach the sidewalk, he's already in his Lamborghini.

The engine roars and he flies down the street.

"Draaaakkeeeeeen!!!" I scream.

Chapter 12

RIVER

I grab my purse from inside before running to the parking lot behind the bungalows.

"Where are you going?" Stone shouts, jogging up behind me.

"After Drakken!" I jump into the blue Audi convertible.

"You're not gonna catch him in that thing. I saw his Lambo."

"His what?"

"His Lamborghini?"

I hiss, "You're not helping, Stone."

He rolls his head, "Try calling him."

My eyes pop open. "Great idea!" I grab my phone from my purse. "Shit! I forgot! The battery is dead!"

Stone pulls his own phone out, "What's his number? I'll call him."

"I don't know!" I say, panicked.

"Plug your phone in, in the house."

"Yeah!" I run back inside and plug my bedroom charger into the phone. It takes a few seconds to come on. I call Drakken.

The automated answering lady speaks immediately. "The number you are trying to reach, three one zero, blah blah blah, is unavailable. Please leave a message after the tone."

Fucking beep.

"Drakken, Drakkozsha. Please call me. I love you. I don't want to say goodbye. I don't want to let you go. I don't care about your dad or whatever. I care about you. I love you. Please, please, please, don't leave me." I start to sob. "Please, Drakken. I can't live without you. I need you in my life. It doesn't matter about your dad. Please, Drakkozsha, I—"

The rude robot lady interrupts, "If you are satisfied with your message, press one. If you would like to record a new message, press—"

I press one. Then I end the call and text Drakken.

"Drakken, my love. Call me. Please. Don't leave me. I need you. I need us. Call me."

My phone rings in my hand. I nearly drop it. I answer it.

"Where are you?" Jocelyn demands. "Luciana is pissed! You didn't call in to say you'd be late. You've got clients waiting for you."

"Oh shit!" I blurt. "Tell her I'll be right in. I'm on my way right now."

"You better make it quick—"

I hang up on Jocelyn.

Too many robot bitches on the phone today. The next one will probably be Luciana herself.

I jump into my white spa uniform before running to my car. I speed down our driveway toward the street. I brake and look both ways for traffic.

Something whacks the trunk of the Audi.

I twist around.

"Are you okay to drive?" Stone asks.

"I'm fine."

"No you're not. Let me drive."

"No, Stone. I need to go. Drakken might be heading to the hotel. I can catch him if I go right now."

He shakes his head, "Be careful, sis. You can't catch him if you're dead." The concern in his voice is obvious. All of his usual bluster is gone.

I chew my lips for a moment. "Okay. I'll go the speed limit."

"Don't run any reds. Some dumb shit is liable to T-bone you if you do."

"Okay," I nod. "I'll be safe."

Stone smiles. "Here's my car charger. For your phone." He hands it to me. "Go get him."

"Thanks, Stone." Despite my anguish, I can't help but smile. "I love you, Stone."

"I love you too, sis. Don't get killed."

"I won't."

He grins and chuckles, "If you do, I'm gonna fucking kill you."

I smirk, "I won't get killed. Promise."

I pull onto the street and head toward destiny.

Chapter 13

RIVER

After thirty minutes of careful driving, I arrive safely at The Beverly Hills Resort and stumble across the parking garage like a zombie from The Walking Dead. My body literally feels like it's falling apart. Despite my mind racing a thousand miles an hour during my drive, the sedate pace of traffic gave me plenty of time to reflect on my hangover.

At this point, it's too soon to call it a hangover. I'm definitely still buzzed. If a cop had stopped me on my way to work, I doubt I would've passed the drunk test.

Wow, today is not my day.

A minute later, I'm rushing down the hallway on the 20th floor. I pound on the double doors of the Sunset Suite and keep pounding.

Karina finally opens the door. She wears an ankle length black lace nightgown. Her lithe body is easily visible through the lace. She is incredibly beautiful.

"Okay, okay," she whines. "What is so important you wake me up? You are too early for maid."

"Have you seen Drakken?" I demand.

Her eyes are sleepy. She blinks them several times and examines my face. "You were with him yesterday, yes?"

"Where is Drakken?"

"I don't know," she pouts.

"Is Svetlana here?" I doubt Svetlana would tell me anything if she was, but I have to try. She may be my only link to Drakken right now.

"No. She is out."

Fuzz. "Do you know when she'll be back?"

"I don't know. I'm not her babysitter. Now you wake me up," she pouts. "I am trying to sleep from jet lag." She slams the door in my face.

Total bitch.

Well, at least I know Drakken isn't here. So where is he? He could be anywhere. But where would he go if he was leaving for good?

LAX.

I hate to think he would just hop on one of his planes and fly away forever, but after the way he left me back at the bungalow, and after all the things he said, anything is possible.

I run down the hallway toward the elevators. My phone rings in my purse.

"Yeah?" I answer hopefully.

"Where are you?" Jocelyn prods.

I don't have time for her right now. "What do you want?"

"Uhhh, duh?" she chides. "You have a client waiting for you? In the spa? How long are you going to make him wait?"

"Him? Who is it?"

"I don't remember his name. He's that hot guy I told you to bang."

Drakken.

She has to be talking about Drakken.

Hope floods my veins. I'm suddenly filled with energy. "Okay, I'll be right there."

I run to the elevators and punch the down button.

Did Drakken change his mind? Or did he want to see me one last time before he leaves? It doesn't matter. He came back for me. He came back!

When I arrive in the spa, Jocelyn smirks at me from behind the reception desk. She leans back in her chair and crosses her arms over her tit balloons. "Make sure you don't fuck him too loud. Luciana is keeping an eye on you."

I roll my eyes and jog to the massage room and open the door in a rush.

"Hey, Riv," Cage smiles. He holds up a bouquet of roses and sits on the edge of the massage table.

My heart drops.

Shizz.

"No," I whine.

"No?" Defeated, he drops the bouquet to his side. "But I booked a massage just so I could see you."

I shake my head and feel tears coming. He's supposed to be Drakken. Not Cage... Oh no! Last night and this morning come crashing back. I woke up in Cage's bed! He probably thinks I want to get back together. No, no, no! I want Drakken!

Cage sighs. "Is this about last night?"

"What about last night?" I ask frantically.

"If it is, I'm sorry."

"Sorry? Why are you sorry? What did we do? Wait, I don't want to know." I just need to get out of here. I back up a step.

He frowns. "We didn't do anything."

"We didn't?"

"Well, we made out for awhile. But you started acting weird so we stopped. I wasn't sure what was going on with you, but it was something. Anyway, after I made sure you weren't gonna drown in puke, I slept on the floor."

"You did?"

"Of course I did, Riv. I love you. If you're not in the mood for sex, I'm not gonna push it. If you're not ready to get back together, I'll give you space. All that heavy shit I laid on you last night is a lot to take in. I get it."

The heavy shit I heard from Drakken this morning is even more to take in, but I can't tell Cage that.

"Anyway, you ran out this morning so fast, I knew something was wrong. I knew I had to talk to you. Last night, I spent so much time telling you what I went through, I never stopped to ask what *you* went through. I hurt you, Riv. I get it. I'm sorry. You have no idea how sorry I am."

Not sure what to say, I merely nod. How long is this going to take?

"Yes, I abandoned you," he says. "Yes, I should've called. Yes, I should've trusted that you wouldn't judge me." He sighs heavily. "And yes, I still love you."

"No, Cage."

He gulps a hard swallow. "What?"

Unable to speak, I shake my head. I don't want to hurt Cage. After what he told me about his dad and his mom, he doesn't deserve it. He's a good person. He deserves kindness. I can't give him that right now. My heart and mind are elsewhere. "Cage, I can't. I have to go." I turn around and rush out of the massage room.

"Riv, wait!" Cage follows me into the hallway and stops. "Wait, Riv! Please!"

The desperation in his voice squeezes my heart. I slow to a stop in the waiting room. I feel awful. Now that I know the full story, I almost feel like I owe Cage a second chance. It's not like he dumped me. We didn't even break up. Not officially. He just had family business that was overwhelming and super stressful. Sometimes, people in relationships aren't perfect and do dumb things. It doesn't mean they stop loving you. It took me forever to stop loving Cage.

I turn back to face him.

In a soft voice, Cage says, "I'm sorry, Riv. Give me a second chance. Please. It's all I ask. I'll prove to you how much I love you. How much I need you. How I've never stopped loving you..."

This sucks so much I can't even begin to describe it. There is still a place in my heart for Cage. I can't deny it. That part of me wants to go to him and comfort him.

I close my eyes, trying to blot out the world, trying to give myself time to think.

All I see in the darkness are frightened blue eyes.

Those ice blue eyes...

I may still love Cage, but I'm not *in love* with him. Not anymore.

With my head hanging, I whisper too quietly for anyone to hear, "I'm sorry." I turn away from Cage and take a tentative step forward, heading toward my future.

From behind her desk, Jocelyn smirks, "Still making him beg?" Her voice drips with judgement.

I stop suddenly and frown at her. "What?"

"Are you still making your ex beg? Until you're sure you have him wrapped around your finger?"

I suddenly remember the hateful lecture Jocelyn gave me way back when about how I was making Cage wait. Making him beg and beg until I broke him. So I could control him. So I could feel safe before letting him back in. Because I needed reassurances. Because I was scared. Because I was a coward.

Anger flashes in my heart and floods my veins. I hiss, "Fuck you, Jocelyn. You don't know me."

Her eyes headlight and she shrinks back in her chair.

Luciana strides into the spa waiting room from the direction of the main lobby. Her peep-toe pumps stab the floor with every step. "Where have you been, River?! We have a full schedule today! I don't have time for the sort of unprofessional behavior you've been exhibiting for the—"

"I have to go," I breeze right past her and run out of the spa.

"River! Come back here this instant!"

I ignore her and sprint into the main lobby.

"Riv!" Finch hollers, trotting across the lobby. "Luciana is *pissed*, girl! She just asked if I knew where you were."

"Screw her," I growl. "I have more important things. Have you seen Drakken at the hotel today?"

"The Drakk Attack?"

I can't help but grin when she says it.

She shakes her head, "No, I haven't seen him. Did you check the Sunset Suite?"

"Yeah. He's not there."

"Are you okay? You seem agitated."

I roll my eyes, "You have no idea. I'll explain later."

"Is it complicated?"

I smirk, "More complicated than the internet."

Finch grins, "I get it. But I will need a full report later."

"Deal." I run to the elevators and punch the DOWN button.

I'm going to LAX.

I just hope I get there before Drakken leaves my life forever.

Chapter 14

RIVER

"I'm sorry, miss, but if you don't have the proper authorization, I can't let you through this gate," the security guy at LAX says authoritatively.

"But it's super important," I plead.

"I'm sure that it is. But without authorization, I can't let you in."

"Not even this once? Can't you make an exception?" I bat my eyelashes at him. It plays more as comedy than seduction when I do it, but I work with what I've got.

He sighs, "Look, you seem nice. But I could lose my job. I can't let you in."

I groan and let my head fall back against the headrest of the Audi. I look at my surroundings. The entire airport is fenced in. "Hey, are those fences electrified or whatever?"

He rolls his eyes, "Don't try and climb them. You'll hurt yourself on the razor wire. Then you'll get arrested."

"If this wasn't important, I wouldn't even consider it. But you gotta believe me. I need to get to that brown building over there and talk to the people inside."

He looks over his shoulder, then back at me. "Do you know the people leasing the hangar?"

"Yes!"

"So call them."

I frown. "I only have the cell phone number of one of the guys who, uh, leases it. I think, uh, his battery is dead. On his phone. Please. This is a life or death situation."

He rolls his eyes and sighs. "Hold on." He walks into the security booth and pulls a clipboard off a hook on the wall. He flips through the papers for a minute. Then he walks out to me and shows me the clipboard. He points at one of the numbers. "This number is a land line to the building. Why don't you try it?"

My eyes light. "Okay!" I punch it into my phone. It rings.

A deep voice answers, "Hello?"

I take a stab at who it might be. "Hey, uh, Lubomir?"

"Yes?"

"It's River. From yesterday? I flew on the F-18? And the Gulfstream? With Drakken?"

"Yes, I remembers."

"I'm here at the security gate. At LAX. They won't let me in. Is, um, is Drakken there?"

Lubomir doesn't respond. The phone makes a muffling noise. Then I can't hear anything for over a minute. A moment later, he says, "I will come get you."

The phone line clicks and goes dead.

"Well?" the gate guard asks.

"They're coming to get me."

He smiles, "You're welcome."

"Oh, uh, thanks."

A few minutes later, Lubomir drives up in one of those electric cars that looks like a glorified golf cart. He is way too big for it and sits hunched beneath the bubble roof. He steps out and the car lifts noticeably. Lubomir chats with the guard, the gate opens, and the guard waves me through.

I follow Lubomir to the hangar in the blue Audi, park beside the building, and climb out of my car.

Lubomir punches in the door code and holds the door for me.

With the bright light of the morning sun in my face, I can't see inside the office. It's too dark.

I step through the door into the unknown and hope for the best.

Chapter 15

RIVER

"Rivka," Drakken mutters as he folds his arms around me. He hugs me fiercely. "What are you do here?"

I hug him back, pressing my cheek into his chest. "Don't go, Drakken. You're leaving L.A., aren't you?"

He doesn't answer.

We stand in the locker room in the back of the hangar, the one where we changed into our flight suits for the flight in the F-18.

"Let me come with you," I plead. I can't believe I said it, but I did.

I feel his warm breath blow against my scalp. He kisses the top of my head affectionately. "You are strong girl, Rivka. I know it from day we meet. Very strong. Like river."

"That's right. And that's why I'm coming with you."

Am I really going to throw everything away for Drakken? My job? My friends? My life in L.A.? My brother? I don't know. Maybe I am. My heart tells me I should. The only thing that makes me second guess myself is Stone. I can't leave him. We're too close. He needs me. But Drakken needs me too. And I think Stone would understand.

Drakken sighs, "Is too danger, Rivka."

"Dangerous," I smile up at him.

"Yes," he grins, "danger*ous*."

"See?" I say hopefully. "You still need me to teach you English. So I'm coming with you."

His ice blue eyes marvel at me. "You are so strong, Rivka."

In his arms, I know everything is going to be okay. In his arms, I am safe. In his arms, I am strong. In his arms, we can take on the world together. Nothing can stand in our way.

I tilt my head back and stand on my tip toes. I lick my upper lip. "Drakkozsha," I mutter. "I love you. I want you. I *need* you…"

His eyes soften and he leans his head down.

Our lips meet. Our mouths open. Our tongues twine. We breathe each other's breaths as we kiss. Our hands roam over each other's bodies. Our hips press together. Our need and our passion ignites.

We pull at each other's clothes with desperate desire.

Drakken lifts my white top over my head. I loosen his tie. He unsnaps my bra. I unbutton his dress shirt and run my hands over his amazing abs. My bra falls from my chest and he squeezes my full breasts.

"Your breasts is beautiful, Rivka. I miss them."

"But you had them just the other day," I wink.

"I need them ever day."

I smile, "I need this every day." I smear my hands across his muscular chest. I lean forward and kiss one nipple and nibble it while I wrap my arms around his back and pull myself against him.

His erection presses against me.

It drives me wild. I hastily unbuckle his belt and unfasten his slacks. I can't push them down fast enough. I pull his cock out of his boxer briefs and lick the hardened tip.

It's smooth, hot, and throbbing.

I swallow it and caress him with my tongue and lips.

He moans softly, "Oh, Rivka…"

I stand up and push my uniform pants down to my ankles, taking my panties with them. I kick off my shoes and now I'm completely naked.

"You are too beautiful for my word to describe, Rivka." His eyes roam over my nakedness longingly.

"Don't go, Drakka. I love you. I need you. I need us." My heart, body, and mind clash in a maelstrom of desire, love, fear, and hope. "I need you, Drakkozsha. Right now. And forever." I can't believe I just said that, but I don't regret that I did. I've never been this bold with men. But something about these circumstances has brought out a side of me I never knew I had.

That's when it hits me.

I am alive.

With Drakken, I am always alive.

Every moment with him is intense, passionate, magical, and the most amazing thing I've ever experienced.

"Take me, Drakka. I'm yours." I lower my voice to a whisper. "Take me…"

His blue eyes glimmer like stars. He stares into my soul. His heart touches mine. We speak without words.

Our love combines.

All pain fades to nothingness.

All fear disappears.

All is love.

All is us.

"Rivka," he whispers, "I—"

He suddenly lunges toward me and scoops me into his arms. He lifts me up and arches his back. I wrap my legs around his waist.

I am hot and wet.

He is hot and hard.

With one hand around my back, he uses the other to guide his cock inside me. He fills me perfectly. My entire body sings with pleasure. My wetness drenches him.

With his pants still around his ankles, he shuffles forward until my back presses against a cool metal locker. The chill surprises me, as does the name tag mounted on the locker above my head.

Skalakova.

Drakken begins a slow thrusting rhythm while burying his face in my bosom and his manhood in my body.

He pushes and pushes, each thrust sending a pulse of primal pleasure billowing through my body. I float in the clouds, riding on the wings of his heat.

I slide my hands under his dress shirt and rub them up his back, across his—

"Rivka," he whispers hoarsely.

—scars.

He is so sensitive about his scars. I don't know how he got them, but I know they hold terrible memories for him. They're a permanent reminder of the painful demons that still haunt him. I expect Drakken to suddenly stop, to end our love making abruptly, to shut down and run away and hide his true self from me. Forever.

But he doesn't. He thrusts into me harder, more intensely, more desperately. As I open myself to him with body, heart, and soul, I feel him open his heart to me. His soul.

I feel our flow.

I feel his sadness, his pain. I let it flow into me, where it mingles with my love for him. I will heal this man with all the love in my soul. I press my palms against his scars, against his battered flesh, sending a flood of healing loving energy back into him.

"Rivka," he sobs, thrusting yet harder, as if he can't bury himself deeply enough inside of me. As if he is trying to hide from the world by climbing into my body.

I welcome him.

I wrap myself around him.

I will protect him from harm.

I will protect his heart and I will protect his soul.

The inside of my thighs quiver as I squeeze my legs around his waist and sink my hips onto his hardness as far as I can go, as deep as possible. Pleasure fills my body. I whisper in his ear, "I love you, Drakka, I love you."

He thrusts with naked need.

"I love you, Drakka," I whisper.

He grunts.

"I love you, my Drakkozsha."

He thrusts.

"I'll protect you, my love," I soothe.

He cries out.

"I will always be here for you."

His body begins to quiver.

My body begins to vibrate.

All of the pleasure inside us shrinks down to a tiny seed between our legs.

"Rivka," he growls and throws his head back. He thrusts into me again and shouts, "Rivka!"

The tiny seed inside us explodes in a titanic release of energy and I scream with orgasmic ecstasy, "Drakken!!"

"Rivka!!"

"Drakka!!"

We climax at the same time.

Orgasm smashes into both of us.

Pleasure becomes our universe as our bodies unite.

Together, we become the infinite.

Chapter 16

RIVER

"Sir?" Lubomir says quietly, startling me.

I'm completely naked, pressed up against the cold metal locker. Drakken is still inside me, filling me as our fluids flow together. My cheek presses against his as we both pant heavily.

"Sir?"

I open my eyes and turn my head. Lubomir isn't in the room. He must be standing in the doorway, just out of view.

"Sir?" Lubomir asks again. "Your plane is ready. Your flight plan is approved with tower. Is time to go."

"A minute, Lubomir," Drakken hisses. "Give us a minute."

"Yes, sir." Lubomir's footsteps fade down the hallway.

Drakken shifts his hips, trying to pull out.

"No," I gasp, and squeeze him with my thighs. "No."

He eases himself back into me.

"I won't let go," I say desperately.

I squeeze him as hard as I can with my arms, my legs, my core. We remain locked together for several minutes.

He gently kisses my cheek. "Is time."

"No!" I whine.

He backs up carefully and sits us down on a bench. My butt rests on his muscled thighs.

"I need flight suit."

"Where's mine?" I ask.

"In locker where you put it yesterday. I get for you."

"You will?" I ask hopefully.

"Yes."

I climb off his lap and he stands.

He opens a locker and pulls out the bulky flight suit.

"Are we doing this?" I ask.

"Put suit on."

I take it from him.

He pulls up his slacks and boxer briefs without bothering to clean himself up.

I step into my panties and my uniform pants, also not bothering to clean up.

Drakken opens his locker and takes his own flight suit out. He steps into it.

I put on my bra and shirt and hastily climb into my flight suit. "I need help with the buckles. I don't know what goes where."

He walks over and helps me adjust everything. Then he grabs his helmet and mine from the lockers. He holds mine out to me.

I search his eyes. "Are we *really* doing this?" I ask nervously.

"Is time to go."

I take the helmet.

He holds out his empty hand.

I take it.

We walk outside to the runway.

The gleaming black F-18 awaits. It's smooth lines glint sunlight. Several men scurry around it, getting things ready. I recognize Radek from last time. Lubomir stands near the ladder under the wing with his arms clasped behind his back. He nods at Drakken as we approach.

I glance over at Drakken's face. Did I miss something?

Drakken climbs up the ladder.

I almost make a crack about ladies first, but don't.

Drakken drops into the cockpit and I reach for the ladder.

Lubomir grabs my wrist in a steel grip.

"What?" I blurt.

Lubomir stares at me, his face flat.

"Let me go, Lubomir!"

He shakes his head almost imperceptibly.

"Let me go!" I try to yank my arm free, but Lubomir is way too strong. I hammer his arm with the bottoms of my fists. "Let go." I twist around and look up at Drakken.

He gazes down at me, his face sad. "I is—*am*—very sorry, Rivka. Very sorry." His voice is nearly drowned out by the sound of an approaching Virgin America jet flying in for a landing. After the plane passes, Drakken says glumly, "Is to keep you safe, Rivka. Is for best."

"No! I'm safe if I'm with you, Drakken! I need to be with you! Keep me safe, Drakken! I won't be safe unless I'm with you! Please," I beg, starting to cry.

Drakken shakes his head heavily. "You no know my father. You are safe away from me. Only then. Only then, Rivka." Drakken lowers the mirrored visor on his helmet. His face disappears behind a silver shield.

"No! Let me go, Lubomir!" I struggle and yank my arm. I stomp on Lubomir's toes. His boots are made of steel. Or his toes are. He doesn't budge. "Noooo!" I shriek.

"Make her safe, Lubomir," Drakken hollers. "No let my father find her!"

The glass cockpit lowers over Drakken.

Lubomir pulls me away from the F-18.

The other men back away.

The engines whine.

The plane pulls slowly forward.

I fall to my knees on the cement, sobbing against Lubomir's leg.

A few minutes later, I watch Drakken's jet fly west, out over the Pacific Ocean. I watch until it shrinks into a tiny black dot and disappears.

I collapse against the cement and wail, hugging the ground, trying to hold onto something because I feel like I'm going to be thrown into outer space and disappear into the black lonely void of nothingness. My heart is already there, so it only makes sense my body will soon follow.

Chapter 17

RIVER

SCREECH!! SCREECH!! SCREECH!! SCREECH!! SCREECH!! SCREECH!! SCREECH!! SCREECH!! SCREECH!! SCREECH!! SCREECH!! SCREECH!! SCREECH!!

"Are you gonna turn that off?" Stone asks quietly the next morning, leaning his head through my bedroom door.

I lie flat on my bed, my covers up to my chin, staring at the ceiling. When my alarm started going off five minutes ago, I was too weak to move.

I am sick with heartbreak.

I turn my head slightly toward Stone. My eyes are hot.

He looks at me with a mixture of love and curiosity.

I start sobbing.

Stone walks around my bed and turns off the alarm.

He sits beside me on the mattress and strokes my forehead with the palm of his hand.

I reach my arms up like I'm a little girl who wants her daddy.

Stone pulls me into his arms and rubs my back through my T-shirt. "Riv, I'm sorry."

I hug him back.

I want to die.

Drakken abandoned me.

This is a million times worse than Cage leaving. I never thought that could be possible, but it is. I may have loved Cage, but not like I love Drakken. I had no idea how much I loved Drakken until he left. Half of my very being is missing without him.

I am incomplete.

I am a shell of a human being.

I can't live like this.

But I don't have a choice.

I have my brother to think of.

I have a job I need to keep.

I have classes I need to focus on.

Somehow, I manage to drag myself out of bed and into the shower and get ready for work. Stone offers to drive me. I would take him up on it except I won't have a ride home because Stone works tonight.

So I drive the Audi down the driveway alone, toward the street. I look both ways.

That's when I notice Sheena the Chevy is parked against the sidewalk right next to my driveway. Lubomir sits behind the wheel. He stares at me.

Drakken told Lubomir to keep an eye on me. A tiny seed of hope grows inside me. With a small smile on my face, I wave at Lubomir.

He nods once.

I drive the Audi into the street. Sure enough, Lubomir follows me in Sheena.

Okay then.

I drive toward work.

I'm suddenly in a much better mood then I ever would've expected. When I went to bed last night, it felt like Drakken was gone forever. With Lubomir following me, it's proof that Drakken hasn't completely abandoned me. I don't want to jump to any conclusions, but as long as Lubomir is around, I have hope.

Hope goes a long way.

Chapter 18

RIVER

Needles prick every inch of my skin.

Hope can be a dangerous thing.

I stand inside the small staff bathroom in the spa at work. I hold the clamshell case of my birth control pills in the palm of my hand.

I've counted my remaining pills seven times. Every time I count, the result is the same.

I've missed my pill for three days straight.

I forgot to take one at the castle in Calistoga on Sunday morning. I forgot to take one after waking up in Cage's apartment Monday morning. I forgot to take one this morning.

I had sex with Drakken yesterday.

Without a condom.

And no pill(s). Plural.

Drakken came inside me more than two days after I last took my pill. I probably still have some of his sperm inside me. Those things can live up to five days. And it's been three days since I took a pill. His sperm have had almost 24 hours to work their magic.

Oh shizz.

I hope I'm not pregnant.

Panicked, I pop today's pill into my mouth and dry swallow it.

The bathroom door rattles. "Is someone in there?" Jocelyn asks.

"Yeah. Hold on." I consider the other pills. I pop another one into my mouth, just in case. Do I need to go to the pharmacy for a Plan B pill?

Fuzz.

This was not on my agenda of things to do today. Or any day.

"Are you done yet?" Jocelyn demands.

I slide my pills into my purse, flush the toilet for effect, then open the door.

Jocelyn sneers, "What were you doing in there?"

"Trying to avoid you." I barge past her.

"You need to get laid," she mutters sourly behind my back.

If she only knew.

Chapter 19

RIVER

I stop at CVS on the way home from work. I walk straight toward the pharmacy section to get a Plan B pill. At the last second, I balk and walk past it. Past the diapers and the baby formula, because they're making me nervous. I end up in the oral care aisle to examine tooth brushes while I think this through. Tooth brushes are innocuous, right? Everyone likes clean teeth, right?

Even girls who forget to take their pill?

Right?

I clamp my eyes shut.

Oh! I am *so* mad at myself for forgetting! I *never* forget my pill!

Ever.

I'm responsible. I'm not an absent-minded airhead. This isn't like me. Of all the annoying things that come with adulthood, remembering to take my pill was not one of them. I never mess around with birth control. I take it very seriously.

So, what the eff happened?

I cite extenuating circumstances. It's not every day I get whisked away in a fighter jet to fantasyland *and* in a private jet to a princess castle complete with fairy princess gown and princess bed chambers. Where I have sex with an actual prince, not that I knew it at the time. But he is an *actual* prince. Then the Karina bomb dropped in my lap, I dropped the

"Drunk With Cage" bomb into my own lap, and finally Drakken dropped the "Leaving Forever" bomb and blew my heart to pieces. Circumstances don't extenuate any more than that.

Okay, I forgive me.

I'm not a horribly irresponsible teenager pretending to be an adult.

I'm a grown-up adult woman.

I can make decisions for myself and deal with the consequences of my actions.

So I'm gonna go deal.

I walk back to the Family Planning aisle, which should be called the Not Planning On A Family aisle, and stop in front of the boxes of Plan B. I don't remember them being on the shelves in the past, but here they are.

They should change the name to Plan D, for Plan Dummy.

I am such an idiot.

At least medical science has contingency plans for irresponsible children like me.

I sigh and reach out to take a box.

Those ice blue eyes…

I hesitate.

I totally can't manage a kid right now. I need to take the pill, just in case.

I reach out for the box.

Those ice blue eyes…

I can't do it.

It's totally stupid, but I can't.

I drop my hand to my side and walk out of CVS.

Anyway, I doubt I'm pregnant.

What are the chances?

Chapter 20

RIVER

The next morning, after I shower and dress, I walk out to the street. Lubomir sits inside Sheena again.

I wave and walk up to his window.

He rolls it down. The crank squeaks every time he turns it.

I smile, "Are you hungry?"

He shakes his head. "I have food. From Armenian restaurant. From last night."

"Last night?" I scoff. "It's probably cold!"

"Is okay. Is very good." With his accent, he almost sounds like Drakken, and it warms my heart. He even has the same coloring: dark black hair, pale skin, luminous blue eyes. But Lubomir looks more like one of those hulking professional wrestlers on the WWE, which I know all about thanks to Stone. Stone absolutely loves wrestling even though he knows it's fake. Yeah, Lubomir looks like he should be wearing one of those huge fancy gold championship belts around his waist.

I smile at him, "I can warm your food up in the microwave if you want."

He shakes his head, "Is okay. Is good cold."

"Okay," I shrug. "Hey, um, Lubomir?"

"Yes?"

"Do you know where Drakken is?"

"Yes."

I wait for him to elaborate further.

He stares at me.

"Uh, is he okay?"

"Yes." And… nothing else.

"It's just that I tried calling him yesterday a bunch of times, but he never answered his phone."

Lubomir stares at me.

"Drakken is okay, right? I mean, he's safe?"

"Yes."

"Can you tell me where he is?"

"No."

Okay then. I nibble on my lower lip for a while. "Is there any reason why you can't tell me?"

"Yes."

And the reason is? I think it but don't say it.

Lubomir stares.

Okay, this isn't getting me anywhere. I sigh, "Thanks, Lubomir. I need to finish getting ready for work. I'll see you in a bit."

When I drive to work, Lubomir follows like last time. I like knowing he's always there. Not that I feel like I need his protection, because seriously, what do I have to worry about? Mainly, he's comforting proof that Drakken isn't completely gone forever and ever with no chance of him returning.

I drive into the garage beneath The Beverly Hills Resort. I notice the valet area is filled with black Mercedes and black Town Cars. I find a space to park and climb out of the Audi.

A minute later, Lubomir drives past me in Sheena and parks nearby. He unfolds himself from the seat and closes the door. He's so tall he almost makes Sheena look like a toy car. He puts on mirrored sunglasses and a black baseball cap. He wears a plain black T-shirt and blue jeans. Other than his size, he is very nondescript. He stares at me.

I smile and wave.

He doesn't respond. With his mirrored sunglasses, I can't tell if he's even looking at me.

The sound of conversation and shoes clacking on the cement echoes through the garage as people approach from around the corner.

Lubomir turns his head toward the voices.

I start walking up the sloped cement ramp toward the elevators, which are in the same direction as the voices. Whoever is talking is still out of view, but I realize they're not speaking English. They're speaking Drakken's language.

That's when I remember Drakken's father and his men. They're still here at the hotel. Before I have time to think about it, I feel a tingle on my back. I whip around to see Lubomir charging toward me. He looks freaky scary. Panic shoots my heart rate up into triple digits. My eyes pop open in fear.

"Lub—" I blurt and throw my arms up defensively.

His huge hand slaps over my mouth and he literally holds my entire face and head with one hand. My mouth is clamped shut and his thumb pinches my nose closed, cutting off my air.

My eyes bulge in terror.

He wraps a tree trunk arm around my waist and yanks me roughly into his chest. He forces me down low and pulls me behind a parked SUV and a big black Range Rover.

"Mfff mfff mfff!" I can't breathe.

Lubomir folds over and smashes me down onto the ground.

"Mfff! Mfff!"

I'm going to die!

"Shh," Lubomir whispers in my ear.

"Mffffffff!!!!" I can't breathe!

"Shh."

My heart hammers in my head. What is Lubomir doing! Ohmygod, ohmygod, ohmygod! "*Mfffffff!!!!!!*"

I try to struggle, but Lubomir is made of granite. His hard arms are smashing me into his rigid body and grinding my knees against the cement floor. I want to flail my arms and legs, but I can't move.

"Shh." Lubomir releases his thumb from my nose.

I can breathe again. I don't think he's trying to hurt me. He's trying to protect me. From Drakken's father. In the scariest way possible. Maybe Drakken wasn't exaggerating. Maybe I should be as afraid of his dad as he is.

I stop struggling, but I'm too frightened to relax.

The foreign voices continue. Car doors open. Car doors close. An engine revs. Then several more. The cars drive up and out of the parking garage.

I expect Lubomir to release me when they're gone. When he doesn't, I start to worry. He pulls me farther back into the shadows.

"Mfff."

"Shh."

Shoes suddenly crack across the cement from somewhere near the valet parking area.

Lubomir tenses and I freeze.

The shoes walk down the cement ramp toward where we're hidden. They stop near the SUV. I can see them from underneath the back bumper.

The only audible sound in the garage is the ticking of the cooling engines in the blue Audi and Sheena.

The shoes shift toward the sound.

Shizz.

Is this guy going to go investigate? Write down license numbers and a description of our cars? I don't know, but I do know if this guy walks toward our cars, he's going to pass the SUV where we're hidden and probably see us.

My heart machine guns in my ears like I'm a frightened rabbit, which at this moment I basically am.

Seven hours pass over the course of the next seven seconds.

The shoes shift again and walk back up the ramp. A car door opens and closes. The engine starts and the car exits the garage.

"Shh." Lubomir releases his hand from my mouth. His body softens and he helps me to my feet. "Stay here," he whispers.

I nod.

He walks to the end of the SUV. He removes his mirrored sunglasses and holds them out past the SUV. He rotates them around slowly. I think he's using the mirrored lenses to see around the garage. Lubomir is one smart cookie. After a moment of scanning the area, he puts his sunglasses on. He crouches and slides around the SUV. I see his feet move up the cement ramp, but unlike Shoe Guy, Lubomir is absolutely silent. After a minute, he returns. "Is okay," he whispers and motions for me to come out of hiding.

Yeah, based on Lubomir's behavior, I think it's safe to say that Drakken's dad is dangerous. Why? I don't know. But now I'm worried.

What would've happened if those men had seen us? Would I have been kidnapped, like Drakken warned? Or worse?

I shiver.

Thank goodness, I mean thank *Drakken*, that Lubomir is here.

Chapter 21

RIVER

"I'm fired?" I whine. "You can't fire me!"

"I can," Luciana says, "and I am."

I sit in the chair in front of her desk in her faux Zen office with its Japanese decor and bonsai trees. In this case, they should be called BANZAI!! trees because of Luciana's sneak attack.

Luciana folds her hands on her desk. "Your performance here at the spa has left much to be desired in the past several months, if not longer. Your questionable conduct with our guests, combined with frequent absences, outright defiance, belligerence, and tardiness, has left me no other choice. I have to let you go."

"But I need this job!" I whine.

Luciana smiles. Her plastic face stretches out like plastic wrap. She leans back in her chair, a look of vicious superiority on her face. "Perhaps you need to reevaluate your priorities, River. If you *need* a job, I would think you would do everything in your power to keep it."

"But I did!"

"Did you?" she asks archly.

"Ahh!" I huff. I don't know what to say. I'm stunned. I wasn't expecting this. "What about Mrs. Mueller? What about Mr. Skelton and Mrs. Ragsdale? They all love me!"

Luciana shakes her plastic cyber doll head, "Mrs. Ragsdale has made frequent complaints about your bizarre behavior. She feels that you don't have her best interests in mind."

"I totally do! I work my butt off to make sure everyone who comes in here walks out feeling ten times better! Ask Mrs Mueller! She'll tell you."

Luciana sighs, "Oh, River. It's never your fault, is it? It's never because of you. Am I right?"

"I didn't say that!"

She shakes her head, "No matter. My decision is made. Your *bad* decisions have left me no choice but to let you go. You can return your spa uniform when you pick up your final check."

"What?!"

"Now I have pressing business to attend to." She turns toward her computer.

I'm too stunned to stand. How am I going to finish paying for tuition and books at LACC? How am I going to pay my rent? It's not easy to get a full time masseuse position in L.A. There's a lot of competition from all the out-of-work actresses who pay *their* bills by working as massage therapists.

What am I gonna do?

Luciana glances over at me, "Please close the door on your way out."

And don't let it hit me in the ass on the way, right? What a total bitch. I'm so mad now, I want to say, "Fuck you, you plastic-faced bitch!" But I don't.

I do the responsible adult thing and walk out proudly without making a scene.

Plastic-faced bitch!

Chapter 22

RIVER

"I guess this is goodbye?" Finch says morosely.

"More like good riddance," I say sarcastically, trying to lighten the moment. "I'll be glad to never see that bitch Luciana or that bitch Jocelyn ever again."

We stand at the concierge desk in the lobby. I notice Lubomir standing off to the side.

Finch pouts, "I'm going to miss you, Riv."

"Me too," I sigh.

"What am I going to do without my work bestie?"

"We'll just have to make more time to hang out outside of work, right?"

She nods enthusiastically, "Totally. Hey, whatever happened with the Drakk Attack? Did you find him? I haven't seen him around the hotel for the past few days."

"Oh, uh, yeah. Well, the thing is—"

"Miss Barksdale!" Mr. Duchamps growls. "I see very little work being done here." His lips purse, making the line of his grease pencil mustache bend into the letter W.

I notice he didn't mention my name. I suppose Luciana told him already.

Finch stammers, "I was just... uh, saying goodbye to River, she... uh, she was..."

"Yes, Miss Barksdale. I'm quite aware."

It actually makes me sad to think that Mr. Duchamps will never bust my lady balls ever again. Or not. I smile at him.

He flicks his eyes at me before walking away.

Good riddance.

"I should get back to work," Finch says apologetically.

I sigh, "Yeah. We'll talk. I promise." I reach out for a hug.

"Ohhh," she coos and hugs me hard. "You better call me, bitch. And tell me all about your fantabulous sex life. *Your* sex life is all I've got," she sniffles dramatically.

"I will," I grin and start toward the elevators.

"I'm going to need deets, Riv!" she hollers. "The romance novel kind with detailed descriptions of every dripping wet body part!"

I laugh and wave goodbye.

"And lots of thrusting! You have to describe the thrusting!"

I'm going to miss Finch.

Chapter 23

RIVER

I drive down Santa Monica Boulevard early the next morning. My spa uniform sits on the seat beside me, washed and folded. After I turn it in, I'll pick up my final paycheck and probably never see *The* Beverly Hills Resort ever again.

I pass the intersection where Drakken ran me off the road nearly a year ago. I can barely wrap my head around what has happened in my life since then. Back then, I was still hung up on Cage.

Cage.

I hope he doesn't come looking for me. I'm not ready to talk to him. With Drakken gone, I'm in a vulnerable state. I shake my head and pull to a stop at a red light.

On the sidewalk to my right, McJogs runs right by. He's shirtless and gorgeous as ever. He runs like running is the easiest thing in the world, just like I remember. He looks so relaxed. I smile to myself. Yes, he's totally hot. No, I don't care anymore. It's time for someone else to pine over him. Maybe I need to tell Finch or Julietta when and where to park so one of them can bump into McJogs and ask him for a hump.

I grin to myself.

The light turns green and I drive to work. I give my uniform to the lady in Human Resources and she hands me a check. After, I head back to the lobby. Finch isn't around. I'd like to say hi, but I don't feel like hanging around here. Too many memories. I'll have to give her a call later so we can hang out.

I walk toward the elevator landing and notice Lubomir standing beside a post. I smile at him and he tips his head ever so slightly. I press the DOWN button on the elevator and wait.

Lubomir stands politely off to the side.

I've noticed he never crowds me. It's easy to forget he's there, but he always is.

Ding!

The elevator arrives. I step up to the doors as they slowly open.

I step forward and halt abruptly.

Time grinds to a stop.

Drakken's father stands in the elevator. A bunch of men in black suits stand behind him. His gaze locks on mine.

My eyes widen in fear and my body locks, every muscle tensing.

His eyes narrow shrewdly. "I know you." He has the same accent as Drakken. But his voice is low and harsh. He seems like a man who is accustomed to compliance in all things.

Drakken's father creeps me the eff out. Despite his impeccable appearance and his aging good looks, which he obviously passed onto his son, he is super scary. Everything about him conveys danger.

"You were with my son," he says calmly.

Oh no.

Every inch of my skin curls.

After what happened in the garage yesterday with Lubomir, I know this is not good. This is beyond bad. I need to do something fast. Something smart. But in a moment like this, there is no time to plan and strategize. The only option is to go with what you know. I play dumb. "Who?" I snivel nasally, wrinkling my nose into a snout.

"My son."

"Like, who's your *son*?" I hope I sound like an airhead.

One of his eyes narrows further, like he's scanning my brain.

I pretend I have no brain for him to scan. I screw my face into a sloppy knot and pig my nose for all it's worth. "Is your son, like, a surfer?"

He doesn't respond.

I glance to the side and notice Lubomir. He's out of view of the men on the elevator, standing on the balls of his feet, ready to spring into action.

Although Lubomir is gigantic, there's like twelve guys behind Drakken's father. Lubomir can't take them all.

This is bad.

I chuckle nervously, "Are you guys, like, getting off the elevator, or what? I'm totally late for my waxing."

None of the men behind Drakken's father move. But they all watch me like a bunch of hungry alligators. One of the men mutters something in the ear of Drakken's father.

The father listens carefully then nods. He says to me in a demanding voice, "Do you work here in spa?"

Oh, shizz.

Shizz, shizz, shizz!

If they know I work here, they can start asking questions. They can find out where I live. They can sneak into my bungalow in the middle of the night and...

"Work?" I whine. "I don't *work*. My baby daddy won't let me." I back up a step. "I, uh... have to like, go, or, uh... like, I'm going to be in trouble with him later. My bush has gotten *way* out of hand. It's gonna need garden shears. Know what I mean?" I chuckle nervously and roll my eyes. "You miss one waxing and it gets to be a *jungle* down there." I tilt my head down toward my crotch. "And you know how my man feels about a hairy bush. He doesn't like going on a jungle hunt to find my bean. And you know what that means?"

Based on the sour looks on the face of Drakken's father and his men, they're either totally disgusted or totally confused. Either works for me.

I continue, "That means Mama doesn't get her cookie. And if Mama doesn't get her cookie, Mama is like, *totally* crabby." I pause. "I mean, I don't *have* crabs. I did *once*, but that was before I learned to keep my jungle shaved." I laugh nervously. "Know what I mean?"

Drakken's father glares at me. He opens his mouth to speak.

"Excuse me!" Finch hollers, barreling out of nowhere, pushing a loaded bellman's cart toward the open elevator. "Coming through! Wide load! Safety hazard!" She jams the cart into the elevator at an angle, blocking it completely, trapping everyone inside.

My eyes goggle. I'm about to say something when Finch flashes me a glance and shakes her head.

I don't need a second invitation.

I spin on my heel and run for it. I sprint around the corner to the stairs and dash to the underground parking garage. Lubomir is right behind me.

He follows me down the cement ramp to the blue Audi.

Just as I'm about to hop into the car, he grabs my arm.

"No!"

"What?" I blurt, surprised.

"I take Audi. You take you car." He points at Sheena.

Worried, I say, "But—"

"Listen. I take Audi." He grabs the keys from me and drops into the driver's seat. He jams the keys in the ignition and starts the car. Then he flips the switch for the convertible top. It slowly whirrs open, unfolding from the compartment in the back. He hunches down as the top closes over him. He rolls down the window. "Men will follow soon. I pretend I am you. I drive Audi. You hide in old car for ten minute." He flicks his eyes toward Sheena. "Then drive slow away. Okay?"

"Yeah," I nod nervously. "Okay."

"Hide in Chevy. Quick. Men are coming." He hands me the key to Sheena. "Go!" he hisses.

I run to Sheena and hop into the front seat. I slide it all the way back and crouch down in the foot well. I hope nobody can see me.

I hear the Audi rev behind me and back out of the parking space before driving up the ramp. Lubomir revs the engine dramatically. Is he trying to call attention to himself? I think so. But I can't worry about him. I need to worry about hiding.

I'm still in view where I'm crouched down. I would be better hidden if I climbed into the trunk, but I'm afraid to do that. What if I can't get out? Then I remember the emergency glow-in-the-dark safety lever for if you're ever locked in your own trunk. Sheena has one. I always thought it was a joke. It's no joke now. I'm about to open the driver door when I stop.

I hear two things at once.

Lubomir racing the engine of the Audi and tires squealing, followed by the sound of shouting men and running footsteps.

I sink slowly back into the footwell, trying to disappear. I hope they don't see me.

The sound of the Audi fades quickly. The sound of the running men suddenly increases. They're running back into the garage.

Oh no. Are they looking for me?

Fuzz! What do I do?

I hear car doors open and slam shut. More engines rev and tires squeak on the cement. The sounds echo and bounce shrilly throughout the garage.

My panic is so bad, my hands are shaking like crazy. What will those men do if they catch me? What will they do to Lubomir if they catch him? I'm afraid to think about it.

I wait for I don't know how long, expecting to hear footsteps coming up behind Sheena, expecting to see someone staring down at me in the footwell through one of Sheena's windows. Maybe it'll be one of the faceless men in black suits. Or maybe it will be Drakken's father. Whoever it is, I'm fresh out of ideas about what to do next.

I drag my cell phone out of my purse and turn the ringer off. Then I watch the minutes tick by on the clock. The passage of time is my only reassurance, my only life line to a sense of safety. Somewhere in the future, I will be safe. I tell myself this over and over again like a mantra.

After thirty minutes, and the passage of several cars into or out of the parking garage, I finally stick my head up.

The garage is empty.

No men in black suits.

I stick Sheena's key into her ignition and start her up, half expecting the car to explode or something. She doesn't.

Hunched low in my seat, with my old pair of sunglasses on, I drive out of the garage as calmly as I can.

When I make it outside and all the way to the street below the resort, I check my rearview mirror. No black cars follow. I breathe for the first time in what seems like forever and pull onto the road.

While I drive, I have both hands locked on the wheel at ten and two. My knuckles are white and my forearms quiver with latent fear. I check my mirrors every ten seconds to see if I'm being followed.

This is insane.

Chapter 24

RIVER

I sit on my couch, sipping tea, trying to calm down. I'm still freaked out from what happened back at the resort an hour ago.

BANG! BANG! BANG!

I gasp and jump where I sit.

Someone is pounding on my front door.

Is it Lubomir?

Or is it Drakken's father and all his men?

All I know is that Stone isn't here and I'm totally alone. It's the middle of the morning and my neighbors are all at work. Will anyone here me if I scream?

The knock comes again. "FedEx!"

Is it *really* FedEx?

I don't remember ordering any packages. Maybe Stone did?

I stand up carefully and creep toward the front door. I peek through the curtain of the side window.

Relief.

It's a FedEx guy in a purple and black uniform. Or what looks like a FedEx guy. He holds an envelope and an electronic clipboard thingy. Before I have time to consider, he turns and hops off the front stoop and walks casually toward the street, the envelope swinging in his arm.

I open the door. "Hey wait!"

He stops and turns around. "Package for you. You gotta sign." He holds out the clipboard, which I sign with the plastic stylus, then he hands me the envelope.

"Thanks!"

He walks away and I go back inside. I drop onto the couch and examine the overnight envelope. It's addressed to me. River Freeman. The return address is a FedEx store in New Mexico. I don't know anyone in New Mexico. But it's addressed to me. So I open it and shake out the contents.

A red paper origami heart falls into my hand. I turn it over and over. It's not just one heart. It's two hearts. A smaller heart is positioned atop the bigger one. The cool thing is, the two hearts are attached. They're made from one piece of paper. Two hearts that are one, the big one containing the smaller one. It is literally symbolic. One heart that contains another.

I only know one person who would send me an origami heart for a present.

Drakken.

My chest floats over my head and fireflies flutter in my belly.

I notice faint writing showing through from the inside of the paper. There's a message hidden inside. The only way I can read it is to unfold it. I don't want to ruin this beautiful heart, but I need to know what Drakken wrote. The only choice I have is to open the heart. I need to open this heart and find out what's inside.

Carefully, I unfold it and do my best to remember the steps so I can maybe put it back together.

When it's open all the way, I see Drakken's careful cursive script. It reads:

"My heart is heavy as I write this letter. I am sorry for abandoning you like that. You deserve better. You deserve the world. But I am not in a position to give it to you at this time."

I pause for a moment. I don't remember Drakken's English being this good. Maybe my lessons paid off? I continue reading.

"Leaving you behind was the hardest thing I've ever had to do. I did not want to leave you. I wanted to take you with me. But first and foremost, I need to keep you safe. There is no way I can convey to you the danger my father presents. He is capable of things you would not believe. That he tracked me down, despite my every effort to avoid him, is but one example of what he is capable of when he wants a thing. In this case, he wants me. He will not rest until he takes me home and forces me to marry. He will let no one stand in his way. This includes you. I was not exaggerating when I said my father would be a danger to you if he ever found out the connection you and I share. That is why I left my best man to watch over you. I trust that he has kept you safe from all harm, and I trust him implicitly. He will be there for you when I am not able."

My jaw drops and I let my arm holding the letter fall into my lap. The gravity of the situation in the parking garage this morning hits me like a surprise attack. If Finch hadn't shown up when she did, and if Lubomir hadn't been there to lead those men away, who knows what would've happened to me. I shudder at the thought before continuing with the letter.

"More than anything in this world, I want to be there for you. Although I trust my men, I trust myself more. I know my father better than anyone. I know how he thinks. But I can't physically be there for you. That is why I need you to stay safe. Because of the danger my father presents, I must reluctantly ask you to quit your job. I can't risk him finding you. I will arrange whatever money you need to cover your expenses."

Well, that's good news. But I wish I had known sooner. His dad already found me.

"You must know that my secrecy, my reluctance to let you in since the beginning, has been my attempt to protect you. My life verges on insanity on a daily basis. I have kept much of it from you in part to keep you safe and in part because it's very difficult to believe. But more than anything, I want you to know that I have always been faithful to you. We share a special connection, you and I. You have felt it. I have felt it. But I have never had the English words to tell you how much you mean to me or how you affect me. (That's why I had a friend assist with the translation of this letter. But I digress.) My heart beats for you. I have only loved one other woman in my life before you. Sadly, that story ended in terrible tragedy. If you were to know what I went through for her, you would understand my actions in regards to you with much greater clarity. But you must know that my love for you is no small thing. It is everything."

I hold the letter against my chest. I'm going to cry. I sniff back tears and continue.

"Please, do not attempt to find me. Something tells me you will. You are brave and strong and courageous. But you can't underestimate the precarious position I am in at the moment. For now, please quit your job. Stay hidden. When the time is

right, I will come for you, my love. I promise. —With all my heart, Yours."

Now I am crying. I love this man. I love Drakken. He shouldn't have to go through things alone. And I need him. I need to talk to him. I need to see him. I need to touch him. I need to hold him and be held.

But I have no idea where he is.

I jump up from the couch and grab my phone. I call Drakken.

After four rings, the robot lady answers, "The voice mailbox for this number has not been set up. No message can be recorded at this time."

I hang up and try again. Same thing.

Did Drakken change his number? If he did, I have no way to contact him. That's not fair. I want to tell him how grateful I am for him and everything he is doing to protect me and care for me. More than anything, I want to tell him how much I love him.

But I can't.

I don't even know where he is.

Where he is…

I grab the FedEx envelope off the couch and look at the address. It's from a FedEx store. It was sent yesterday. The note from Drakken is hand written. That means he had to have either dropped it off himself or given it to someone in or around New Mexico yesterday so *that* person could take it to the store for him. Then again, Drakken has a frickin' fighter jet and a Gulfstream. He could've dropped it off in New Mexico himself, then flown anywhere on the planet.

But something about New Mexico rings a bell.

That's when it hits me.

I'm going on a road trip. If I'm wrong, I'll find out when I get there.

Chapter 25

RIVER

I'm in the middle of nowhere.

This place is a lifeless red desert wasteland. The scorching sun is high overhead and it's a miserable million degrees outside. The road ahead shimmers from the heat.

The only living thing out here is me.

I'm a little worried about Sheena. She's not used to driving conditions like this. I've got her A/C on full blast because I would melt otherwise. The A/C was broken before Drakken arranged for her to be fixed up way back when. I guess he had the mechanic fix more than the alignment. Still, Sheena is an old car and I'm in the middle of a harsh desert.

I keep hoping at some point I'll glance in my rearview mirror and see Lubomir following behind me. But he has no idea where I went. Worse, I keep fearing I'll glance up and see a fleet of black Mercedes following me. But I imagine if they knew where I was, they would have already caught up and run me off the road or who knows what.

I sigh to myself.

I just hope Lubomir is okay.

My phone rings, startling me. I pull it out of my purse. It's Finch. I'm about to answer the call when paranoia slaps me across the face. What if it's not Finch? What if Drakken's father got her? What if she's tied up somewhere, all beaten up, and they're making her call me?

If that's the case, I guess it doesn't matter. I answer, "Finch?"

"What the hells, Riv?" Finch blurts. "Are you okay?" She doesn't sound tortured or abducted.

"Where are you?"

"I'm at work. It's been crazy all morning. A ton of guests are checking in for some convention. Where are *you*?"

"Never mind that."

"Are you okay, Riv? What was with your showdown with those guys on the elevator this morning?"

"My what?"

"Your showdown. Those guys have been creeping around the resort for the past few days. They totally weird me out. When I heard you talking to them like you were some ditzy bimbo, I knew something was wrong. You aren't *that* dumb." She giggles.

"Hey! I'm not *any* dumb," I grin.

"Anyway, what was going on? Why were you talking to them?"

"I better not go into it."

"Why not?"

"Just trust me, Finch. And don't talk to them. Stay away from them. If they ask you about me, don't tell them anything. Okay?"

"You're worrying me, Riv."

"I'm sorry. Just don't talk to them."

"Hold on a sec." Finch chats with someone at the hotel for a second about incoming guests. "Riv, I gotta go. More people are checking in. It's a zoo over here. You're lucky you got fired," she jokes.

"Yeah," I grin.

"I'll call you later, okay?"

"Okay. Stay safe."

"I will. And you too. Wherever you are."

"I'll tell you all about it when I get back."

"Promise?"

"Totally. Talk soon."

Somewhere in Arizona, I pull into a Shell station for gas and a pee break. I buy a bunch of water bottles and a turkey and cheese sandwich. The cool air inside the shop is refreshing. I press a chilled water bottle against my forehead while I wait in line at the register.

Man, it's hot in Arizona.

Outside, I climb back into Sheena and continue east. Eventually the road turns south toward Tucson. After Tucson, I really am in the middle of nowhere. There are zero cars on the road. You could easily run out of gas out here and die in the desert. I would hate to break down out here.

Lubomir never does show up.

I'm all alone when the sun goes down, but I keep going in the darkness.

After ten hours of straight driving, I pass through the tiny town of Hurley. Hurley looks like it has about ten or twenty people living in it. I would stop to eat, but I don't see any restaurants from the road. I can't imagine living out here. It feels so isolated.

Just past Hurley, I turn onto Airport Road. It leads to the Grant County Airport. The same airport where I flew with Drakken when we delivered that heart or lung or whatever to whoever needed it when we left Calistoga and the castle. Grant County has one big long asphalt runway. I remember Drakken mentioning it because the other runways were just dirt. The Gulfstream landed here, no problem. I'm sure an F-18 could land here too.

I hope Drakken is here. I don't know where else he'd be. If he's not here, I'll be totally alone. Then I'll have to drive back to L.A. and hope that Drakken's father doesn't find out my name or my address or who knows what else.

Well, I can't worry about that now. I need to focus on finding Drakken.

The Grant County Airport isn't like a regular big city airport. It's just a handful of one-story buildings and a couple of airplane hangars in the middle of the desert. It takes Sheena all of three minutes to creep past them at five miles an hour. This late at night, most of them are dark. One group of buildings is surrounded by a fence. A lone lightbulb shines on a sign at the gate that says US Forest Service.

I pull over to the side of the road and park in the gravel so I can consider what to do next. Only one group of buildings has any lights on. Maybe I can check there.

My cell phone rings. It's Stone.

"Hello?"

"Hey, sis. Why aren't you home yet?"

"I'm, uh… studying." I never told Stone I was fired. He probably thinks I went to work this morning like always. I know if I told him I drove ten hours to the middle of nowhere, he'd freak out.

"When you coming home?"

"Soon."

"All right. I left you some dinner in the fridge."

"Thanks. Hey, um, Stone?"

"Yeah?"

"Did anyone come by the house today looking for me?"

"No. Why?"

"Oh, uh, I have, um, some group study thing at LACC. One of my partners was supposed to drop something off," I lie. "We have, uh, a project we're working on and, uh…"

"I'm not believing a word you're saying, sis. Tell me what the hell is going on."

There's a knock at my window.

I gasp and twist in my seat, expecting to see a bunch of faceless men in black suits. Or rapists. It's dark, I'm in the middle of nowhere, and I'm all alone.

It's not them.

Drakken leans down over my window with his palms resting on his thighs.

Thank goodness it's Drakken. I couldn't be happier to see him. My worries dissipate in an instant. "Stone," I blurt. "I have to go. I'll call you later."

"Wait, Riv!"

I end the call and toss my phone into my purse.

Drakken wears jeans and a black T-shirt with the Gravity Unlimited logo on it. His muscled shoulders and chest stretch the shirt material impressively. Several days worth of stubble peppers his jaw. He looks rugged and imposing. Emphasis on imposing. Is he mad I'm here? He did give me explicit instructions to stay away. I sure hope he's not pissed. I'm almost afraid to roll down my window because of the reprimand I sense coming. Oh well, I may as well get it over with. I crank the window down. "Hey."

Drakken's face lights up, "What are you doing here, Rivka?"

My mood goes from vaguely worried to ecstatically happy. I return his smile. "I came for you, Drakken."

He smirks, "I said I would come for *you*, my love."

I shrug. "Does it really matter who came for whom?"

He winks suggestively, "If we both come, is good, yes?"

I blurt laughter. "Ha! Yeah. Coming is always good. Hey, what happened to your face? It's all bruised up."

He smirks, "Is long story. I say later. Okay?"

I nod. "Okay. Hey, um, you're not mad I'm here, are you?"

He shakes his head, "No. All that matter is we are together." He leans his head through the window and kisses me with his luscious lips.

Even though it's awkward, it's the most romantic kiss ever kissed, and I, River Freeman, am doing one half of the kissing. The most incredible man on the planet is doing the other half.

My heart floats to the heavens.

Chapter 26

RIVER

"This is your secret business?" I ask.

"Yes," Drakken answers.

We stand inside the largest airplane hangar at the airport. In contrast to the darkness outside, banks of fluorescent lights on the ceiling bathe the huge plane parked inside in cool white light. The word 'plane' is a bit misleading. It looks more like three or four planes all smashed together. I'm not even sure how to describe it other than to say it looks super sleek and futuristic, like something from a science fiction movie. A number of men and a few women mill around it, doing who knows what. I recognize several faces from Drakken's crew back at LAX. I guess they came out here with him.

"What is it?" I ask.

"It is a suborbital space plane," Drakken smiles.

"A *what*?"

"It is airplane that flies in air and in space. Is for private spaceflight."

"No way! So it's like, a spaceship?"

"Yes." Drakken grins. "Is really a spaceship."

I notice the Gravity Unlimited logo is emblazoned on the side of the plane. I guess I was wrong about Drakken being in the business of manufacturing breast implants filled with liquid heroin. Silly me. "Did you build it?"

Drakken nods proudly, "With help of my team. I create main design, but many very smart engineer make it better, and many more build it. Is too much for one man to make by alone."

"Wow. It's amazing, Drakken. I've never seen anything like it."

"No one in world has see anything like it. Is why is secret," he grins.

"Are you gonna fly it?"

"Yes."

"Into space?"

"Yes."

"What?! I can't believe it!"

"Is true. After maiden voyage, if all go well, it will fly many passenger into space. For space tourism."

"Wow, that's amazing! Hey, isn't this kind of like that Virgin Galactic thing?"

"Yes."

I swallow hard, "The one that just crashed? I read about that online."

Drakken bows his head somberly. "Yes, is like that."

"Didn't one of the pilots die or something? Didn't the plane explode?"

"Plane break apart for turbulence," Drakken mutters. "One pilot is killed. Is miracle other pilot survive. Plane is torn apart around him at 900 mile per hour, but somehow his seat is thrown clear. He black out because oxygen at 50,000 feet is very thin, too thin for breathe, but his emergency parachute open automatically at 20,000 feet, so he survive."

My eyes goggle.

Drakken sighs. "Experimental aircraft is all ways dangerous business. Test pilot is very brave men."

A disturbing tingle tickles my scalp and icicles in my chest. My voice clicks as I ask, "Are you a test pilot, Drakken?"

He lifts his head and pins his eyes on mine. His face is flat. "Yes."

I stare back at him. My stomach rolls. I just went through the torture of thinking I lost Drakken forever, and that was just because he left L.A. without telling me where he was going. Now I have to face the idea of losing him permanently? Because he's in the business of doing incredibly dangerous things and he might actually die? I shake my head, tears brimming. "No," I whisper.

Drakken's face softens. "Rivka, is okay."

"No."

"I am good pilot, Rivka. Very good."

I shake my head weakly, "No, Drakken."

He steps toward me.

I want to step back. I want to turn and run away. But I'm too frightened of the future that is now pressing in around me from every direction. "I need you Drakken." My voice catches. "I can't live without you. I love you, Drakkozsha. I don't want to lose you." I'm crying as I say it.

He pulls me into a hug and squeezes me tightly. "It is okay, Rivka. My space plane is very safe. We test it many times. I will be okay. I will no get hurt."

I'm too choked up to respond.

Chapter 27

RIVER

"When are you going to fly it?" I ask.

"Not for few weeks. We have more test before first suborbital flight."

I stand at the stove in the kitchen of the small two bedroom house Drakken is renting in Hurley. I flip sizzling hamburger patties in the frying pan with a spatula. We literally drove two towns over to Silver City to find ground beef. The only thing in Hurley is a gas station.

Drakken sits on a folding chair beside a card table. There is almost zero furniture in the ultra-plain and dingy house. The bedroom has a queen sized air mattress and the tub in the lone bathroom has rust stains around the drain. It's a stark contrast to the luxury of The Beverly Hills Resort.

"How do you like living in Hurley?" I ask.

He shrugs before tipping back the water bottle he is drinking from. "Is okay. Very quiet. I like quiet."

"Don't you miss all the action in L.A.?"

"I have all action I need right here," he winks.

"Who, me?" I grin.

He nods. "Why do I need Sunset Strip and Rodeo Drive when I have you, Rivka?"

"You're such a charmer."

"What is charmer?"

"No English lessons tonight!" I joke. "Burgers are ready." I tear open a bag of Lays potato chips and shake some onto our paper plates beside the burgers and buns. I add a dill pickle to each plate and walk everything over to the card table.

Drakken hops up and pulls my folding chair out for me.

"Thank you, Drakka," I smile and sit down.

"For you, Rivka, I do everything." He sits down next to me so we are knee to knee.

"You don't have to do *everything*," I grin dismissively. "Just the gentlemanly things."

"Is okay. I do everything for woman I love," he winks and pops a potato chip into his mouth.

It's so weird being here with him. It's like we're on vacation or something. "Does it bother you that I'm here?"

"Bother?"

"You know, me coming without telling you?" I take a bite of my burger.

"Oh, yes. I understand. No, I am happy you come."

I wait for him to make a joke about coming. It's hard *not* to think about sex when I'm around Drakken. He has that effect on me. Even while eating his potato chip, he looks like a TV commercial titled 'Sexy Guy Eats Potato Chip'. Feeling naughty, I quip, "I haven't come in forever."

He snickers, "You come only few days ago. Or did you not come? Was fake come?"

I shake my head, "No! It was the real deal! Real come!"

He laughs, "Is good."

"Very good," I purr and stare at him. His eyes burn me alive. Other parts of me are on fire too. I squirm on my folding chair.

"Eat your burger," he smiles and takes a big bite of his.

We chew for awhile in silence.

He asks, "How is job? Is okay for you to be here?"

I frown, "I got fired."

"Fired?"

"Luciana said I wasn't doing a good job. So she fired me. I lost my job."

"Oh. I understand. I am sorry," he says compassionately. "But is for best. For you to be safe."

I can't help but think about his dad and what happened at work. I don't want to mention it and spoil the moment. I joke, "Now that I'm out of work, how am I going to pay my bills?" I wink at him.

He wipes his lips with a paper napkin. "Maybe I need personal masseuse. My job is very hard. Do you know any girl good with massage?"

"I might know someone..."

"She has to be pretty. Very pretty."

"She does?" I ask innocently.

"More pretty than every girl in world."

"Oh, I don't know anyone *that* beautiful."

"No? I see very pretty girl with seed on nose right here." Drakken leans forward.

I look down at the tip of my nose and notice a stray sesame seed from the burger bun. "Whoops!" I reach up to grab it but Drakken swoops in and kisses it off.

"Is best seed I ever eat," he smiles.

"Drakken," I giggle and roll my eyes.

He chuckles. "Will you be my pretty massage girl? For personal massage from hard day of work?"

"How *hard* is it?" I wink.

Drakken leans back in his chair and folds his arms behind his head. "*Very* hard."

"*How* hard?" I slide my hand up his jeans. "Oh! *That* hard." I tease his cock through the fabric. When I find the tip, I massage it with my thumb.

He leans forward and we kiss. Our lips smack together wetly and our tongues tangle. My head spins pleasantly in one direction while my stomach spins in the other. My body is a corkscrew of sexual energy.

I break the kiss to take a breath. I resume moving my hand across the bulge in his jeans. I snicker, "When did you sneak this pickle into your pants, Drakka? It's huge."

"Pickle?" he scoffs.

I nod, "I bet it's salty."

He chuckles, "Yes, juice is salty."

I can't decide if comparing Drakken's enormous cock to a pickle is a total turn on or just plain weird.

Drakken doesn't seem to be in doubt, "You want to taste juice?"

"Since you asked..." I hood my eyes and lick my lips expectantly.

He unfastens his jeans and arches his butt off the folding chair so he can slide them down past his knees. His heavy cock lays across his thigh, hot and hard.

I lean forward and press my palm against it. "Mmmm..." I grin. "This is quite the pickle." I grab his shaft and pump it lazily while I massage his balls. "What are we going to do about it?"

"What you do with any pickle. You eat it."

"Is that an order?"

He grins. "You work for me, yes?"

"Yeah. I'm your private masseuse."

"Then you do my order, yes?"

I nod seductively, "Are you ordering me to eat your pickle?"

"Yes," he grins.

"Well, if you're giving me an *order*..." I offer a sexy smirk and lean forward. I touch my tongue to the underside of the tip.

He moans.

"You like that?" I tease.

"Suck it," he grunts.

"Yes, sir," I grin. I smother his cock with my tongue, working the hot head until it's slippery and wet. It's not the only thing slippery and wet. I'm totally turned on myself. I lean forward and take him deeper into my mouth, still working the shaft with my one hand while caressing his balls with the other.

"Is good," he moans. He slumps down in his chair.

I lean over his cock, working it hungrily. I'm incredibly turned on right now. I think partially because only yesterday I wasn't sure if I'd ever see Drakken again. Also because I can't escape the nagging feeling that something terrible could happen at any moment. Between his creepy dad and his dangerous space plane, everything hangs on the edge of disaster. Knowing this drives me wild, like this might be the last time we ever have sex. It doesn't matter that we're in a rundown rental house in the middle of nowhere. Amazingly, it's just as good if not better than when we were in a fairytale castle during our dream-date getaway.

The burning desire between my legs is proof.

I lick and squeeze his cock as I lift my head. My lips smack when I release the tip. "Drakken. Drakka. I need you inside me. I need you to fuck me." I surprise myself with my own dirty talk.

He nods and gazes at me through slitted eyes. "We need condom."

Oh, shizz. I forgot about condoms. "Uh, are you sure? We didn't use one last time at the hangar."

He nods, his brow darkening. "Yes. Is mistake. I am sorry, Rivka."

I shake my head, "It's okay I'm on the—" I stop myself, remembering that I forgot to take my pill for three days. Right now, I don't want to think about it. That ominous feeling that tomorrow or the next day might spell disaster pushes it away. I want to focus on right now, on being here with Drakken. Not 'what ifs' and tomorrows.

"Yes, I know. You are on pill. But to be safe, we should use condom."

"I don't have any condoms," I sigh with disappointment.

"Is okay. I still have some from weekend."

"You do?" I smile hopefully.

"Yes. In bedroom."

I stand up, "Do you want me to get them?"

He stands and pulls his pants up without fastening them. He picks me up by the butt and I wrap my legs around his waist.

He smiles a smokey smile, "I take you to them." He carries me into the small bedroom and lowers me onto the air mattress. It squishes and bunches noisily beneath me as I start taking off my clothes.

Drakken fishes through a small duffel bag on the floor beside the bed. "Found them." He holds up the roll.

I grin.

Drakken hands them to me then stretches his Gravity Unlimited T-shirt over his head, revealing all his muscled glory.

I eye lick his chest and hard abs. Such an incredible body. I don't think I've ever wanted a man so much in my entire life. I thought I had been hot and bothered when he had me in golden handcuffs back at Chateaux de l'Amour. But that doesn't compare to this moment. The simple truth of Drakken's beauty and the knowledge that life is short and fragile is a complete aphrodisiac. I am soaked.

He kneels onto the air mattress and parts my thighs. He slides his fingers across my entrance, his middle finger dragging through the center of my slick folds. "You are very wet, Rivka."

"Only for you, Drakka."

He slides down between my legs and lowers his mouth to my lips and licks my slit.

I instantly feel that intense flow that I have only ever felt with Drakken. My head falls against the mattress and the ecstasy between my legs overwhelms me. Our connection is primal and essential. Within seconds, I am coming. "Oh, Drakkozsha!" I moan. The orgasm is warm and fluid, washing through my body like waves on a hot sand beach.

Drakken raises his face and slides up my body, his chest tickling my breasts. We kiss deeply and lovingly while his hardness throbs between my legs.

"I need you, Drakken," I whisper desperately.

"I need you too, Rivka."

"I need you *inside* me. Right now."

We put the condom on him and he fills me with his heat. I feel his need. It's as desperate as mine.

"Rivka," he mutters softly in my ear as he thrusts into me. "Rivka." His voice is strained with fear and potent desire.

"I'm here, Drakka. I'm here for you."

"Rivka," he pleads as he forces his way ever deeper into me. Into my body and into my heart. Into my soul.

"Rivka," he begs. "Don't leave me, Rivka."

"I'm here, Drakkozsha," I whisper. "I'm right here." I caress his back, feeling his scars. His tender scars. The wounds that never heal.

"Never leave me, Saz—" Drakken suddenly stops.

RIP!!!!

Imagine the sound of a record needle being torn across the record, amplified by the P.A. speakers at a super loud heavy metal concert. Or bombs going off two feet away from your ear. Take your pick.

"What?" I whisper.

Drakken doesn't move.

His body weighs on top of me. His face is buried in the mattress.

"Drakken?"

He doesn't move.

"What did you just say, Drakken?"

His body starts to shiver. "Is too much," he whispers, his voice squeaky and barely audible.

"Drakken?"

"Is too much," he hisses louder through gritted teeth. He slams a fist on the air mattress.

My head bounces once then settles. I stare at the ceiling, afraid to speak. 'Is too much' is how his meltdown started on that fateful day in the Sunset Suite when he flipped out. But that was different. I had zero idea what was going on then. Now I have a much deeper insight into Drakken. But I don't know the whole story. I have to say something. I have to understand what's behind his pain. His letter mentioned another woman. His letter said their relationship ended in tragedy. Was he thinking about her just now? Whatever the answer is, no matter how much it may hurt *me* to find out, I have to know. I whisper in a tender voice, "Drakken, did you just say someone else's name?"

His body tenses.

"Drakken?"

He jumps up from the mattress. The room is dark and he's silhouetted against the full moon shining through the bedroom window. His face is obscured in the darkness. He whispers, "Is too much."

I can't read him. I don't know what's going through his head. I just know that his heart is aching. I gather my courage. "What's too much, Drakken?"

He breathes heavily, overcome by emotion. For a moment, I feel our flow increase, I feel him opening up to me in a deeper way than he ever has. He is truly letting me in.

Suddenly, the flow is cut off. He bends over and grabs his pants.

"Drakken? Can we talk about this?"

He shoves his legs into his jeans and pulls on shoes and storms out of the bedroom without a shirt.

"Drakken?"

The front door slams.

Gone.

Chapter 28

RIVER

The streets of Hurley are dead empty at night. The full moon silvers the houses and casts long black shadows everywhere. I notice that none of the yards have lawns. Just gravel or dirt.

I'm surprised I actually see a few darkened trees scattered here and there. But they don't disguise the fact that this place is a ghost town.

Somewhere out here in the chill night air is one very sad shirtless ghost. If only I could find him. He must be freezing because it's frickin' *cold*.

I have heard that the temperature drops at night in the high desert, but this is ridiculous. My teeth are chattering and I'm wearing the only sweater I brought. Luckily, the town really is very small, so I'm sure I'll find Drakken around here before I freeze into an ice statue.

I stroll up and down the gridded streets for about half an hour before I end up on the east side of town. There's some kind of factory or rock quarry or something past the edge of town. It's got smokestacks and a bunch of conveyor belts and tin buildings. I'm not going out there. It looks haunted. Plus I can't feel my fingers and toes. Time to turn back before I get frostbite.

I spin around and bump right into Drakken.

"Oh!" I gasp. "I was wondering where you went."

He gazes at me silently.

"Did you see me standing here or something?" I ask.

"I follow you."

"Huh? I was following *you*. I've been trying to track you down since you left the house. Why didn't you say anything?"

"I want to be alone."

I frown, "Then why were you following me?"

"I no want to leave you alone."

"Oh." I'm not sure if that makes any sense, but I'm not going to ask. "What happened, Drakken?"

He shakes his head, "I no want to say. Is too much," he mutters.

IS TOO MUCH!!!

I feel his pain as if it were my own.

A million questions race through my head. Questions about *her*, about his scars, about his past. Although knowing more might ease my own fears, I don't know that his telling me is going to help *him* any. Not at the moment, anyway. Right now, all I care about is that I am with Drakken. I don't know what tomorrow will bring for us, and I don't need to know what the past held for him. I just need right now.

And I need Drakken.

I fold my arms around his naked torso and rest my cheek against his chest. His skin is unbelievably warm to the touch. "How are you not freezing out here?" I marvel.

"Is not cold for me."

"Right, right. Your country is very cold. I remember."

He kisses the top of my head. "Yes, my homeland is cold. And dark…" His voice fades away ominously.

"Let's go home," I whisper. Not that some random rental house in this desert wasteland is home for either of us, but somehow it seems like an oasis compared to wherever Drakken came from.

Chapter 29

RIVER

It's official.

It's been four days since I missed my period.

If things don't kick in downstairs in the next few days, I'm driving to the nearest pharmacy to get a pregnancy test. Wherever that is. I've gotten to know the desolation that is Hurley quite well in the past few weeks. The only thing to do out here is stare at the wall in the rental house, stare at the rocks and gravel in the yard outside, or hang out at the hangar with Drakken. He's always super busy working on the space plane with his team of engineers when we're there, so I take a lot of walks around the airport, or drive along the surrounding desert roads in Sheena to look at more rocks and dirt.

I haven't told Drakken about forgetting my pill or missing my period. He has a lot on his mind. If he's going to risk his life by flying his space plane up into space soon, I don't want him worrying about it. I can tell him after he arrives home safely.

In the mean time, I have other pressing problems.

Stone has been freaking out. He calls every day. I tell him I'm okay but I haven't told him where I am or what I'm doing. Something tells me it's best he doesn't know. I mean, what would happen if Drakken's dad came by our bungalow and started asking Stone questions? I hope that never happens. But isn't it better not to worry Stone needlessly? I know Stone can take care of himself. He's got plenty of street smarts. If twelve guys in suits show up at our door, he's not going to invite them in for tea or whatever. I've also talked to Finch a couple times since I've been here, and she confirmed that she hasn't said anything to anybody. I don't think Drakken's dad ever saw me talking to Finch, so there's no reason why they'd bother her. I hope. So I tell her and Stone not to worry about me and that I'll be home soon.

I really do want to get home soon. I'm going to flunk out of my classes at LACC this term if I stay here much longer. I'd ask Stone to mail my books to me, but I know he'd just drive them out here and try to convince me to come home. Not that I'd mind. Each day that I'm here, I find myself longing more and more for a return to normalcy.

The only thing keeping me sane is how slow things are in Hurley. It's hard to worry about boogie men when you're surrounded by a vast and silent desert. And silent Svetlana. It turns out she's staying in the other room at the rental house.

I see a lot of Svetlana. Since she's not into the actual building of the space plane any more than I am, she's at the house quite a bit.

So far, we've barely spoken to each other. Not because of me. Whenever I'm in the house without Drakken, she stays in her room. I don't think she likes me. Why, I have no idea.

One afternoon, I'm sitting at the card table in the kitchen reading through texts on my phone when Svetlana walks in the front door with a bunch of shopping bags in hand.

"Hey," I smile at her.

She wince-smiles but doesn't say anything. She wears a cowboy hat, tank top, cutoff denim shorts, and super expensive boots. All of it is brand new. She must've just bought it today because I haven't seen this outfit before. Instead of looking like a Hurley local, she looks like she belongs at a photo shoot for a sexy cowgirl calendar. She's managed to get quite a tan here in the desert. With her dark hair and fine features, she's stunning.

She sort of glances at me as she walks toward her bedroom without acknowledging me. She quietly closes her door.

I stand up from the card table and go knock. "Svetlana?" After a minute, I knock again. It's only a ten by ten bedroom. How long can it take her to walk from one side to the other?

Finally, the door opens and she leans her head through the gap like she's hiding something. "Yes?"

"Um, hey. Can I ask you a question?"

"What?"

"Do you know who Saz is?"

"Who?"

"Drakken mentioned someone named Saz. Does that name ring a bell?"

Svetlana's beautiful face is inscrutable. If she knows, she's not saying anything. Not to me, anyway.

This feels so high school. I should just ask Drakken. It would probably be easier than enduring Svetlana's judgmental stare. But I don't want to bother him. He's got enough on his mind with the space plane. I smile apologetically, "Sorry I bothered you. I'll leave you alone." I turn to go.

She sighs heavily. "Did he tell you about her?"

I stop in my tracks and turn to face her.

Her bedroom door drifts open and she leans her hip against the doorframe.

I glance around randomly, not wanting to meet her eyes directly. "Um, he mentioned her name, but he didn't really say anything about her."

"My brother has very strong feelings for her."

Does she mean present tense? As in, *still* has feelings for her? "Uh, is Saz a nickname for Karina?" I'm pretty sure I already know the answer, but I want to make sure.

Svetlana shakes her head and smiles, "No. Karina is not her."

That's good to know. Without thinking, I blurt, "Who is she? Who is Saz?"

Svetlana sighs, "Is not for me to say. You must ask my brother."

I thought she might say that.

A sudden stab of jealousy hits my heart. Now my conversation with Drakken can go like this, "I might be pregnant with your baby, so why are you saying some other woman's name during sex? Oh, and considering you're officially engaged to Karina, are there any other secret women I need to know about?"

Yeah, that'll go over great.

Gosh, road trips sure are fun.

Chapter 30

RIVER

Two pink lines.

I hold the First Response pregnancy stick in my shaking hands. I had to drive all the way to the Walgreens in Silver City to get it. Now I'm in the dim bathroom in the rental house in Hurley.

Two pink lines.

I'm pregnant.

Shizz.

What am I going to do?

I hear the front door of the house bang open.

"Rivka?" Drakken hollers.

I shove the test stick into the bag with the box and stash everything in the tiny vanity cabinet beneath the crummy sink. I cram it behind the rolls of toilet paper. I'll have to move it later. I flush the toilet and run the sink like I'm washing my hands, even though I already did.

"Rivka!"

"I'm in the bathroom! I'll be right out."

I can hear him stomping around the house. Is something wrong? When I open the door, he sweeps me up in his arms. He kisses me repeatedly on the cheeks, the mouth, my chin, my nose, smothering me with love and excitement.

"Drakken!" I can't help but giggle. His affectionate enthusiasm is contagious.

"Rivka! Is ready!"

"What's ready, Drakken?"

"The orbiter. The space plane!"

"It's ready?"

He nods excitedly, "Yes. Is ready for first test flight into space!"

"No way!" The only thing Drakken has talked about since I got here weeks ago was going up into space. I have to admit, it's exciting. I mean, frickin' space. "That's amazing, Drakken!" I jump up into his arms and wrap mine around his neck.

He twirls me around in the narrow hallway. We spin and laugh joyfully until he sets me down. When my feet touch the ground, my fears rocket into the stratosphere. Drakken is going to test pilot his space plane into space for the first time. He might not make it back in one piece. He might not make it back at all. He might never get to meet his own child.

Now I *really* don't know what I'm going to do. This is crazy. No, this is *beyond* crazy. My life has upheaved in a matter of weeks. I feel like the ground has disappeared beneath my feet. My life is totally out of control. And yes, it's making *me* crazy.

I blurt, "Take me with you, Drakken. Take me to the stars."

His face freezes.

I'm about to freak out. No, I freaked out back in the bathroom five minutes ago. But seriously, what the fuzz am I thinking?

"You remember," he marvels. "I tell you at winery I take you to stars. In royal bedroom, when I watch full moon."

I nod, "I remember. I want to go with you."

"But is not stars. Is only sub orbit. Stars very far away."

"Take me anyway."

"But—"

"If it's safe enough for you, it's safe enough for me." What am I thinking? I have a baby on board! Oh well. I never claimed to be sane. I'm totally blaming my hormones.

"But—"

"I'm going."

He smiles and frowns thoughtfully. "You are strong woman, Rivka. I all ways know it."

"Hells yeah I am," I grin.

Just because I'm an adult doesn't mean I'm not crazy. Finding out I'm pregnant is also a contributing factor. When life flies out of control, you have to fly with it. Even if it means flying to space.

Frickin' space!

I'll get to go before Angelina Jolie *and* Lady Gaga!

Take that, bitches!

"When are we going?" I gasp.

"Tomorrow."

Oh, shizz.

Chapter 31

RIVER

"Is okay?" Drakken asks after adjusting my white flight suit in the locker room inside the hangar at the Grant County Airport.

"Yeah, it's fine," I smile.

"Are you scared?"

"Of course I'm scared! We're flying to space! My hands are totally clammy. Feel." I grab his hand and squeeze it. His hand is warm, strong, and comforting.

"I keep you safe, Rivka." He helps me to my feet. "In white flight suit, you look like angel."

"I do?"

"Yes. You even have wings." He points to a patch on the breast of the flight suit. Yup, it has wings.

"Drakken," I snicker. "In your black flight suit, you look like a devil." I wink, "A *handsome* devil."

He grins.

Vladan, the man who piloted Drakken's Gulfstream when we flew up to Calistoga and the castle, leans his head into the locker room. He too wears a flight suit, although his is red. He grins from ear to ear, "Are you ready, sir?"

"Yes, Vladan," Drakken grins. "We will be outside in one minute."

"The wind is good, sir. We should take off as soon as you are ready. Before wind changes."

"Yes, Vladan. One minute."

Vladan nods once and walks away.

Drakken turns to me. "You hear Vladan. Are you ready to fly to space?"

"Uh… This is really happening, isn't it?"

"Yes. You are going to be first woman to fly as passenger in commercial space plane to outer space."

"What, really? But haven't there been like a bunch of women who have gone into space?"

"But not one who go in space plane as private passenger. You are first."

"No way!"

"Yes. But to be official passenger," he arches his eyebrows, "you must pay for ticket."

"Oh. How much is a ticket?" I hide my disappointment.

"$250,000."

"What?! I can't pay that!"

"Is what Angelina Jolie and Lady Gaga pay. Rocket fuel, component parts, testing, development, all is very expensive," he says seriously.

"I don't have that kind of money," I whine.

He grins, "Okay. I give you discount."

I smirk, "How much of a discount?"

"You pay me with kiss. Deal?" He grins.

"Deal." I lean forward and smooch him. The next thing I know, his tongue is in my mouth. I heat instantly inside my flight suit. Especially between my legs. Who needs space when I have Drakken?

"Sir?" Vladan asks, leaning into the locker room again.

Drakken breaks our kiss. He stares at me for a moment, then kisses the tip of my nose. "We go."

My heart races. "Okay."

Outside on the runway, the morning sun glimmers across the space plane. To me, the plane looks like it could fly to the rings of Saturn and back, but what do I know?

Painted on the nose of the plane in cursive script is the name 'Anastazie'. The script reminds me of Drakken's handwriting in the letter he sent me. I suddenly wonder, is Saz a nickname for Anastazie? I hope not. I don't really like the idea of flying in a plane named after the woman whose name Drakken blurted out during sex. I kind of wished he'd named it after me. I mean, I don't mean to be greedy. But if he loves me so much, shouldn't he have named the plane Rivka or something? And not some woman from his past?

Before I have time to think about it, a bunch of people rush up to us. I recognize most of them from seeing them at the hangar. Others, I don't. All of them have cameras. They start asking for photos.

Great. I get to fake smile for the camera while wondering if I'm going for a space flight inside Drakken's ex-girlfriend. You know what I mean.

Radek, whom I recognize, positions Drakken, Vladan, and I in front of the plane. He makes sure to get the three of us and the name Anastazie in the photo. Jolly good.

All the people with cameras press in around us and start snapping photos.

Fake smile.

Drakken wraps his arm around my waist.

Vladan stands on my other side, his arm over my shoulders. He squeezes the arm of Drakken's flight suit and grins at both of us. "Is good to have you with us, Reka."

I remember Reka was what Drakken called me way back when we first met, because it means 'river' in his language. "Thanks, Vladan. I'm glad to be here." Mostly glad but also confused. I think the confusion shows on my face. This whole thing is totally overwhelming.

"Don't worry," Vladan grins, "Drakken is best pilot I ever know. He will get us home safe."

After the photos, we board the plane by climbing up a staircase, much like we did for Drakken's Gulfstream. Considering I'd never been on a plane before a month ago, I've come a long way real fast. Fighter jets, luxury jets, now a frickin' space plane?!

Inside, I'm freaking out.

When we reach the top of the stairs, Drakken stops and turns to me. "Are you sure you want to do this Rivka?"

"Uh..." Maybe I should at least call Stone and tell him what I'm about to do. At least that way he'll know. Come to think of it, I haven't heard from Stone in a couple days. That doesn't seem like him. I hope he's okay. I mean, imagine if Drakken's dad *had* found out where I lived and sent men looking for me? And found Stone instead? And what if instead of twelve guys in suits knocking at the door, just one guy showed up wearing a Department of Water & Power uniform? And he was hiding a gun? I shudder at the thought.

"Sir," Vladan says, "wind is changing. If we wait too long, we might have long delay."

"Um," I bite my lip nervously.

Drakken smooths his hand over my hair, which is tied back in a ponytail. "You don't have to do this, Rivka. Is okay."

Now I'm totally worrying about Stone. "How long is the flight again?"

"Whole trip take maybe two hours."

I glance at Vladan.

Vladan is anxious to get going.

I remind myself that Stone has been safe for the past few weeks. He should be safe for another two hours, right? I can call him as soon as we land. I say nervously, "Drakken, do you think it's safe?"

"What, the plane?"

"Uh, yeah."

Drakken smiles confidently, "I know is safe. I build it. I fly it many times. Is very safe."

"I trust you, Drakken. My life is in your hands." I almost add that our child's life is in his hands, but I can't. I only took one pregnancy test. What if it was wrong? Sometimes they are. What if for some reason the baby doesn't come to term? You never know. I don't want to worry Drakken needlessly. Wow, who knew flying in a space plane could be so fraught with anxiety? Duh.

"Is something wrong, Rivka?" The concern on Drakken's face is obvious.

"No, uh, everything is fine." I nod vigorously.

"You are sure?"

If ever there was an ultimate YOLO moment, flying on an experimental space plane has to top the list. I feel a surge of confidence. "Yeah, I'm sure. Let's do this!" I grin and barge into the space plane. The cabin inside is super futuristic. Stylistic seats resembling loungers line the length of the interior. They look super comfy. "Where should we sit?"

"I will be in cockpit," Drakken says behind me.

"Can I sit with you? It would be totally awesome to watch how you fly this thing."

Drakken smiles, "Vladan is co-pilot. He will sit next to me. Is only two seat in cockpit. But you can sit in front passenger seat, close to cockpit."

"Oh." I kind of imagined us holding hands on the flight up.

"Is okay," Drakken smiles. "I sit next to you until 50,000 feet."

"What happens at 50,000 feet?" I suddenly remember that 50,000 was when the Virgin Galactic space plane blew apart. And one of the pilots died.

"Carrier plane release space plane."

"Huh?"

"You will see. For now, buckle in."

I slide into the comfy lounger seat and buckle up. It doesn't take long for Vladan and Drakken to get strapped in.

Unlike at LAX, there's no planes ahead of us waiting to use the runway. We're already lined up, pointing down the runway.

I hear the engines turn on and spin up to speed.

A minute later, Drakken twists in his seat and smiles at me. "Here we go!"

The plane rolls slowly forward.

Holy shizz!

This is it.

Space, here I come!

Chapter 32

RIVER

I don't know what I was expecting.

I guess after flying in the F-18, I was expecting us to rocket up into space in like five seconds. Nope. The space plane takeoff is as gentle as the Gulfstream.

"How long will it take to get to space?" I ask.

"It will take one hour to reach release altitude," Drakken calls back from the cockpit. "Then ten more minute to reach space."

I'm not sure what he means by release, but I know what an hour and ten minutes means.

Wow.

I'm incredibly nervous. I try to take deep breaths. My heart hammers in my chest. I close my eyes, trying to imagine I'm not about to die a tragic death that involves exploding things and bits of me flying in every direction for hundreds of miles.

"Are you okay?" Drakken mutters in my ear.

My eyes pop open. "Drakken! Aren't you supposed to be flying the plane?!"

"Is okay. Pilot in carrier aircraft is flying right now."

"You mean Vladan?"

"No. Matej. He is in carrier plane. Above." He points toward the ceiling.

"What's a carrier plane?"

"Is big plane to carry space plane up to 50,000 feet."

"Oh," I nod, not entirely understanding.

"I sit with you for now. We still have hour until separate."

"Okay."

He slides into the lounger seat across from me and buckles in. He reaches across the aisle and grabs my hand in his.

Wow, that helps a lot. I glance out the window. So far, this flight reminds me of our flight on the Gulfstream. Slow and smooth. No big deal. But I can't imagine it's going to be like this the whole way. I keep thinking about the Virgin Galactic crash. Suddenly, I'm not in any big hurry to get into space. I did a little reading about the crash online during all my down time. The VSS Enterprise, which was the official name of the Virgin Galactic test plane, had flown and landed safely plenty of times before the day of the crash. But it was torn to bits during a routine test flight. The National Transportation Safety Board—the people who investigate airplane crashes—are still trying to determine exactly what happened. They have some ideas and theories, but that's it. Like Drakken said, being a test pilot is dangerous. Things can go horribly wrong despite taking every precaution. You never know. It's the price people pay for living on the cutting edge.

Why am I up here again? You only live once? Unfortunately, YOLOing this moment is not helping me feel any better. Oh well. Too late now.

I glance over at Drakken.

He smiles sympathetically, "Is okay, Rivka. You no worry. You are safe with me. All ways safe."

It amazes me how all Drakken has to do is talk to me and the sound of his voice is proof that everything is going to turn out okay. His supreme confidence is incredible and totally reassuring.

I gaze deeply into his ice blue eyes. That sense of flow I always feel with him ignites.

Our souls connect.

His eyes comfort me and give me the peace I need. It only takes a few minutes with him holding my hand and gazing into my eyes for my nerves to completely calm.

As the plane flies higher and higher, my mind wanders all over the place. I think about everything Drakken and I have been through together since we met. It's all so weird. Yet he's still a big mystery. If there's a slight chance we don't make it home, I'd like to know a few things. Since Vladan is at the controls, and whoever and wherever Matej is is also at the controls, I figure it's now or never. I turn to him. "Drakken, who is Saz?"

Drakken closes his eyes and turns his head away.

Our flow stops.

I start to panic.

But he doesn't release my hand.

He sighs heavily, "Sazkia Pokojska is my one true love."

Is? Ouch. I wince. I pull my hand from his but he squeezes it, holding on.

He turns his head back to face me and opens his eyes.

Our flow ignites.

He sighs. "Until I meet you Rivka, I think I never find love again after Sazkia was stolen from me."

My heart is thudding in my chest. I'm not sure what to make of this. I want to believe that when Drakken finishes his story, all of my worries will finally be set to rest.

"I know Sazkia from very small. I love her from as long as I can remember. I think I was to marry her when I grow up. As boy, Sazkia is my whole world. I see her every day. I love her so hard it hurt."

Wow, hearing him say that hurts *me* way more than I would've expected. The love in his eyes is obvious. It's powerful, and I have to wonder if he loves *me* that much. I don't know. How can you ever be sure? Who could ever compete with a first love?

Drakken looks at me with the saddest face I've ever seen in my entire life. Tears fall silently down his face.

Is he sad for Sazkia? Or sad for me? I don't know, but I do know that right now my entire body is shaking with absolute fear. I have a very bad feeling about what part I will play in Drakken's life from this moment forward. I'm afraid to hear what he says next. I don't know if I can deal with it, and I don't even know what he's going to say. But based on the terror in his eyes, I'm totally freaked out.

"When I am seventeen," Drakken says, his voice tortured and thick with abject agony, "I make Sazkia pregnant." He swallows hard. "When my father find out, he kill our daughter."

Chapter 33

RIVER

"Wait, what? He *killed* your daughter? Do you mean like an abortion?" I can't believe what I'm hearing.

Drakken shakes his head minutely. "No," he whispers. "My father killed my daughter Anastazie."

Anastazie.

I gasp. I can barely get my head around what Drakken is saying. But I suddenly realize that once again, I assumed the worst about him. I assumed this space plane was named after his first love instead of me, which made me feel like a second class citizen somehow. I was so wrong. Now I'm tearing up. "Drakken, did you name this plane after your daughter?"

He nods morosely. "Yes. I name for her. To honor her spirit. Is my angel plane. So I can fly up high above earth and be with her. Maybe she see her name and visit me in space."

"Oh my god." That is the saddest and most poignant thing anyone has ever told me. I don't know if he means he *literally* wants to see his daughter in space. But it doesn't really matter. The sentiment is the same. The next thing I know, I feel my tears spilling and I'm bawling quietly. "I'm so sorry, Drakken."

He looks at the ceiling. Tears dribble down his cheeks. He speaks absently, as if he's barely occupying his own body. "When I am small, I see Sazkia every day. She is best friend. I no understand I am prince and she is nothing. To me, she is everything."

"What do you mean, she is nothing?" It sounded so weird I had to ask.

"Sazkia is daughter of maid in castle."

"You grew up in a castle?"

"Yes," he says with no joy whatsoever. "When I am twelve year old, my father see that I spend time with Sazkia every day. He no like for me to be with her anymore. One day, Sazkia and her family are no longer at castle. I am very scared. I sneak out of castle to look for her. I am happy when I find her at air field. Is where we all ways watch plane take off and land. I come back next day, and she is there. We meet at air field every day I can go. Some day I go, she is not there. Some day I am not there. But we all ways go back. We love each other. Love like biggest love ever." He looks over at me.

I feel a pinch of jealousy hearing him talk about how big his love is for another woman.

"I love you same big, Rivka. Same as Sazkia." His eyes gaze into my heart.

I feel our flow. I sniff, "I love you too, Drakkozsha."

"When I know Sazkia is pregnant, I am very scared. I know my father will be very mad. She is peasant, I am prince. We can no ever marry. If my father find out, he will be mad because he no want uh, what is word?"

"Um, bastard?" I say it reluctantly. I assume that's what he means.

"No. Is, uh, pretender. Pretender to throne. My country is much political disagreement. People try to take throne from my family. My father all ways stop them. If he know I have child with peasant girl, he will kill her. Child is danger to him. I know it. People in power in my country get killed. Is part of life. Politics in my country is danger business."

This is insane. I mean, I know people are assassinated in foreign countries all the time. But I guess when you read about it on the news, it's not the same as someone who lived it telling you about it first hand. What's weirder is that Drakken grew up this way like it was normal.

"Sazkia hide her pregnant as long as she can. But kid in my school find out. I go to rich private school. Only children of richest people go to my school. One boy, is name Slavoj, he know I love Sazkia. When he find out Sazkia is pregnant, he tell his father. His father know my father, so he tell him. One day I come home from private school in limousine. We drive across drawbridge into castle. When I get out of car, father stand in courtyard with Sazkia. She look very scared. I am scared too. I know my father is very bad man. He ask me if baby is mine. I say yes. I hope if he know baby is mine, he will protect my child. I am wrong. But I no know this because I am young and stupid." Drakken winces, holding in his pain. His fists clench at his sides.

"You're not stupid, Drakken," I whisper. "You just wanted to do what's best for your child." I squeeze his hand reassuringly.

"My father have men take Sazkia away. When people in my country are take away, they never come back. I scream at father 'No hurt Sazkia, no hurt my child!' He ignore me. He take me inside castle to throne room. I am very scared. Is when he whip me."

"Your own father *whipped* you?" I gasp.

"Yes," Drakken croaks.

Chapter 34

DRAKKEN

Age 17.

"On your knees!" my father shouts.

I want to resist him, but I can't. All of my life, my father has been a demonic figure. A terrible force to appease. He is a brutal man, capable of atrocities that are indescribable. I am so accustomed to bending to his will, I am unable to say no.

I fall to my knees.

"Remove your shirt. I will not have my clothes soiled by your betrayal."

He speaks of my clothes as if they are his, which of course they are. He paid for them. He pays for everything. He owns everything. This castle, the people who work in it, the land around it. Me. My father owns me. I know this like I know that snow falls in winter or that the fox is clever. It is a basic fact of my existence.

I weep silently as I remove my shirt. I hate my father for making me do it. But I hate myself more for obeying him. I am his pawn. I am not my own person. I am an extension of him. He drives this idea home every single day of my life.

My feelings are irrelevant to him.

My wants are irrelevant to him.

My needs are irrelevant to him.

I often think my life is irrelevant to him.

Like the slave that I am, I fold my shirt and place it neatly beside me. There is no defiance in my actions. Defiance equals death. Since I was born into this world, it seems normal. But a secret part of me, the part that loves Sazkia, is horrified by my weakness.

A waiting servant wearing the royal livery holds a whip by his side. The man stands apathetically, staring straight ahead, as if unaware that I am about to be beaten.

My father waves his hand.

The servant trots forward, across the criss-cross pattern of delicate wood inlay. He kneels and offers the whip to my father as if it is the greatest gift this man has to offer.

My father takes the whip and stretches it in his hands. He begins to circle me, loosening his arm, spiraling the whip quietly against the floor.

"You have disobeyed me, boy."

I am not even his son. To him, I am a stranger. I say nothing. It is the only act of defiance that won't get me killed.

He flicks the whip against the floor.

CRACK!!

I refuse to move, refuse to wince, refuse to show my fear.

"You have betrayed me, boy."

He flails the whip again.

CRACK!!

"You have committed treason. Boy. Do you understand?"

I don't want to speak.

"DO YOU UNDERSTAND????!!!!" he roars.

CRACK!!

"Yes. Father," I hiss.

"Then you understand why I must punish you…"

I won't answer. I won't, I won't, I won't.

"DO YOU UNDERSTAND????!!!!"

I won't answer.

SLASH!!

The whip bites my back and glues into the skin.

I grunt.

He rips it away, tearing flesh. Blood flows.

I scream.
He whips me again.
And again.
And again.
And again.
And again.
And again.
And again.
And...

Chapter 35

RIVER

"Drakken..." I weep.

His mouth quivers as he stares at the ceiling. His face shakes. He looks so alone, so lost, so helpless.

"Sir," Vladan calls from the cockpit. "We approach 50,000 feet. Release in five minutes."

Drakken doesn't respond.

"Sir? I need you up here in cockpit."

"Drakken?" I whisper.

His face hardens. He sits bolt upright in the lounger style seat and unbuckles himself. He turns to me. The stone mask on his face is blank. "Is time."

I'm still weeping. I don't understand how he can tell me that story and be able to function. I'm a wreck. "Drakken? Are you up for this? I mean, maybe we should turn around and try again tomorrow? When you've had a chance to calm down?"

Drakken stands up. "For Anastazie, there is no tomorrow." He leans over me and pulls several more straps out from beneath my lounger, strapping me in with a bunch of different seat belts, much like in the F-18, so I'm safely immobilized.

"Drakken?"

"I keep you safe, Rivka." He steps into the cockpit. He and Vladan immediately start talking intensely in their own language. I'm guessing they're talking about airplane stuff.

I look out the window. We are super high in the air. Much higher than we went in the Gulfstream. All the clouds are far below. I spot a jet airliner flying just above the scattered clouds, a thin white tail unfurling behind it. From here it looks tiny. Usually I see tiny airliners passing by high overhead, not way down below. Wow.

"Rivka?" Drakken calls. "Are you ready for space?" There is excitement in his voice. I wish I could be in the cockpit next to him.

"Yeah!"

"Release in five, four—"

Geez, he didn't give me much of a warning.

"Three, two, one. Release!"

Something really loud thunks in the roof of the plane.

"Oh!" I gasp. I have no idea what's going on. I hope the plane isn't breaking. Suddenly, I feel like we're falling. I spoke too soon! I swallow hard and my stomach clenches. I look out the windows to either side and see the big wings suddenly going up. But we're going down.

Oh shizz! Did the wings just fall off?

I start to panic.

BOOM!

There's a really loud explosion and I'm suddenly thrown back in my seat.

"Ignition!" Drakken roars.

I can barely hear him over the thundering at the back of the plane. Is this thing going to hold together?

After a few moments, I realize we're not dying. We're accelerating. Like, really, *really* hard.

"Breathe, Rivka!" Drakken chuckles.

I remember the breathing thing Drakken taught me in the F-18 and I start doing that.

"Mach one! Is speed of sound!" Drakken calls.

I clamp my hands around the arm rests.

"60,000 feet!"

Without warning, the plane rolls to the side. "Drakken!" I scream. "What's happening!"

He doesn't answer.

The plane starts to shake really hard. It's going to come apart.

I look out the window to my left and all I see is ground. To my right is sky. Only it's dark. It's night blue. But it was day time a minute ago. Early morning, in fact. Am I seeing space?

Before I can ponder this, the plane whips around in another roll and I'm looking at the ground.

I'm totally going to be sick if this keeps up. Unless we all die first.

Slowly, the plane rolls back to level.

"70,000 feet!"

I look out the window. Even though we're level, the sky is *below* us. It's a blue haze around the earth. Oh my gosh. I can see the curvature of the earth. It really is round! Columbus or whoever wasn't lying!

"Mach two point zero!" Drakken shouts. "Twice speed of sound! 100,000 feet!"

"Are we in space yet?" I shout. I'm freaking scared but I'm also exhilarated.

"Not yet." Drakken's excitement is obvious.

"Mach two point five!"

I look out the window. We are *way* higher than we went in the Gulfstream or the F-18. New Mexico is shrinking, and there's a pale haze over everything. Is that the atmosphere?

"150,000 feet!"

"Are we there yet?" I quip, like I'm a whiny brat. I'm trying to act like I'm not super scared because it's the only thing I can think of to do.

"Not yet! Mach three point zero!"

I'm not sure how fast we're going, but I'm pretty sure bullets can't catch us at this speed.

"250,000 feet! Burn out in ten, nine, eight—"

What's burn out? Space planes who smoke too much pot?

"Seven, six—"

"290,000 feet!" Vladan shouts.

"Three! Two! One! Now!!!"

The plane suddenly shudders and I think we're about to die. The loud noise of the rocket engine or whatever suddenly goes silent.

"Are we out of gas?" I shout nervously. I'm pretty sure you don't want to run out of gas this high up.

"Yes," Drakken calls.

Oh shit. As in, actual poop. "Really?"

"Yes."

He isn't kidding. Shit, shit, shit.

"Is okay. We coast for long time."

"Coast where?"

"Into space."

"We're not there yet?"

"No. Space is officially at one hundred kilometer."

"Officially?"

"Yes," he chuckles.

Outside the windows, everything above the blue earth is black.

"Look up!" Drakken calls.

Now he tells me. There's windows on the roof. Everything is black. Holy crap. I'm seeing space! "This is epic!"

"320,000 feet," Vladan calls.

"Almost there," Drakken laughs.

I'm literally shaking in my boots.

"325,000 feet!"

"326!" Drakken calls.

"327!" Vladan hoots.

"328,100 feet!" Drakken cheers. "We are in space!"

"Oh my god!" I laugh.

"Rivka, you are officially astronaut!"

"What?"

"Yes!" he laughs.

"No way!"

"Yes! You are astronaut! And first commercial female spaceplane passenger in history of world! You will be remembered forever, Rivka! You are pioneer!"

I bark laughter. I can't speak.

I'm a fuzzing astronaut!

Woo hoo!!

Chapter 36

RIVER

Drakken floats into the main cabin from the cockpit. Yes, he *literally* floats.

"What?!" I blurt.

"Is zero gravity," Drakken grins. He reaches down and unbuckles all my belts.

When they're all loose, I notice them floating randomly like tentacles on a sea anemone. But we're not under water. I shift in my seat and suddenly I start to float upward.

"Oh my god! I'm floating!"

Drakken grins from ear to ear. "Yes, Rivka. We are weightless. But only for few minutes. So make fun while you can!" Drakken kicks off the seat and starts to somersault in the air. He laughs the entire time.

"Don't make yourself sick!" My stomach already feels queasy. Good thing Drakken made me skip breakfast. I push off and missile toward the back of the small compartment. "I'm flying, Drakka!" I laugh. "I'm flying!" I turn myself around by grabbing some handles on the back wall.

Drakken has stopped somersaulting. He stares at me, his face sagging.

"What's wrong?" I ask, worried.

"Sazkia say that to me when we are very small. We play to be bird. We *pretend* to be bird."

"Oh, Drakken," I sigh sadly. Compassion *and* jealousy flicker through me. I can't help but feel that Drakken is a million miles away right now. Because his heart rests in the hands of another woman.

He floats toward me across infinity and wraps his arms around me. "Is okay, Rivka. I am here."

Is he? He never told me if Sazkia is alive or not. Not that I'm going to ask if she's dead. That would be beyond rude, thoughtless and totally insensitive. I *can't* ask. Too bad the not knowing makes me nervous. What if she came back into his life somehow? I can't think about it.

He kisses the top of my head.

My pony tail flutters around into my face and brushes my check. I wrinkle my nose.

Drakken chuckles.

Trying to shift my focus away from my own thoughts, I look out the windows at the curved surface of the earth. "It seems so far away. So fragile. So delicate."

"Yes."

"It puts it all into perspective, doesn't it?"

"Is like magic. Is make you want to protect planet."

"Yeah," I sigh.

"Look up, Rivka," he whispers. "You can see forever."

I look through a round window overhead and I see thousands of stars. *Billions* of stars. I see eternity. Awe overcomes me.

"Anastazie is out there somewhere," Drakken mutters. "One day, I will see her again."

I squeeze him in my arms. "Thank you for bringing me here, Drakkozsha. I can't tell you how much it means to me to be here with you."

"I feel same way, Rivka. I am very happy you are here with me."

"Have you ever heard that saying, 'When you love someone, you follow them to the ends of the earth'?"

"No. I have no heard that. But I understand."

"Well, this pretty much constitutes the end of the earth, doesn't it?" I grin.

He chuckles, "Yes it does, Rivka. Yes it does."

He kisses the tip of my nose. Then he kisses my lips.

Our mouths part.

Our tongues touch.

Our flow consumes my awareness.

Our connection becomes everything.

We float in heaven.

We are two souls connecting cosmically, connecting across the infinite expanse of space and time. For *all* time. This is easily the most profound kiss I have ever had, and probably ever *will* have, in my entire life.

We float and spin slowly, he in his black flight suit, me in my white flight suit. We are twined together, two cuddling teardrops, one of black and one of white, a circle of yin and yang. Inside my womb, like the two small dots in the yin yang symbol, a piece of each of us has combined to make a new being.

At some point, we break our kiss and I snuggle my check against the chest of Drakken's flight suit. "I'm pregnant, Drakkozsha."

He tenses.

After hearing his story about Anastazie, I realized why he was so afraid of getting me pregnant. He was afraid of what his father might do to me and the baby. But Drakken needs to know. "I'm pregnant with our baby, Drakka." When he doesn't respond, I say, "It happened at your hangar at LAX. I forgot to take my pill when we went to the castle. And the day after. I was so frazzled, I just forgot. When I met Karina, I got so mad I went out and got drunk. I—" I don't want to explain what happened with Cage right now. I trust that Cage was being honest when he said we didn't sleep together. I know in my heart that this baby is Drakken's. "I forgot to take my pill again. Then we made love. It wasn't until after you left that I remembered."

Drakken doesn't respond.

Is he mad? Is he anything? Or is he just in shock? Slowly, I lift my head.

He looks down at me, his eyes full of tears. "I love you, Rivka. I love you," he whispers.

"Sir!" Vladan calls. "We start re-entry procedure soon. I need you in cockpit."

Chapter 37

RIVER

I'm strapped into my space age lounger chair.

The space plane is shaking like crazy.

Just because I'm now officially the first female space plane passenger in history doesn't mean I'm not going to die up here or crash into the ground at a million miles an hour.

Under the circumstances, I'm glad I told Drakken I'm pregnant. Whatever happens, at least he knows.

The plane shakes so hard there's no way it's going to hold together.

Drakken and Vladan talk back and forth frantically in their language.

My heart pounds in my head.

I can't look out the windows at the ground. It's too scary.

So I look up. It's still blackness above.

I see into forever.

WHAM!

The plane slams into something.

WHAM!!

What the hell did we hit?

WHAM!!!

All I see is blackness.

Eternal blackness.

Chapter 38

DRAKKEN

"Engage air brakes!" I shout.

"I am sir!" Vladan shouts.

"We're dropping too fast!" I'm forced back into my seat by the high G's of deceleration. The meter reads 5.9 G's. It's a lot, but I'm accustomed to more. I squeeze my legs and keep my breath high in my chest.

The stick bucks in my hand. Re-entering the atmosphere is like ramming into a mountain of gravel. Although it moves, it does so reluctantly. There is every chance that some portion of the airframe will fail.

I can't let that happen.

Rivka is on this plane.

My child is on this plane.

I can't let anything happen to them.

I fight the stick. If I can get her under control, she will hold together.

A warning buzzer starts chirping from the control panel.

"The rudder assembly is not responding!" Vladan barks.

"Try it again!"

"I did sir! I think there's a short in the electrical!"

"Try the back up system!"

"It's not responding!!"

I glance at the control panel. There is a red X blinking below the tail on the schematic image of the plane.

The hull shakes violently around us. If the intensity of the vibration increases, we are going to lose more than just the rudder. We may lose other control surfaces. We could even lose an entire wing. If that happens, we are finished.

I close my eyes and pray.

Help me, Anastazie. Help us. I named this plane after you. Don't embarrass your father by letting us be torn to pieces.

I can't help but smile as I picture Sazkia's face in my mind. Our daughter would have looked like her, I'm sure of it.

"Sir!" Vladan shouts. "It's back on line! The rudder is back on line!"

The stick calms in my hand and the vibration eases to manageable levels.

Thank you, Anastazie.

Thank you.

Chapter 39

RIVER

"Rivka! Wake up!"

Am I dead?

I blink my eyes open.

Sun light beams into the cabin. I look out the windows and see the desert far below. I don't think the afterlife is a desert. Well, maybe for some people, but not for me. "Did we make it?" I ask.

"Yes!" Drakken cheers. "We glide in for landing soon!"

"Holy crap!" I cheer. "We made it!"

"Only few more minute to landing."

I relax into my seat and watch out the window as we descend the rest of the way.

"That is strange," Vladan says ominously.

I hope we're not about to crash again. Once was enough.

"What?" Drakken asks.

"Do you see line of black cars? Turning onto Airport Road?"

"What?!" Drakken asks, his voice tense.

"Black cars. Six of them. East of runway."

I can't see the runway. It must be in front of us. "Why are there cars on the runway?" I holler.

Drakken doesn't answer.

"Drakken? Is something wrong?"

"Yes," he growls. "My father is here."

Oh fuzz.

What is his dad going to do when he finds out I'm pregnant?

Is this bad?

Yeah, this is bad.

"Drakken?"

"Yes?"

I wish I could see his face, but he's way up in the cockpit. "Uh, can we just fly to another airport? So he doesn't find us?"

"No."

"Why not?"

"Plane has no fuel. We are gliding in. We land here or we crash."

Okay, I'll say it.

Fuck.

Chapter 40

RIVER

Our landing is smooth but the second we step off the space plane, everything goes nuts.

The crowd outside is whistling and cheering when Drakken opens the cabin door and lets the sun and heat into the plane. The photographers are snapping pictures. People shout congratulations. When Drakken descends the stairs first, he's rushed by his team. They're ecstatic.

When I descend the stairs, people start congratulating me and jostling into me.

A new face appears in the crowd. It's that guy Charles, the one I saw Drakken buy hookers for way back when at The Beverly Hills Resort. The guy who Drakken told me was investing a ton of money in Drakken's business. He claps Drakken on the back. "Congratulations, Drakken! Customers have been calling in since you descended safely down to 40,000 feet! They're demanding to buy tickets!"

Drakken laughs, "Very good! How many have we sold?"

"Two hundred and seventy seven seats in the last twenty minutes."

Drakken grins. "At $250,000?"

Charles shakes his head. "No. *Three* fifty."

Drakken's face lights up. "*Three* fifty?"

Charles snarls, "Three fucking fifty!"

I do the math in my head. That is almost one hundred *million* dollars.

Charles grins, "Supply and demand, baby!" he cheers and slaps the tops of Drakken's shoulders enthusiastically. "Supply and *fucking* demand!!"

Svetlana squeezes through the crowd and kisses Drakken on the cheek. She smiles at him with pride, "You are hero, Drakkozsha! Your business will be huge success!"

He grins at her, "Thank you, Sveta!" He flicks his eyes toward me. "Rivka…" He reaches an arm out for me, but before he can say anything, several people from his team surge toward him and start asking questions about the flight and the performance of the plane.

Svetlana turns to me and throws her arms around me.

I shrink back defensively, expecting her to attack me.

Instead, she gives me a huge hug and kisses both my cheeks. "You are okay!" she laughs like we're best friends. I can barely hear her over the noise of the crowd. She leans into my ear, "My brother loves you. You must not hurt him. He is tender man."

I pull back and search her eyes.

She's smiling at me. Somehow, in a weird way, I feel like she's giving me her blessing. And I thought she hated me.

I don't know what to say. I return the smile. "Thanks, Svetlana. Seriously. Thank you."

Her face withers.

Was that the wrong thing to say? All I said was thanks. What the eff?

Her eyes drift to the left and I follow her gaze.

A line of six black Mercedes sedans drive onto the runway.

"No," Svetlana gasps.

The cars stop. Twenty-four doors open in unison. A bunch of men in black suits step out of the cars.

One of them, larger then the others, tumbles to the black asphalt.

Lubomir. He struggles to his knees. His face is battered and bruised, but he shows no fear.

"No!" Svetlana whines. "Drakken!"

He is immediately beside Svetlana and I. "Father," he growls.

Svetlana is suddenly pale and deathly afraid. She shrinks behind Drakken.

"Stay here," Drakken warns.

The mass of men are now lined up in front of the sedans. In the center of them stands Drakken's father, still as stone. Lubomir is on the ground in front of him.

As Drakken shoulders through the people on his team, they all begin turning toward Drakken's father. Several of them mumble.

"Ivan."

"The king."

"How did he find us?"

"He will ruin everything."

The general tone of all the men and women is fear. My own fear is amplified by theirs. All I can think about is the life forming inside me.

And whether or not Drakken's father will try to steal it from me.

Chapter 41

DRAKKEN

"Leave here now!" I shout at my father as I stride across the runway. I stab my hand toward the road.

My father stands motionless and stares at me, his lips welded together in a white hot line.

I glance briefly at Lubomir.

He has been beaten by my father's men. I was hopeful they would release him unharmed. I should've known better. But the hard glint in Lubomir's eyes tells me he's not seriously injured. He is a resilient man.

I stop several feet away from my father.

Several of his men move their hands inside their suit jackets, no doubt grasping the butts of their concealed automatic pistols. The other men leave their arms hanging free at their sides, prepared to intercept me or anyone else who comes too close to the king.

"Go." I growl at my father.

He sneers. "You play with these toys and think you are a man now?" His question is loaded with doubt and judgement.

"More than you will ever be. I built my kingdom." I glance behind me at my team of men and women, and the space plane parked behind them. I level my eyes at him. "You inherited yours."

"You built this...toy" he says sourly, "with MY money. It is not even a military vehicle. It is a complete waste."

I smile defiantly. "YOUR money is untouched. I courted investors and raised all of the capital on my own."

He chuckles, "I don't believe that."

"Check my accounts. Yes, I know you're aware of most of them. That money is untouched for seven years. Everything you see here is paid for by private investors. Not one cent of this is yours."

My father attempts to maintain his chagrined smile, but I see it falter.

He knows.

He smirks, "Well, well, well. So my son has finally made a man out of himself." He says it like it's an impossibility.

"Not with your help, you bastard," I hiss.

He chuckles. "Bastard? You are the one who knows all about bastards."

I start to shake.

He went for the throat.

Of course he went for the throat.

Dangerous men always do.

I feel a soft hand touch my elbow.

Rivka leans against me.

I glance down at her.

Love shines from her eyes. She gives me strength.

I smile back. Then I smile at my father. My happiness will hurt him more than my anger or hatred. He doesn't understand happiness.

My father stares at Rivka for awhile with obvious amusement. Then he smiles at me. "Did you make another bastard with this little girl?"

His words stop my heart.

How could he know?

A secret voice in the bottom of my heart mutters:

He always knows.

I explode.

Chapter 42

DRAKKEN

"You killed my daughter!"

Rage roars from my mouth like dragon fire. I fly at my father, my hands hooked into talons. I will tear his heart from his chest. If I can find it. His has no doubt shriveled away to nothingness.

His men are too slow to stop me.

I slam into my father and crush him into the ground. My fists fly.

Men descend on me like darkness.

They are bowled aside by Lubomir, who knocks at least six men off of me, despite his hands being bound behind his back.

"You killed her!" I rage as I pound my fists into my father's face.

I am going to kill him.

"Drakken, no!" Rivka screams. "You're killing him!"

I don't care!

I don't care!

I don't care!

I punch and pound and punch.

His face is a bloody mess.

He is a murderer.

"No!" he shouts, his voice full of command.

I'm no longer his slave.

I punch again and again.

"Stop, Drakken!" Rivka screams. "Stop!"

My father is a very strong man. He shouts, "She!"

I pound.

"Is!"

And pound.

"Not!"

And pound.

"Dead!"

I hesitate, my fist hovering above.

Despite the red mess I have made of my father's face, he projects absolute command. "Your daughter is alive," he growls.

"You lie!!" I shout.

"I am the king. The king does not lie."

"The king only lies!!" I shout.

I will never believe a word this man says. Everything he says, everything he does, is to manipulate, to control, to bend others to his will. He is a horrible liar. He is unfit to be king. He is unfit to be a worm. Worms spit upon him.

I glance around and realize that all of my team are surrounding my father's men. Several of his men have their pistols out, but none, thank God, have fired on my people.

I suddenly realize this situation is far more precarious than a battle between father and son. These people are my responsibility. I can't allow my father or his men to harm them too.

I stand up and stare down at my father.

He struggles to sit up.

He will have to do it on his own.

When he is sitting upright, one of his arms gives out and he falls to his elbow.

In my glory, I am disgusted with myself. I have sunk to my father's level.

I am no better than him.

My father tilts his head up and stares at me. For the first time in my life, he looks weak. He extends his hand, "Help your father."

No.

"Drakken," *Rivka nudges my elbow,* "Help him."

I project bitterness as I glare at her.

Her face saddens.

Why am I hating her?

She leans down and takes my father's arm.

I can't believe what I'm seeing. She doesn't know him. She doesn't realize what he is capable of.

She lifts him to his feet.

He stumbles, and two of his men rush to his side, supporting him. He looks at me, pain straining his face. He is breathing hard. "I... I couldn't do it."

"Do what?" *I demand.*

For a moment, his face softens.

I have never seen this look on his face before. It frightens me. It doesn't belong to my father. He is a deceiver.

Breathing hard, he says, "I couldn't kill my own granddaughter."

"You lie!!" *I shout.*

He shakes his head, panting. "She is alive, Drakkozsha."

"Don't call me that!" *I roar.* "You don't love me!!"

"Your daughter is alive. She lives in a decrepit old convent. Far away from the capital city. To the north. She is eleven years old."

"No! You took her away! You killed her!!"

He shakes his head, "No, Drakkozsha. She is alive."

My world crumbles beneath my feet. I have built my life on hatred for twelve years. Everything I have become was a reaction to my father and his hatred. I became his hatred. All for nothing. "Why?" *I plead.*

"I had to keep her a secret. You know how the game is played. No sign of weakness. No one could know. Imagine the danger she would be in? Imagine the danger her mother would be in? Or you? Imagine the danger our kingdom would be in?"

He is right. I know he is right. "What about Sazkia?"

My father looks away.

"What about Sazkia???!!!" *I roar.*

"She went to the convent."

Hope thrums through my heart and body.

My father continues, "That is where she gave birth to your daughter. To Anastazie."

Hearing my father say my daughter's name is both the foulest sound to touch my ears and the strangest.

My father hangs his head. It is a gesture I have never seen him make. Not once. He bows to no man. He mutters, "A few years ago, unbeknownst to me, Sazkia fell ill. The old nuns at the convent are... antiquated in their understanding of modern medicine. They have both feet firmly planted in the past. They believed she had taken on vapors. Or perhaps been possessed by a minor daemon." He shakes his head. "Such ignorance. It is a miracle she survived as long as she did. The nuns prayed, as they do, for a speedy recovery."

Dread crawls out of my stomach and suffocates me.

"Without modern medicine, there is no speedy recovery from a burst appendix. When word finally arrived to me in secret of her ill health, it was too late to transport her to a proper medical facility. She perished shortly thereafter. The autopsy confirmed the cause of death. I am sorry."

This is too much. It sounds like the tragic ending to a horrid fairy tale. But my father was never one to tell fables. Or apologize. He has never apologized for anything. Ever. That's why I know he's telling the truth.

He looks into my eyes. A tear runs down his cheek. I have never seen him cry. Not once. I did not believe that he could.

"You have to believe me, Drakkozsha." His voice trembles.

I slump over, my hands on my thighs. I can't breathe. This is too much. TOO MUCH!!

I shake my fists. I am going to explode in a column of fire.

Then I remember my angel.

My prayer during descent.

Some angel answered my prayer. Of that I am certain. There is no reason why the actuator in the rudder would have recovered if it was damaged. But if it wasn't Anastazie that answered my prayer, if she was not the guardian angel watching over my Rivka and our child, then who was it?

Who saved us?

Sazkia.

I know it with all my heart.

Sazkia saved us.

I begin to shake and sob uncontrollably.

I fall to my knees and weep.

Chapter 43

RIVER

"Drakken?" I kneel beside him. His head hangs against his chest.

"She's alive," Drakken mutters.

Fear tingles across every inch of my skin. I have no idea what Drakken's father just said to him, but I recognized the name Sazkia and Anastazie several times. Drakken must be referring to one of them.

If his daughter is alive, this is cause for celebration. If Sazkia is alive, I think my heart will break. He will go back to her, won't he? His first true love? The mother of the child he lost? I can't bear to think about it.

If I were Fate, the goddess who chooses when to end one life and let another begin, I would have a terrible decision to make in this moment. The mother or the child. Thank goodness the decision is out of my hands.

But I need to know. "Who's alive, Drakken?"

"My daughter."

"Oh my god," I gasp.

"But Sazkia is dead," he moans. He leans against me and wraps his arms around me weakly. "She is dead, Rivka. Dead." He hitches and sobs, holding me tight. "She is dead!"

There is no happy ending for Drakken today.

I feel awful for him. My compassion washes away every bit of jealousy I felt a moment ago. Although news of Sazkia's death should uplift me, it only leaves me feeling guilty, like I somehow took her from him. But I didn't. This is all too confusing and I don't want to think about it right now. I need to focus on *this* moment. On Drakken. I squeeze him into my chest and hold him while he cries. When a loved one dies, the pain lives on.

A sudden motion catches my awareness. I glance over at Ivan.

He sags in the arms of the two men supporting him. They lower him to his knees. Both men are clearly frightened that he can't support his own weight.

I can't help but think this is the first time they've ever seen their king crumble.

Chapter 44

DRAKKEN

"My heart," my father wheezes, squeezing his hand to his chest. His men have lowered him to his knees. He lifts his head as if it is an unbearable weight and stares at me.

With both of us on our knees, we truly see eye to eye for the first time. Man to man.

He whispers, "Forgive me, Drakkozsha."

I search his eyes for a long time. Then I stand up tall and look down at him from on high.

If he dies, I am king.

I will inherit his fortune and I will inherit his throne.

My sister is now beside me. I gaze down at her. She meets my eyes and nods. She must have overheard everything my father said. She too knows the truth of things. She lived through all of the atrocities my father visited upon our family and our people. She also understands the gravity of this situation.

She gives me a subtle nod.

We are in agreement.

I have but one choice.

"Vladan!" I shout.

Vladan is instantly beside me. "Sir?"

"Get the Gulfstream ready."

"Yes, sir." His brow furrows with determination and he runs toward the Gravity Unlimited hangar, still wearing the red flight suit he wore as co-pilot of the Anastazie.

"Radek?" I call out.

"Sir?" Radek asks, pushing out of the crowd.

My countrymen all stare wide-eyed at the tableau before them. They all know what is at stake. They know the fate of their nation hangs in the balance. They watch me expectantly.

I say to Radek, "Call 911. Get an ambulance here on the double. Then find the closest hospital with a Life Flight helicopter on standby. Tell them we can meet them at the nearest airport if necessary. Then we will transfer my father to the helicopter."

"Yes, sir," Radek nods.

"Quickly! Time is of the essence!"

I turn to Rivka.

"I'm here for you, Drakkozsha."

I pull her into my arms and hug her with all my might. "I love you, Rivka. I love you." I kiss the top of her head.

"I love you too, Drakka."

Chapter 45

RIVER

The world glows dimly white all around us.

I am freezing.

For once, Drakken is actually wearing a jacket. But he doesn't seem to notice the cold at all.

"Aren't you cold?" I ask. I'm wearing a winter parka that is warmer than a sleeping bag. I have the fur lined hood up, big mittens, fur lined boots, wool pants, and I'm still shivering.

He turns to me and smiles, "I grow up with cold. Is normal for me." He squeezes me against his side on the bench seat of the sleigh with one arm while casually holding the reins with his other hand.

Our sleigh is literally being pulled by four reindeer across a winter world. Snow covers everything. The trees are all buried under cones of snow. Everything is snow, snow, snow.

"Hey, Drakken, would you care if I broke into song and sang 'Let It Go'?"

He grins at me, "Is Disney song, yes?"

"Yeah."

"Sing as loud as you want. No one hear you out here."

I smack his arm, "Are you implying I can't sing?"

"No. I never hear you sing. You can be very good, yes?"

I roll my eyes. "I'll spare you until next time."

We kiss briefly and I snuggle into his side.

An hour later, we see a low building in the distance. It's really just a long hump of snow with a few golden pinpoints of light shining from tiny windows and a chimney with a curl of smoke lazily drifting out the top.

When we are close, Drakken reins in the reindeer and the sleigh slides to a stop. Plumey clouds puff from the mouths of the reindeer as they shift from foot to foot like they want to keep going. They're used to this.

I'm not. My teeth are chattering.

Drakken hops out of the sleigh and helps me down.

"Whoa!" My boots sink into the snow up to my knees. "Good thing I'm wearing mukluks or whatever!" I laugh. I take a few steps. I've never been in snow before today. "Wow, it's hard to walk!"

Drakken chuckles.

"Don't laugh! You have an advantage because you're so tall. The snow doesn't come up as high for you!"

He bends and sweeps me off my feet. "I carry you. Okay!"

I'm not going to argue.

Drakken trudges toward the stone building. It looks really old. It's made of thousands and thousands of smaller stones stacked together. I can't tell what the roof is made of because there's like three feet of snow covering it. The snow on the ground is packed down around the middle of the building. I see a door in the center of it. A stone cross juts out of the snow near the door. Several inches of snow are piled on the upward facing surfaces of the cross.

There is a faint clunk behind the door. It creaks open. Three nuns walk outside. Two older women and a young girl. They wear white habits which look really old school, like they were made in 1884.

Drakken stops in his tracks.

I slide down his body until my feet touch the ground. It's like he forgot he was carrying me. I don't mind. I feel kind of weird being carried in front of a bunch of nuns.

When I gain my footing in the snow, I look at the three nuns.

The little one runs three steps forward, then stops. She stares at Drakken, who is still ten feet away.

Those ice blue eyes...

"Are you my father?" she says in Drakken's language.

He has been teaching me words and phrases whenever we have spare time. I've picked up the basics, but that's about it.

Drakken drops to one knee so he's at the same level as the little girl. *"Yes. I am your father."* He holds out his arms to the girl.

I don't know if his expectations are too high. She's never met him before this moment. I don't want Drakken to get hurt if his daughter views him as a stranger.

"What do they call you?" Drakken asks. Drakken and I had wondered privately if her name had been changed for secrecy.

"I am called Angel,"—she says it like 'An-djell'.

I glance at Drakken's face. His expression is soft and open and hopeful. I haven't seen his hard stone mask in weeks. Not once. It's as if the walls around his heart have finally crumbled. Since his father's heart attack, it's as if Drakken is no longer at war with the world.

My own emotions get the best of me as I watch Drakken closely. I am so in love with him, my heart feels ready to burst with happiness as I watch him hope for a connection between himself and this little stranger.

She stands still, her eyes searching his, unsure of what to do.

The hope on Drakken's face fades slightly and his arms drift down to his sides.

I smear a tear from my cold cheek. His daughter may not feel a connection with him today, but I trust in time, she will come to love Drakken in her own way.

The girl takes a step toward him. *"Mother called me Anastazie. She told me you would come for me."* She takes another step forward, and another, until she is face to face with Drakken. She reaches out tentatively toward him and touches his cheek with her little fingers. She marvels, *"She said I have your eyes…"*

Drakken starts to weep silently. *"Yes. And you have mine, Anastazie. You have mine."*

Those ice blue eyes…

Epilogue

RIVER

I am *so* exhausted.

Like a loon, I insisted on taking no drugs during childbirth. I almost changed my mind part way through labor, but with Drakken by my side, I powered through. Now I lie in the hospital bed, holding our angel in my arms.

Drakken sits in a chair beside my bed, leaning forward, his elbows on his knees and a brilliant grin on his face. "She has your beauty, Rivka." His hand rests on my shoulder.

I smile warmly at him and nod, still too tired to say much of anything.

He squeezes my shoulder affectionately.

Anastazie stands beside him. She wears a Disney 'Let It Go' T-shirt and blue jeans. Her shimmering black hair is pulled back in a long pony tail. She has seen Frozen a hundred times and knows all the songs. "Is my sister?" she asks in accented English.

I've been amazed by how quickly she has picked up English since coming to live with us. "Yes," I say and smile at Anastazie, "This is your sister."

"What is her name?" she asks curiously.

I glance at Drakken. We have gone back and forth about what to name our daughter, but none of our choices seemed quite right. "Any thoughts, Dad?" I grin at him.

He chuckles, "Is too many good names to pick only one."

Anastazie grasps the handrail on the side of the hospital bed with both hands and leans over the baby to get a better look. "You should name her Sazkia," she says thoughtfully. She turns to Drakken. "After Mama."

Drakken and I gaze into each other's eyes for a long time.

Flow.

I feel our flow.

Our magical and incredible flow that makes me feel so alive, our flow that tells me everything is as it should be, our flow that is proof that everything in life happens for a reason.

I look down at the angelic face of my sleeping daughter and murmur, "Yes, we will name you Sazkia, for all the joy and light you bring into our lives."

Her eyes flutter open.

Those ice blue eyes...

Drakken stands beside the bed and rests his hand on our daughter's head. A tear slides down his cheek and he mutters:

"My angel..."

Want to get an email when Devon's next book is released?

Sign up here: http://eepurl.com/B7crf

Personal thanks from Devon Hartford:

Thank you, dear reader, for taking the time to live with River and Drakken for a while! If you enjoyed One Year Love, please leave a review wherever you purchased this ebook, on Goodreads, or any book blogs you frequent. Be sure to tell your friends about it!

Contact me and let me know who you want to hook up with McJogs:

Julietta Fabiano OR Finch Barksdale

Like me on Facebook

Friend me on Facebook

Follow me on Twitter @DevonHartford

Follow me on WordPress at devonhartford.com

ABOUT THE AUTHOR

Devon Hartford spent most of his life in Southern California frequenting many of the locations in One Year Love. Devon drew upon his passion for foreign languages while writing One Year Love. He is also an artist and musician, and drew upon his experiences with both while writing his previous romance series The Story of Samantha Smith and The Story of Victory Payne.

OTHER BOOKS BY DEVON HARTFORD:

ROMANTIC COLLEGE COMEDY:

Fearless (The Story of Samantha Smith #1)

Reckless (The Story of Samantha Smith #2)

Painless (The Story of Samantha Smith #3)

ROCKER ROMANCE:

Victory RUN 1 (The Story of Victory Payne)

Victory RUN 2 (The Story of Victory Payne)

Victory RUN 3 (The Story of Victory Payne)

BILLIONAIRE ROMANCE:

ONE YEAR LOVE - Part One

ONE YEAR LOVE - Part Two

ONE YEAR LOVE - Part Three

ONE YEAR LOVE - Part Four

ACKNOWLEDGMENTS

A HUGE thanks to all my passionate and fantastic beta readers: Emaleth Morrigan (mermaid), Neicy Cassidy, The REAL Julie England, Hayley Picknell, Sandye, Tamara Clark, Renee Julian, Kimber, Mandy Jamerson, Michele McKenzie, Maria Combee, Jordan Bault, Crystal, Mylinda Abraham-Powell, Natasha Slater, Michelle Crane, Wendy Boyer, Melanie Starr (My favorite Comma Bomber), Rosanne Triegaardt, Muriel Garcia, Stephanie Svajgl, Steffini Walker Texas Ranger, Tania Clark, Sarah Patton (Yak enthusiast), Jini Perez, Her Highness Samantha Sheeley (Queen of All Typos), Bethanie Melander, Mandy Karsa, Nicki Hewitt-Hart, Megan C Christmas, Anna Lamonica, and The Ever Special Mel Bushell for invaluable feedback and encouragement! You guys rock the typo sauce!

Annemie Stuer for inspiring the idea of the translated love letter!

Becs Glass and Sinfully Sexy Books for dedicated book pimping love!

Chrissy Zent Sharp for awesome book pimpery via The Book Whoreder's Delights. Be sure to check them out if you're a Romance reader.

Hayley Picknell for awesome reviews everywhere!

Everybody's ever luvin' cowbag, Lindsey Melia for ghetto ghood pimpin'.

And thanks to everybody else who has helped make this book a reality!

www.ingramcontent.com/pod-product-compliance
Lightning Source LLC
Chambersburg PA
CBHW030802260626
47169CB00001B/156